The Convent

MAUREEN McCARTHY

ALLEN&UNWIN
SYDNEY·MELBOURNE·AUCKLAND·LONDON

Australian Government

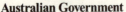

*This project has been assisted by the Australian Government through
the Australia Council, its arts funding and advisory body.*

This paperback edition published by Allen & Unwin in 2015

First published by Allen & Unwin in 2012

Copyright © Maureen McCarthy 2012

Allen & Unwin – Australia
83 Alexander Street, Crows Nest NSW 2065, Australia
Phone: (61 2) 8425 0100
Email: info@allenandunwin.com
Web: www.allenandunwin.com

Allen & Unwin – UK
c/o Murdoch Books, Erico House, 93-99 Upper Richmond Road, London SW15 2TG, UK
Phone: (44 20) 8785 5995
Email: info@murdochbooks.co.uk
Web: www.allenandunwin.com
Murdoch Books is a wholly owned division of Allen & Unwin Pty Ltd

A Cataloguing-in-Publication entry is available
from the National Library of Australia
www.trove.nla.gov.au
A catalogue record for this book is available from the British Library

ISBN (AUS) 978 1 74331 834 8
ISBN (UK) 978 1 74336 669 1

Cover design and photography by Astred Hicks, Design Cherry
Photograph of girl by Luisa Brimble

Set in Bembo

Printed in Australia by McPherson's Printing Group

1 3 5 7 9 10 8 6 4 2

The Convent is a work of the imagination. Apart from some known aspects of my mother's early life no resemblance to real people is intended nor should be inferred.

As far as possible I have tried to make the personal dates of my characters tally with the historical chronology of the Abbotsford Convent, but I have taken some liberties. For example, Peach's story – the 'now' of the novel – takes place in 1999. At that time the fight to save the Abbotsford Convent from development was only just beginning; there were no painters' or writers' studios. The Convent as it appears when Peach works there is very much how it is today – a vibrant, bustling, artistic community with cafes and galleries and bars.

Any mistakes made regarding convent conventions, in dress, ceremonies, speech or anything else are entirely my own.

Maureen McCarthy, 2012

For Sadie, the grandmother I never knew

You may find in that far-off land to which you go, sorrows which may often fill your Chalice to the brim. Yet I say to you, Go! my dear daughters, go with great courage where God calls you!

St Mary Euphrasia Pelletier
Foundress of the Congregation of the Good Shepherd

Peach

My sister and I often rode past the convent that summer.

I'd been trying to get her to do some exercise every day – apart from the three hundred daily trips she took back and forth from the chair to the fridge – and bike riding was the one thing she didn't mind. Most evenings I was able to cajole her out when it was still light enough to see but dark enough for her not to feel too exposed.

We'd head down the backstreets to the river, and at Dights Falls we'd turn right onto the bike trail and follow the river towards the city, zooming under the Johnston Street bridge and through the Collingwood Children's Farm. It was a nice easy ride, a winding track with little hills and flats and corners, not too hard on the muscles and plenty to look at on either side.

At that time of day there usually weren't too many people about to stare at the large olive-skinned girl with the wild black mane, cycling in stately fashion behind her slim, fair-haired sister. The brown river was on our left; on our right was a cliff face dotted with natives, the odd palm and clumps of peppercorn trees, or concrete walls covered in wild graffiti. When we came to the farm there were horses and goats and cows, even bee boxes and a few wonderful old oaks. Once we were through to the open space of the river flat, we could look up to our right at the massive grey building that was known locally simply as 'the convent'.

We got into the habit of stopping there so Stella could catch her breath. She liked to lean against the fence and wax on about the spires and turrets visible through the trees, and how interesting it would be to go back in time and see *what really went on there.*

It was all a bit of a ruse, I think, to stop me getting her back on the bike too quickly, but I liked looking at the convent too, especially towards evening when some of the lights were blazing, and the beat from a band playing outside the cafe and the smell of cooking would waft down to the bike track.

We knew it had been set up by French nuns back in the 1860s and from then until the early seventies it had operated as an industrial laundry, a farm, an orphanage and a school, as well as a home for destitute women and girls in trouble. Once the nuns left and the place closed down there was a long fight to save it from the housing developers.

But all that was long over by the time Dad and Mum shifted to Collingwood to be nearer their work in the city. The place had stood empty for years. Now the old dormitories and refectories and parlours were in the process of being renovated and let out to health practitioners and theatre companies, artists and writers.

But when Stella and I stood musing in the middle of our bike ride, it was mostly the past we were trying to conjure up.

Why would anyone choose to become a nun? Who were the orphans? What about the *bad* girls who'd been locked up there? What crimes had they committed?

We were not from a religious family, so the lives of the women and girls who'd lived there were enticingly remote.

I liked the way the building seemed to change mood. Against a pale blue sky or a pink-and-gold sunset it looked full of magic, as pretty as a castle in a young girl's fantasy. But when the sky was low and grey with cloud, the buildings took on the menacing undertones of a jail.

Sometimes we'd wander through the gate and up along the gravel path through the garden that had been laid out in the French style. The renovations were only partly completed, and large parts of it still weren't open to the public. But it was easy enough to peer into the big industrial spaces where the girls had worked the laundry, eaten meals and gone to church.

The gate through which the trucks had driven every day to collect the laundry from the St Heliers Street entrance was still there, battered and rusty. You could see where they'd stored the coal and wood, and the huge iron boiler that had heated water for the whole place.

One evening we snuck past the developer's wire fence, through a door and upstairs to wander through the Magdalen dormitories. The few rows of abandoned iron beds, the sinks along one wall, the battered cupboards and dusty shower cubicles made the huge rooms eerie, as though everyone had left in a hurry. Apart from thin shafts of late-afternoon light coming through the cracks in the boarded-up windows it was more or less dark inside.

It got a whole lot more eerie when Stella swore she could *smell* the girls who'd slept there, that she could feel their spirits, too, hovering with the dust mites in the corners of the empty rooms. I told her she was crazy, that the place had been closed for almost thirty years, and yet ... I believed her. Stella couldn't tell a lie if she tried.

I had no idea then of my own connection to the convent. I'd only just turned nineteen and, to tell you the truth, I didn't *want* to know. There was enough on my plate already. Mum and Dad were overseas. I had my studies, a summer job, a best friend in the middle of a huge drama of her own making and a sister I was meant to be caring for, who, for reasons of her own, seemed intent on doubling her size.

And there was Luke, too, of course. Luke 'the Fluke' Robinson, my former boyfriend with the smoky grey eyes, who had been saved from drowning when he was three years old by his mum who couldn't swim until she found out she had to.

He used to tell me that there was no getting away from the past; that wanting to know your own history is as basic as the need to take your shoes off at the beach. That first touch of icy water, the million sand granules squishing between your toes, the vast expanse of sky above, and you know ... *you just know* you have a right to be there.

Well, he was right in a way. The past does come after you whether you like it or not. It blusters in like a noisy drunk off the street, tapping you on the shoulder, demanding to tell his story. You resist at first because you have better things to think about, then you make an excuse to slip away, and when that doesn't work you listen out of politeness, impatient for the end because the story doesn't make much sense. There is none of *this* followed by *that*, the way a story is meant to go. People and events drift in and out as they please, running together like drops of water on a grimy windscreen, reforming, breaking apart and flying off in different directions.

But you get hooked anyway, and when the story is over you see it makes its own kind of sense.

It is then you understand that all you've ever known about yourself and your particular place in the world has shifted position. You're left wondering how you're meant to deal with it.

But you do. That's the good part. You do.

Sadie, Ellen, Cecilia and now ... *me*.

Sadie 1915

It began at daybreak with three hard knocks on the door, and light sneaking like a thief through the holes in the blind. Sadie woke on the third knock and reached for her dressing-gown. She was two weeks behind with her rent and the old skinflint who owned most of the street made it his business to call early if someone needed a warning.

Not to worry. There was three pounds ten in the pocket of her gown, and a little more in the drawer near her bed. With a bit of luck she'd have enough to pay the milkman as well. She could hear the faint clip-clop of his horse in a nearby street. *Whoa there, girl . . .*

She smiled through a thick head and dry mouth and felt for the extra money in the side drawer. Bill the milko had cut her plenty of slack over the years; she'd see him right.

By the time she had opened the door of her tiny Carlton terrace her feet were freezing. She was met with thick white fog and two people, neither of them the landlord. A heavy, red-faced woman dressed in some kind of grey uniform was closest. She had short, steel-grey hair and narrow eyes, hard as splinters, and she was carrying a blanket over one arm. Next to her stood a fresh-faced copper, all done out in brass buttons, a cap and shiny black boots. He had a long baton in a holster by his side.

Sadie held firm. It didn't do for a woman living alone to show fear. Her first thought was for the boy, William, living with his father now, cutting stone in some godforsaken place up near Echuca. She clutched tightly at her dressing-gown and snarled a quiet prayer to the God she had no time for these days. *Let the kid live.*

It was only then that she saw the third person. Lurking behind the other two, his hat pulled down over his eyes, pretending he wasn't there, was *Frank*! What the hell was that sanctimonious little bastard doing knocking on her door at six in the morning? Sadie caught his eye and he edged further back. She had to stifle the jeer that rose like bile from her guts. Under the thumb of a hypochondriac wife for twenty years and run off his feet with two carping sisters, it was a wonder he'd managed to get himself off the chain for the early morning outing.

'Yes?' Sadie said.

The copper shoved some kind of document under her nose.

Sadie waved it away. 'I can see you're a copper,' she said. 'What you here for?' Reading wasn't her strong point, but that wasn't for him to know. Let that slimy little bastard Frank tell them if he must.

The copper didn't say anything at all, and neither did the other two, but they looked at each other, shifty and sly-eyed, as if they were unsure how to proceed seeing as she'd refused their bit of paper.

She folded her arms and waited, apprehensive but righteous. It was freezing, she had over a month of rent in her pocket and this was *her* front door.

'You should read it,' the copper said uncertainly, trying to sound as if he knew what was what, when everything about his silly young face told her he was out of his depth.

'Why?'

'It's the law.'

'Is that a fact?'

'Yes.'

'What law says I've got to read it?'

'Otherwise you won't know what we're here for.'

'Can't you *tell* me, Officer?' she mocked. He would have joined the police as a face-saver when all his mates were volunteering. Not that she blamed him, of course. Why get your head blown off if you didn't have to? Even so she wanted to jeer, *Decided to keep your skin on, did ya, shirker?*

The other two were looking at her with curled lips and it angered her. Maybe her dressing-gown was grubby and she had no slippers, but it was six o'clock in the morning *and* ... Sadie pushed her shoulders back, pulled her belt tighter and reminded herself that she'd never pretended to be anything she wasn't. She fed her little girl well, kept her clean and kept a decent roof over their heads. Sometimes only just ... but still. What right did they have to look down their noses?

'And what brings you here, Frank?' She was already imagining telling Dottie about this later. *Too gutless to come on his own! He brings the jacks and some fat bitch from the government to my door at daybreak and expects me to stand there trying to guess what he's about.*

The words were spilling around in her head, but her mouth stayed tight. Dot was going to love this. Snatch a laugh or two when you could else you'd go barmy was her theory, and as far as Sadie was concerned it wasn't a bad one. Stories that stuck it to the jacks sent them both off like tops.

Frank was behind this, whatever it was. If the copper hadn't been there she would have given him a piece of her mind, told him to keep the few measly quid he gave her every month if that meant she never had to look at him again.

He still couldn't meet her eye.

'You are Mrs Sadie Reynolds?' the copper asked stiffly, as if he had the baton up his rear end.

'Yes.'

'Where is your husband?'

'That's my business.'

'Where is your husband, Mrs Reynolds?'

Sadie knew she'd better start toeing the line or there'd be more trouble. 'If you must know, he is up north, working.'

'You keep in contact with him?'

'Yes,' she spat. 'Of course I do.'

It was a lie but so what? Joe turned up for a feed every now and again, and for whatever else took his fancy. Last time it had been the boy, and they'd fought cat and dog over that one but … what use dwelling on it? She didn't have the money to feed a growing boy and they both knew it. Joe would let her starve without blinking an eye, but that shouldn't mean the kid had to. To all intents and purposes her husband was *gone,* and he'd taken their son with him.

'Well, Mrs Reynolds, we don't want any trouble now,' the copper said uncomfortably.

'Nor do I.'

'So where is Ellen?'

'*What?*' A shaft of ice went straight to her guts, and her bowels began to churn.

'Ellen,' the young man said again, triumphant now he could see her fear. He looked down at his bit of paper. 'Ellen McIntosh Reynolds. Three years old. Where is she?'

'Where do you think?' Sadie said loudly, trying to still the panic, but her voice sounded hollow as if she was in some kind of cave. 'In her bed asleep.'

The three of them looked at her impassively. She almost told them to go and take a look for themselves if they didn't believe her, except that would be inviting them in and that was the last thing she wanted.

'May we see her please?'

'No.'

'Mr McIntosh wants to see the child, Mrs Reynolds.'

'Well, he can't!'

'He is the child's father, Mrs Reynolds.'

'So?' For the millionth time she cursed her own stupidity. In a crazy fit of honesty she'd put his name on the birth certificate. The child had her husband Joe's surname, of course – that was the law – but seeing as she'd hardly seen Joe over these last few years she decided to stick Frank's surname in the middle. *The poor little mite needs to know who her real dad is.* Oh why had she done that? It gave him ideas above his station, made him think he had rights far and beyond what was the case.

She turned to Frank. 'What do you mean bringing people here?' she hissed, trying frantically to grab the doorknob without taking her eyes from his face. Her father had been a tough Scot, and he'd taught her that the chances of winning are always better if you stand your ground. But the door had swung wide open behind her and she was unable to catch the knob.

Sadie's heart had begun to beat in her chest like a terrified bird trying to get out of a cage. She swallowed and swallowed but couldn't seem to get the lump out of her throat. There was slipperiness under her arms, too, in spite of the cold, and at the back of her neck sweat had begun to trickle down like tears.

They were moving towards her, crowding in close.

'We have evidence, Mrs Reynolds.' The copper was talking.

'Evidence?'

'You have no male support.'

'But I have a . . .' She looked at Frank frantically.

'That you are an unfit mother.'

'An unfit— Show it to me!'

'That you consort with unsavoury characters.'

'Like who?' She looked from one to the other, the panic bubbling through her now like poisonous gas.

'You keep company with . . . fallen women.'

'What are you talking about?'

'Prostitutes,' he said under his breath.

Sadie stared at him, barely able to breathe. It was as if someone had punched her hard in the side of the head and she'd forgotten how to suck the air in again. They must mean Mona who stayed over sometimes, poor downtrodden little Mona, with three mites to feed, who gave her a couple of quid every now and again just to have somewhere to flop when she needed a rest. The johns never came anywhere near the house. That had been understood right from the start.

Suddenly the three of them were pushing past her. They walked straight through into the narrow passageway of the little house and it took her a few moments to realise what was happening.

'Get the hell out of there!' she yelled after them. But the copper was opening the first door on the left and poking his head in. 'You have no right!'

'We have every right, Mrs Reynolds.'

Sadie ran past them, down to the second door on the left where the child was asleep, and tried to bar the door with her body. 'Don't you touch her!' she said in a low voice. She didn't want to wake the child with angry voices outside her door.

But in a couple of swift movements the young cop had grabbed both her wrists and pulled her away from the doorway. He pushed both her arms up behind her back and held her there while the other two went in to where the child was sleeping.

'No, no! Don't wake her!' Sadie struggled to get free. 'You mustn't do this!'

But the woman and Frank had already closed the door behind them.

In a matter of a few moments the shrill cry of her daughter sounded from behind that door.

The fat woman in grey reappeared, carrying the half-asleep Ellen, who was grizzling now, with one thumb stuck in her mouth, all soft and warm in her little nightdress and socks, her half-empty bottle of milk in the other hand. Her big blue eyes were staring around at the strangers. But when she saw Sadie being held by the policeman she let go of the bottle, held out both her plump little arms and began to yell.

'Mumma!'

The fat woman spoke soothingly and tried wrapping the little girl in the red blanket. But Ellen wasn't having a bit of it. She was kicking and squirming like a sleek little seal, trying to free herself and shouting for all she was worth.

Sadie caught a strong whiff of urine and somehow that set her desperation off down another tunnel. They were going to take her without even changing her, without putting clean clothes on her or brushing her lovely dark silky curls that were all mussed up at the back!

'Mumma!' she wailed. 'I want my mumma!'

Sadie gave up all pretence of trying to keep things civilised. She lashed out at the young copper with her feet, kicking him, bending to bite his hands where she could. When that proved ineffectual, she began to scream, and spat into his face.

But the copper held on, puffing and grunting against her efforts, occasionally swearing under his breath.

'Too gutless to go to the war? Rather fight women, would ya?'

'Shut your mouth, whore!' he growled under his breath.

'Found your soft spot, have I?'

'Shut your mouth.'

'I'll shut my mouth when you leave me and my child in peace.'

'Mumma!'

But Sadie couldn't free herself from the young man's strong grip and so she had to watch her baby daughter disappear out the front door in the arms of a strange woman, squirming, shouting and pleading for her mother the whole way.

'Mumma!' Ellen wailed. 'I want my mumma!'

Still holding Sadie in a tight grip, the copper walked her outside. By the time she was on the footpath, Frank was closing the car door on the woman who'd settled into the back seat of a black Ford with the howling child on her knee.

'Please don't do this, Frank,' Sadie gasped. 'Anything but this, I beg you. I'll tell the government that he's deserted me and you can move in. Or I'll come to you. We'll live as man and wife! Anything!'

'You had your chance,' he said, walking carefully around to the other side.

The copper let Sadie go, hurried around to the driver's side, got in and started the motor.

Sadie ran to the window where the child was looking out and pulled uselessly on the handle.

'Give her back!'

'Mumma!' Ellen screamed.

The car took off and Sadie, sobbing and cursing, ran after it as long as she could in her bare feet. When the car was gone and she couldn't run any longer – her feet all cut about and bleeding – she stopped to lean against the bakery's brick wall, gasping.

'Help me,' she mumbled. 'Help me, someone. Please help me!'

But there was no one to help her. The street was as empty of people as it had been half an hour before, and the grey light was as inadequate and miserable as a soldier's blanket.

She stumbled back along the footpath to the empty house, the door still hanging wide, and climbed the stairs up to the front door. She fell inside, crawled along the passageway to the child's room and buried her face in the bedclothes. They might as well have ripped her arms off and thrown her to the dogs, or put her in a cage for people to come and jeer at. She was done for now.

Even as she lay on the floor, all curled up like a stillborn calf, the child's blanket stuffed in her mouth and her dressing-gown wet with tears and snot, she could feel the hinges that held her together loosening with each passing minute. Soon she would be just a rubbery shape on the floor. Some weird-looking thing that only vaguely resembled a woman, a sack of blood and bone, tissue, hair, muscle, barely human.

My baby … Give me back my baby.

On the fifth morning after Ellen had been taken, Sadie received a letter from Frank.

Mrs Joseph Reynolds
McPherson Street
Carlton

Dear Sadie,

By now you will have had a chance to gather yourself, and I pray that you see the wisdom of my decision. For your information, I have placed the child with the nuns in St Joseph's nursery at the Abbotsford Convent, but be warned you no longer have any legal rights regarding her. She is now a Ward of the State and you are not permitted to see her.

I have agreed to pay all extra costs both now and into the future, and so the child will have education and not be put to menial work. The Reverend Mother has made me aware of the future tuition fees, all the extras such as music lessons, extra milk and special uniforms for this and that, and although it is a lot on my wage I am prepared to carry the costs.

I'm sure you will be comforted to know that after the initial fretting, Ellen is already laughing and smiling and chattering again. The Sister in charge of the babies' section at Abbotsford, Mother Mary Help of Christians, is a kindly soul and in my opinion well suited to looking after babies and toddlers.

Try to put this behind you, Sadie. Before God, I am convinced I've done the right thing.

Yours faithfully,
Frank McIntosh

Ellen 1926

'You're not happy to be back with us, Ellen?'

'Yes, Mother.'

'Then why the long face?'

'No reason, Mother.'

'Come and see me after Benediction.'

'But I'm all right, Mother. I am. Really.'

'I'll expect you in St Cecilia's room at six.'

'Yes, Mother.' Ellen panicked as she watched the nun's retreating back. It was the last place she wanted to go. She was fourteen years old and was desperate to keep the shame to herself. *But how?* Nuns were so good at prying everything out of you. They asked questions and you had to answer. Could she pretend to be ill to get out of it?

She decided to wait for the Benediction bell under the old oak tree at the front of the convent. At least she'd be alone there. She took the shortest route past the Sacred Heart enclosure, which contained the Magdalen laundries – something she wasn't meant to do because it was out of bounds.

The Sacred Heart girls were enclosed behind a twelve-foot

high wire fence topped with six strands of tight barbed wire. There was no way in or out except through a locked iron gate.

Ellen watched the girls pouring out of the laundry from their afternoon work, their shouts and bursts of laughter and chat ringing out in the unseasonably cold air. Most of them were older than Ellen by a few years, dressed in drab pleated skirts and bulky hand-knitted jumpers with pinnies over them. They formed small gossiping groups, slouching, their arms folded across their chests against the chill.

Ellen started in surprise when a ball flew over the fence right in front of her.

'Hey, chuck us the ball, will you?'

Three of them were staring through the fence at her, their hands clutching the wire.

Ellen ran for the ball and threw it back over the fence.

'Thanks!' A cheerful chorus went up.

One of the girls motioned for her to come nearer to the fence. 'Hey, over here, Ellen.'

Ellen hesitated. How did this girl know her name? Interaction between the Sacred Heart girls and the St Joseph's girls was totally outlawed. The 'roughies' were not to be trusted under any circumstances. But Ellen was feeling so confused, so low, she didn't care. She didn't even look around to see if anyone was watching as she walked over.

'I thought you'd gone,' the girl of about eighteen said. The twinkle in her bright eyes made Ellen think she might be on the point of telling a joke or bursting into laughter. There was something familiar about her.

'I'm Margie,' the girl explained.

'Oh.' Ellen flushed, remembering their encounter earlier that year. Margie worked in the bakery, and when Ellen had been sent down to get the soft loaves for the old nuns two mornings in a row they'd talked while Ellen waited for the bread. 'You've cut your hair.'

A dark look crossed the girl's face and she lowered her lovely eyes. 'Mother Mac,' she said savagely, letting her eyes rest on Mother Mary Immaculate, who was standing with her back to them at the far end of the enclosure.

'Why?' Ellen remembered the girl's hair. Coal black, thick and wavy it had been, tied back into a ponytail for work.

'Swearing.'

'Oh.' Ellen nodded.

'So what happened?' The bright eyes were back. 'Did they give you the bum's rush out there?'

Ellen flushed and backed away. 'I should go ... I can't really talk ... here.'

'Don't go.' Margie's low breathy voice was hurried, her eyes darting constantly over to the nun on duty. 'Do something for me?'

'No ...' Ellen looked around nervously. 'It isn't allowed, and I have to go.'

'Oh, come on.' The girl fished under her jumper with one hand, and brought out a small fat envelope. She curled it up and poked it through the wire fence. It straightened out, and Ellen saw that there was a name and address and even a stamp on it. 'Post this for me?'

The nuns were always warning them against this kind of thing. *Under no circumstances will you have anything to do with the Sacred Heart girls.* Many of them were at the Magdalen laundry instead of in jail, others were soft in the head or, worse still, they had 'pasts' that could only be hinted at.

'I got no other way of getting to him,' the girl implored, holding the letter out with two fingers.

'Your boyfriend?' Ellen whispered, intrigued in spite of herself; she moved closer.

'We're planning a break-out.'

Ellen's mouth fell open. 'Who?'

'Three of us.'

'When?'

'Can't tell you that.'

'Why not?'

The girl looked her up and down dispassionately. 'You'll tell.'

'No ... I won't!'

'I can't risk it. We're going to swim the river at night. And we need the fellas waiting on the other side.'

'Oh,' Ellen breathed, 'but you're locked in at night.'

'Look,' Margie said impatiently, 'I've got to get this to him. Are you going to help or not?'

'How will you know if he gets the letter?'

'He'll get it if you send it.'

'So who else is ...?'

'I can't tell you. Just post it. We need them waiting with a car.'

'A *car*!'

She couldn't *not* take it now. Just the idea of a boyfriend with a car was too enticing. She slipped the letter into the pocket of her pinny and ran off.

The old oak tree was Ellen's favourite place. She looked around to make sure she wasn't being watched and lay down on her back to stare up into the swaying canopy and think about how it would be to have a boyfriend with *a car*.

She imagined the three girls swimming the river and shivered. What if there were strange creatures in there? Ellen had never learnt to swim. The river down at the edge of the convent grounds was out of bounds. She'd never even seen the sea.

The convent had been her only home for as long as she could remember. Her father had come every Sunday without fail to take her out for a few hours, but until recently she had never been to his house, or met his sisters, and had always been back at the convent by five p.m. for Benediction. In fact, she had never spent even a night away from the convent *until* ...

Ellen shuddered and tried to concentrate on the blue patches of sky.

She'd passed her merit with flying colours. She'd won first prizes for elocution and piano, third prize in history, second in French. Her father wanted her to do at least two more years of schooling before she went for a job, and because St Joseph's at the Abbotsford Convent stopped at Grade Eight, he'd booked her into the Academy of Mary Immaculate in Nicholson Street, Carlton.

The plan had been that she would live with him and his two sisters in their terrace house in Grattan Street. She would walk to school every day from there. And oh how she'd looked forward to it. For six months she had marked the days off, one by one, praying for the time to pass. To live in a proper house in a street with other ordinary houses, like a normal girl in a family would be … *wonderful*.

Ellen waited outside St Cecilia's music room listening through the heavy oak door to the last few bars of a simple piece being played over and over again. The succession of chords right at the end was proving difficult for the student, whoever she was. Again and again she almost got there, only to be cut off with that sharp tap of Mother Seraphina's ruler followed by the admonishment, 'No, child! That is a C-sharp followed by A and then another C-sharp!'

'Yes, Mother.'

'From the beginning of the bar, if you please.'

Ellen shuddered. How many times had she been in there doing that?

At last, the scraping of chairs and the heavy door swung open to reveal the music teacher and a thin little girl of perhaps ten.

'Nothing magical about it, my dear,' the old nun was saying sternly. 'You have the ability. You must practise. Do I make myself clear?'

'Yes, Mother.' The girl's eyes were darting about as she waited for her chance to escape.

'Off you go then, and God bless you.'

'God bless you, Mother, and thank you.' And the little uniformed girl was away.

'Come in, dear. Come in.'

Just the smell of the room made Ellen want to cry. Polish and wax and the soft soapy smell of the nun, with her dry, ageing fingers and starched veil. It was a small room with just the upright piano, a stool, a wooden chest where the music was kept and a straight-backed chair for Sister Seraphina. On top of the piano was the same old blue vase that had been there forever, along with the metronome. There was a picture of the Christ kneeling in the garden of Gethsemane on one wall, and a crucifix above the piano, but these two were overshadowed by a large plaster statue of the patron saint of music, St Cecilia, standing on a long wooden pedestal in the corner. Her hands were joined in prayer, a small harp propped at her feet along with a few sheets of rolled-up music. A bunch of fresh flowers from the convent garden were in a little glass jar at her feet. *St Cecilia pray for us.*

All the heavy wood gleamed in the late afternoon light coming in through the long window, which was open as always. Mother Seraphina believed that fresh air, even in autumn and winter, was important for keeping her students' minds on the job.

She was a plump woman of medium height; her soft Irish skin was virtually unlined although she was well into her sixties. She adjusted the piano stool to face her own chair and then motioned for Ellen to sit down.

Ellen did as she was told and took a deep breath. The hours she'd spent in this room seemed to rush at her, to surround her in a mass of sticky tangled feelings she didn't have a hope of unravelling. It wasn't just floor wax and polish and soap she could smell, but the deeper smells of effort and pain, exhilaration and humiliation, frayed nerves and blind terror. Hundreds of girls had been taught here over the years. Learning new pieces, practising for exams and concerts, all the scales and arpeggios and exercises, the prodding and the carping. So much of Ellen's own life had been lived *here* in this room with this old woman. The long pieces, the short, the light-hearted and the sad; the fury and frustration when her fingers refused to do what they were meant to.

And what are those lumps on the end of your hands, Ellen Reynolds?

Bits of wood from a tree, are they? Turnips perhaps? But there were bursts of warmth too, which lightened Ellen's spirits for days afterwards. If she got through some difficult piece, the nun would clap softly and laugh. *Ah, you have it, my dear. You have it. Well done!*

Once she'd told Ellen, 'You remind me of my mother, child. Bless her soul. Her hair was dark like yours, and her eyes blue and bright too, and she was a great one for the jolly pieces.'

Ellen had been delighted. It was a running joke between them that Ellen found the light, joyful pieces much easier to learn, even if they were more complex than the sombre ones. Mother Seraphina was always trying to make her see the beauty of a serious piece by Beethoven or Elgar, and Ellen would scowl, which always made the nun shake her head and laugh under her breath.

'Did your mother play well, Mother?' Ellen had ventured shyly.

'She was … *competent.*' Seraphina smiled. 'Let's just say what she lacked in technique she made up for in enthusiasm.'

Ellen would have loved to know more. She'd been on the brink of asking how many brothers and sisters the nun had, and if they all played and what, if any, instruments they'd had at home, and where was her home in Ireland, but … in the end she didn't dare. It was an unwritten rule. The Sisters rarely spoke about their former lives. Questions from the girls were out of place.

'So, my dear?' The nun was settled into her chair now and looking at Ellen keenly.

But Ellen turned away, unable to meet her gaze.

'You went to stay with your father?'

'Yes, Mother.'

'And his sisters, I believe?'

'Yes, Mother.'

'What were their names, child?' the nun asked softly.

'Rose and Mary,' Ellen gulped, willing the terrible constricting feeling to leave her alone. It was as if some kind of crustacean with great horrible claws was crawling up her throat. 'And Rosalind … except she was my sister.'

'Your *sister*?'

'Half-sister. I didn't know I had one.'

The old nun was confused for a moment. 'So how old was this sister?'

'Old,' Ellen mumbled. 'Thirty-two, I think.'

'And *her* mother?'

'She died. She'd been sick a long time. And she died last year. But I didn't know that ... I didn't know anything about her either. She wasn't *my* mother.'

'No,' the nun said softly. 'So you'd never met this sister before?'

'No. I'd never met my father's sisters, either, or my ... I'd never met Agnes. Not before I went there, Mother.'

'Oh dear.' The old nun shook her head. 'So you went into a house with your father, his two sisters and his ... other daughter?'

'Yes, Mother.'

The nun sighed and drew both her hands into her lap, twisting her thumbs around each other.

Ellen's head was still lowered, but she watched the thumbs moving around. First one way and then they'd stop and do an about turn. Nothing was said for some time. Outside, the day was sliding away and the room was growing dark. Ellen wondered if she should suggest that she turn on the overhead light, but the dark was comforting in a way. It helped the awfulness fade a little. The longer she sat there in silence, the easier it all became. The terrible months became like scenes from a book that she'd read. Being in this room had always made her feel as though the world outside didn't really exist, and it was the same now.

'So they were unkind?'

'Yes ... Mother,' she mumbled.

'And you were there for six weeks?'

'Two months, Mother.'

'And your father?'

'He went to work.'

'And you were home during the day?'

21

'The new term hadn't started.'

'I see.'

Ellen kept her mouth tightly closed. She'd sworn on pain of hell that she would never tell a living soul what had happened in that house. And now she was blurting it out to a prying nun. But what else could she do?

'So how were they unkind, child?'

'They said that...I...That my mother was...That I was...' Ellen closed her eyes.

'Come, child,' the nun said softly, 'come now.'

'They said I...I had bad blood in me,' she whispered, 'that I am a daughter of sin.'

'Did they now?' The nun took a sharp breath.

'And that I would turn out just like her.'

'Her?'

'My mother.'

'Oh.'

Tears rushed into Ellen's eyes without warning. She knew nothing about her mother, only that she was alive, that her name was Sadie and that she had dark hair. Apart from that she was a ghost, a ghost that Ellen loved nevertheless. Oh, she loved her, there was no doubt that she loved her. Occasionally, in the middle of the night, Sadie would appear at one end of the dormitory, a transparent floating vision of a dark-headed woman in a worn blue coat, right next to the statue of St Therese, the Little Flower. She was there and yet not there. Ellen would sit up and stare down past the other beds of sleeping girls, a wave of relief washing through her. Her mother had come at last!

Mother Seraphina reached out and gripped Ellen's right hand in her own. This in itself was quite shocking. Ellen couldn't remember ever touching a nun before. She wished that her own hand didn't feel so damp and warm against the nun's dry, papery skin.

'And your sister?'

'The worst.' Ellen gulped and wiped her eyes with her other

sleeve. 'I had to share a room with her and she never spoke to me. She would just stare at me and sometimes throw my things about. And she tipped things on me.'

'Tipped... what kind of things?'

'Water.' Ellen raised her head and looked at the nun. 'Once she threw a cup of tea in my face when I was lying on the bed reading. Hot tea. It burned. They wouldn't let me sit with them after dinner... so I would go outside or try to read on my bed. I... I didn't have anywhere else to go!' Ellen began to sob, and she turned her face away into her other hand.

'Oh, dear child.' The old nun's grip tightened and she felt in the pocket of her habit for a hanky and passed it across. 'So, you told your father?'

'No, no... I didn't... he... no.' Ellen took the nicely laundered white hanky but hardly dared use it. 'He knew a bit, I think.'

'Wipe your eyes now, dear,' the nun said.

'Thank you, Mother.' It felt wrong somehow to use a nun's hanky, but she didn't know how to say that.

'So what brought things to a head?'

'I couldn't eat. He took me to a doctor and I had to drink a tonic and... that made me sick too. I overheard them talking one night, the three of them in the kitchen, screaming at him to get me out of their house. They kept saying I was a *whore's* child.'

The nun shuddered.

'What *is* a whore, Mother?' Ellen whispered desperately. 'Please tell me what it means?'

'Oh, my dear.'

'Do I have bad blood?'

The nun shook her head but said nothing. Then she let go of Ellen's hand and searched in the folds of her habit for her rosary. Ellen opened up the hanky and wiped her eyes and blew her nose properly, all time watching the nun's hands fingering the cross.

'We'll say a little prayer now, Ellen, shall we?' Mother Seraphina said softly. 'Just a little prayer to Our Lady.'

Ellen gulped and nodded as the nun kissed the cross and blessed herself with it.

'And we will remember always that the Blessed Mother is with us, especially in our sufferings.'

'Yes, Mother.'

'That she had to watch her only son die on the cross, and so she knows what it is to suffer, my dear.' The old woman stood and faced the window. 'We'll say the Memorare together,' Mother Seraphina muttered softly. 'To ease the pain.'

Ellen stood up and began to pray alongside her teacher.

Remember, O most loving Virgin Mary,
that never was it known in any age,
that anyone who fled to thy protection, implored thy help
or sought thine intercession was abandoned.
Inspired with confidence, therefore,
I cry to thee, most loving Virgin Mary.
To thee do I come, before thee I stand, sinful and sorrowful.
Do not, O Mother of the Word Incarnate,
despise my prayers, but graciously hear and grant them. Amen.

The nun stopped and put her rosary aside. She took a couple of deep breaths and then sighed.

'Will you play the Mozart sonata for me now, Ellen? The one you learnt for your exam.'

'But I haven't practised!' Ellen was genuinely aghast at the thought. She hadn't touched a piano in months. 'And Mother...it's Holy Week!' Could the nun really have forgotten that no bright, joyful pieces were played in the week leading up to Easter?

'I think Our Lord will understand, dear,' the nun said. 'I really do. I think Our Lord and his Blessed Mother will love to hear you play that particular piece.'

Ellen began tentatively, quietly and self-consciously, but the music took over. It was a piece they both loved. The nun had told her about Mozart as a young boy, not much older than Ellen was, careering around Austria in his lovely velvet clothes and wig, that he was known to be a wag, boisterous and cheeky, playing tricks on people, and all the while writing the most wonderful music in the world. And that was what Ellen thought about as she played. She pretended Mozart was sitting behind them both, listening and smiling, clicking his fingers and tapping his fancy heels on the polished wooden floor, glad that it was her, Ellen Reynolds, playing his notes.

It was by no means her best rendition, but for most of the way through she was halfway pleased. Not too many notes went missing, and every time she came to the end of a page of music and Mother Seraphina leant forward to turn it Ellen saw she was smiling. Ellen's fingers flew over the notes. By the end she knew she was making all kinds of mistakes, but it didn't matter because they were both laughing by then.

'Bravo, my dear girl! Bravo!' Mother Seraphina clapped a couple of times before gently putting down the lid of the piano. 'With no practice, you did very well indeed.' She sighed and checked the time on the small silver watch under her guimpe.

'Well, we must be going, dear.'

'Thank you, Mother.'

The nun took her hand. 'Tell me what it is you want to do in life, Ellen?'

Ellen could only look at her in shock. No one had ever asked her that before. Not even her father had asked her that. What did she want to do?

'You mean...?'

'When you leave school and become an adult.'

'I don't know, Mother.'

'Think, child.'

'Well...' Ellen began shyly, 'I would like to have my own family one day, Mother.'

The nun's old face lit up. 'Then you will, my dear,' she said softly, 'you will. You'll have a beautiful family.'

Ellen was surprised that the nun seemed so certain, because she wasn't at all sure herself. She'd never in her whole life spoken to a boy, and she knew nothing about babies or families for that matter.

'Oh yes.' The nun closed her eyes. 'You'll meet a good Catholic man. And you'll have a wonderful family of your own.'

'With my own house,' Ellen added softly.

'Of course, my dear!' Mother Seraphina stood up. 'A house full of lovely children. You'll bring back your first child and show me, if I'm still alive?'

'Oh I will, Mother! I will. I won't forget.'

They both stood up. Ellen waited as the nun packed up the music books into a neat pile.

'Now, Ellen, I have some time on Saturdays around three. We don't want all that practice going for nothing, do we?'

'You mean a lesson, Mother?'

'What else, child? Of course I mean a lesson. As long as you're here, you'll have lessons.'

'Thank you, Mother.'

When everything was shipshape, she turned to Ellen, her face softened into a whimsical smile. 'What will you call your first child, do you think?'

Ellen smiled and didn't hesitate. 'Dominic,' she said, and the nun frowned thoughtfully as though the name invited deep consideration. Ellen waited, hoping that the nun wouldn't disapprove. But why would she? After all, it was a Great Saint's name. Ellen secretly didn't care much for the saint but rather loved the sound of the name. *Dominic*.

'Dominic is a wonderful name,' the nun said at last. 'And what about if you have a girl first?'

Ellen looked at the plaster saint in the corner. 'Cecilia,' she whispered.

'Of course!' This time Mother Seraphina laughed in delight. 'And she'll have the gift, too, like her mother. I don't doubt it. Now don't you forget,' she said. 'If I'm not gone to God I want to see her too. Dominic *and* Cecilia.'

'I won't forget, Mother.'

Cecilia 1964

He has placed his seal upon my forehead and I will admit no other lover but him…

The day had arrived and she was ready for it.

Today. Everything that was meant to happen would happen: hour by hour, minute by minute. And at the end of it, when she lay down to sleep in this bed again, she would be changed. Transformed. No longer nineteen-year-old Cecilia Mary Madden, the only daughter of Ellen and Kevin from Wongabbie Farm near Bendigo but … *someone else entirely.* The first step had been taken just on a year ago when she'd first walked through the gates, but today was the one that mattered. Today was serious.

Cecilia lay in her narrow bed, staring at the pale-green ceiling. There were eight beds, four on each side of the room, seven of them occupied. There was the huge crucifix down one end, and the big round clock on the wall opposite. She saw the time and smiled. Five minutes to six. An extra hour's sleep. The night before, Reverend Mother had granted the sleep-in because of it being a special day for the whole community. But to wake *before* the bell was a first if ever there was one! That terrible clanging sound usually crashed in on her dreams with the force of a hundred stampeding horses, making her hate everything in her new life for a few moments until she managed to gather herself and remember where she was … and why.

There were no pictures in the dormitory, no ornaments, and no mats on the polished wooden floor. The uncovered windows were open in spite of it being winter. All the bedcovers were white.

But Cecilia's future spread out before her like an exquisite piece of finely worked cloth, with all the different coloured threads making a pattern as subtle and varied and difficult to read as the night sky. *Poverty, chastity and obedience.* There would be hard times, she didn't doubt that, dark nights when she lost her footing on the steep narrow road she'd chosen, but there would be joy too. Of that she was even more certain.

Downstairs in the large locker next to the communal basins, the lovely satin wedding dress her mother had made waited on a hanger. It had beaded embroidery around the neck, and a lace veil with three satin roses to hold it in place. *Oh, Mum!* she'd protested. *I won't be a bride for long.* But secretly she'd been glad it was so beautiful.

Now the day had arrived she couldn't wait to put it on. Nor could she help hoping her family would come in time to get a front pew so they would see how lovely she looked in that dress, walking up the aisle with six other postulants to meet her future. *Such vanity, Cecilia!* This morning she planned to ask the Novice Mistress, Mother Mary of the Holy Angels, if she might leave her hair to hang loose, for this … *her last day in the world.*

For the past twelve months the honey-blonde curls had been scraped back from her face into a tight little bun, held with pins under a little thing that was more like a bird's nest than a veil. During today's ceremony the postulants would file into the sacristy for a few minutes to have their hair shorn off. When they came out again into the main body of the church they'd be dressed in their new habit: wimple, bandeau, white veil and guimpe. Proper nuns for the first time!

Her father had always called his only daughter's hair her *crowning glory,* and she so wanted him to see it this last time.

'This is it, kid.'

Cecilia turned to smile at the impish face of Breda Walsh, who was poking her head out from under a pillow in the bed beside hers. There were seven postulants in the dormitory, all more or less the same age as Cecilia and Breda, except for Joan who was twenty-seven, and the rest were still sleeping soundly. Cecilia put a finger over her mouth to remind her friend that it was totally against the rules to speak. The Great Silence was observed from the end of evening recreation until after breakfast the next day – on this of all days it must be so.

'You having second thoughts?' Breda whispered in her deep, throaty voice.

Cecilia shook her head. 'You?' She mouthed without uttering a sound.

'A few.' Breda nodded seriously.

Cecilia had to stifle a cry of dismay. Four of the original group of eleven had left, just disappeared without a word of goodbye, because that was the way it was done. One, everyone was sure, had been asked to leave because there was something not right about her, but … *but not Breda. Not today! Please.*

'Only kidding!' Breda whispered. 'You seriously think I'd want to miss out on Babs's slice?'

Cecilia's mouth fell open in relief and a giggle escaped before she could hold it back.

Babs was Sister Barbara, the convent cook, and there was no more warm hearted and cheery soul in the world. Everyone loved her, but unfortunately that didn't change the fact that she couldn't cook. Her specialty was making meals out of thinly disguised leftovers. Not, of course, that any of the postulants or novices complained. To do so would be to bring the wrath of Mother Mary of the

Holy Angels down on their heads. But just occasionally they'd stare down at the food in front of them and look at each other or give a small private sigh that the rest of the table understood. On special Feast Days Sister Barbara let herself go with an array of sweets that were nothing short of amazing: lopsided sponge cakes, soggy puddings with lumpy custard, trifles awash in so much port that a decent serve was liable to make a young Sister tipsy. But it was with the slices that she outdid herself. The chocolate ones were bitter and the lemon slice so sweet it made their teeth ache.

'We might get the *bruise* today if we're lucky!'

'Shhh ...' Cecilia was laughing so hard that tears were running down her face.

On the Feast of the Sacred Heart, Babs had gone all out to make a marble cake, but instead of using pink and gold food dye, she'd used darker colours and it had turned out black and blue, and to top it off the icing was red, like blood. When out of the Novice Mistress's hearing, the postulants referred to it as *Bab's bruise*.

Once Cecilia started giggling she couldn't stop. Every time she caught Breda's eye gleaming at her from under the pillow a new spasm of laughter would ride up from her belly into her throat, until the two of them were curled up under their bedclothes biting their fists to stop from shrieking.

'Shhh.' Cecilia turned back to Breda. 'Breda! *Shut up,* please.'

The bell sounded on the floor above where the fully professed Sisters slept. It would be only a matter of a minute before the Novice Mistress was walking down between their beds, and if she sensed any shenanigans at all there would be hell to pay.

Mother Mary of the Holy Angels had made it very clear over the last year that she saw it as her task to subdue any vestiges of ego in the postulants before they were received into the noviciate proper. As Mother put it, by then *they'd better know what they'd got themselves into.* After two years as novices it would be time to make their First Profession. A few years later came the Final Vows, a solemn commitment to stay for the rest of their lives.

The aim was to become empty vessels open to God's Will and that meant obeying every rule set out for them by Mother Superior, from how and when they were to speak, smile, pray, walk or open a door, to the way they ate, knelt and lay in bed. Any kind of laughter, giggling or gossip was actively discouraged, along with close personal friendships. Nothing about their lives was deemed personal or off-limits or, for that matter, above suspicion. At the end of every week each postulant was required to confess to the rest of the group her own shortcomings at the Chapter of Faults, always in the spirit of complete humility. Every misdemeanour, from an incorrect attitude to botched practical tasks like dusting or cleaning one's shoes, to any unkindness or impatience towards another Sister, was considered serious enough to confess and sometimes worthy of chastisement and punishment.

The Novice Mistress was finding Breda an unusually hard nut to crack. The short, bright girl was very devout and always took her punishments cheerfully, never for a minute seriously questioning her Superior's right to dish them out, and so one had to assume she had a genuine vocation. But Mother Holy Angels still held serious doubts, because her personality was turning out to be very hard to subdue. It bubbled up in the most inappropriate ways. For a postulant to question practices that had been part of convent life for centuries was unusual enough – but for her to find these practices *amusing* was unheard of. That she always apologised in the most respectful manner after letting out one of her irreverent giggles somehow made it even more infuriating. The truth was that if it weren't for Reverend Mother's obvious liking for the girl, Mother Mary of the Holy Angels would have sent her packing months ago. As far as she was concerned, if the likes of Breda Walsh slipped through the cracks then the Order might not see the century out!

Only the night before, when Mother Holy Angels had come in to wish the postulants goodnight, she'd found Breda standing in her nightdress looking out a window. The main convent building was in a square and completely hidden from the street beyond the ten-foot-high walls. The postulants' and novices' dormitories were on the second floor. Their windows looked out over a pretty internal garden with a huge liquidambar tree in the middle of the lawn, the top of which reached their floor.

'Just what are you doing, Sister?' Mother fumed.

'Er … just standing here, Mother. I'm sorry.'

'*Standing?*'

'I love the tree at night, Mother. I'm sorry.'

'Sisters of the Good Shepherd do not stand about … looking at trees!'

'I know, Mother. It's just that …'

'Just as we do not run, or speak unless it is absolutely necessary,' the older woman fumed. 'We are never late and we open and close doors silently at all times!'

This was in direct reference to Breda's misdemeanour earlier in the day when she'd come late into the Church Doctrinal class and in her consternation had left the door to clatter shut behind her. Bad enough that it caused everyone to look around, which put them all in the wrong, too – part of the Custody of the Eyes Rule stipulated *never* looking up when someone came into, or left the room – but the banging door had made Breda forget another even more important Rule. Instead of immediately dropping to her knees to kiss the floor in front of Mother Bernard, who was giving the class, she'd stood at the door mumbling about being *ever so sorry to be late!*

Mother Bernard had simply exploded, going so far as to question Breda's vocation right there and then in front of everyone. If she couldn't get such a simple thing right, then what hope was there for her?

And here she was, the same girl, the night before she was to be formally received into the convent, standing about *looking at trees!* Mother Holy Angels's cheeks flamed red with indignation.

'Yes, Mother. Thank you, Mother.'

'As we do not look at our superiors!'

'I'm very sorry, Mother.' Breda's head fell immediately.

'Do you *still* not understand the Custody of the Eyes?'

'I do, Mother.'

'Are you sure? Tomorrow you will ask to be received into this Community of Sisters for the next two years, on the understanding that you fully intend making vows to live here with us for the rest of your life!'

'I do realise that, Mother,' Breda said with her eyes downcast. 'And with the Grace of God I will try to correct myself.'

'Very well,' the Novice Mistress sighed, 'then I ask each and every one of you to pray for Breda Walsh as well as yourselves, because she does seem to be taking a very long time to learn the most basic aspects of our Rule.'

'Yes, Mother,' the six other voices chorused.

Special friendships were discouraged, and Cecilia seriously tried to comply with this rule. But Breda sometimes seemed to be more a force of nature than a person. How could you not love the sun or thrill to the sound of thunder? She and Breda no longer sat next to each other in the refectory, nor knelt together in chapel and they avoided each other at recreation as Mother Holy Angels had requested, and yet their friendship blossomed. In the main it was unspoken. When something struck them as funny they would turn to each other before they had time to think. Neither of them seemed able to help it.

All meals were taken in silence, apart from the Sister whose turn it was to stand at the rostrum to read to the whole congregation. At breakfast the week before, Mother Holy Angels had rushed in from outside to interrupt Mother Mary John of the Transfiguration, who was reading aloud from *The Lives of the Saints,* to give two *serious announcements*. Everyone had put down their cutlery and waited, eyes on their plates, all of them very alert. Cecilia had tingled with excitement but also with dread. The one other time the Silence had been interrupted in this way was when Reverend Mother had come in to tell them that the American President,

John Kennedy, had been assassinated. So something momentous must have happened. Had war broken out? Was some other terrible disaster unfolding as they sat there quietly eating their meal? Could the Holy Father in Rome have taken ill?

But Mother's first message was that Sister Cyril would be teaching correct shoe-cleaning procedure after Benediction that evening. And the second was that as St Augustine had deemed excessive eating and drinking unholy, the postulants were not to have more water than what was absolutely required when they were cleaning their teeth.

Cecilia's and Breda's eyes had met across the tables. When Mother left the room, they had both raised an empty hand to their mouths at exactly the same time, as though gulping down water from a glass. For the rest of the day they'd had trouble suppressing laughter every time they'd caught each other's eye. Perhaps it *was* wrong, but until someone showed Cecilia the papal decree that outlawed laughter she thought … *what harm?*

Just on six-thirty a.m. the door to the dormitory creaked open, a two-second flicker before the place was blazing with fluorescent light, and the rotund body of the Novice Mistress was among them, walking up the aisle between the beds calling, '*Praise be to Jesus,*' her stern face expressionless as she waited for each half-asleep postulant to return the phrase.

The mumbled responses were thick with sleep. *Praise be to Jesus.* They pushed off their bedclothes and sank to their knees by their beds. *O praise be to Jesus.* All kneeling now and praying together. *O praise be to Jesus …*

It's on. I'm on the way. Cecilia wanted to yell out the excitement that bubbled up inside her; instead she buried her face in her hands and tried to concentrate on the prayer.

O Jesus, through the most pure heart of Mary, I offer thee all the joys, prayers, work and sufferings of this day …

At the end of the morning offering, she rose from the floor, drew the curtains around her bed, pulled off her long nightdress and slipped the long black petticoat over herself. Then the black stockings, followed by the black serge dress pulled in at the waist by a leather belt. The cape and white collar would come later.

She picked up her towel, pushed back the curtains surrounding her bed and took a moment to stare at the light beginning to break outside. She longed to look around at the others, if only to give them a smile of encouragement. But this too would be against the rules, and anyway it was important to get down quickly to have a good wash in the little warm water allowed in the mornings.

When she'd first arrived at the convent, one bath a week had seemed outrageous. Her own sour smell under the black dress still occasionally distressed her to the point of tears, but as the days and months wore on she got better at accepting it. Putting aside such petty concerns brought her closer to God.

When everyone was washed and dressed, the postulants formed a single straight line behind the novices at the top of the stairs to wait for Mother Holy Angels, who would lead them down to the chapel for Lauds, the first liturgy of the day. The Profession ceremony would be part of a High Mass celebrated by the Archbishop later that morning. Cecilia tried to quell the rumbling in her stomach as she stood with the others, hands clasped and eyes down. There would be nothing to eat until the afternoon. She said a quick prayer that her stomach would not betray her during the ceremony.

'You nervous?' whispered Breda.

Cecilia nodded. The ceremony would last for at least two hours and, apart from the vows and the sermon, it would be conducted completely in Latin and she was nervous that she'd get something wrong. There was so much to remember. The Novice Mistress had trained them thoroughly, of course. Over and over again they'd sung the hymns, the responses and the order of ceremony, but what if she got tongue-tied when it was her turn to answer the Bishop, or what if she dropped the veil when he gave it to her? *What if…?* There would be no end to it. Mother Holy Angels would consider any mistake a personal slight.

'You?'

Breda nodded and then grinned.

'Are *all* your brothers coming?' Breda whispered. Cecilia nodded. 'Even Dominic?'

Cecilia nodded again and smiled. Breda had been brought up in the city, the eldest of three sisters; she found Cecilia's stories of growing up on a farm with so many brothers fascinating.

'Can I meet them today?'

'Yep. At the lunch when—' Cecilia flushed when she saw one of the older novices turn around to frown at them. It was so easy to forget about the silence. The words just spilt out. Even now after a whole year!

During the last family visit, three months before, her mother assured her that all six of her older brothers and the younger twins, Declan and Sean, would come to the ceremony. Even Dominic – the eldest, who had more or less cut himself off from the rest of the family, and made it plain that he didn't approve of what Cecilia was doing – was coming. Her mother had written to him especially, told him that it would mean the world to his only sister. He'd reneged on his hardline stance and had actually written Cecilia a short note to say that he would come and that she could rest assured that he would behave himself, that he loved her and always would. Cecilia had been so touched by the rough note that she'd had to stop herself from crying. She handed back to Mother Holy Angels the two other letters she'd received that day – one from her favourite aunt who was dying in a country hospital, and the other from her mother – but against all the rules she'd kept the note from Dom. What harm would it do to keep something which meant so much to her and nothing to anyone else? She would hide it under her mattress and pull it out occasionally when the loneliness got too hard.

But the Novice Mistress had a sharp eye. That evening Cecilia was chastised in front of the whole community. Punishment for her insubordination was to lie face down on the refectory floor while the rest of the Sisters ate their meal. At the end, every one of the other Sisters in the congregation had stepped over her without a word. Photos, mementoes, letters, any private possession, was against the Rule. To try to keep anything so frivolous as a note from a brother was a serious offence.

Over the past year Cecilia had come to love the Liturgy of the Hours. Entering the ethereal space of the chapel every morning with the pure voices of the Community of Sisters surrounding her in chant and song never failed to lift her spirits. She was often tired from not enough sleep, cold in the winter and occasionally hungry too, but the gloomy recesses and the majestic archways under the high vaulted ceiling made all bodily concerns recede and exhilaration took over.

Benedictus Dominus Deus Israel; quia visitavit et fecit redemptionem plebi suae...

Blessed be the Lord God of Israel because He hath visited and wrought the redemption of His People...

After all, God was present before her on the altar, and later that morning she would be taking the living Christ into her own body. The miracle of it suffused her innermost soul with joy. *Make me worthy to receive you,* she prayed over and over. *Only say the word and I will be healed.* She stared at the mural of Our Lady ascending into Heaven that was above the altar, and then over at the big wooden crucifix nailed to the side pillar where the tortured body of Christ hung, and her whole being was filled with a deep, melancholy joy.

Oh my dearest Lord. God of all the heavens! Today I will share your burdens with an open heart. Today I pledge my life to you!

Illuminare his, qui in tenebris et in umbra mortis sedent, ad dirigendos pedes nostros in viam pacis.

To enlighten them that sit in darkness, and in the shadow of death: to direct our feet into the way of peace.

Four hours later, the swell of the organ created a buffer against the mass of curious faces turning to watch the seven postulants, all dressed beautifully as brides, begin their slow, single-file walk up the central aisle of the Convent Chapel, eyes downcast and hands joined.

Behind them came the novices who were to be professed. The whole congregation was singing.

Veni, Creator Spiritus
mentes tuorum visita,
imple superna gratia
Quae tu creasti pectora...

Come Creator Spirit
Fill the minds of Your People
Enkindle in them the fire of Your Love

Cecilia tried to concentrate on the words she was singing, but mixed in with her prayers was an awareness of the soft white lace around the neck of her wedding dress, the nipped-in waist, the covered buttons down the back and the rather spectacular sight they must be making for those watching in the pews.

In the end, Mother Holy Angels had baulked at loose hair, but as a compromise Cecilia had been allowed to let a few stray curls frame her face. There were no mirrors in the convent, but she was able to see in the window reflection that it looked pretty. Her father would see and be pleased.

The male clergy and half-dozen altar boys had made their entrances some minutes before, and the Archbishop, resplendent in an embroidered mitre and magnificent scarlet robes, was waiting by the altar. Stooped and frail, he sat motionless in the enormous carved chair, staring impassively ahead as the fifteen Sisters in all – seven postulants dressed at brides and eight novices in white habits – made their way slowly into the two front pews. In his right hand he held the gold shepherd's staff of St Peter, and on either side of him stood clusters of priests, eight in all, some old and some young. They were dressed in white lace surplices over long white linen cassocks. One of the younger ones – Cecilia thought it might be Marie Claire's brother who was a recently ordained Oblate – stood in front of the others swinging a gold thurible of incense. Sweet-smelling smoke drifted in small grey clouds down into the body of the church, and the soft clanking sound made a steady backdrop to the singing.

Most of the Community of Nuns sat in special seats on either wall of the church, but some were up keeping order among the Sacred Heart girls in the section to the right of the altar, and others were at the back singing in the special choir. The centre pews of the church were filled with seculars – the families and friends of the postulants and novices. The enormous space, lighted by masses of candles and the red light from the ruby windows, was alive with the beautiful psalms set to music.

Who is she that cometh forth as the morning rising,
fair as the moon,
bright as the sun
terrible as an army set in battle array.

In the few minutes it had taken to walk up the aisle, Cecilia's focus had shifted from feeling nervous and shy and conscious of how she looked, to an utterly joyful sense of being in another world altogether. By the time the first triumphant hymn had ended and the Bishop was making his slow way over to the pulpit, her joy had ripened into a state of mystical ecstasy such that her whole being was yearning to glide like a bird into that other realm of spiritual harmony with her Beloved. She was ready now, and couldn't wait to discard the beautiful irrelevant dress and put on the habit.

'*These young women will remember this as the greatest day of their lives ...*' The Bishop's address was the only part of the ceremony said in English.

Cecilia sang, letting the rich harmonies of the voices around her, the sweet smell of burning incense and the rich organ music assault her senses. Never had she felt more alive. The Latin, so alien when they'd first arrived in the noviciate only twelve months before, had now become almost as familiar as their mother tongue.

Dominus vobiscum
Et cum spiritu tuo

One by one the postulants ascended the altar steps to kneel in front of the Bishop and pronounce her free intention to join the Community of Sisters. *My child, what do you ask?*

Cecilia looked up at the Blessed Sacrament he was holding in front of her and her voice was strong. *My Lord, In the Name of Our Saviour Jesus Christ and under the protection of His immaculate Mother Mary ever Virgin, I, Cecilia Mary Veronica Madden called now in Religion Sister Mary Annunciata, most humbly beg to be received to the Holy Profession ... In this, the year of our Lord one thousand nine hundred and sixty-four.*

May God grant you perseverance in this your holy resolution ...

Veni Sponsa Christi,
Accipe coronam, quam tibi Dominus praeparavit in aeternum

Come, Spouse of Christ,
Receive the crown which the Lord hath prepared for thee in eternity.

And then it was the novices' turn, making the first of their solemn vows.

I do vow and promise to God, Poverty, Chastity and Obedience and the Zeal for Saving Souls, and to preserve until the end of my life in enclosure in this Institute for the charitable care and instruction of poor women and girls ... I will make my vows to the Lord in the sight of all His people in the courts of the house of the Lord.

The Bishop sprinkled each newly received novice with Holy

Water and handed her a folded white veil, a long white candle and a small, silver, heart-shaped locket in which those same vows were enclosed.

Receive this holy veil, the emblem of Chastity and Modesty. May you carry it before the judgement seat of Our Lord Jesus Christ that you may have Eternal Life and live for ever and ever.

The novices and New Professed responded to the words of the Antiphon *Vota mea* in unison.

I am espoused to Him whom the angels serve and at whose beauty the sun and moon stand in wonder.

They filed off the altar in procession to the sanctuary where the capping would take place as His Grace intoned the *Regnum mundi*. Mother Superior, along with the Mistress of Novices, supervised the cutting off of their hair and the putting on of their new habits, all the time singing in Latin.

I have despised the kingdom of the world, and all the grandeur of this earth, for the love of Our Lord Jesus Christ, Whom I have seen, Whom I have loved, in Whom I have believed and towards Whom my heart inclines.

There were so many pieces of clothing and so many prayers to remember as each garment went on. Cecilia was not the only newly professed novice who had difficulty fitting the bandeau properly and pinning the white veil in place. So many archaic undergarments before the voluminous outer dress. How was it going to feel in summer? And where was her chord and how were you meant to tie it?

She swung around so a stern Mother Holy Angels could set her guimpe straight as they continued singing the psalm.

He has placed his seal upon my forehead and I will admit no other lover but Him.

After assessing each new novice for imperfections, the Mistress of Novices motioned for them all to fall back into line. One by one they knelt before the Mother Superior and took a long white flickering candle.

Cecilia risked a small smile as she caught the eye of Marie Claire, now Sister Mary Scholastica, and Breda, now Sister Mary Perpetua. *How different we all look!*

Breda nudged Cecilia. 'We made it, kiddo.'

'We did.'

A massive organ and the singing of Psalm CXXXIII accompanied their return into the main body of the church.

Ecce quam bonum
Quam jucundum
Habitare fratres in unum

Behold how good and how pleasant it is
for brethren to dwell together in unity.

Cecilia sensed a rustle of disquiet as the congregation, who'd been sitting and waiting for them for some time, craned forward. She went on singing and didn't raise her eyes, but for the first time she thought of her own family sitting somewhere in the body of the church. Mum would be fine, but her father and brothers would be finding this long ceremony difficult. She wished suddenly for it all to be over, longed to hug them. No matter about her new religious name, she was still Cecilia, the same person that they'd always known.

And yet the blunt truth was that she had left them, and she knew they knew it too. Apart from a couple of hours every six weeks, after this day she would be effectively gone from their lives. The new habit said it all. Only her face was visible. A sudden stab of sorrow shot through her, as an image of the home she'd grown up in filled her mind. Never again would she see that house, sit in the kitchen or smell a cake cooking in the oven. Nor would she ever ride again with her brother Dom, race across the paddocks towards Auntie Mon's back paddock, clearing Patterson's Creek near the bridge that they'd been warned a thousand times was too wide and dangerous for a horse – then up the hill to the finishing line, neck and neck, the horses wet with sweat, both of them breathless with laughter.

Never again would she sit on the verandah and drink mugs of tea, listening to her brothers scrapping and fighting and joking with each other. No food or drink would pass her lips in front of any other person for the rest of her life except her fellow sisters. The twins – those two boys who'd arrived after her mother thought she'd finished having babies – were now only eleven. She would never know them, nor they her.

Nor would she ever have a family of her own. No man to love; no babies to hold.

In a final act of submission, the line of professed Sisters lay face down in front of the altar. The funeral pall that would be placed over her coffin one day was draped over her body to signify her retreat from the world. She could smell the floor wax and feel the cool of the wood, and she hoped she wasn't going to sneeze or cry. Already her shorn head felt itchy.

The new novices walked single file down the aisle joyfully singing the *Te Deum* along with the other Sisters.

Te Deum laudamus: Te Dominum confitemur.
Te aeternum Patrem omnis terra veneratur.

We praise thee, O God: we acknowledge thee to be the Lord.
All the earth doth worship thee: the Father everlasting…

And it was over.

After a quick lunch with her fellow sisters – they were all ravenous, having not eaten since the night before – there were two and a half hours of sitting about in the convent gardens with her parents and brothers. Dominic really had come, and although he'd been distant with them all, his smile for her was warm. They'd all started off shyly, probably because they hadn't seen her for months, and the new habit hid the sister that they remembered. But as the afternoon wore on, when she linked arms with them, laughed and joked like old times, they all relaxed. For Cecilia it was such a joy to be with her family. She would never go home again, nor eat another meal with them, but this was the next best thing.

At one point there'd been a lull in the conversation. Her father had looked up from his paper to the big brick buildings. 'This place will kill you,' he'd muttered sourly.

Cecilia laughed in dismay. 'I'm happy here, Dad.'

'I heard you telling your mother just now that you couldn't take your cardigan off without *asking* the Reverend Mother,' he growled. '*That* is just plain ridiculous.'

'Oh, Dad!' Tears sprung to her eyes. 'It's nothing.'

'You could be using that head of yours.'

'But I am!'

He slumped down in the chair, closed his eyes and shook his head slowly. 'My only daughter,' he said to no one in particular, before turning back to the pink *Sporting Globe,* 'cooped up like a bloody chook! I never thought I'd see the day.'

Cecilia tried to laugh along with her brothers. But his blunt ridicule cut deeply, all the more because he'd intended that it should.

It was later, when Cecilia pulled the curtains around her bed and began to take off the new habit, that panic hit her. It came in waves, ebbing and flowing around her like the cold green ocean on a bleak day. The new robes were confining and hot, much heavier than the postulant dress. The starched linen encasing her head had chafed both sides of her face and a sharp line across her forehead. It diminished her hearing too. She missed half of what people were saying unless she was facing them directly.

As she felt for the pins that held the whole set in place, she made herself take some deep breaths. *Calm down!* If only she had some oil or lotion for the sore bits. But it was when her hands touched the short stubble where her hair used to be that some deep part of her stilled, and her head became a roll of panicky drumbeats, all out of rhythm. *What have I done?*

During the ceremony it had been exciting seeing the soft golden clumps fall about her feet, but now, feeling her bare head, and picturing again the grim satisfaction on the Novice Mistress's face as the curls massed on the floor, something inside her mind gave way. The soft shapes turned into slivers of glass about her feet, and she wanted to cry out. *I'm nineteen years old, and I have no hair!* She fell to her knees and prayed. *Oh God, let me see that it is leading me closer to you!* But all the certain calm joy that had carried her through the day had vanished and in its place was a pit of black terror.

Her heart was rattling, her skin clammy with dread. She put both hands up to her prickly skull and a silent scream echoed around and around her head high above the drumbeat. *Oh, what have I done?*

She longed suddenly for human contact. If she could just talk to someone! If she could only pull the curtains aside and sit on the end of Breda's bed. Ask her if she felt the same about losing her hair. But doing that would make a mockery of all that she'd decided to do that very day. To breach the Great Silence with such an inconsequential matter would be a very grave fault.

Thou has made us for thyself, O Lord, and our hearts are restless until they rest in thee.

Oh, but it was true! It had to be true. How many times had she said it? And so she must do so again and again and again. They were St Augustine's own words written during his own dark night of the soul. *Thou hast made us for thyself, O Lord, and our hearts are restless until they rest in thee...*

Ever so slowly her equilibrium returned. *Yes.* She knew who she was. She was Annunciata, a newly received Sister in the Order of the Good Shepherd. She knew who she was, and why she was where she was. *I do. I know who I am. I do. And I know why I'm here.* Eventually she rose from her knees, pushed back the curtains and got into bed. She was overwrought, that was all. Overwrought.

It had been a big day.

At last the overhead lights were out. Cecilia listened to the quietness of the others asleep around her, and thought of her father and his curt dismissal of everything she held dear. But that didn't upset her as much as Dominic. Dom was troubled. Anyone could see it in his face, and it tore at Cecilia's heart. Her eldest brother, who used to put her up behind him on the white pony when she was very little, make up funny little stories for her and whistle tunes for her to guess. When she was old enough, he'd taught her to ride. Now Dom was … lost. If only she could help him. If only she could sit with him, tell him a joke, make him smile.

'Have you been riding?' she'd asked shyly that afternoon during a quiet moment.

'Nah.' He'd shrugged and looked away.

She lay on her back staring at the ceiling, letting the tears leak from the corners of her eyes down onto her thin pillow. Most nights someone cried herself to sleep in this room. So now it was her turn.

She shifted onto her side in the bed and was just dropping off to sleep when she realised that Breda's bed was empty. Alarmed, Cecilia sat up and looked around.

Breda was standing by the window, her small bald head bent to one side in the light coming in from the cold moon. She must be up looking at that tree again. Cecilia couldn't help smiling. Just then the moonlight caught a glint of something silver in Breda's hand and the smile froze on her lips.

Oh my God! Cecilia pushed off the bedclothes and tiptoed over. 'Where did you get that?' she whispered in awe.

'Dad,' Breda said simply, holding out the small transistor radio so Cecilia could see. 'Today.'

'But Breda!' Cecilia was genuinely shocked. 'If Mother sees it she'll have a stroke.'

'Footy,' Breda said matter-of-factly. 'I'm sick of relying on Guido.'

Breda's only source of information about her beloved team, Fitzroy, was old Guido, a sixty-year-old Italian refugee who worked with Mother Benedict in the garden. Every week she risked the Novice Mistress's wrath to grab five minutes to find out the Lions' weekend score. But he didn't work Mondays, so it meant she had to wait until Tuesday.

But they weren't allowed to own anything. *Poverty.* 'The female has a natural inclination to make a nest,' Reverend Mother told them time and time again. 'My dear Sisters, housewifery is part of our very natures and so must be resisted at all costs. We are not housewives but vehicles for God's Grace in the world. As such, we own nothing except the sacred vows we have taken and keep as the sweetest flowers near our hearts. They are kept fresh every day with the pure water of prayer.'

Nothing. We own nothing.

Indeed, each novice had to humbly beg the community every few weeks to use the simple trifles that she needed to survive, such as crockery, prayer books and the shoes on her feet. If a sister broke anything out of carelessness, then she had to wear it about her person for a whole day as a reminder to be more careful with property that didn't belong to her. Only the week before, little Sister Paula had had to walk about all day with four broken cups hanging from her belt. The week before that, Cecilia herself had had to carry around a chipped tray that she'd dropped when she was taking one of the old infirm Sisters her breakfast.

So what could Breda be thinking?

Cecilia tried with everything in her to hold back the laughter. But when she gave in to it, Breda joined her, and suddenly they were clinging to each other, doubled over and helpless, barely able to stand up.

'You can't keep it,' Cecilia gasped. Their lockers were open for inspection all the time by anyone who cared to inspect them.

'Watch me!'

'But *how* ... I mean?'

'I'll hide it.'

'But what if she finds it?'

Oh but it was good to laugh, to feel the knots loosening inside, to feel herself just nineteen years old, with all that energy spluttering to life again.

'So how ...?'

'Today. Dad slipped it into my pocket.'

'Breda!'

'I know, I know.'

'But it's so ... neat,' Cecilia whispered.

Breda pushed it up against Cecilia's ear. 'Listen to this,' she commanded.

Love me do.

The simple cheekiness of the tune bounced along Cecilia's raw nerves like a tennis ball, making her weak suddenly with a dull longing for all that she didn't know.

'The Beatles,' Breda breathed excitedly, 'from Liverpool in England. They're coming to Australia. Dad's going to take my two younger sisters.'

Cecilia nodded. The yearning in her friend's voice made her want to weep all over again.

'Where will the concert be?'

'Festival Hall.'

'They'll tell you all about it at the next visit,' Cecilia whispered encouragingly. 'It will be the same as being there.'

They stared at each other in the light coming through the window, and Cecilia saw then that Breda had been crying too.

They both knew that hearing about the Beatles concert from her sisters a month after the event would not be the same as being there.

'It's so hard sometimes, isn't it?' Breda whispered and Cecilia took her hand.

'It is,' she murmured.

It was after eleven and very cold, but the two newly received nineteen-year-old brides of Christ were on their wedding night and there was a Beatles special on 3UZ. They stood side by side at the open window, taking turns with the radio, dressed in long plain flannelette nightgowns, their shorn heads turning occasionally, smiling at each other in the darkness, their fingers thrumming along in time with the music on the heavy wood of the window frame.

Peach

Fuck! This can't be. But … yes, it is. I'm awake now. Well and truly awake, and I know what I'm hearing. It's the creak of the cutlery drawer followed by the fridge's soft slam, then the slow shuffle of my sixteen-year-old sister's slippers along the kitchen floor. *Oh God, here goes.*

Yep. Now it's the low but definitely discernable sound of the television, some strung-out seventies rock band of course, interspersed with bursts of manic applause. *Oh please,* not the Sex Pistols *again!* I can't stand it. They'd have to be grandfathers by now.

It is three a.m. for Christ's sake! I have an interview in the morning for a job I want. What to do now? What *can* I do, short of going down and throwing a fit, slamming a few doors and screeching at the top of my voice for her to shut the hell up?

In normal weather the creaks, rattles and groans of this old terrace shuts out whatever is happening downstairs, but tonight is so completely still, and so hot, that nothing is moving. When I hit the sack around midnight I left my door wide open hoping to get some air. *So why don't I just get up and close the door?*

For some reason I can't move. I lie here as rigid as a dead

sailor, hammered to the deck by the weird kind of inertia that disappointment creates. That last plan took us both the best part of a day to work out. All those solutions, strategies and promises written down so meticulously and pinned to the back of her bedroom door. The *DOs* on the left-hand side and the *DON'Ts* on the right. They'd looked so damned *convincing* spread across two large white pages. Mum and Dad were going to be so proud of her, *of us*, when they got back. It's only two days later and she's cut loose again, hurtling along that infamous paved pathway, stepping on all the good intentions in the world!

I sit up and stare out the open window at a dark clear night full of stars, feeling the frustration begin its slow miserable journey down from my brain into my throat and chest. Maybe I should go down there and yank her up by the hair. Smack her around a bit. She deserves it. Fifteen key points. She crossed-her-heart-and-hoped-to-die on every single one of them. Number one on the right was *No secret eating in the middle of the night*.

An electric guitar riff strides into my ears as if it has a perfect right, followed by drums, then some screeching angst about purple sunsets. Is this sneering Johnny Rotten telling everyone what a hero he is, or The Clash vomiting over the crowd in some forgotten English club?

Stella's musical tastes are fixed strictly in the seventies. She also loves Neil Diamond, the mature Elvis in his white-studded jump suit, grim-faced Patti Smith, Joni Mitchell with her jutting teeth and early Sting.

'He lost it after The Police,' she told me recently.

'Really?' The sarcasm went straight over her head.

'Yeah,' she sighed, like it cut her up to have to say it. 'There was only one good album after that.'

I lean across to the bedside table, grab the glass, gulp some water then flop back down. I turn over and look at the fronds of the top of the Jacaranda tree playing along the bottom edge of the window sill and try hard to think about something else.

But it's not working.

This can't go on. It has got to stop ... *now*.

I feel along the bed for the cotton nightie I threw off earlier. Thick tendrils of hair have escaped from the knot at the top of my head and lie in damp curls around my ears and neck. Sweat runs between my breasts and under my arms.

After I've dealt with my sister, I'll go have another cold shower.

I creep downstairs, past my mother's photo collection and out into the wide front hallway, stopping for a moment at the bottom of the stairs. Moonlight is shining straight through the stained glass panels set into the front door, making flecks of gold, deep-blue squares and patches of ruby red float along the polished wood floor.

I make a mental note to tell Det about this when I see her next. She'll laugh at me, but she'll like it. She is an artist and light is her thing: moonlight, fluorescent light, candlelight, sunlight, old gaslights and inner light too.

Sure enough, Stella is in the family room at the back of the house. Wrapped in a sheet, propped against one of the heavy chairs in front of the telly – and yep, it's some old bootleg video of the Sex Pistols. She's spooning ice-cream from the tub into her mouth as though someone has switched on the automatic button. I stand in the doorway a moment because I don't want to frighten her.

'Stella,' I say.

She doesn't turn around, but she stops spooning the ice-cream so I know she has heard me. I take a few steps towards her. 'Stella, it's after three a.m.'

'So?'

'Bedtime.'

'No need to crack the shits,' she grumbles sourly, still not looking at me. 'It's not exactly against the law!'

'I'm not cracking the shits.' I walk over to her and hold my hand out for the ice-cream.

She heaves a deep sigh and gives it up.

I look down at the extraordinary mass of coal-black hair she inherited from Dad. It is springing out in tight curls from her head at virtual right angles, almost blocking a view of her shoulders, and I wish I could play some role other than big-sister-who-knows-best. *She* used to set *me* straight about a whole lot of stuff not so long ago.

I put the tub of ice-cream down on the coffee table and take the thick pink hairband from around her wrist. Using both my hands I drag as much of her hair as I can up into a rough ponytail.

'Much cooler like this,' I murmur.

'I know,' she sighs.

'So why didn't you have it up?'

'It makes me look ridiculous.'

I have to smile. I twist her shoulders around so I can see her from the front and we grin at each other. It does look ridiculous. The ponytail, I mean. It looks like some weird black plant sticking straight up out of her head.

'And there are so many people here to see you, Stella, and all of them with cameras. You and your freaky hairdo with be all over the internet before you know it.'

She giggles and gives me one of her gorgeous bright-dark smiles, her enormous eyes twinkling in the low light from the flickering television. I have to wonder (for the millionth time), if her burgeoning weight means she is in the middle of some deep inner crisis, then how come she seems so cheerful most of the time?

'You never know who might be watching,' she says, mimicking Nana, who tried to teach us about being groomed at all times. *When you least expect it, girls, the man of your dreams will be coming around the corner of the street!*

'Yeah. Even at three a.m., someone might call,' I say, then take both her hands and pull her up. 'Come on, switch that off.'

She allows herself to be led until we reach the foot of the stairs, then she stops and pulls her hand away. I turn to see that she is frowning.

'Come on,' I say sharply, about to turn off the light.

'So how come?' she whispers, lifting her eyes to my face. 'How come you don't have them anymore?'

'What are you talking about?' I snap, pretending I don't know what she means, but of course I do. She knows I do, too, which makes it all the more crazy to be standing here denying it at three a.m. on this hot, airless night. But I know this much about myself, that if I let her embark on one of her big rambling monologues about my dreams now, I'll start screaming.

'Those dreams were so ... *you*, Peach.'

'Bed,' I say again, sharply.

'But I won't sleep,' she whines. 'I won't.'

'You just tell yourself that.'

'No, I honestly won't sleep,' she sighs miserably.

'You will.'

'Can I sleep with you?' she whines. 'Please, Peach?'

'It's too hot.'

'I swear I won't touch you.'

'Promise?' I sigh, too hot to fight her.

She nods happily and hurries up the stairs like a little kid. 'I'll bring the big fan in,' she calls over her shoulder. 'Okay?'

'Okay,' I say sourly.

I walk up the stairs behind my sister watching her bum bounce up and down. There are rolls of fat around her neck. She pauses on the stairs and tries to sound offhand.

'When are Mum and Dad coming back?'

'Six weeks on Saturday.'

'Oh, I can't wait,' she sighs. 'It will be soooo great to see them again, won't it?'

'Yeah. I guess.' Our parents have only been gone two weeks, but Stella is already missing them. She'll be like a bloody caged cat by the time they get back. She goes straight for the shower, comes out stark naked and goes to her room for the big fan.

'Wear a nightie,' I yell after her.

'It's too hot!' she calls back.

'Stay in your own room then!'

'Such a prude.'

'Yeah, well ... cop it.'

When she comes back in with the fan she is wearing a cotton nightdress like mine, except hers only just fits her.

I head for the bathroom and stand under the lovely cold water, gasping as the cold enters my bones. I know I won't get much sleep now. It is a double bed, but once she's asleep my sister's legs and arms often fling out in odd directions. She'll grunt and sigh and snore a little. She is actually liable to push me out. But she'll be happy. And I'll be doing the job that I agreed to do and ... that's important.

'Tell me stuff,' Stella murmurs sleepily.

'Too late.'

'Just tell me anything.'

'What?'

'I like listening to your voice.'

'Well, I don't want to talk.'

'Hate it when you go all quiet on me, Peach.'

'Please shut up, Stella. I have to get up early in the morning.'

'It's just a stupid old boring cafe job.'

'But it's a five-minute bike ride and I need money for the trip.'

'Have you guys bought your tickets yet?'

'No, we haven't and please ... shut up.'

'Okay.'

The full blast of the fan is good on my freshly showered skin. I watch the way it makes the curtains flutter in the dark and I am lightly and fleetingly happy.

It is too hot for even a sheet and we are both spreadeagled on our backs as far away from each other as we can get. My right arm is above my head and my left dangles over the edge of the bed. Just as well I'm thin or there wouldn't be room for us both. Within a minute I hear my sister's deep, even breathing. I turn over on my side and close my eyes.

Stella and I are so different physically that it is funny. People who don't know the situation just about fall over when I introduce her as my sister.

'*What?*' Their mouths open in disbelief. 'But you don't look anything like each other!'

Then come the wisecracks about Mum having had a fling around the time Stella was conceived, because oddly enough Mum and I look pretty similar, which is funny, really, because it's me who isn't the blood relation.

I was adopted as a baby when my parents thought they couldn't have any children of their own. They had their names down for another child when Mum became pregnant 'out of the blue', as she likes to say. Stella came out looking just like Dad, a bit stocky, olive skin, with dark eyes and thick curly black hair.

Sometimes we don't bother to tell people the truth. We just smile at each other and let them rave on. Of course, all our friends know. Most of them were initially intrigued about what it felt like not to be 'real' sisters. I stopped getting annoyed about what that question implied a long time ago. Stella too. We figure we were so damned lucky to get each other that all that crap isn't important. Everyone has family issues, why should we be immune? When our friends met our parents and saw that we live in a normal family – that me being adopted is not an issue – they soon lost interest.

My hair is naturally blonde and wavy, and although Mum and I have quite differently shaped faces, and her skin is fairer than mine, I pass as her birth daughter without comment, because I'm fine-boned too, and we both have blue eyes. I'm tall for a girl: 172 centimetres when I last measured myself.

Stella was pretty too, but in a completely different way. She still is, of course, only it's getting hard to see it. Her coal-black hair, bright-dark eyes and husky voice make you think of Spain (even though none of us has been there!). People pick up on her warm, gutsy vibe as soon as they meet her, and they either love it or avoid her like the plague. Stella wears her heart on her sleeve. It's just the way she is. She is fantastic and ridiculous in equal measure. We're so close that she tells me I am her *other side,* the ethereal, cerebral guardian angel who lives in her head. If that is true, then she has to be *my* other side, the tempestuous, brave, wild side that I'm too uptight to let out most of the time.

People have all these strange ideas about what being adopted must be like. For the record, let me just say that I don't sit around yearning to meet my *real* parents, nor have I even wondered much about them. I don't spend time thinking about how my life might have been different. Maybe I simply lack imagination, but it has never been something I've considered important. Oddly enough, it's Stella who is more intrigued by it all than me. One of her favourite pastimes is weaving complicated stories about my origins. *Your birth mother was a priestess in a faraway land ... She couldn't keep you because she was doomed to die when she turned sixteen.* My lack of interest in these bizarre scenarios never fails to infuriate her.

'I wish it was *me* who was adopted,' she often moans to Mum and Dad. 'The romance of it is wasted on boring old Peach!'

'Will you look after her for us, sweetheart?' Mum and Dad sat side by side on the deep-pink velvet two-seater couch under the window; it had belonged to Nana who'd lived with us until she died the year before. 'We don't *have* to go if it's going to be too much for you or if you feel that you won't be able to cope.'

It pissed me off a bit that they thought they had to ask. As though I wouldn't look after my sister while they were gone!

'Of course,' I said, not bothering to sound enthusiastic. 'I'll have her sorted out by the time you get back.'

'We realise it might get difficult,' Dad was looking down at his fingers, 'but you can ring us any time. We'll come home early if needs be.'

'Don't sweat.' I shrugged. 'It will be okay.'

'Thanks, love.' He gave me a tired smile. 'But understand, you are not responsible for everything she does. And it's only a couple of months.'

'I know that.'

'You think you'll be okay at Christmas?'

'We've been over this a million times!' I said irritably. 'I am nineteen years old!'

Christmas has never been that big in our house, mainly because we don't have any close relatives apart from Mum's sister, Claire. It was all arranged for us to go to go over to Claire's place for Christmas Day. But I knew it wasn't really Christmas that was worrying them. It was Stella.

My sister's slide into a strange malaise over the last year had us all stumped. There was Nana's dying, I suppose – they were so close because of the music thing – and then the teacher stuff, but it still didn't make any sense to the rest of us.

'Your sister is almost seventeen. You must continue to go about your normal life.'

My normal life! I felt like laughing, and then I wanted to cry, because I was suddenly thinking about Fluke. The way he'd smiled at me through the smoke and bouncing lights and loud music, straight across the heads of the other girls, some of them my friends who were dancing so fast and mean and sexy that I couldn't keep up.

'Go see your friends and have fun, okay?' Mum was nodding seriously. 'All we're asking is that you keep an eye out for her.'

'Just as long as I can still bring home hot guys to party all night?'

Dad grinned. 'Just make sure Stella doesn't get hold of them first!'

The same week that Nana died, Stella got a new music teacher. I'd already left school by then, but I heard about her. Spiky and vivacious Ms Beatrice Baums, she of the striped red socks and sharp tongue, had decided that she was going to make Stella a star. What sixteen-year-old can resist that? To say Stella developed a crush on her teacher would be the understatement of the year. Stella didn't just want to be *like* Ms Baums, she wanted to *be* her.

Mum stood and propped her bum on my desk. She put one hand on my shoulder and ran her other fingers through my hair.

'I might have to come back early,' she said, resting her chin on the top of my head and holding me around the neck. 'Wild men in the middle of the night sounds too good to miss.'

'Hang on!' Dad laughed.

My parents are both doctors, specialists in different fields. Mum is in women's health and Dad is a surgeon, with a speciality in oncology. Although he's short for a man, Dad has a lovely, warm open face, dark skin and a long straight nose. He is one of those guys who shaves *twice* a day. He's got patches of hair on his back and shoulders and his legs and arms are thick with it. When Stella and I were really little, we'd sit on the mat of curly black hair covering his chest and belly and he'd tell us that he'd grown it especially for us two and we believed him.

Stella used to say quite seriously that she'd never go out with a guy who wasn't covered in hair like Dad, because she'd be afraid he wasn't the real deal. I secretly agreed of course. Dad is the best.

Mum is two inches taller than Dad, quieter, gentler, with beautiful fair skin. She is the most honest person I know, and the kindest. It's not just me who thinks so. Everyone who meets my parents loves them.

They were both looking at me, waiting for me to say something or ask something, but all I was thinking about was the lines of tiredness and stress I saw around their eyes and the fact that whatever happened I wasn't going to call them back early. They really needed a break.

Of course, we'd all been away together heaps of times, but this would be their first proper holiday together, just the two of them, since I came along. First they were off to Paris, where Mum had gone to university and still had friends, and then over to England to see Dad's very old mother. It was all arranged that as soon as school finished Stella was going to do an intensive music summer school and I was going to get a cafe job and save for an overseas trip with my mates.

Then two weeks before they left, Stella declared that she wasn't going to do the summer school because she wanted to spend more time 'with friends'. We all knew that was bullshit because she didn't have friends any more.

They'd fallen by the wayside like most other things in her life. She was just piking out on the thing that she was best at, and it didn't make sense. But none of us knew what to do about it.

'Just make sure you come home safely,' I said stiffly. I couldn't seem to swallow the lump that had formed in my throat. *What if something happens to you?* Just looking at them was freaking me out. I'd never thought of them as *old* before. Maybe it was just because they'd spent such long hours at work recently. I wished Mum hadn't cut her hair so short and let it go grey. I wished she cared about her clothes; I wished she would laugh more, too, the way she used to.

'Of course we will, darling.'

I wanted to get nasty, tell her bluntly that if she wanted me to look after Stella, then at least she could start caring for herself again. I would shame her into it. Nana was nearly eighty when she died, but she looked good to the end. You never saw her without her hair coloured and styled, or without her lipstick. We all adored Nana. I wanted to tell Mum that her mother would absolutely hate to see her in an unironed fawn shirt, boring old thongs and a daggy haircut. I opened my mouth to say it all, but nothing came out. I just ... couldn't.

'Tell us what you're thinking, Peach,' Dad said slowly. 'Come on, sweetheart.'

'Just come home safely,' I mumbled again.

'Of course we will, darling,' they said again in unison. 'We'll be home before you know it.'

Watching them walk out of the room talking about what we'd have for dinner, I was overtaken with an *unnerving* feeling that my life was about to be shaken loose from its foundations. I desperately wanted to call them back again, make them sit down and tell me again that they'd be back and that everything would be fine.

As though sensing something, Dad stopped at the door and looked back at me.

'She'll come good once Year Twelve starts. The new school will do the trick. Give her a fresh start.'

'Yeah.' I nodded.

He grinned at me.

'Just don't let her change her name to Beatrice while we're gone!'

It's after eight when I wake, the sky is already blazing and I'm alone. Stella must have gone back to her own bed. The job interview is in an hour and I have to ride there, so I haul myself up and into the shower.

I wash my hair because it will dry before I get there, but I have no idea what I should wear to a job interview on a scorching day. I end up in a short cotton skirt, a loose, black linen top and flat-heeled sandals. I tie up my damp hair in a style that says I'm a practical hard worker, which I suppose I am.

In the kitchen, I pull down the blind to keep out the sun and pull out my phone to text Cassie, who will already be there, serving the coffees and selling bread. I cross my fingers as I turn on the kettle and get bread out of the fridge for toast. It would be so cool for us to work together. I want this job.

Remind Sam-the-man that I'm his girl! I write.

Within about six seconds she replies.

Already have but be warned, he's expecting favours!

I laugh and pop the bread into the toaster and text back.

Okay, but no sicko stuff

Whips okay?

Of course, but no spurs.

I'll let him know.

Cassie is my other best friend, along with Det. She is opinionated, short, fast and she gets things done. Always has. She started at my school in Year Nine and by the end of the first day she'd organised the class into groups of five to compete with another class to raise money for a dance competition. If a concert has sold out, Cassie can have tickets within the hour. Need something impressive to wear? She'll find you an outfit you really love before you finish the phone call. She's doing Commerce at uni, but she'll end up running a business. I'm convinced of it. She loves fashion and parties and knowing where people fit in, who is important and who isn't. Oddly enough, this doesn't make her shallow or heartless. She's just someone who happens to be really good at knowing how the world works, and making sure she gets a slice of the action. Det and Cassie don't always see eye to eye, but with me in the middle, our threesome somehow works out.

Sam-the-man is the guy who runs the bakery and cafe at the Abbotsford Convent. He's nice, apparently. When he said he needed someone reliable for the early-morning shift, Cassie suggested me, then told him a whole lot of lies about all the experience I'd had working in cafes. In fact, I've never even made a coffee but I have pulled beer and washed dishes, so ... I suppose it can't be that hard.

I text her again. *Do I lie about the coffee?*

But this time she doesn't get back, so I guess she's busy. Damn. I meant to get down there before now and get her to teach me on the sly.

I'm in the middle of a physiotherapy degree majoring in accidents and emergency care. Both Cassie and Det think this is hilarious, bordering on bizarre, seeing as the subjects I got the highest scores for were French and History.

'How can you stand it?' Det asked recently when I was settling down with the books to study for exams instead of hitting the party scene with them. 'Learning by rote is for parrots!'

'So a parrot will look after you when you have your bike

accident?' I snap straight back. Det rides a Honda motorbike and she knows the stats are not in her favour.

'Touché,' she laughed, 'but come anyway, my serious, sweet and conscientious Peach. No fun without you.'

'Not everyone can be an artist,' I grumble, shaking my head. 'I want to be useful.'

She puts one hand over her heart and pretends to topple over as if she's been mortally wounded.

'So cruel.'

'You asked for it.'

'Okay, nerd. Don't come!'

I'm standing at the kitchen bench stuffing segments of an orange into my mouth and waiting for my toast to cook when Stella saunters in, bleary eyed and yawning widely.

'Where did you get to?' I ask.

'Went back to my bed,' she mumbles, then goes to the fridge, opens the door and stands in front of it for ages, staring in as if something in there might be the answer to all her prayers. 'Did you know you radiate heat when you're asleep, Peach?'

'Really? And you don't?'

'Touchy this morning, aren't we?' She grins at me, then pulls out the milk and juice and goes for the bread. 'What do you think they'd be doing right now?'

'Well, it would be the middle of the night so probably sleeping.'

'Maybe, they're out late and as they are walking back to their hotel, some guy has a heart attack in the street and they save his life?'

'Maybe,' I murmur, rolling my eyes.

'And what about my other mother?' Stella says, shifting the packet of bread from one hand to the other as if she is playing with a ball.

Oh God, here we go. I sigh and don't answer.

'What do you think she'd be doing?'

'You don't have another mother, Stella,' I say bluntly.

Stella gives me a hurt look. 'I have a *spiritual* mother,' she says.

'Whatever,' I sigh.

She looks at me as though I'm the one who is being deliberately thick.

I just shake my head, letting her know that I will not be a party to this turn in the conversation. Of course it doesn't stop her.

'I think she's singing.'

'At eight-thirty in the morning?'

'She might be planting something in her garden and singing to herself.'

There is no real point telling her to stop this crap.

'You think one day she'll want to hear me sing again?'

'Probably not,' I say.

Stella sniffs and puts a slice of bread in the toaster and I wish for the millionth time there was something I could say to snap her out of her craziness.

'Stella Bella,' I say gently, 'I'm going for that job interview at the Abbotsford Convent this morning.'

'Hmmm?'

'You got any plans?'

'How long will it take?' she asks.

'Not long, but I'm going to wait for Cassie to finish her shift and we're going to fetch Det and maybe hang out together for a while. Lunch and stuff.'

'Sounds good.'

'But what will you do?'

'I'll be fine.' She frowns at the cooking toast. 'I don't really want toast. What should I have for breakfast, Peach?'

'What do you feel like?'

'Nothing.'

'Remember—' I begin my lecture, but she grabs me around the middle and shuts me up by gagging me with her other hand. I squirm and giggle, and we chorus together, 'Breakfast is the most important meal of the day!'

'I hate breakfast,' she grumbles, letting me go, as though I haven't already heard it a million times. 'It's the one time in the day I don't feel like eating.'

I nod and continue buttering my toast. Another conversation about Stella's intake of food is not what I need right at this moment. 'Let's not talk about it now, okay?'

'Fine with me.' Stella grins. 'Let's never talk about it again.' She lunges across the bench, pinches a half-slice of my toast from the plate, stuffs it in her mouth and leans over for my mug of tea too, but I hold it well away from her.

'Stella!'

'What?'

'Get your own.'

'Oh come on, Peaches. You're nearer.' She giggles. 'Please pour me a cup of tea!'

I pull a mug from the shelf and push over the pot and the milk. 'Here. Do it yourself.'

'So scratchy,' she mumbles to herself.

'What *are* you going to do today?' I persist.

'Maybe go see Ruby.' She gives a bored sigh.

'That's a good idea!' I say, too enthusastically. Ruby is one of the few friends she has left. 'Maybe you could have a swim?'

'Hmmmm, maybe.'

I've been trying to make her do something every day. She won't swim in the local pool any more because she's self-conscious about her size, and she doesn't walk much any more either. Ruby lives only a few streets away and the pool in the family backyard is this little rubber thing, but at least my sister would be doing *something*. If I don't nag her she'll just stay at home in front of the television and … eat.

Stella blows on her mug of hot tea.

'I woke up with this feeling about today,' she says dreamily, looking out the window.

'What kind of feeling?' I look at my watch, go to the sink with my dishes and wash the orange from my hands.

'That something truly amazing is going to happen.'

'Yeah?' I smile, shaking the water off my hands. 'To us or to the world?'

'To you.'

'To *me?*' I laugh. 'Nothing ever happens to me, Stella.'

'But today it will.'

'Will it be good?'

She looks thoughtful and then frowns. 'I ... I think so.'

'Don't freak me out!'

'It's just a feeling,' she says simply.

I laugh, but I'm curious in spite of myself – a touch alarmed too, if I'm truthful.

Stella operates on a different level to the rest of us. I'm not saying she is a mystic or anything like that. Only that she seems to have an uncanny ability to *twig* to stuff that other people miss. Mum, Dad and me acknowledge Stella as the soul of our family.

One afternoon she rang up to say she had a feeling that something had happened to Mum. When Mum got home that night she told us that she'd had a nasty prang in her car and had just missed being seriously hurt. Another time, Stella predicted that Det was going to come into some money by the end of the week. None of us even knew when the results of the grant applications were being announced. Even Det had forgotten all about it.

Stella often finds things when no one else has any idea. She found Dad's passport recently when he'd been beside himself searching the house all day. It was tucked away inside a plastic bag, inside the lining of another bag in the garage. It just didn't make any sense that she knew where to find it. Mum thinks Stella has some kind of *gift*.

'Maybe it means I'll get the job,' I say lightly.

'No no.' Stella shakes her head quite seriously. 'It will be far more important than that.'

'What makes you say that?' Her sureness unnerves me.

'Things can be one way in the morning, Peach,' she frowns and looks out the window, 'and by evening they're another. I've got the feeling that today is going to be one of those days for you.'

'For me?' I feel uneasy.

'For you.' And she isn't laughing.

I wait to see if she'll tell me more but she just sits there, sipping her tea, staring out the window.

I rush upstairs, clean my teeth, get on my bike and head off down to the end of our street. I cross Hoddle Street and ride behind the old Collingwood football ground and onto the bike track, pedalling towards the convent and thinking about Stella. It doesn't seem so long ago that she was an amazingly confident kid at Fitzroy North Primary School, full of bounce and bravado . . . I can almost see her: the queen of Grade Six, dressed in pink tights, a green pleated skirt and a purple-and-green striped jumper, her thick black hair knotted up into a number of little buns at the back of her head. Mum always says that Stella knew exactly how she wanted to dress by the time she was three. On her first day of school she insisted on wearing her pink tutu with green socks and runners. Mum and Dad tried to dissuade her, thinking that she'd feel silly in front of the other kids, but there was no way Stella could be convinced. There was no uniform at Fitzroy North Primary, but the other girls turned up in nice new cotton school dresses, with white socks and school sandals. At the end of the day, when Mum came to pick her up, a bit worried that she might have been picked on for looking odd, Stella had made fifteen new best friends and wanted to know if she could stay at school for the night because she was having so much fun. On the way home she declared casually that she was glad she wore the tutu because, *'I looked better than everyone else.'*

Then, in secondary school she found her voice. Literally. Was it only two years ago that she came home grinning from ear to ear?

'Guess what?' she whispered dramatically.

We looked at her and waited. Her eyes were glowing.

'I got the lead part in the musical.'

Her singing voice was outstanding, just like Nana's. Mum's mother had been an opera singer and Stella inherited the deep contralto voice. It's the kind of voice that sends shivers down your spine. Not that I've heard it in a while.

I get to the entrance of the Abbotsford Convent five minutes early. I stop a moment to peer around at the odd collection of buildings, the trees and the people coming and going. I've never actually walked through the Clarke Street gates before.

I walk in further and stare around, no idea where to go. About to check the directions board, I notice the Boiler Room sign straight in front of me. There are a dozen wooden tables set up outside with people sitting around talking and drinking coffee. So far so good. I walk towards the big brown doors and push them open.

The wonderful smell of fresh bread nearly bowls me over. Inside the large dark room, two big glass counters are filled with pies and tarts, glistening cakes and long baguettes filled with avocado, cheeses and salads. All different kinds of bread are stacked on the shelves behind. The first person I see is Cassie, serving coffee to a couple sitting at a small round table to the side of the room. There are probably a dozen of these small tables. Cassie grins and motions me towards the door behind the glass counter.

'He's expecting you,' she says in a low voice. 'Don't say anything stupid, okay? Make sure you get the job.'

'Okay.'

Then I see Nick serving bread. He's a guitarist in a local band, Slick City, and I'd forgotten that he's working here. I used to see a lot of Nick because he and Fluke are friends. We smile at each other.

There are two other people serving the small crowd: a tall guy with long blond hair tied back with an elastic band and a dark skinned girl in a headscarf. They also smile as I edge past them and through the door into the room behind. There is a wood-fired oven set into the wall down one end, a couple of big square tables covered in flour, and over by the far wall sit big containers.

A small, neat swarthy man sits down the end of one of the tables, drinking coffee and frowning over figures.

'Can I help you?' he asks in a perfunctory way.

I suddenly feel nervous.

'I'm Peach, er, I mean Perpetua. I've come about the morning job.'

He stands up and holds out his hand. 'I'm Sam. Come and sit down and tell me about yourself.'

I perch on a long bench running along the opposite side of the table. 'Well, I'm a student at the moment,' I say shyly, because he is taking me in now, noticing my hair and skin, my legs in my short skirt. 'I've just finished first year at Melbourne Uni. I live locally.'

'Good for you,' he says, and I breathe an inner sigh of relief. Nothing sleazy here. He doesn't edge closer and start telling me that I'm 'way too cute' to work behind a counter, or that my face should be on the front of some magazine and that he knows just the person who'd make sure it happened, or if I'm doing nothing later how about we go out for a drink and dinner. I'm not kidding. It's the kind of crap I sometimes get from older guys. Det reckons it's because I'm blonde.

'So what do we call you?' he asks, looking at my application. 'Peach or... Perpetua?'

'Peach,' I say quickly, 'definitely.'

'Cassie says you actually like mornings.'

'I do.' I smile. 'I'm a morning person.'

'Can you be a seven a.m. *every* morning person?'

'Yes,' I say without hesitating.

'Good.' He takes a deep breath and frowns. 'Then you have the job until you don't turn up, okay? I mean it, unless you have a very good excuse.'

'Okay.' I hesitate. *Is this all?*

'Why don't you go out now and learn the ropes with Cassie for a bit and then turn up tomorrow morning? I'll be here and we'll iron out the details then.'

'Okay.'

And that is it. I have the job.

For the next couple of hours I hang out behind the counter with Cassie and Nick, learning the names of all the cakes and their prices, and how to make the different coffees. They teach me how the cash register works and the particularities of the warming oven and the microwave. The other guy, Max, and the girl, Yalna, are really nice about taking over the serving while I learn, until it gets on for lunchtime and it's too busy for them to manage. But by then I feel confident that I have the hang of it all, more or less.

I step outside to wait for Cassie, parking myself at a table near the door under a big canvas umbrella to keep off the bright sun. But it's still very hot.

'Get this into you, Peaches!' Nick appears over my shoulder, plonks a bottle of cold juice in front of me, and heads back to the brown doors.

'You're an angel, Nick,' I call back.

'Yeah? Tell that to my mother!' He disappears inside. But his head pokes around the door again almost immediately. 'You coming tonight?'

'Where?'

'Night Cat at eleven. We're on.'

'Oh wow! Hit the big time now, have we?'

'You said it, babe.'

'I'll be there,' I say, wondering if I will in the end. Will I be able to sneak Stella in, and if she refuses to go would it be okay to leave her? Nick is a stocky guy, going bald way too prematurely – he's only twenty-three – with crooked teeth and a voice like a gravel truck unloading. And yet ... he has these warm, twinkling eyes that look straight at you. I love that.

'Thanks, Nick,' I call. That he thought to ask me along suddenly makes me feel really good.

'Good one!' He gives me the thumbs-up and disappears.

After Fluke and I broke up I stopped going out because it

seemed that everywhere I went I ran into him, and seeing him was like rubbing salt into my wounds. So I sort of closed down the hatches, hung out with Det and Cass and tried to help my parents out with Stella. Of course, running into *me* didn't seem to affect him at all, which only made it worse.

It's not long before Cassie finishes her shift. She and Nick come out together, chatting and laughing. Nick has a bag over his shoulder and his guitar case in his other hand.

'See you tomorrow, Greek,' Cassie calls.

'Should do, wog girl.' Nick grins. 'If I survive rehearsal. So where are you chicks going now?'

'To see that mad artist starving in her garret.' Cassie holds up a brown paper bag. There are three filled baguettes poking out the end.

'Tell her if she needs to do a serious portrait one day then my rates are very reasonable.'

'Will do.' We wave him off in the direction of the bus stop. 'See you tonight.'

Cass and I walk along the path towards the bluestone church.

'This place is pretty amazing,' I murmur looking up at the tall gothic buildings. The long arched windows are edged in red brick.

'Det knows all about it,' Cassie replies.

'Of course.' We smile at each other and take a swift left turn from the main path into an enclosed square courtyard surrounded on three sides by a lovely three-storey building in the same grey brick as the other big buildings.

'Wow.' I look up in wonder. 'Make a good film set.'

'I think this was where the nuns lived,' Cassie says. 'Every window up there was a nun's cell.'

'So where does Det hang out?'

Cassie stops in the middle of the lawn and points up. 'See that second window from the end on the top floor? That's her room.' She puts her two hands around her mouth and calls loudly, 'Hey, Det!' No answer. She shrugs. 'I saw her this morning. She knows we're coming.'

The ground floor has a high vaulted ceiling, and we walk past a dark lobby with an intricately tiled floor. I stop to look at the light coming in through the stained-glass windows set around the heavy wooden door. The central one at the top is of a shepherd in a red cloak holding a lamb in one arm and his staff in the other.

The carpet and the walls are shabby, with holes and peeling paint, but the actual structure is awe-inspiring. Up we go to a long empty corridor with more shabby walls and more flights of stairs. The place sort of smells of another age.

I follow Cassie along yet another wide, high corridor with dozens of identical heavy wooden doors leading off either side. Some of the doors have names and occupations on them – artists and writers and playwrights and puppeteers. Some are pinned with pictures, photographs and notes.

'This is her.' Cassie stops outside one of the doors.

In typical style, Det has written her name in black ink and nothing else. No indication of what she does.

Cassie knocks loudly. 'Hey, Det,' she calls.

There is the sound of garbled talking from inside the room and the door is pulled open.

Det, dressed in a dirty shirt over a red skirt and rubber thongs, motions us in with one paint-splattered hand and a distracted smile. The other hand is holding her mobile to her ear. She mouths *Hang on* and walks off into a corner to argue with someone about her phone service.

I follow Cassie into the room, and the intoxicating smell of paint and paper and art materials fills my nostrils. I take a deep breath and look around. This is unlike any other place of Det's I've seen. It's so ordered and neat. Two open steel cabinets sit along one wall. The shelves hold tins of paint, jars of all kinds, packets of paper, pens and charcoal, all carefully set out. On the large wooden table in the corner sits a kind of raised drawing board with piles of paper pads and charcoal and pens and inks. A number of ink-wash drawings of a funny-looking kid in a strange hat are stuck up on the huge pin-board near the table. Two piles of CDs sit on a small table near the window along with a player and a couple of speakers.

Det is thin, bordering on scrawny. She has long straggly red hair, which she should wash more often, fair skin and sharp, even features.

We met her in our last year at school, and she's a bit older than us. She was brought up in Mildura. Her father committed suicide when she was twelve and her mother's reaction was to drop the ball completely. Mrs Donovan apparently took off with some guy twenty years younger and more or less stopped coming home. Det was left in the house with her three older brothers. The only part she willingly talks about is her need to escape. With the help of a sympathetic teacher she sat the entrance test for Mac.Robertson Girls' High at fourteen years old. When she was accepted, she applied for government support to move to Melbourne and lived with the same teacher's grandmother for four years while she completed school.

Det was dux in Year Twelve doing languages and humanities subjects. Then she came back the next year and did all the science subjects and was dux again. Perfect scores two years in a row. Unbelievable. Her second Year Twelve was when Cassie and I got to know her. Naturally she was accepted into all the prestigious university courses, but in the end she chose Fine Art. It seemed a completely crazy choice at the time. She'd never talked about art, and none of us had ever seen her draw anything or even pick up a paintbrush at school. The teachers were beside themselves and went into overdrive trying to dissuade her, but Det stuck to her guns.

As far as we know she has nothing to do with any member of her family in Mildura, and ever since we've known her she has carried a knife with a carved ivory handle in a leather sheath in her bag. I've never seen it in use, but ... I have no doubt that it has a purpose.

'Why?' I asked her once.

But she only shrugged and made a face. 'Why not?'

By that stage, I knew it was the only answer I was going to get.

It's the huge unfinished canvas on the easel that grabs my attention now. I walk over, captivated by its dramatic central image. Three young men, faces turned away, arms raised in the act of throwing small canisters of ... something. Tear gas? A thick fog hovers over and around them like a cloud. The misty whiteness covers most of the painting, making the men's bodies seem caught in a dream. In the distance, through the fog, I make out dilapidated walls and buildings with bits of plaster hanging off open door-frames, the bricks and boards worn and battered. In the foreground, some space away, are three children – boys, I think – squatting down and playing in the dirt at the side of the road. The eldest, maybe ten years old, holds himself apart looking out. He has a gun slung across his back. In spite of myself I'm intrigued. Even unfinished the image hauls me in and makes me anxious. Who are the kids? And the men? What are they doing? What does it mean?

'Good, huh?' Cassie goes to the window and pulls up the sash, allowing the hot air to rush in. 'She's done a whole lot more on the kids since I saw it two days ago.'

I study them more closely and see one of the younger ones is a girl. She's in a windcheater and worn sneakers and is writing something on the pavement with chalk. The barely discernable words *Here I am* are scratched in a childish scrawl. *Oh Jeez, what is that meant to mean?*

Still on the phone, Det must have noticed me studying the painting, because she grabs a newspaper photo off the wall, gives it to me, points to the painting and retreats to her corner to continue her increasingly acrimonious call.

'But I rang yesterday and the day before!' she shouts. 'Don't give me that bullshit!' She is quiet for a while and then she sighs heavily. 'Then take me off the plan, because you said it was going to cost fifty-nine dollars a month, not seventy-nine dollars.'

I tune out and stare at the photo. It is a shot of three men throwing their canisters of tear gas. I can't really tell what nationality they are. Is it the Middle East, or maybe Vietnam? There is no caption. But I see now that Det has used the basic composition of the photo as the starting point for her painting, adding in her own elements: the buildings, the walls and the children.

'Did she tell you that I'm going to be her agent?' Cassie whispers to me.

'What does that involve?'

'The business side.' Cassie waves at the painting. 'She got so ripped off at that last exhibition.'

Det was invited to exhibit with these older, more experienced artists and she was the only one who sold every painting. But she didn't see enough of the money. Most of it went to the agent and the gallery owner.

I look around the room at some of the drawings lining the walls. Some are only half finished but still they take my breath away. Her renderings of faces and figures, trees and cityscapes are so realistic that they are almost scary. She uses them as her starting point. I didn't understand the process or the finished paintings at first. I'd see them at various stages and I couldn't see why, after all the painstaking detail was completed and the whole image was as perfect as a photograph, she set about subverting it, as if she was wilfully trying to wreck her own work. Once I seriously tried to stop her from scratching in stripes of thick green paint over this amazingly realistic face of a child. 'Don't ruin it,' I protested.

But she kept scraping on the sick green stripes. I had to walk out of the room because I couldn't bear to watch. *So what is the bloody point?* I wanted to yell. *What is the point but to be beautiful?*

But when I came back the next week I saw that it wasn't ruined at all. She'd finished the whole painting, and I saw that it was beautiful in a tougher, more interesting way. The child wasn't just a lovely child anymore. He was peering out through a curtain of weird foliage at what looked like a totally alien landscape. There was the dark shadow of a man's profile over half his face, giving the finished image a menacing feel. Someone horrible was threatening the kid. It had the power of a vivid, disturbing dream, and the more I looked at it the more I understood that by scratching on that paint and messing with the perfect sky she'd done something sharper and more remarkable. The initial meticulous paintwork was still there underneath, like perfect machinery. That painting that I'd been so keen for her not to *ruin* had been the first to sell at the exhibition.

I join Cassie by the window. The view out into the square court is lovely, the enormous tree growing in the centre is spectacular, and I'm suddenly filled with gladness for Det that she has this wonderful place.

'This place will be so good for her,' I say quietly.

'I know.' Cassie takes a quick glance back at Det, who is still on the phone. 'That grant is a life-changer.'

Det has lived in a number of crumby share houses with other students – her present one is no different – and she has never been able to afford a separate studio to work in.

I don't know what it says about me that my two best friends are exact opposites. I'm the lynchpin, I suppose. It's a weird thing to say, and maybe totally egotistical, but I don't think they'd be friends it weren't for me. Det has always been the dreamer; even when she was passing those exams with flying colours you had the feeling that she had her eye on something else. Something bigger, deeper, more … difficult. The practicalities of everyday life are pretty much outside her realm. Which is the opposite of Cassie. Every now and again Det will have a go at the day-to-day stuff, but she can never sustain interest for long, and the truth is she often just makes things worse.

Det clicks off the phone, throws her head back and gives an almighty groan of frustration. She comes over, puts her arms around our shoulders, and kisses us both hard on the cheek.

'Did you get the job, Queen Peach?' she asks.

'I did.'

'Good for you!' We smack palms. 'Isn't it so great that we're all going to be here together! Well … sort of. You pathetic dudes will be slaves downstairs, while I . . . I'm up here being the greatest talent of the age.'

'While you're up here being an *arty farty wanker*, you mean!'

'Isn't it fantastic!'

'We'll be able to plan stuff!'

'We can nick off and go to the movies!'

'We can sip gin out on the balcony!'

'And chuck stuff down at people we hate!'

'Det, this place is fantastic.' I throw my arms around her. 'It's just what you need and you deserve it. I'm so happy for you. You're going to do some great painting here.'

'Perfect, isn't it?' She smiles.

'You've already started.' I point to the big canvas.

'Yeah.' Det pulls away from us and takes off her work shirt. Underneath is a tattered T-shirt over the red skirt. 'Let's eat. I'm completely famished.'

Cassie pulls a small grainy photo of a man standing against a wall and squinting into the sun from the pin-board. 'Who's this?'

'That is my old man,' Det says dispassionately.

Cassie and I are quiet as we stare at the photo, but Det takes it back and pins it up where it was. 'I found it in my stuff months ago.'

She has her thongs on now and is wandering around her studio frowning. She suddenly seems edgy and out of sorts.

'What are you looking for?'

'Ciggies.'

'How old was he in the photo?'

'About thirty.' She smiles when she spots her tobacco under some screwed-up paper in the corner. 'Come on, girls! Got me fags; I'm starving.'

'Do you remember him?' I risk asking.

'Yeah.'

'So how old were you when he died?'

'Twelve.'

'What was his name?'

'Martin. But everyone called him Marty.'

'So what was he like?' I ask curiously.

'What can I say?' She shrugs. 'He was … my dad.'

Cassie pulls the baguettes from her bag along with the drinks. 'I got freebies!'

'No shit? Oh man!' Det yelps in delight, grabs one and takes a couple of huge ravenous bites before putting it back in the bag. With a guilty laugh she wipes her mouth with one paint-splattered hand. 'Sorry, but I just had to do that! We'll eat them downstairs then?' She runs back and opens the window wider. 'This place needs air too. Let's get out of here.'

At the door, Det takes a moment to stare at her canvas. 'I've been working on this fucker all night,' she mumbles, 'and I've hardly got anywhere.'

'Did you have any sleep?'

She points ruefully at the corner. Two grimy sheets and a rumpled doona.

'You slept here?' Cassie is appalled.

'Well, I did last night.' Det is defensive. 'I have a key. We're allowed in to work at any time of the day or night. How would they know if I sleep here? It was actually good. I had some sleep then got up and worked like a maniac all morning.'

'It's good, Det,' I say, looking at the painting again. 'At least, it will be.'

'You think?' Her face brightens momentarily. 'I'm not sure yet.'

'Are all the rooms here the same size?'

'I got a big one,' Det replies. 'Most of them are half this size. Apparently the painters get a choice if one comes up.'

'So, back when it was a convent would a more senior nun have had this room?'

'No, half a dozen postulants would have shared this one,' Det says.

Cassie and I look at each other. 'What the fuck is a postulant?'

'When they first went into the convent they were called postulants. They had a year or two to try it out.'

'How do you know all this stuff?'

Det pokes me in the chest. 'Old Peach hates not to know, eh?'

'Well?'

'My dad's sister was a nun. We used to go see her when I was small. I know all about postulants and rosary beads and all the rest of the bullshit. Come and I'll show you around.'

'So you grew up Catholic?' Cassie asks.

'Yeah …' Det grimaces as though already bored.

I grew up in a completely non-religious family, and Cassie's is more-or-less the same, I think, although her dad is Greek. I can't say I mind that I never spent a zillion boring hours in church when I was a kid.

When we get downstairs again, to the dark lobby with the polished-wood door and the stained glass, Det points to the adjoining room.

'The Bishop's Parlour. This is where the Bishop used to come in and see the Mother Superior and take tea.'

I smile, lost for a moment trying to imagine the scene. 'So they'd both be dressed in the weird gear?' I ask, loving the whole idea of being in the very room where it took place. 'Was the Bishop in one of those pointy crimson hats?'

'How the fuck would I know, Peach?' she says dryly. 'I wasn't there.'

'I wonder what they talked about!' I mutter, running my hand over the inlaid woodwork around the fireplace. 'And I wonder who did this. It's so lovely.'

'Well, you can bet whoever did do it isn't around now.' Cassie is in practical mode. 'Come on.' She pushes me out of the lobby. 'You can look another time.'

'Did they wear ordinary clothes on weekends?' I ask.

'Who?'

'The nuns?'

Det stares at me. 'It wasn't a *job*, Peach.'

'So what was it?'

'A *vocation*,' she says. 'They were called by God.'

'*What?*' I start laughing. This coming out of *Det's* mouth is just too bizarre.

'Called to the religious life,' she says seriously. 'It's full-on. No wages and no getting away on the weekends.'

'And … do you believe that?' I ask as noncommittally as I can. 'I mean the bit about God calling them?'

She doesn't say anything for a while and then she chuckles softly. 'Yeah. In a way I do. Yeah. I do believe that.'

'But you don't even believe in God!' I splutter. 'You told me you didn't.'

'So?' She grins at me. 'Just because I don't believe in God doesn't mean that *he, she* or *it* doesn't exist, does it?'

Cass and I glance at each other behind her back and raise our eyebrows and I decide to let it go. I've never been one for talking around in circles. But a picture of a girl on the phone taking *the call* from God fills my head. Then afterwards, explaining it to her friends. *Hey guys, sorry I can't go to your party because … God called me! He said I have to go to this place and put on all these funny clothes. I don't get any time off and I earn no money. What do you think? Good career move? Can't afford to pass it up, can I? The opportunity might never come around again.* Yeah, right.

'You look troubled, Peach.'

'Were they allowed *out*?'

'No. They were enclosed.'

'Jesus,' I whisper. 'Did other people come in?'

Det shakes her head and then grins. 'Hey, I'm not a world expert on nuns and I'm hungry.'

We find a long bench under the cover of the verandah, and Cassie deals out the baguettes and the drinks. The three of us are quiet for a few minutes as we get stuck into the food. It's still hot but the clouds have begun to gather.

'Okay, what's up then?' Cassie turns to Det with a hard, in-your-face stare. 'You look shithouse.' She takes another bite and hands Det what is left of her baguette. 'Go on, have it. I've had enough.'

I look at Det and see that she *is* even more pale than usual. Trust Cassie to notice.

'I'm okay.'

'When did you last eat?'

'Back off,' Det mumbles.

'You look pale and you're edgy,' Cassie persists.

'Jeez, Cass!' Det laughs awkwardly.

'Well?'

'I'm fine, but ... I've got something to tell you both.'

'What?'

'Don't worry.' Det looks away uneasily. 'No one has died or been attacked or anything important like that.'

'Well, that's good to know,' Cassie says.

Cassie and I snatch another conspiratorial glance and go back to eating. We know that if we start firing questions at Det she is likely to clam up completely. So we just sit there and watch her demolish the last scrap of food.

'So.' Det sighs as she looks up at the church spire. 'Looks like I'm pregnant.'

I watch Cassie's face. It is still for about three seconds, then her eyes narrow, her mouth tightens and she begins to heave, as if she is going to be sick.

I turn away, not trusting myself to look at either of them at this point. I know what is going through Cassie's head, because the same thing is going through mine. For this to happen *again* is too much. I chuck what is left of my roll out onto the concrete for the birds and crumple up the paper bag into a tight ball.

Cassie gives a deep, furious moan that sends an echo around my own brain. *This – is – too – much.* I almost just get up and walk off. I so much want to be somewhere else right fucking now. Seriously, I wish I'd never met Det. She's too mad, too irresponsible. She lacks even the most basic street smarts. I'm totally and utterly sick of her.

The cold horrible truth is that Cassie and I have seen Det through two abortions already, and she is only a year older than us. The first one was understandable. She was a green country kid who'd never had any kind of social life at all until she left school. She hadn't been interested in going out and it had worked well for her. She was a student who got top marks two years running. School and the friends she'd made had been enough. But after school the old lady she was living with became ill and retired to a nursing home. Det had to find accommodation elsewhere.

Her first place was a share house where everyone was older than her – and things were pretty wild. There were loud parties and lots of drinking and drugs and hangers-on. She went a bit wild too, got involved with one of the guys and ... the inevitable happened. That termination knocked her around enough, but it was the second, last year, that affected her so deeply.

She let herself get run-down after it was over, and then she got physically sick and then she got really, seriously and very deeply depressed. Within a few weeks she literally couldn't get out of bed in the mornings. Cass and I brought her food every day for three months and made her eat it. We washed her, talked her through everything, again and again and ... *again*. We helped her dress; we took her to shrink appointments; we gave her money. I'm not kidding, we did everything we could; she was a total mess and there was no one else to do it for her. I honestly think if it weren't for us she would have died. She was that bad.

After a few months the black fog lifted; gradually and without fanfare she started to come good. She got back to her day job at a cafe in Collingwood and that helped. She started painting again and two of her lecturers let her know that they saw her as someone with exceptional talent. This gave her confidence. She started seeing people again. Slowly, slowly she pulled her life together.

Then she was invited by a small, prestigious gallery to exhibit with two older, well-known male artists who were initially miffed to be exhibiting alongside a young female student – until they saw the work. The gallery owner added a nought to the price of each work, and much to everyone's surprise – and to some people's chagrin – Det's work sold really well, way better than the other artists'. She was on her way. She had a few grand in the bank and her spirits had climbed right out of that terrible hole. Then she got the government grant at the end of the year. She was on a roll.

'Well, say something,' Det mutters. 'Yell. Scream.'

For the second time inside twelve hours I do want to scream. I want to rant and rave and throw stuff around. Not only do I have my sister at home to look after, but now there is my best friend … *all over again.*

'This is crazy, Det.'

'I know.' She bites her lip. 'It's ridiculous.'

'It took you *ages* to get over it last time,' Cassie says. 'You know what you were like.'

'Yeah. I know.'

'It was hard on us too, Det. Then you got the grant for this year and this wonderful place to work at last.' Cassie's voice breaks. 'Every blasted thing is going so well for you!'

'I know, I'm a complete idiot.'

'So who is the—'

'No no. That's not important. I think—'

'It *is* fucking important!' Cassie snarls. 'Because at the very least he can help pay this time.'

'It's just that I'm not absolutely sure how to find him. I mean … it was just casual.' She's blathering.

'Well, start looking.' Cassie cuts across the bullshit.

I'm with her on this. In fact, my bet is that Det knows very well how to find him but is too proud to involve him, so I dig my boot in too.

'As far as I am concerned, this time whoever *he* is can be part of the whole bloody thing, Det, because the termination procedure is just the beginning. Then there's the follow-up visits to doctors, medicines to pay for, time off work.'

'I know. I know. I'm sorry.'

Cassie and I forked out last time and I'm not going to again unless I really have to. And what if she crashes again? Of course that's what we really fear. I just don't want to even think about all that happening again.

'I just ... had no idea ...' Det mumbles but doesn't finish the sentence. 'We only fucked a couple of times. He said he'd go get condoms ... I said it wouldn't matter 'cause I'd just had my period. So it's all totally my fault.'

I look at her and see that she is absolutely miserable and my heart melts – against my will. I still want to scream at her, but I also want to cradle her in my arms because, well, she is Det – so funny and wild and different to anyone else I have ever known.

Cassie is obviously feeling the same thing. She edges closer and puts one hand on Det's knee.

I put one arm around her skinny shoulders. 'What's done is done,' I say softly, 'and we'll help, won't we, Cass?'

'Of course,' Cass sighs.

'Thanks,' Det sniffs.

Cassie takes her diary out of her bag. 'You've been to the clinic?'

'Yeah.'

'Okay, that's good. And they've given you a date?'

'Yep.'

'So when do you go?'

'Next week,' Det mutters. 'Tuesday, I think.'

'Okay, good. We'll get it over with and then you can start picking up the pieces again.' Cassie looks at me. 'There is no need to assume that it will be as bad as last time.'

I murmur in agreement.

'This time will be different, Det,' Cassie says sternly. 'You won't go down the way you did before.'

'Will you go to the same place?' I ask.

'Yep.' Det bends down and takes her packet of tobacco out of her backpack and begins to roll one of her thin little cigarettes. 'Except that this time, I'm not going to have a termination.'

'What?'

'I'm not going to have an abortion.'

Neither Cassie nor I speak.

As horrible as another abortion is to contemplate, the alternative is simply *impossible*. Det is the best person, generous, and kind to a fault, but her life is a total train wreck. She has never lived in the same share house for more than about six months. She takes drugs, she drinks, she smokes, she has no family behind her. Or none that she has anything to do with, anyway. She doesn't know how to eat or look after herself.

Probably more important than any of that, she has never wanted children. It isn't a matter of her being ambivalent about it. She was adamant when we first met her. *I will never have a kid*. She explained that some people just know in their bones they are not cut out for it. I believed it then, and I believe it now.

'If you don't have an abortion then you'll have a baby,' I mutter.

'Yeah, well ...' She smiles weakly. 'I guess that is the way it goes.'

'And you don't want a baby,' I went on relentlessly. 'Do you?'

'No, that's right ... I don't ... want a baby.'

'Because you are an artist who loves her work,' I push on. 'You love music, dancing all night, getting off your face on whatever is around. You are twenty-one years old, Det, and you have never wanted a baby. *Ever*. You have no boyfriend or partner. It would be really irresponsible for you to have a kid.'

She nods. 'You're right,' she says in a small voice.

'So ... what are you really saying?' I persist, more gently now, thinking that she is just overreacting to the idea of having to have another termination.

She turns and looks at me directly. 'I guess I'm saying that I'm going to have a baby.'

'What do you mean?' Cassie shrieks. 'You *guess* you're going to have a baby? Det, that is exactly what will happen if you don't have a termination. You *will* have a *baby*! A screeching tiny human being that needs attention around the clock! It has to be fed and changed and ... rocked all the time. Have you any idea how boring that is? Well I do! My sister's first kid sent her absolutely spare for six months. It never shut up.' Cassie is yelling, her hands flying around Greek style. 'And *she* has a husband, a house, the whole friggin' shebang *with bells on* ... an army of people to help her! You don't get to give it back when you get sick of it, Det. It's not a dog. I'm telling you that you must *not* have a baby. It will ruin your fucking life.'

'I'm pregnant, and I'm going to have a baby,' Det says firmly, and takes a long drag of her cigarette.

'Look at you smoking! Look at you. You have no money. You're are a drug addict.'

'I am not a drug addict, Cassie,' Det cuts in mildly.

'It will be born damaged! All the alcohol and the cigarettes you consume. And you don't eat properly.'

'I know,' Det mutters.

'What do you mean, *you know*?' Cassie is virtually hyperventilating. 'Do you know that all that stuff affects how the kid will turn out?'

'I know. I've got to change some ... stuff.'

'Some *stuff*? What the fuck does that mean? It's too late. Vital stuff has happened already to that foetus. Ask Peach. She knows all about biology. Peach, isn't that true?'

I nod uneasily.

'See! *It's too late.*'

'Hey, calm down,' I say. People walking past are staring at us. 'Come on, Cassie. Screaming doesn't help anyone.'

Cassie glares belligerently at a middle-aged couple and their two pre-teen kids who seem amused by us yelling at each other.

'Fuck off!' Cassie snarls. They turn away in embarrassment. She stands up, her face ferocious and unforgiving. 'Listen, I can't handle this. I really can't.' She looks at me. 'For Christ's sake, talk some sense into her.' Then she picks up her bag and flounces off towards the entrance gates.

Det and I sit and watch her neat little figure as she disappears out the gate. Cassie hardly ever goes off the deep end. She prides herself on always seeing things through. She likes being in control. So ... this is big.

Eventually Det gets up, gives me an apologetic smile and mumbles something about needing to go back to work.

'How pregnant are you, Det?'

'About nineteen weeks.'

'*What?*'

'I haven't known for that long.' She shrugs helplessly. 'I thought it might be something else.'

Something else?

I get up to leave too. There doesn't seem to be a lot to say.

Cecilia

Cecilia shifted in her seat and tried to stretch her legs, but it was impossible to get comfortable. Since the Singapore stopover she'd been stuck halfway down the plane between two men. One had some kind of breathing difficulty – he wheezed constantly. The other, in the aisle seat, took every opportunity to engage her in conversation. Cecilia had been friendly at first until she realised that he was flirting with her. He couldn't have been more than thirty-five! She looked at her watch. Three hours to go. She was due to land in Melbourne at nine p.m.

'Excuse me again,' she said apologetically and stood up. It had only been an hour since the last time, but she couldn't sit still any longer.

'Getting excited, huh?' He stood up to make room.

She smiled without meeting his eyes and edged past, cursing her own naiveté. When they'd first sat down together she'd made the mistake of telling him that it had been fifteen years since she'd set foot in the country of her birth. Whenever she looked up from the book she'd long since finished reading, he was ready with suggestions about the bars and restaurants she should go to, along with interesting places that had changed or been built since she'd last been home. It wouldn't be long before he was offering to show her around.

She made her way slowly up the aisle to the toilet, stepping past row after row of tired, cramped people trying to sleep, the evidence of the long flight strewn about them – bags full of duty-free alcohol, shoes, earphones and plastic cups.

Cecilia was over fifty and still an attractive woman who looked at least ten years younger than she was. She thought it was ironic that at precisely the stage in life when her looks were fading, she'd finally realised that she was beautiful. She was slim with a good curvy figure. Her hair was honey blonde and curly with only occasional strands of grey. She had bright blue eyes and a full mouth. Apart from the crow's-feet around her eyes when she smiled, and a few lines etched into the corners of her mouth, her skin was as fine as ever – one of the few positive legacies of spending her twenties in the convent when most of her generation were at the beach.

She noticed a couple of empty seats near a window and she bent down to peer out. She saw the red sun making the clouds pink and gold. Then the plane dipped a little and swung around and she was looking down on red earth. *Australia.* Her stomach lurched with apprehension.

Why? After all this time. *Why?*

But she knew why. Breda had written. *Breda.* After all these years she had hunted her down and written a quick breezy email with promises of more 'juicy info' when and if Cecilia wrote back.

Hey there, Annunciata, is that you? Cecilia had stared at the screen disbelievingly. It had been so long since she'd been called by her religious name. She hadn't set eyes on Breda since that last evening in the convent. One morning, just two days before they were to make their final vows, Cecilia woke to find that Breda was gone. Not a word to anyone and no note. Her bed was made neatly with just her black lace-up shoes at the end. Not a thing was out of place. It took a whole morning before it became clear that she'd done a bunk in the middle of the night. It turned out that not only Breda was gone, but one of the girls from the laundry had gone too. Cecilia smiled as she remembered how *shocking* it had been at the time.

Listen, kid, you got to write back! I know some of what happened to you, but I need to know the rest.

But how could she? Her years as a nun had been wrapped up so tightly and thrown into the do-not-disturb section of her brain. She knew that opening the package after all this time might not be wise. What if after sorting through the contents she didn't know where anything fitted? But Breda had sounded as quirky, sharp and full of fun as she remembered her, and so of course Cecilia hadn't been able to resist writing back.

And I want to see you! Come home, why don't you?

A couple of years after leaving the convent, Cecilia decided to give herself a clean break. Dominic was dead and Patrick had fled to Darwin after his acrimonious divorce. She would make a new life for herself in whatever way she could, even if that meant deliberately blocking out her family, the convent years, Peter and the child. It was time to become someone else.

In spite of some lean years in England the strategy had worked, more or less. Even at her lowest ebb she was never tempted to return home. And when she met the Canadian, Jack, she knew it was the best move she'd ever made. The seven years she'd had with him had been the happiest of her entire life. But Jack had died of cancer too soon and somehow after that her life stopped working. For five years she'd been wandering the globe like a nomad, teaching here and there, taking on photo assignments. She made friends easily but lost them just as quickly.

She was adrift in a vast lonely space of her own making. In her darker moments she saw it as her due, the payback for a series of wilfully stupid decisions she'd made in her life.

Then Breda had found her. The email had crashed into her life like a gate left open in a wild storm. No way could she ignore it. *Wake up, Annunciata. Wake up!*

1965

'What is troubling you, dear?'

The Novice Mistress's hand was on her arm. Cecilia turned around and lowered her eyes. They were red, but surely not enough for anyone to notice. At least, that's what she'd hoped when she'd splashed her face with cool water an hour before. It was a grey evening and she was walking out from evening prayers in the chapel with the rest of the community. Cecilia was hungry. In Lent the meals were sparser than usual, and there'd been no afternoon tea. The others were passing by on their way in to supper and she longed to join them. But here she was alone with the formidable Mother Holy Angels and no idea how to explain herself.

'You're unhappy, Sister Annunciata?' the old nun said gently, but her eyes were scouring Cecilia's face critically.

'No, Mother,' Cecilia said. 'I'm very happy here.'

'Then why the tears?'

Cecilia took a deep breath. 'I find one bath a week insufficient, Mother,' she whispered, looking at the ground. There was no reaction at all, so Cecilia continued. 'And fresh underwear only once a week feels unhygienic.'

It was at the word *unhygienic* that the Novice Mistress's face tightened with fury. She threw her shoulders back as though preparing for battle, and Cecilia stepped back in dismay.

'How dare you!' The Novice Mistress's voice was low. 'The impudence of a twenty-year-old novice calling into question practices that have been part of our Rule for centuries! How dare you!'

'Oh Mother.' Cecilia slumped with mortification. 'I'm so sorry. I didn't mean to ... I wasn't ... It's just that ...'

'In case you haven't realised yet, this convent was not set up to service your personal needs. And if that is what you expect, then why don't you walk out right now and save everyone a lot of time?'

'Oh no, Mother. Please don't send me away!' Cecilia was blinded with panic. 'I'm so sorry ... I wasn't thinking at all.'

'Then perhaps you should begin thinking!'

'Yes, Mother.' Cecilia's stammered apologies sounded inadequate even to her own ears.

'Go back to the chapel right now!' Mother Holy Angels said. 'Kneel in front of the Blessed Sacrament, with both arms extended, until I send someone for you.'

'Yes, Mother.'

It was torture after ten minutes, but Cecilia remained determined. Within half an hour she was woozy with pain and exhaustion, but she kept her arms extended as she'd been ordered, alone in the dark church.

When Breda was sent to bring her up, she found her lying unconscious on the floor of the chapel, blue with cold.

'Wake up, Nuncie! Come on, wake up.'

Cecilia jerked awake but didn't immediately recognise Breda. Her limbs were heavy and she could hardly move her face, but she was nevertheless filled with the overwhelmingly delicious feeling of having died and gone on to another life. Could that red flame flickering in front of the gold tabernacle be the Holy Spirit?

'What happened? Where am I?'

'Hush. Mother Angels sent you down here.'

'Oh.' Cecilia sat up a little, leaning her back against the polished wood of a nearby pew. The scene with the Novice Mistress flooded back. She groaned. 'How long have I been down here?'

'An hour at least,' Breda whispered, rubbing Cecilia's cold hands with her own warm ones. 'What did you do?'

'Complained about there not being enough baths.'

'You idiot!' Breda gave a low chuckle.

Cecilia looked into Breda's warm smiling face and felt a sudden infusion of energy run into her lethargic limbs. She tried to get up.

'Stay a minute.' Breda caught her arm. 'Take a few deep breaths.'

Cecilia did as she was told as Breda set about straightening her veil.

'How long did you last for?'

'I don't know,' Cecilia whispered. 'I think I passed out.'

'I only lasted two minutes,' Breda chuckled.

'But …'

'Too painful,' Breda went on casually. 'I snuck a look behind to make sure no one was there and put my arms down.'

Cecilia smiled. *What about obedience?* she wanted to ask but didn't have the energy.

'Don't let her get to you, Annunciata.' Breda's face had become serious. She took Cecilia's hands in her own and rubbed them some more. 'She's not that important.'

'You seem so happy,' Cecilia whispered wearily.

'Well, I stink too!'

'But you're happy.'

'I *am* happy,' Breda admitted.

'Even though …'

'Even though I stink and can't manage most of what I'm meant to manage …'

'So …?' Cecilia waited.

Breda met her eye with a shrug. 'This is what God wants of me.'

Cecilia nodded. Yes. She understood that. It was what she felt herself. She looked across at the Blessed Sacrament and prayed for strength.

Within minutes she was on her feet again. Breda helped her up and they made their way together up the wide gloomy stairs to the dormitory.

On their way back from chapel they stood back as Reverend Mother passed them on the stairs with only the coolest of nods.

Cecilia took this to mean that news of her misdemeanour had been reported and that the Provincial would be keeping a closer eye on her now. *Oh God!* She might not get the votes needed to get through to the next stage. Some novices were taken aside and told that that they were unsuited to the life and should go home. Their relatives were called and asked to come and fetch them. Imagine that! The humiliation of knowing that she'd failed. More than anything in the world Cecilia wanted to be professed.

Breda nudged her when the nun was out of view.

'Sour old biddy,' she whispered, laughing under her breath. 'Don't let them get to you, Nuncie.'

'But how do you manage that?'

'Because I'm loved,' Breda said softly. 'I know God loves me, and he loves you too.'

Cecilia stared at her wonderingly. Breda broke more rules than all of them put together and yet she seemed happier than all of them too. Somehow that was difficult to fathom. It didn't add up.

'Pray!' Breda said as they tiptoed along the corridor towards their dormitory. 'You'll be okay if you pray. God listens.'

Peach

Before I put my key in the door I stop, close my eyes and offer up a prayer to whatever God is on duty that day.

'Please let her be at Ruby's. Let my sister be out doing *something*.' I open the door and I'm immediately hit with a blast of Roy Orbison's 'Pretty Woman' and hope dies an instant death. I head for the stairs. To say I don't need Stella right at this moment is a gross understatement.

'Is that you, Peach?'

I stop on the fifth stair and sigh. 'Yep,' I call back, 'it's me.'

'What you doing home?'

I go back down to the family room. Stella is lying on the big couch. There is an empty cardboard noodle container on the table nearby, a crushed packet of chips and a number of lolly wrappers around her. She smiles at me, but I ignore it and turn to the screen. She's watching an old concert of Bruce Springsteen, Roy Orbison, Jackson Browne and Bonnie Raitt. Stella senses my mood and turns it down.

'What's up?' she says. 'I thought you were going to hang out with Det and Cassie all day.'

'So did I.'

'So what happened?'

'I dunno.'

'Has anything amazing happened to you yet?' she asks casually.

'*What?*' I look at her blankly, and she gives me a knowing smile. I remember her pronouncement that morning.

'Not yet,' I say sourly. Det's pregnancy does not come under the *amazing happenings* heading as far as I'm concerned. It's more suited to *diabolical tragedies*.

Stella looks at her watch. 'Plenty of time.'

'Whatever you say, Stella.' I stare at the old stars jiving around with their guitars and wonder, not for the first time, why the hell a sixteen-year-old on the edge of a new century wants to watch a pack of performers from her parents' generation.

'I got an email from Mum,' she says, switching off the telly and looking at me.

'And?'

'Everything is fine. Loving Paris. You know the drill. They're going to call us.'

'What time?'

'Tonight. Late.'

'Okay,' I sigh. I go to the fridge and take a long slurp of milk straight from the plastic bottle. I would kill Stella if she did the same thing in front of me, but seeing as how I'm running this domestic situation, I don't care. I pick up my big canvas pool bag from the hook and check it. Shampoo, conditioner, soap, face moisturiser, bathers and a towel. Stella watches me intently.

'What are you looking at?' I say sharply, as I pull a comb from my other bag. I need to get out of the house. I'm no good to anyone like this.

'What's the matter, Peach?'

'Nothing,' I say. *You, Stella. You are the matter!* 'I'm going to the pool now.' I head towards the hall. 'And then I'm going out again later as well, so I might not be home to talk to Mum and Dad.'

'You're going swimming *now*?'

'Yes. You should come,' I say, knowing she won't and that I don't really want her to either.

She shakes her head. 'Where are you going later?'

'To see Nick's band at the Night Cat,' I say. 'You wouldn't like it. Too loud.'

'Okay,' she returns mildly.

I turn my back and walk out to the front hallway, hating myself because, apart from Mum and Dad, I love Stella more than anyone else in the world, but right at this minute I'm finding it hard to be even civil to her.

'I brought the mail in,' she calls after me cheerfully, as if I'm meant to congratulate her. 'I left it all on the table in the hall. There's a letter for you.'

'Who from?'

'I don't know,' she says, 'but the writing is vaguely interesting.'

'Okay, thanks.'

'Have a good swim, Peach.'

'Shall do!' I try to sound light, but then I can't help myself. I turn around and walk back into the room. 'Did you even ring up Ruby?'

'It's going to rain.' She looks away.

'You could have hung out together.'

'Yeah, well … I think she's got stuff happening.'

You used to make stuff happen too, Stella! I'm on the point of yelling.

'I'm going swimming now!' I shout at her. 'A bit of rain won't kill me and it wouldn't kill you either!'

'Okay, okay,' she says. 'Don't take out your hang-ups on me!'

Hang-ups! I go back into the hall and it's then I see the a mauve envelope sitting innocuously on the hall table. The loopy letters of my name and address on the front have been written in blue ink with a fountain pen. Apart from official letters from banks and phone companies and the university, I don't get any mail. But here it is, a fat letter addressed to me. I turn it over in my hands.

No name, but an address in Castlemaine that I don't recognise. It's obviously from an old person, but ... what old person do I know, and why would they be writing to me?

I put my swimming bag down and set the envelope back on the table next to the little vase of white flowers and stand looking at it a while. It's almost as if I've stumbled on an artefact from long ago, or received a message from another planet. As far as I'm concerned it has value, sealed up tight as it is. Why actually *open* it? Why spoil the delicious sense that all kinds of possibilities are hidden inside that sealed square?

But of course I have to open it. I go out onto the front porch, tear open the envelope and take out eight pages of cheap, lined writing paper that have been carefully filled back and front with the same blue-ink loopy scrawl as on the front of the envelope. As I read each page I let it drop onto the brown tiles, one by one, and at the end I'm left staring down at them.

Eventually I pick them up and sit down on the top step to read them again.

To my dearest granddaughter Perpetua!
My only daughter's only child!

I think of you every single day. Every day I wonder what became of you, if you are happy and healthy, if you are good at school, if you have friends. Lord, if I could just see you!

My own daughter, Cecilia, your mother – who used to slam down the phone whenever she heard my voice, and now I don't even have a phone number for her – her brothers think she has left the country, but where would she go? It feels just as though she has disappeared off the face of the earth. I am eighty-eight years old; I'm not a fool. I know I don't have much time left.

Forgive me for writing, Perpetua. I woke up one morning with

98

this strong conviction that I must contact you. So I got onto little Evie, who is Declan's girl, and I asked her to see if she could find you. I won't go into how she did it but I don't think it was strictly above board. Anyway, after I had the address I prayed long and hard before I sat down to write. But I decided in the end that there are things that need to be said. There are things you need to know.

I never knew my own mother. I was brought up by the Good Shepherd nuns, in a convent in Abbotsford, quite near where you live. So you and I have that in common, not knowing our mothers, I mean. All I know about her was that her name was Sadie. When I left the convent I lived at the Catholic girls' hostel of St Anne's on the corner of Rathdowne and Victoria streets, which burnt down some years back. I worked for the public service in Melbourne for nearly eight years at Treasury Place. They were by far the happiest years of my life. I mean the ones after school and before I got married. Maybe one day I'll get a chance to tell you more.

Please keep reading! I'm not just some crazy old woman. I am old but I have all my wits about me! If you saw me you would be proud of me! I stand quite straight and every day I walk to the shop. Until last year I was able to kneel by my bed on the mat to say the rosary every night. My knees have gone now so I've taken to sitting in the chair while I pray. The man Louis at the shop is my best friend now that Evelyn has gone. He is from Greece and has had a sad life. He tells me he has no faith because of all the terrible things he saw during the war in his home village, and who am I to argue or try to convince him? He helps me up the steps and I sit with him a while before we decide what I need that day. If I'm there before eleven in the morning he gives me a cup of that strong coffee. I don't tell him that I'd rather a cup of tea because it might hurt his feelings. He saves me something every single day. Sometimes it's a choice apple, the next day it's a banana or some of those big black grapes that I love. When he gets things on special then he tells me. I tell you, he is more use than any of my damned sons and their interfering wives! A terrible thing to say I know, but it is the truth.

You get to my age, Perpetua, and you can't be bothered with anything but the truth.

I had six sons before a longed-for daughter, your mother, and then twin boys. The first son, Dominic, is dead now. He died in tragic circumstances but I won't go into that now. I have seven sons left, and none of them want to listen to me or know what I have lived through. Not that I blame them. They're busy with their own lives. They come by and they drop things off that I don't need and make me food I don't like. They try to boss me around. 'Mum, you should do this!' 'Mum, you should go there.' 'Mum, you'll be cold if you don't wear this, or hot if you don't use this fan or that air conditioner.' 'Mum, you should sell this house and move to a hostel.' Mum, why don't you try this food or that.' 'Yes, yes,' I say but I don't take a bit of notice. I go ahead and do what I want. Do they think I was never hot or cold before?

Every year on your birthday I think of you, and the way she gave you away, and every year around that time I had Father Duffy say Mass for you and your mother. When I get home from that Mass I light a candle and pray to Our Lady to keep you from harm. Sometimes I think that Our Blessed Lord is just too busy for an old woman like me, what with the world being the way it is, so it's best to go straight to Our Lady, who understands better what it is like for a woman and how hard it can be. I wonder if you pray. Most of the young people don't these days. Remember you don't have to go on and on or say anything fancy. Our Blessed Saviour knows your heart and so does his Mother.

I have secrets to tell you, big things and small things. And things to give you, too, if you're interested. They're useless to me now. I can't even read very well anymore.

Did you know you were called after Cecilia's best friend Breda? They entered the convent more or less together. Cecilia was given the name Mother Mary Annunciata when she was received. And Breda got Mother Mary Perpetua. But you might know that already? I have no idea what you know.

Oh that ceremony! The music was out of this world. I felt as though I'd died and gone to heaven because I was back in the same chapel I'd known as a girl, watching my own girl dedicate her life to God! And having the Bishop there and all those priests serving on the altar, all done up in their fine regalia, the embroidered gold albs and silver crosses! The High Mass went on for three hours. It really was something. Seven beautiful girls all dressed as brides dedicating their lives to God. And your mother, well, you should have seen her. She was the most beautiful of all of them. What a picture! Nancy Morgan from out near Woodside helped me make the dress for her and it fitted perfectly.

It was just about the only I ever saw Kev cry. 'If only she really was getting married,' he whispered, the tears streaming down his cheeks. 'If only there was some bloke up there at the altar with her!' People sitting in pews around us heard him and so I told him to hush up, the fool, he was disgracing us all.

Those last couple of years in the convent were very difficult for Cecilia. Dominic had died, you see, and I think that was the beginning of the end for her. She wasn't allowed to go to his funeral because it was an enclosed order. But it was very hard on her.

Everything in the Church seemed to change around that time. Have you heard of Pope John 23? He was a good man but he started all the trouble. Maybe he had to do it. I don't know, anyway it was like they opened the windows and once everyone got a whiff of fresh air they decided to climb out and run away. The old rules didn't apply any more. It seemed like every week some rule or other was relaxed and none of them knew where they were. One week if you ate meat on Friday you were in a state of mortal sin and would burn in hell forever, then the next week they told us it wasn't the case.

Well, what were we meant to think? It wasn't a clean cut either. The old ways had to co-exist with the new for a good few years and so half the time we didn't know what was going on.

When she finally left the convent I think your mother was

terribly confused. She didn't seem to know who she was. One day she'd be in a miniskirt, her face plastered in thick make-up, and the next she'd be in a dress that made her look like a grandmother. I probably wasn't any help at all.

We do things we think are right but they turn out to be wrong. Such genuine holiness in a little girl is not common, so naturally I encouraged her to enter the convent. It seemed the natural thing. Later, when she told us that she planned to give up her child I knew in my heart that it was wrong to give away your own flesh and blood, but I said nothing. Maybe she blames me for that.

You'd think at my time of life I'd accept everything that has happened, including my own mistakes, but I don't. It's hard to see the point of any of it.

I'm worn out now. I had planned to write different things to you, Perpetua. Brighter things. But somehow the pen just took off on its own. I hope you will forgive me if I have said anything wrong or if I'm not cheery enough. Maybe you have met your mother already and will be able to tell me she is safe. That would be enough for me.

I am longing to hear from you, Perpetua! If I could just see you once I would die happy.

Love from your grandmother,
Ellen Mary Madden (nee Reynolds)

I fold the pages up carefully and slip them into my pocket; then I go back into the house. The front door bangs behind me as I head up the stairs to my room.

'Peach, are you still here?' Stella calls after me.

I am acutely aware of a number of things all at once: the darkening sky outside my window, my neatly made bed, the books on the desk, the curtain falling to the floor in folds, and my skin getting tight across my scalp, as if it might be about to peel away. I cross my arms tightly over my chest to keep myself in one piece, and I turn around slowly and stare hard at all the familiar objects. There is the dressing table with the photos of my friends stuck to the big mirror. There is my bag where I chucked it on the cane chair last night, the shoes I took off yesterday, the glass of water on each side of the bed. Everything is familiar but ... somehow strange. Things seem to move in and out of focus. I turn to the Chagall print above my bed. The bright colours of his dream seem to be crumbling at the edges, just like a sandcastle at the end of a day at the beach, all the edges and straight lines slowly collapsing. I swallow, but my mouth feels stuffed full of dry sticks.

'Peach?' Stella calls again.

'I'm here,' I call back, but my voice is off-key.

'Are you still going swimming?'

'Yeah. I think so. Maybe.'

'If you do, bring me back something?'

'Okay.'

I grab the edge of the desk. I don't know *what* I'm thinking exactly, only that the little systems inside my head seem to be cutting out, one by one. As if someone has turned off the power supply and all the pulleys and levers are creaking to a standstill.

'Something really yummy, will you,' Stella yells from the foot of the stairs, 'like one of those burritos. No beans, but extra cheese.'

'Okay,' I say, but she won't have heard. I can't seem to raise my voice above a whisper. A splatter of rain hits the windowpane and that sort of brings me back. Am I going swimming in the rain? I take the letter and stuff it away into the shoebox inside my wardrobe.

I wait a while, then I tiptoe downstairs and out into the backyard. Our big tree is already drooping a little as a smattering of rain hits its thirsty leaves and branches. I run through the warm heavy air and shelter under it. *I already have a grandmother. I have the best grandmother in the world.* The fact that she is dead is not the point.

She is still Nana. *My nana.* And there is Dad's mother in England, too, although we don't really know her. I don't need another one.

Stella and I adored Nana. She took us to piano and dancing lessons. She was at every school concert and every sports match. Mum was her first child and born late in her life. Before she married, she sang for ten years with the Australia opera. Her voice was a low, rich contralto. She'd be at the piano for hours with Stella; they'd be laughing and singing together, chatting over new pieces. *If you love music then you'll never be lonely* was one of her sayings. Her musical genes had passed over Mum and into Stella.

I'm not musical like Stella, but I always felt adored by Nana anyway. *You're the brains around here,* she used to tell me. *One day you'll show the world!* I loved being told that. It made me study hard at school because I didn't want to let Nana down.

She sang at weddings and funerals and she kept busy seeing all her friends. Most of them were old ladies like herself, full of fun with plenty of money. They drank sherry and had card nights. They went to films and plays and concerts and enjoyed their lives. Our nana was … perfect.

I sit on the back verandah, comforted by the lovely soft rain.

A decent downpour will mean I can stop worrying about Mum's garden for a few days. I've been collecting shower water and carting it out in buckets to the plants every morning, along with what I save from the kitchen sink. Stella helps, but it isn't in her nature to take such things seriously.

A long roll of thunder in the distance sends a shudder through me, and then the sky is alight with two sharp forks of lightning. Another loud crack of thunder and the rain picks up pace. I shut my eyes. It is so dark inside my head. I listen hard to the sounds around me, the soft hiss and occasional crack as the rain hits the leaves, and the creaking of the shed door. I can't hear my own breath going in and out, but when I put one hand over my heart I feel it pumping.

'*Sadie, Ellen and … Cecilia.*' It feels odd to say these names aloud, oddly *familiar*. I've never heard them before, but it's as if they've been sitting there all along, waiting for me to open the door and let them in.

'Peach, is that you?'

'It's me.'

'What are you doing?' Stella is standing at the back door holding a bowl and a wooden spoon. Her hair all is all over the place and she's wearing a big white apron. 'Didn't you go swimming?'

'Just watching the sky.'

She puts down the bowl and spoon and comes towards me, both arms stretched out. I let her pull me up.

'Come inside!' she says. 'You'll get wet.'

'Okay,' I laugh.

'What's the matter?' She is dragging me through the back door.

'Nothing.'

'You look weird. Like you've seen a ghost.'

'Nothing's wrong.'

'Don't lie!'

'Okay.'

Once we're inside I tell her that I feel a bit strange, and that I'm going up to my bedroom to lie down. The truth is, I'm scared.

Stella never minded me waking her when I had the dreams. I'd crawl into her bed, or she'd come into mine, and I'd tell her the dream in as much detail as I could remember. Then I'd go back to my own bed and sleep peacefully. Sometimes weeks would pass without one, then, out of the blue, they'd be back, three nights in a row. I was always lost somewhere, abandoned and alone, with crowds surging around me. When I opened my mouth to scream no sound came out.

'It's your soul talking, Peach,' she used to tell me. 'Your soul is wandering around looking for answers.'

Well, maybe. But what I do know is that I haven't had one of those dreams in more than a year, and although Stella might miss them, I certainly don't.

Lying here on the bed I have to wonder if maybe Fluke was right after all. Maybe it is gutless to not even want to find out your own mother's name.

I remember coming home from school once in Year Nine and finding Mum on the couch reading. I'd developed a passionate hatred for my name over that year, and I wanted to have it out with her.

'Why did you call me this crazy name?' I complained as soon as I came in the door. 'Nobody, absolutely *nobody,* is called Perpetua!'

Mum took her glasses off and looked at me. I was at the fridge pulling out cheese and tomatoes and slamming them onto the bench, giving her snaky little looks while I did. I used to get so ravenous after school. It was probably hunger as much as anything else that put me in such a bad mood.

'It was the name your birth mother gave you,' Mum said. 'Remember, we told you that?'

I shrugged. She had told me about being adopted, of course. Right from the start my parents had been totally open with me. But I suppose I wanted to have a fight. 'So why didn't you change it?'

'Because you were a gift!' Mum put her arm around my shoulders, but I shrugged her off. So she just stood there alongside me picking cheese from the plate. 'The most precious gift in the world, and we were so grateful that we wanted to pay her that respect.'

'Respect?'

'It seemed the one thing we could do to say thank you.'

'Did you ever meet her?'

'No.'

'So who decided that I would go to you two?'

'She did. She was given a list of profiles of different couples and photos but she didn't want to meet anyone.'

I knew this already, but I suppose I needed to hear it again.

'We just felt so lucky that she chose us,' Mum said.

'Why did she choose you?'

Mum shrugged and smiled as if she still couldn't quite believe it.

'No idea! She might have liked the idea of us both being doctors. I don't know.'

'Did she take long to decide?'

'Not sure about that one, love.'

'I just hate my name,' I whined. 'You have to spell it for people all the time. And they give you these weird looks. *Perpetua?*'

'Well, I suppose it is different,' she said hopefully.

'I don't want to be different.'

Mum went back to the couch and picked up her book again. She didn't start reading but continued to look at me.

'Do you want to try to find out more, darling?'

I sighed. Whenever the topic was raised, both she and Dad went into positive overdrive about helping me find out more about my origins. 'Find out about *what?*' I snapped.

'Your mother.'

'You are my mother,' I said quickly.

'Of course I am.' Mum smiled. 'But one day you might want find out more about your birth mother. You might want to try to make contact with her. Of course I'll *always* be your mother. Always and no matter what.'

'Did she see me?'

'Probably.'

'So I was loathed on first sight?'

'No. She would have *loved* you on first sight,' Mum said forcefully. 'Life can be hard, sweetheart. It was impossible for her to keep you for some reason, but I'm absolutely positive she would have thought you beautiful, and she would have loved you.'

'Yeah, yeah.' *No need to go overboard.*

'I mean it.'

'What about her name?' I knew the answer to this too. I just wanted to hear it said.

'Don't know,' Mum said. 'She didn't want us to know anything else about her.'

'Why not?'

'Maybe she thought it would be easier like that. We could find out, of course, by getting hold of the original birth certificate but ... I haven't done that.'

'Why not?'

'Just out of respect for her privacy.'

'Was she married?' If my birth mother was some hazy forlorn figure, then my father was simply a dark, mysterious blob.

'We're not sure.'

'God, Mum, you don't know much!'

'Well, we can try and find out more now, if you like.'

'Why didn't you at the time?'

'What she was doing was huge,' Mum said hotly. 'We didn't want to make it harder for her. She wanted to stay anonymous, but she might well have changed her mind by now. She might really like it if you contacted her.'

I thought about that for about three full seconds, then wrinkled my nose. 'Nah.'

'Why not?'

I shrugged, pissed off that I'd even brought the subject up. The earth revolved around me that year, so what did I care about what *she* might like?

'Just don't.'

'Okay. Maybe another time.'

'Maybe.'

I love the Fitzroy Swimming Pool, and so let me count the ways. It's Olympic size, so the laps you do are proper ones. It's open all year round. The water is virtually cold, with just the chill taken off. And best of all it's outside. Indoor pools make me feel like I'm swimming in a soup.

The sky is lighter by the time I get there. Dramatic streaks of white light are breaking through the low cloud, but the rain has scared off the crowds. Suits me. I head into the change rooms. Around me there are women of all shapes and sizes and ages in varying stages of dress. Any body size or shape fits in here. I tell Stella this and she still won't come. I'm changing into my black Speedos right next to a large muscly woman in her sixties with grey hair and tatts on both forearms. She is having an animated conversation with a really old skinny woman – must be about eighty – about hip-replacement operations. They're cackling about how bits of their bodies have begun dropping off. The really old one has plastic daisies hanging from her ears. Her bathers look plastic too.

There is the pack of teenage girls gossiping and preening in front of the mirrors in their skimpy underwear. And next to the showers are two stunning black-skinned women, dressed in bright purple and orange, with wild turbans wound around their heads. They're laughing as they muster about half a dozen little kids who don't want to go home.

I pick up my towel, walk out, pick the fast lane and hit the water.

One lap, two, four, eight. I surge angrily through the water, the frustration rushing through my arms and legs, making them strong. Before I know it I've done fourteen laps and it feels like I've just started. I could swim forever.

Stella. Det. Ellen.

Where do *I* fit in?

No one even asks how *I* am anymore. No one says, *Hey, Peach, what's going on in your life? Are you happy? Are things working out for you, kid?* I know why. It's because *my* particular drama is so bloody *yesterday*! Who in their right mind would want to talk about a love affair that ended months ago? Who would want to talk about the way I continue to allow him to eat away at my heart? And because I don't talk about it, because I don't shove it in people's faces, everyone assumes it's over, but it's not over. *I'm not over it.*

Time to move on, Peach, they'd say. *Time to put all that behind you.*

But what if I can't even imagine doing that? What if the very idea makes me feel shaky? What if my heart feels as smashed as a melon fallen from the back of a truck? No one bothers to stop because there are plenty more where that came from. The back of the truck is full of friggin' melons! Will my heart be left to rot by the side of the road forever?

I remember that first time, standing with a drink against the wall of a bar in Johnston Street, watching my friends dance. I looked up and there he was, watching me. Fluke. We'd met briefly a few months before, and I'd seen him around the traps, always on his own, or at the edge of someone else's crowd. He would stand by the wall watching the band, in his own world, quieter and more self-possessed than the rest of the crowd. And I was always aware of him in some strange way.

This night felt different for some reason. I knew something would happen. As soon as I saw him standing there my heart leapt to life and without warning the words *You're the one* blasted through my head. *Stop it.* I was panicking a bit. *For God's sake, don't be so uncool. You're not in a Jane Austen novel.*

But as I watched him making his way through the throng to the bar, something in me knew he would turn around before he got there.

And he did.

He hesitated and, without buying a drink, turned and walked straight towards me.

I want you.

'Hey there … Perpetua?' He held out his hand, his eyes raking over my tight jeans, high-heeled red boots and the cream lace top that I'd bought that day, landing back on my face, a strangely serious expression in them.

'Hey,' I laughed and shook his hand, just as though I played these kinds of flirty games every day. 'How do you know my real name?' No one ever called me anything but Peach.

'I made it my business to find out.'

'So, are you going to dance with me?'

'That's what I'm here for.'

We danced all night and then went for a coffee, and as each minute passed I had this delicious sensation of *falling away* from all I'd ever known. It wasn't that we talked about much. It was just bits and pieces of our backgrounds, where we lived and the music we liked. But the way he smiled, so quietly, as if there was a secret life going on inside him that he was inviting me to share ... And his hands, those strong fingers tapping the table in time with the music coming from the nearby speakers. He had calluses on both thumbs and he laughed when he caught me looking at them.

'Old blisters, and a splinter I can't get out,' he said matter-of-factly.

I dug the splinter out of his palm with the tiny pair of scissors I keep in my purse.

He was twenty-two, and working down on the docks, but he'd just finished his Year Twelve at night school. Getting a grip on Luke's past was like trying to catch a fish with your hands. It slipped away before you could take a proper hold.

But I gradually learnt that his mother had had problems with drugs and money and men. He'd left school at fifteen, barely able to read and write. Teaching himself to read properly by buying the newspaper every day was the best thing he'd done *by far,* he told me. He'd look up words and write them down in a small book he kept in his pocket. He told me this without shame or pride. It was just the way things were.

'Am I hurting you?'

'Nah. Ouch! Keep going.' He laughed when I held up the bloody splinter. 'You're a surgeon like your dad.'

'Split it?' I said when the bill came.

'No need,' he said, picking it up. 'I'll see you home.'

'But—'

'Please,' he said with that smile. 'It's late.'

'Okay,' I said.

And so he walked me home along the dark Collingwood streets. Past the rows of tiny cottages and the enormous cleaned-out shells of factories and disused warehouses waiting for the developers who had already begun changing them into edgy little apartments for the young professionals moving into the area. It was such a still night. A crane on a half-finished building loomed above us and trucks, graders and building materials lined the narrow streets. In a few hours the place would be filled with guys in yellow hard hats and overalls shouting at each other, but right then it was ... perfect.

It is five to three on a Saturday morning. I am eighteen years old and my life is about to begin.

I will never forget the peculiar fragility of that night. The over-stuffed rubbish bins, the stray whiff of jasmine in the air, the cans thrown carelessly in the gutter. Not that anything was happening. We were just two people walking three feet apart along a street after a night out, moving like shadows through the soft air. Any moment it might come undone. Any moment it might smash open and fall away. Lost forever. I knew that. I might have been half expecting it, and I suppose he was too.

At my door I was desperate to kiss him, but he took both my hands in his own and said formally, 'I'd really like to see you again, Peach.'

'How about tomorrow?' I laughed, amazed at my own boldness.

'You're on.' He grinned.

And then he did kiss me. Very quickly, as if we were signing a deal.

He was the first guy I'd ever seriously wanted. That he wanted me too seemed nothing short of a miracle.

Fluke and Peach. Peach and Fluke. In love ... in love ... in love!

In the beginning love is so easy.

I swim and I swim and *I swim*.

At twenty-five laps I'm completely done in, spent, wrung-out. I pull myself out of the pool feeling empty and much calmer.

'You were really fanging it in there!' the lifeguard exclaims with a grin.

I like his open face and his stocky hairy legs. I can tell he'd rather be doing anything else but standing around waiting for someone to drown, and I can sympathise with that.

He points at the dark sky. 'You got a car?'

'Nope.'

I rush to the change room and into the shower feeling exhausted but easier somehow. Lighter. *What if I went back out there and asked the lifeguard out?* I giggle to myself. I just know he'd say yes. *Oh do it, Peach! Do it!* My sister's voice is in my head.

The hot water is wonderful. I want to stay in the shower forever but I don't. I'm the only person left in the change room, so I stand naked for a few moments, looking at myself in the mirror. I push my head back and raise my arms and pretend I'm a ballerina.

I can hear the clatter of rain beginning again. Is there anything better than a summer storm after a few really hot days? Life becomes loose and unpredictable. My position in the universe suddenly feels utterly arbitrary, but it doesn't matter. I'm one of those wooden toys bouncing on a bit of elastic, and I don't mind at all.

I pick up my bag, drape my towel around my shoulders and head out. There is quite a crowd standing about in the entrance lobby waiting for a break in the rain. Some have come from the gym upstairs, but most, like me, have been swimming and have wet hair. The walk home is only about ten minutes and I don't mind getting wet, so I push my way through the crowd towards the glass doors.

And run straight into Fluke.

He is in loose jeans and a faded blue T-shirt. He has a bright yellow towel draped around his shoulders. We're up close and facing each other.

'Peach.'

There is the strong smell of chlorine and wet bodies, but I get a whiff of him anyway, and it sends a shiver of longing straight through me. I step back, but we are in the middle of the small crowd so I can't move very far. We are physically closer at this point than we have been in months.

'Oh!' I gulp nervously. 'Hello.'

His eyes in this low light are as dark as I've ever seen them and hard to read.

'Hi.'

'Hello.'

'How are you?'

'Good, thanks. You?'

'Good,' he says and then laughs. 'Oh, you know, okay. A bit of this and a bit of that.'

'Yes.'

I love eyes that change. My eyes are bright cornflower blue and people tell me they are beautiful – but they're always the same. In normal daylight Fluke's eyes are a soft smoky grey but when the light changes they change too. *You're a man of smoke and mirrors,* I used to tease him, and the longer I knew him the truer it became.

But here in the late afternoon, in the swimming pool lobby, with the summer storm beginning again outside, they're as dark and mysterious as charcoal dug from the ground.

Black bristle almost hides the scar running down the middle of his chin, but not quite. I was there the night he got that scar. He fell during a fight outside a pub in Collingwood. I took him to the Saint Vincent's emergency department and after three excruciating hours of waiting he had twelve stitches. We laughed all the way home. I remember grabbing his face between my hands before I left in the morning and staring hard into those smoky eyes.

'Oh, sweet Peach, What you looking at?'

'Just you.'

'And what do you see?'

'Not telling.'

Everything was up for grabs then. Everything was sweet and waiting to happen.

'You been for a swim?' he asks now.

'Yeah.'

I look away over the heads of the people in front of me towards the glass doors where the rain is bucketing down.

'Got to get home,' I say. At least leaving first will give me a shred of dignity.

'You're not going out in *that*?' He smiles.

'Oh yeah … I am.'

'One tough girl, eh?'

'Not so tough,' I say sharply and push past him.

But he grabs my arm. 'Wait, Peach,' he says, 'you'll drown.'

'I don't care.'

'So you're in a hurry?'

'I'm in a hurry.'

'Can I ask why?'

We're staring into each other's eyes. He is friendly, cool and sure of himself, and I am nervous and hostile and weak with longing.

'I'm just … in a hurry,' I say again.

'Then I'll give you a lift.' His hand is still on my arm and his eyes are on my face. 'Come on, my car is just outside.'

Why have my insides gone to water? Why are my knees weak when *I actually hate him*?

I picture the car he shares with his mother, the inside with all her rubbish strewn around, her cigarette packets, the empty cans on the floor, parking tickets and food containers, and I remember the way he always cleaned it so carefully for her. Such a good son to such a shit mother. That was his role and he knew how to play it. Now he's in nice-guy mode with me. Offering a lift to some chick he used to know. *Some chick he used to like but who now doesn't even register on his radar.* He's already feeling like a hero, I can tell. Nothing he likes better than to do someone a good deed.

I pull away blindly and by the time I get to the automatic glass doors and out into the rain I'm sobbing. Thank God he can't see, because it feels as if my whole life is in my head and gushing out my eyes; the tears feel hot and alive, and I can't stop them. *Is this what they mean by bleeding profusely?*

But as I head blindly down the steps and onto the footpath I feel a hand on my shoulder.

'Peach.'

He doesn't immediately realise that I'm crying but when he does his shoulders slump, his mouth loosens and the easy, confident smile disappears. The grey eyes flit to his feet. He's embarrassed for me. One hand grabs my elbow like a vice.

'Let me give you a lift, Peach,' he says quietly. His eyes lift to my face and they stay there. 'Come on. My car is just around the corner.'

'No.' I shake my head.

'But why not?' He moves closer.

I stare back at him. There is something genuine in his voice, a sincere bewilderment, and a long terrible moment passes where I realise how much I love him still and how that makes me hate him like crazy.

'Because you're the *last* fucking person I'd ever want to get a ride with. You hear me, Fluke? The last! Don't *ever* try to be friendly to me again. Don't even speak to me. Don't even say hello.'

He drops my elbow and steps back, reeling as though I've hit him. The suddenness of my anger has shocked him. I can see that.

I turn and dash through the rain, almost colliding with a bike rider on the footpath. 'Hey, watch out!' the man yells. I turn right down a small street towards home, sensing that he is still there in the rain looking after me. I don't turn around.

All the way home I'm on a mad high. *Did I say that? Did I just yell at Fluke?* I'm elated in a sick, crazy way. I have never let go like that before with *anyone*. If I've hurt him, then I'm glad. It's out there anyway, isn't it? Of course I know I'll crash, probably sooner rather than later, but this high is real. Road rage. You're driving and someone does something stupid and dangerous but instead of thanking your lucky stars that you missed out on being killed, the adrenalin kicks in and you start yelling and screaming and gesticulating *after the event*. It doesn't do any good, and later when you think back you're appalled at yourself, but I'm not there yet. This bit feels too good.

By the time I get to our front door I'm soaked through. I bounce up and down in my squishy sneakers and fumble in my bag for my keys.

Once inside, I call out to Stella to let her know I'm home. But there's no answer.

I walk into the kitchen, seeing it properly for the first time in about a week. What I see is grot everywhere. There are half-finished bowls of cereal and unwashed cups and glasses on the sideboard, and newspapers scattered all over the table. I pull open the fridge to check if we have any milk, only to find Stella's hairbrush, thick with hair, sitting on a rack next to the yoghurt. *Yuck!* I pull it out and shut the fridge door too hard. I grab my phone, itching to scream at her to come home *right now* and start cleaning up. But there's a message from her saying she's gone to the movies and will be turning her phone off.

I think about cleaning up the mess myself, but instead I dump my swimming bag in the middle of it and head upstairs, where I pull off my wet clothes, and crawl under the bedcovers.

My mother was a nun for ten years.

I have a grandmother in the country who is desperate to see me.

I reach for the box where I stuffed the letter, but just then my phone rings. It's Cass.

'I'm sorry for walking off like that earlier.'

'That's okay,' I say, 'but I'm busy at the moment. Can I ring you back?'

'Peach, we can't let it happen.'

'But what can we do?'

'She can still get the abortion, but she has to do it soon. Like this week.'

'But she doesn't want—'

'It's the Catholic thing,' she cuts in breathlessly. 'Her family.'

'She hasn't seen her family for years.'

'I don't believe in abortion either, except in extreme circumstances,' Cassie says defensively.

'Hmmm,' I murmur evasively. But I don't agree with her. Not really. Why should the reason have to be extreme? If a woman doesn't want a kid, then she shouldn't have to have one as far as I'm concerned – it's her body. But I don't want to get into a discussion about it.

'Det is an extreme circumstance,' Cassie goes on. 'Agree?'

'Yep.'

'I'm going round to see her again and try to talk some sense into her.'

'Right,' I sigh. 'Well, good luck.'

'But you've got to come with me!' she cries. 'You and me together. We've got to do something... She *can't* have a baby. She doesn't have a maternal bone in her body. She won't be able to manage it. You know that. She'll get sick of it and then get depressed and then maybe suicidal. And you know what will happen then, don't you?'

I wait. *No. Tell me what will happen then, Cassie.* I've never heard her so agitated. It isn't like her.

'You know what will happen?' she says again and waits.

'What?' I say, only because I know she wants me to. I just want be left alone.

'They'll take it away from her!'

'*They?* Who is *they*, Cass?'

'The government, of course,' Cassie wails. 'They take kids all the time from people. Don't you know that?'

I say nothing. I'm getting cold now, and I wish she'd just get off the phone.

'Peach, are you there? Will you come?'

I want to stay curled up for a while and forget everything. Then I want to have something to eat and go to Nick's gig and dance all night.

'No,' I say.

'Why not?'

'I just can't.' My voice cracks and I don't trust myself to say anything else.

Cassie takes a couple of seconds to register it. 'But we can't just give up on her?' she says in a quieter, more reasonable tone.

'Cassie, listen to me. She'll do what she wants to do, the way she always does what she wants to do.' Having said this, I realise that it's true. Det is the strangest person I know, and the best. She's always known her own mind.

'Peach, this is different.'

'How?'

'Can you see her with a ... *baby*?'

'No.'

'And can't you see that this will affect us too?'

'I'm going now, Cassie. I'll ring you later. I just can't come, okay?'

'I guess I'll go on my own then,' she says huffily.

I hang up and burrow under the covers.

When Det phones a couple of hours later she sounds so damned cheery and ordinary, so much like she always sounds, that I wonder if the pregnancy is a figment of her imagination. Or else one of my bad dreams.

'Peach, you coming to see Nick? Cass has bailed.'

'Yeah, okay,' I say.

'Will I meet you there?'

'Yep.'

'You sound weird.'

'I was asleep,' I say. 'I'll see you there in about an hour.'

Det laughs. 'Attagirl.'

Cecilia 1962

It was ten past one on a Sunday morning, and Cecilia was travelling home from a local dance with her brother Dominic. Her matriculation results were yet to come out but she had the feeling that she'd done well. Dom was pretty drunk, driving too fast and roaming over to the other side of the road occasionally, but it didn't worry her unduly. There wasn't anyone else on the road, and all her brothers got sloshed whenever they had a chance. Drink wasn't allowed in the dance hall, but the boys stood outside for a while before they ventured in, sufficiently inebriated to ask the girls to dance.

Cecilia was sitting on the passenger side, with her whole left arm hanging out the window, thinking about the boy she'd danced with most of the night and kissed briefly under the stars before she'd got in the car to go home with her brother.

The boy had slicked-back hair and green eyes. He'd been wearing tight black pants, desert boots and a short-sleeved checked shirt. He'd been home all summer helping his father with sheep. Muscles rippled down his arms in small hard waves, and he knew how to dance. It was a fifty/fifty dance, which meant half rock-and-roll and half old-fashioned numbers for the oldies.

They had danced well together, and talked easily. He was three years older than she was, already at university studying engineering. Cecilia was intending to go to university herself if she was accepted. When the dance was over he'd walked her to the car, and while they were waiting for Dom, he'd put his arm around her shoulders, which felt awkward until, quite naturally, they moved closer and began to kiss.

Cecilia remembered the rush of warmth she felt in her belly when his arms first pressed her to him, the strong hard hands moving up and down her back and holding her about the waist. Her hands had felt so soft and small inside his large rough ones and that was lovely, but confusing, too. Because although it was exciting and part of her wanted to go on kissing him, at the same time she felt an odd reluctance. *This is not enough for me. It's not interesting enough. If I go for this, then nothing interesting will ever happen to me again.*

'So what gives, sis?' Dom suddenly asked.

'About what?'

'What you thinking about?'

'This and that.' She grinned at him.

'You like that bloke you were dancing with?'

'Yeah. He's all right.'

'You see yourself married some day?'

'No,' she said without thinking.

'Girls always say that,' he mocked, 'and it's the one thing they want more than anything.'

'Not me,' she said.

There had always been something recklessly honest about her brother that brought out the same in her. He turned the car from the main road onto the dirt track that led up to the farm, almost scraping the big rivergum that had stood in the same spot for at least two hundred years.

'Dom, I should be driving.'

'Relax!' He tapped on the wheel. 'So come on, why not? Why don't you want to get married?' The cabin reeked of alcohol, but his voice was steady enough.

She brought her arm in from the window and looked at him. 'I don't know, really. I just don't.' She wanted to tell him that she couldn't imagine herself in love. That when she listened to her friends talking about it and saw them with their boyfriends something in her recoiled. She liked the boys well enough, but she hated the way the girls were when they were with them. The way they simpered and giggled to win attention. Then, when she saw their older sisters, girls that she'd actually looked up to only a few years before, with babies in prams, their spark and prettiness submerged in domesticity, she'd think, *Not me. Never.* But how did you talk about that kind of thing with your brother?

'What about you?' she asked to divert him. 'Do *you* want to get married?'

'Yeah,' he grinned, 'of course. But … it's different for blokes.'

'How so?'

He shrugged. 'A woman sort of … gives up everything.'

Cecilia said nothing, but she was stunned. A wave of pure love washed through her. Trust Dom to put his finger on feelings that she didn't even understand herself. She looked over at his profile in the dark. With the long face, straight nose and high forehead he was like a Roman senator.

He'd been whistling along with the radio, one hand on the wheel and the other on the outside mirror. But he turned the music off suddenly and looked at her.

'I mean, look at Mum,' he said quietly.

'Yeah.' Cecilia turned away. *Look at Mum.*

There were only a few photos of their mother as a girl, but it was hard to match that bright young thing with the dark wavy hair and slim build to the worried woman whose fair skin had weathered so badly in the harsh sun and whose legs were plaited over with thick, painful varicose veins. With nine children and a difficult husband, she was at everyone's beck and call night and day, and no one ever even said thank you. Not properly. Thinking about her mother always made Cecilia guilty and angry in a way she didn't understand.

'Mum is the best mother in the world,' Dom cut in to her thoughts. 'But she's done it hard.'

'I know,' Cecilia said quietly. She loved her mother, but from the age of about twelve Cecila had stubbornly refused to be close to her, knowing that was what her mother wanted more than anything. Cecilia had coldly and calculatedly turned her back. On some unconscious level she knew that if she allowed herself to stay close to her mother, she would be dragged down into that compliant domestic cesspit of never-ending meals and cleaning and looking after other people's wants before her own. Her mother's acceptance of her lot had become totally *repugnant* to her.

But her mother wasn't just a drudge, and Cecilia knew that too. She was warm and spontaneous in a way that Cecilia was not. Cecilia envied her mother's capacity for joy. The way Ellen would burst into song for no reason other than that she felt like it. Right in the middle of making piles of sandwiches for school lunches or taking scraps outside for the chooks she would break into a Latin hymn from her schooldays, or a sad song about missing loved ones, home and family.

Cecilia and her brothers would go quiet. Even their father would sometimes stop to listen, shake his head and smile, because she had a wonderful voice, strong and rich and full of passion.

Dominic had once shouted at their father that it was totally outrageous that there was no piano at home for her, but Kev Madden had shrugged off the comment. He had enough to pay for without buying pianos. Nor was he about to take advice from his ne'er-do-well eldest son. Besides, Ellen never complained.

'Are you looking forward to being married?' Cecilia asked her brother.

'Oh yeah,' Dom laughed, and turned the music up high and began to thump the steering wheel. 'If I find the right girl.'

'You will.'

'So if you don't want a husband,' he said, 'then what?'

'Not sure.'

'Teaching?'

'No.'

'Nursing?'

'God no!' Cecilia shuddered. 'I just want …' She held her arms out wide. 'I want to understand things.' She laughed, because it sounded so lame.

'You've always been deep,' Dom said. 'Even when you were really little.'

Sister Jane Francis, who taught Cecilia Literature and Religious Instruction, was the only person she knew with a truly inquiring mind. Cecilia loved watching and listening as the nun pulled apart poems and plays, bits of scripture. Getting the class to discover the hidden truth lying dormant under words was her gift.

'So, university?'

'Maybe,' Cecilia sighed. University would be great, but in a way it was just more school. Eventually you had to decide what to do with your life.

'Come on!' Dom grinned.

'I don't know.'

'Politics? You want to be Prime Minister?'

'No!' They both laughed.

'What about being an actress? You were good in that play last year.'

'No.'

'So you don't want to be famous?' He was teasing now. 'Come on, don't all girls want to be Liz Taylor?'

'No.' Cecilia shook her head, thinking of the way the girls at school pored over pictures of actresses and models and fashion and secretly longed to be discovered and whisked off to Hollywood. With her fair hair and slim build, some of the girls suggested to her that she could be *the next Grace Kelly*, and they meant it. The fact that it didn't attract her in the least puzzled them.

'You're good-looking, sis. Play your cards right, you could marry a really rich bloke.'

'I'm not interested in that.'

'Well, I give up,' he said finally. 'You'll work it out.'

'Or I won't,' Cecilia sighed.

The three-mile trip on the dirt track ended when Dom tried to turn the vehicle into the drive leading up to the house and fell short of a clean turn. There was a horrible sound of metal on cement. He'd scraped the side of the car along one of the pylons flanking the cattle pit. Dom groaned loudly and flung the door open, leaving the engine running. Cecilia got out too and they stood staring at the damage in the light from the full moon. Dom crossed his arms, leaned up against the car and closed his eyes.

'Shit! He'll kill me.'

'Yep.' Cecilia grimaced. 'You should have let me drive.'

'You don't have a licence.'

'But I'm not drunk.'

'Ah well, better get going. Face the music in the morning.'

'Yep.'

But neither of them moved. They stood alongside the car, staring up at the brilliant soft night alight with stars around them. Her brother pulled a packet of cigarettes from the top pocket of his shirt. Cecilia hesitated before taking one, more to keep him company than anything else. The moon cast shivering silver light on the leaves of the nearby tree. The only sounds were the low male voice on the car radio and in the distance a howling dog.

Cecilia recognised the Buddy Holly classic and smiled.

She thought of the boy she'd kissed and felt sad suddenly, cut off and different to everyone she knew.

'Do you believe in God, sis?'

'Of course I do,' she laughed.

'Do you believe that Christ died for us?'

Cecilia turned to look at him. Where was this leading? They'd never talked about such things. He shrugged when he saw her looking at him, pushed his hands deep into his pockets and stared up at the sky.

'Well ... do you?'

'Of course' she said quietly. It was like asking if she believed she had skin encasing her flesh, or if night followed day, or if there was blood running through her veins. Evidence of God was all about her, in the trees around the house, the paddocks and hills and valleys, in the change of seasons and in the music from the radio. She risked another drag, blew out and tried not to let the slightly nauseous feeling take over from the enjoyment of having the burning thing between her fingers.

'So where does it come from?'

'Where does what come from?'

'Faith.'

The question stopped her in her tracks, because she knew where *her* faith had come from. And it wasn't from anything anyone had *said*. All those boring sermons she'd sat through in church, along with the rubbish those small-minded, narky nuns in primary school had dished up, had left her cold. They had nothing to do with this living *thing* that burned like a hot coal at the core of her being. No.

It was her mother who had first made God real to her. Her poor, downtrodden mother had been the one to show her the beauty and mystery of life in the simplest of things. When Cecilia was very little, her mother would call her outside to witness the overnight opening of a bud, or the beauty of the sunset, or the way everything grew and changed after rain. They'd walk hand in hand down to the creek, the mother with her only daughter. She told Cecilia softly, as if it was the most wonderful secret in the world, that the natural world all about them was God's creation, and that it was important to give thanks for it every day.

On those walks her mother had also taught her lovely long rambling prayers and told her dramatic stories about the angels and saints. Some of it Cecilia didn't understand, and yet they became part of her life along with God and his Son who died on the cross.

She looked at her brother, who'd been silent for some time.

'What about you?' she ventured.

'I don't know.' He sounded genuinely baffled. 'I've been told all this stuff by people who know more than me, but if I really seriously believed what they told me, then surely it would have to change my life, wouldn't it?'

'How do you mean?'

'Well, if I really believed Christ died for *me,* then I'd have to take it seriously, wouldn't I?'

'You don't?'

'I mean, I'd have to try and *repay* the debt. I'd be a missionary or a priest or something, wouldn't I?' He looked at her. 'If it's true, then shouldn't I give up everything – career, footy, marriage, kids, the lot?'

'And?' she said curiously, because she knew he was trying to understand something important.

'And ... throw in my lot to go *follow Him.*'

The simple logic of what he was saying appealed to her. 'And have you thought of doing that?'

'Shit no!' He laughed.

'You've never considered it?'

'You must be kidding!' He roused himself and got back into the car. 'When you're ready sis,' he called out the window as he turned up the radio.

Cecilia said nothing. She walked away towards the dam and stood watching the way the moonlight streaked across the water.

An image came to her of Sister Jane walking among the house teams on sports day, her face lively with good humour, laughing, talking and patting girls on the back and congratulating them, and yet on some important level she wasn't even there. You only had to talk to her for five minutes to know she had a deep, interesting *inner* life that didn't depend on other people at all. She wasn't trying to prove anything to anyone. She was above it all … in a different world altogether.

I want that.

The realisation came to Cecilia as fast and furiously as a clap of thunder. Why should she bother with all the tedious and accepted intermediaries, the boyfriends and social life, university and career, husband and family? Why not leave all that behind and *go for broke like Sister Jane?* Why not? Excitement suffused her brain and rushed down into her chest and shoulders.

For he who loses his life for my sake shall save it.

Unable to stay still, she walked around in little circles, crossing and recrossing her arms across her chest to stop the tingling feeling. *Am I going crazy? Maybe I'm just … What about …?*

But no! Her brother was right. If you believed, then something huge *was* called for.

By giving we receive, by dying we find … life!

How many times had she heard those words? Words that made no logical sense and yet she had always recognised the wild truth behind them.

Anything worthwhile had to be fought for. Think of the hours a great ballet dancer had to put in before she could pirouette her way around the stage. Think of that party of adventurers making their way through the blizzards, the ice and the fear to the South Pole. Think of Christ Himself on His mission to save mankind. He'd accepted His terrible fate on the cross.

The easy way, the comfortable way, the sensible way was … *no way at all.*

Cecilia could smell the leftover heat in the grass around her, and all was quiet, but her mind was shooting off in all directions. *Oh yes.* A fire had been lit in her head and she was being pulled ever deeper into it.

She looked over at Dom, who was sitting in the car, staring straight ahead and looking so dejected that she only just managed to refrain from running back and blurting out her thoughts. *Do I really believe? Well ... why not find out?*

Cecilia sat on her decision for a week before she told anyone. She went first to Sister Jane, who only smiled when Cecilia blurted out the news.

'You've always been an interesting girl, Cecilia. It doesn't surprise me at all to know you have a vocation,' she said mildly. 'Are you thinking of joining *us*?'

'No, Sister,' Cecilia said shyly. 'Teaching isn't for me. I've been looking into it and I'm thinking about the nuns who brought up my mother. The Good Shepherds in Abbotsford.'

A frown crossed the nun's face. 'The French orders are very austere.'

'Yes.'

'And the work they do is ... very difficult.'

'Yes.' Cecilia smiled. 'That is why—'

'You know they take in girls from the courts? Some from very rough, sad and desperate backgrounds.'

'I *want* to work with girls like that,' Cecilia said vehemently, 'with girls who have nothing. The ones who need a new chance in life.'

The nun nodded thoughtfully.

'And Mum always speaks so well of those nuns. I would like to do it for her.'

'But it is your life, Cecilia.'

'I know,' Cecilia said defensively, 'but to help girls who are on the wrong path would be ... useful.'

'Oh yes, indeed,' the nun sighed. 'But you'll be lucky to see the inside of a university lecture hall, Cecilia. The Good Shepherds are not big on education, and you're so bright.'

'It's what I want, Sister,' she said, more sure than ever. *What is university compared to changing a life? Maybe a whole lot of lives?*

When she told her mother and father they looked at her in complete shock.

'No.' Her father banged the table with one heavy fist. 'I won't allow it.'

'Dad, I have to.'

Out of his depth completely, he looked at his wife. 'She's too young. It's wrong.'

'I'll be nineteen soon.'

'Go to the university first,' he yelled and stormed out of the room. Within two minutes he was back and to her utter dismay angry tears were streaming down his weathered cheeks. 'Please!' he begged. 'You are the brightest girl in the school. Think how wonderful it will be to go to Melbourne University!'

She had never seen him cry before and it broke her heart. He'd had virtually no education himself, and she knew how important it was that any of his children who had any aptitude got a chance at it. But she held firm.

'Dad, I have to do this.'

'You don't have to do anything.'

'But it's God's will.'

He closed his mouth abruptly.

She knew then that she had delivered the fatal blow. To go against the will of God in such an important matter would be putting himself at risk of mortal sin, and so there was nothing he could say.

Still, he did his best. They fought head to head for a week, upsetting her mother dreadfully, but Cecilia stayed firm, and in the end he gave in.

'Go then and get it out of your system,' he muttered one day on his way out to check the lambs. 'I can't stop you.'

Cecilia laughed and pretended not to care that her father would not give his blessing. He could always hurt her and he knew it too.

When she told Dominic, he said nothing for a full three minutes; he kept looking at her, opening his mouth as though he wanted to speak and then closing it again.

'Are you sure?' he said at last. 'I mean, it's so bloody *drastic.*'

'I'm sure. What do you think?'

He shrugged unhappily and looked away. 'Well, if it's what you want,' he muttered.

'It's what I want,' she said. But she knew what he was thinking.

How would she go without those slow walks home after a gallop through the paddocks, the sun sinking low over the hills against a brilliant summer sky splattered in crimson and gold, the quiet of evening settling in around them like a blanket? How would she manage not watching out for the first star coming into view over the roof of their house?

'Well then.' He tried to smile, but she could see that her news had brought him undone in some deep and terrible way. 'I hope that you'll be happy.'

She was unable to sleep that night thinking of the hurt that she was causing to the people she most loved. In desperation she got up at two a.m. and read again from the booklet on the Order of the Good Shepherd's worldwide mission. It was in the words of the Foundress that she managed to find her resolve again.

To save one soul is worth more than the whole world.

That idea had set her heart on fire the moment she'd read it and it was working its magic now. It was her life. The only one she had.

She would do what she must do.

You may find in that far-off land to which you go, sorrows which may often fill your Chalice to the brim. Yet I say to you, Go! My dear Daughters, go with great courage where God calls you!

Peach

Det is waiting for me at the bar. I'm wearing my new high heels with jeans and a loose red top, and I feel very jittery. My hair is pinned back and I've got on my red lipstick. When I left the house my eyes in the hall mirror looked too bright. They were glittering. And my cheeks were uncharacteristically pink.

I'm flushed, as though I might be coming down with something.

Det is pale, as usual, and is dressed in an old black trench coat. She notices my colour and mood immediately.

'What are you on?'

'Nothing,' I whisper.

'Peach!'

'Oh, I'm just … Nothing. What about you?' I ask in a bid to get her eyes off me.

'Brilliant.' She grins.

'How come?'

'It's called food.' She flips my hair a couple of times playfully. 'I'm actually trying to cook food and it's working wonders!'

'God,' I murmur and take a look around at the crowd, 'bit dramatic, isn't it?'

'I chuck a lot of it up every morning, but still … Hey, you look hot, Peach,' she teases.

'I need me a drink,' I say, pulling out my purse. 'Seriously.' I have this nervous edgy feeling in my guts that won't leave me alone.

'Okay,' Det says wryly.

'Vodka,' I say to the young barman. 'Double shot.'

Det tucks my purse back into my pocket. 'My shout.' She grins. 'Least I can do is buy my mate a drink when she needs it. So what's up?'

I shrug, on the edge of telling her everything, but I pull back because … well, if I start actually discussing the letter, it will become real and I might have to do something about it. Part of me thinks if I keep it private then it might just fade away.

I notice Det's glass full of ice and a clear liquid which looks blue in the bar light.

'*Water?*' I ask disbelievingly.

'Well, yeah.' She grimaces. 'H2O certainly is a new experience for me.'

'So, not even a splash of happy juice?'

'Just water.' She laughs. 'Can you believe it, Peach? Me and *water?* Water and me!'

'Doesn't sound right,' I agree, and we both laugh.

We're joined by Nick and two of his fellow band-members. Dicko, whose real name is Richard Head. Can you believe his parents would be that stupid?

The drummer, Kooloos, is commonly known as Screwloose. He is a forty-year-old classical guitar lecturer at the VCA, but moonlights as a heavy rocker in Nick's band, when they get a gig.

They sit alongside us at the bar. Nick picks up Det's glass and smells it, then pretends to fall off his chair, but she only shrugs.

'Just trying to stay nice.' She smiles, her eyes sliding past him to the crowd of guys who've just come in.

'A first for everything, eh?' Nick winks at me. 'You're looking hot, Peach!'

I slide one hand over his balding head and hug him. 'So you'll dance with me?' I ask.

'Thought you're never ask.'

I scull my double vodka and we walk through to where the band is playing. I'm feeling very cool, very sharp, very much on top of things. Admiring eyes run over me and I know I must be a little inebriated, because for once in my life I like it.

'Great arse,' someone murmurs into my ear.

I toss my head and think, *Yes. I do look good in jeans. Hey, this might just be fun. Better than being a fucking nun anyway! I wonder how old she was … when she became one.* I pull out my long blonde hair and fluff it out with both hands, and I feel every male eye around me taking it in. Nick is right behind me, calling out to people he knows. He is proud to be with me, and I like that too.

The music blasts into my head like steam, setting my blood alight. Tonight I don't care who the hell is watching. Nick grabs my hand and we let rip. He's a good dancer too, and I'm so far gone with that quick double shot on an empty stomach that I figure I am too. By the end of the set I'm wrecked, drenched in sweat and loose, and I'm not thinking about nuns or brides or old women, or babies either. I don't see much of Det until midnight when Nick's band comes on. She and I dance for about another hour, then I remember I have to start my new job in the morning.

'I'd better go home, Det.'

'Me too,' Det says.

We edge our way through to the bar and then over to the corner where we left our coats with a couple of girls.

'Stay at my place?' I suggest, putting my coat on.

Det pauses. 'Okay,' she says, which surprises me. She is usually so determinedly independent. Never needs a ride, won't stay overnight; doesn't want a meal unless she is bringing half of it. Then you find out later that she had to catch a taxi or she had no food in the house. It's almost pathological. Det is the quintessential loner.

'Good.'

At the door someone yells goodbye. I turn around and lock eyes with Fluke, who is standing at the bar. Was it he who called? But he gives no indication. We stare at each other for a couple of seconds before I turn away. I walk out into the wet night feeling oddly pleased that he would have seen my raunchy dancing.

The rain has stopped and the streets are gleaming, but it's not cold.

'So how is ... everything going, Det?'

'I gotta get out of my place,' she mumbles, 'find somewhere else. The guy bought another dog yesterday. I just can't stand it. I'm the only one who cleans up the fucking shit.'

'That is *still* going on?'

'Oh yeah.'

Det has lived in some crumby places, but the current one is the worst. The backyard is the size of an envelope and the kitchen is disgusting. She lives with two guys who simply don't know the meaning of a clean sink, and one of them has some miserable mongrel who not only whines and barks day and night but shits everywhere. The other guy, Travis, isn't so bad, but he has a demented girlfriend virtually living with him who is constantly pissed and who doesn't know how to clean up either.

'Cassie is seriously bugging me too,' Det complains. 'She called me this afternoon, after she stormed off. I don't mind her opinion, but I don't want orders.'

'Fair enough,' I mutter.

'She thinks the only reason I'm keeping the baby is because I feel guilty about the other two abortions.'

So why are you having it? I want to ask.

She must know what I'm thinking, because she stops to look me squarely in the eye. 'I don't care what *anyone* says, Peach. I'm going to have it.'

'Okay,' I say.

'Just okay?' She grins.

'Yeah,' I say. 'Okay.' I can see her determination. It's the same as when I first met her. She told me then that, yes, she had a family, but she sincerely hoped she'd never see them again. It was there when she insisted on doing Fine Art against the wishes and advice of everyone. Det is so tough that it's scary. Maybe I'm still a bit drunk, but I am suddenly genuinely glad for her. One way or another, she will pull this off. I take her by both shoulders and shake her gently.

'Good for you,' I say.

'Yeah?' She searches my face for any hint of sarcasm or dishonesty and when she sees none her face relaxes. 'I'll probably be a terrible mother!'

'Yeah,' I agree. I'm not going to start lying to her just because she's got a kid on board. 'But I reckon if you can just keep it alive for, say, three or four years, maybe till it gets to school, then I think you'll be okay.'

'*Really?*'

'Yeah.'

'So … have you got any hints?'

'Hints?'

'On how to keep it alive until I get it to school?'

And that's when we both crack up laughing. Giggling and snorting, we continue along the wet footpath towards my home.

'Sorry, Det. I failed Babies 101 first year uni. Forgot to turn up for the exam. Hey, where did you go for *your* examination?'

'The Women's.'

'And what did they say?'

'Just to look after myself. Try to eat and all the rest of it.'

'Fags, drugs, alcohol?' I say softly.

She shrugs ruefully. 'I told them everything.'

'And?'

'They were so nice. No sermons. Just told me to do the best I can. So I will …' Her voice catches in her throat. 'I really appreciate how nice those nurses were. They did preliminary tests, but it's still too early to tell if something is wrong. They'll do more tests later.'

'What will you do if … they find something wrong?'

'Have it anyway.' She shrugs.

'Yeah?'

'Yeah. I don't care if it's got flippers. I'm having it!'

'*Flippers!*' I burst out laughing again. Trust Det to think of flippers. She gives me a dark look.

'Don't tell anyone yet, okay? It might decide to check out early when it realises who it's got as a mother.'

'But if it does manage to hang in there it will have a good mum,' I say quietly.

The one thing Det hates more than bullshit is sentimentality. But I know my words have touched her because she goes quiet. Then she pulls a hanky from her pocket and blows her nose. It's very dark, but it's actually nice walking along in the day's leftover heat. I feel like we might be in Singapore or Bali.

We turn the corner into my street and walk in silence, arm in arm.

A baby!

There is a note from Stella on the table when we get home.

Oh Sister Peach!

Queen of my heart, mistress of my soul! I'm in bed pining but where are you, luscious one? (Please accord me absolution. I have seen the error of my ways. I promise. As proof of this I hearby swear to clean out the cupboard under the stairs tomorrow morning. Notice that it smells of rats! I kid you not.)

You missed Mum and Dad, you total absolute wanker! They hung on for as long as they could but when you didn't turn up ... they had to go. Anyway, they send their love and lots of kisses and will try again in a couple of days.

But I need to know if it happened! Tell me!

Oh pleeeese, Peach, don't leave me in the dark, you blonde goddess! I know you've got to leave in the morning for your job so tick the box below, else I'll come and haunt you in your sleep. I'll pester you in your new job.

With love from your biggest fan,
Sister Mary Stella of the fat Arses! XXX

There are two crudely drawn boxes under her name with *yes* under one and *no* under the other.

Det reads the note over my shoulder. 'What the hell is she talking about?'

I shrug dismissively and go out into the hall to grab bedding from the cupboard. Det is already pulling out the sofa bed.

'There's a spare toothbrush in the downstairs bathroom. You want a nightie or something?'

'No, I'll sleep in my undies.'

While she is brushing her teeth I run upstairs and grab the envelope from my wardrobe. Then holding it carefully as if it might contaminate my fingers I rip it in half and take the two halves out the back and dump them into one of the big green recycling bins. The council rubbish truck will take it soon and then it will be gone for good. Not very nice, I know, but I can't let it happen. I won't let my life be blown apart.

Det looks at me from the open bathroom door, her mouth full of toothpaste.

'So tell me what Stella was on about,' she mumbles.

'She said something momentous was going to happen to me today.'
'And did it?'

I straighten the freshly made bed

'What do you think?' I wave at the same old room, and Det gives me her famous raised eyebrow which tells me that she knows something else is up but that she is deciding not to push it. She climbs into the bed.

'You want a drink?' I ask. 'Hot milk or something?'

She bursts out laughing. 'Yeah, hot milk and a water bottle and fluffy slippers!'

'Really?'

'On the double!'

I go to the door and we smile at each other before I switch the light out. Then I remember Stella's note. So I sneak back into the room and pinch her note and take it upstairs with me. Once in my room I take a pen and tick the *yes* square and then slip the note under her door.

That night I dream that I am lost in the convent. I am hurrying along dim corridors and pushing open doors into dusty, empty rooms, trying not to panic, desperate to find someone who can tell me the way out, but there is no one. Occasionally I hear the faint sound of furniture being moved, occasionally the soft murmuring of female voices and then a telephone ringing. But as soon as I turn towards the sound it fades.

I come to a wide wooden staircase leading down. At the bottom is a huge stained-glass window of Jesus holding a small lamb. It frightens me for some reason, but I descend slowly. I am aware that I do not belong and the longer I stay the more afraid I am that I will be caught here. When I'm halfway down the stairs there is a sudden loud, terrible scream.

I wake up terrified, my heart beating like crazy, my pillow damp with sweat.

Sadie, Ellen, Cecilia.

They are uninvited guests trying to set up camp in my head. Strangers. Why should I care about any of them? Stella's words from the morning come back to me, sending an eerie tingle down my spine.

Things can be one way in the morning, and by evening they're another.

I climb out of bed and creep downstairs, past the still-sleeping Det, and out the back door. I retrieve the letter from the recycling bin. I find sticky tape in the kitchen and join the pages together again. Then I take the letter upstairs and lie on the bed and I read it again.

My mother was a nun for ten years.

I have a grandmother who is desperate to see me.

Sadie, Ellen, Cecilia ... and me.

Cecilia

Cecilia came through the sliding door into the crowded airport lobby and looked around. It was like every other such place in the world. Loose groups of people were lined up with expectant faces, waiting to connect eyes with loved ones coming in on the evening flight. There were a few welcome-home placards, and someone had a string of pink balloons. Children, some in pyjamas and propped on their parents' hips, were looking around sleepily. One by one they found each other and the tired, anxious faces broke open in relief. The couples and little family groups moved away from the strangers to embrace each other in a little huddle, to kiss and laugh and talk excitedly.

Cecilia moved through the crowd towards the doors, dragging her luggage behind her, telling herself she was lucky. She had Breda's address in the pocket of her coat. She would catch a taxi straight there. The key would be under the clay pot on the right of the front door. She was to go inside and make herself comfortable. There would be bread on the table, fruit and cheese and even wine in the fridge if she felt like it. She could go to bed in the spare room if she wished – everything would be ready for her – and

Breda would get home from work just as soon as she could. All would be well. *And yet...*

And yet, after all this time, not one person to meet her. She had told no one but Breda that she was coming home, and yet the terrible feeling persisted as she made her way outside. *I am alone in this world.* The same feeling that had dogged her in those last difficult years of being a nun, struggling with her faith and having nowhere to turn. *I am alone, so alone, and it is terrible.*

It didn't matter that she was the one who'd burnt all the bridges with family and friends. If she'd taken a risk, lifted the phone and rung one of her brothers before she left London, there might well be a contingent to meet her. *Maybe not.* Maybe she'd have been met with silence, coldness and accusations. She took her place at the end of the long taxi queue.

'Hey!'

Cecilia turned around. Some crazy person was bounding towards the line of tired, patient travellers, waving frantically. As she got nearer, Cecilia saw it was a stocky, badly dressed woman with grey hair.

'Hey! It's me. I made it, kid!'

Cecilia dropped out of the taxi line and stood looking down at the small, excited woman in dazed wonder.

'I couldn't stand the idea of you catching a taxi!' The bright eyes shone exactly the same.

'Oh, Breda.' Cecilia fell into her arms. 'Thank you. Thank you! You shouldn't have, but... thank you.'

'Come on.' Breda was laughing. She grabbed the big case. 'Let's get out of here.'

Once in the car, with Cecilia's luggage in the boot, they turned to each other again.

'You're the same.' Cecilia smiled. 'Exactly.'

'You too!'

In fact, Breda's face was lined and her dark hair was streaked with grey. She'd put on a bit of weight and her clothes were very ill-fitting and ordinary, but the essential her was very much there. The liveliness of her mouth, the quick smiles and wonderful eyes, dancing under the black lashes, were as bright as ever.

'How are your boys?'

Breda groaned and started the car. 'Don't ask! They drive me bonkers.' She grinned at Cecilia. 'Mad as cut snakes but, you know, they're fine.'

'Youngest still sleeping all day?'

'And partying all night! And Sean told me today that he was going to spend the money he'd saved for a car on a *luxury* holiday. Luxury, if you don't mind! At twenty! Backpacking isn't good enough for him. *Excuse me*, I said, *but...*' She laughed at herself. 'Sorry, I'm raving.'

'It's okay!'

They'd exchanged basic information by email, but had agreed to leave the past for when they met. After leaving the convent, Breda had retrained as an intensive care nurse. She'd married but had recently been left a widow with four boys. Three of the boys were in their early twenties, had left home, were at university and were doing well. The fourth one was in his last year at school.

About to reverse out of the parking space, Breda suddenly flipped the car back into neutral, clasped the steering wheel with both hands and began to squeal with laughter.

'Oh, God, I just can't believe this!'

'Me either!'

'Do you remember us, Nuncie? *Do* you?'

'I do. I do.' Cecilia smiled with delight. 'Of course I do.'

'Remember how clean our shoes were?'

'Oh yes!'

'Remember sneaking the extra bath when we knew Holy Angels had gone to that conference?'

'Yes!'

'Remember us going together to ask permission to say our final vows in English instead of Latin?'

Cecilia threw her head back and began to laugh properly.

'Remember what she said?'

'*How dare you!*' Cecilia mimicked the Novice Mistress.

'That's right!' Breda chortled. '*How dare you!*'

They were both rocking with laughter now inside the car in the airport car park, harsh fluorescent light blasting from the cement ceilings.

'It was you who asked,' Breda gasped.

'Me? No! No. It was you. I would never have dared'

'*You* said, "Mother, I *think* Rome has just recently given official approval for the vows to be said in English."'

'Did I?' Cecilia squealed.

'And she said...' Breda had tears running down her face. 'She said, "You are not here to *think,* Sister Annunciata."'

'Oh God. Did she say that?'

'*You're not here to think!*'

It was as though the last few decades hadn't happened. All that time simply collapsed into a thin wedge of complete ease.

'So much to catch up on, kid,' Breda said at last. 'But let me get you home in one piece first.'

They remained quiet until they were out of the airport and on the freeway heading back into town. Cecilia wound down the window and took a few deep breaths of the cool evening air. Oh it was good, so good, to be home.

The laughter had done her good too. She stared out at the billboards, at the slick guys in their sunglasses and the girls in their underwear, and wondered if her daughter wore such things. She would be the right age now. Nineteen.

'You never made your final vows, Breda.'

'No.'

They went quiet for a while, thinking.

'I missed you so much,' Cecilia said quietly. 'You were my rock.'

'Annunciata, I was a ratbag!'

'But... we needed you'

'Yes.'

'You never said goodbye.'

'I just couldn't, Nuncie. If I didn't leave then, I knew I never would. She loved me, you know?'

'Mother Gabriel?'

'Yes.'

Cecilia nodded and smiled. 'You were her favourite. Everyone knew it.'

'I loved her too,' Breda said passionately. 'She was a complex woman, but in the end I thought ... if I stay here she's going to eat me alive! I loved you all. I wanted to be a nun so much. I truly did believe it was what God wanted for me.'

'Me too.'

'And I loved the girls,' Breda went on. 'I loved our work. But I could see it was all wrong ... I was angry all the time.'

'Yes.'

'Just furious ... all the time.'

It had been against the Rule for anyone to speak of any Sister who left the Convent. Only Reverend Mother was told, and after arrangements with the family were made the Sister simply disappeared without speaking of her decision to anyone else. The other Sisters might raise an eyebrow at the empty space at table where once a dear friend had sat, or the empty bed in the dormitory, or the new space in the chapel every morning, but nothing official was ever said and no discussion among themselves was permitted. Convent life went on as though that Sister had not existed.

But the Rule couldn't stop them from privately wondering and grieving. Sister Jane Francis had found the stepladder by the back gate, along with the laundry girl Ida's nightdress and Breda's rosary beads, and the news spread like wildfire around the noviciate. Perpetua had gone with Ida Bakewell from the laundry.

'Did you really jump over the wall?'

'Yes.' Breda giggled. 'Ida held the ladder for me because I was smaller and we thought there would be more chance I would break my leg! Then she came after me and we made a dash for it.'

'Where to?'

'To the nearest busy road.'

'Did you have any money?'

'Ida had a few quid that her aunt had given her, so we jumped in a cab and went to my aunt's place in Moonee Ponds.'

'Did she know you were coming?'

'No ... but, apart from home, it was the only address I knew.'

Cecilia had missed Breda deeply. She'd been unable to believe it at first, and was incredibly hurt. But after some time passed she began to see that Breda had had to do it like that. It was who she was. She didn't want to have to explain herself to anybody – probably least of all the Provincial Mother Gabriel.

'Not far to go now.' Breda squeezed her hand. 'Tell me about you.'

'Two years after you.'

'Really?'

'You were my inspiration.'

'Oh, so blame me!' Breda laughed. 'So when did you first ...?'

Cecilia shook her head. 'Right back in the noviciate odd thoughts would fly in from nowhere and then ... when my brother ... they didn't let up.'

'That was so tough for you when he died.' Breda took her hand briefly.

'Snatches of his letters would come into my head. Why did we stay for so long, Breda?'

'We hung on because we believed we should, Nuncie. The doubts were part of it. And we were happy a lot of the time, weren't we? We were part of the Renewal. Remember Mother reading out that missive from Angers telling us how everything was going to change. I remember being so excited. And happy too ... so much of the time!'

'That's true.' Cecilia smiled. 'There was great happiness.'

'So many good days.'

'And bad days.'

'Remember the tennis?'

And they were both laughing again.

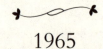

1965

'I'm going to ask her,' Breda said. The four other novices, Cecilia, Paula, Jane Francis and Beatrice, looked up in surprise. *What?*

It was evening recreation and they were sitting down one corner of the community room on straight-backed chairs pretending to concentrate on their needlework. It was Reverend Mother's Feast Day the following week and every novice was expected to have worked at least one item especially for the occasion. The pieces would be set out on the ornately decorated table as an offering to Mother, and then gone over with a hard eye for detail by all the older Sisters.

'When?'

'Tonight?'

'You'll go over Holy Angels's head?' Jane Francis whispered disbelievingly.

'Yep.' Breda giggled. 'Straight to the power zone!'

'You won't!' Paula was only eighteen, and her eyes were wide open, bright with merriment. 'I bet you won't be game!'

'Shhh, Paula,' Beatrice pretended to chide, 'Perpetua knows exactly what she's doing.'

Paula was an incessant giggler. The slightest excuse and she was off. She often got the whole group of novices into trouble for being unable to suppress her giggles, but no one could find it in themselves to mind, because her high spirits were so infectious.

'Just watch me,' Breda said.

Recreation was after the evening meal, and Cecilia looked forward to it. Although everyone was required to sit and do something constructive – needlework usually – there was a full hour to do it in and freedom to chat. After a whole day of prayer, work and silence, when Reverend Mother's bell rang to announce the commencement of recreation the Community room came to life with the sound of female chatter and laughter.

'Oh damn!' Paula's young face fell as she looked down at her needlework. 'Damn,' she muttered again. She'd been so busy laughing that she'd pricked her finger and a drop of blood had seeped onto the altar runner she was working on. 'Holy Angels will have me on toast!' She looked at Breda hopefully. 'Help *please*.'

Breda's mother was a beautiful seamstress, and Breda must have picked up some skills without even knowing it. She took the grimy, lace-edged cloth from Paula's hands and considered it.

'We can't all be gifted in every field, my dear,' she mimicked the Novice Mistress's dour tones. 'But we can at least start well by washing our hands!'

'Shut up, Pep! Just fix it for me.'

'You'll have to wash it.'

'Okay. But what about the stitches?'

They all knew the Novice Mistress would take it as a personal affront if the offerings this year were inferior to previous years. Cecilia's doily depicting the Ascension of Our Lady into Heaven in blue tones had been keeping her busy for months and was far from finished, but Paula's altar runner was in a much worse state. As the Feast Day got closer, Mother Holy Angels was at them the whole time, demanding to see progress every day.

Breda checked to see that the Novice Mistress was nowhere, then threaded a needle and began working on Paula's runner.

'Oh thanks, Pep,' Paula sighed in worried relief. 'I'm so hopeless.'

'You have other gifts, Paula!' Cecilia smiled.

'Such as?' Paula moaned despondently.

'Paula's gifts have yet to be discovered,' Beatrice declared dryly.

'You might be surprised to know,' Paula was giggling happily again now that Breda had taken over her sewing, 'Mother said I was making some headway at last!'

'That's only because Pep does it for you,' Jane Francis grumbled. She looked around at the others. 'Wouldn't it just knock you rotten if Mother chooses Paula's as the best piece when she's barely done a stitch of it herself?'

'Sour puss!'

'Don't think we need to worry on that score,' Beatrice murmured.

And they were all off again, laughing and teasing each other.

'Shhh,' some sisters in a nearby group cautioned them. Mother Provincial was frowning and looking their way, which meant they were making too much noise. They bent their heads and pretended to concentrate on their work.

'Mass got interesting this morning, didn't it?' Beatrice whispered, and the rest of them dissolved all over again into gales of silent laughter.

Cecilia, who had been in charge of snuffing the candles after Mass, had gone about the task too strenuously. First she'd caused one brass candlestick to fall with a crash onto the stone floor, and then, completely unnerved, she went back to her seat the wrong way, bumping into the beautiful vase full of Mother Holy Angels's lilies sitting one of the wooden pedestals. The whole congregation of one hundred and fifty nuns had watched breathless as the vase had teetered left and then right before steadying. Father Mac had come out of the sacristy to see what the kerfuffle was about, and by the time Cecilia was back in the pew with the others, her face was like beetroot.

It might have ended there, but while they waited for Mother to begin the *De Profundis* after Mass, Sister Paula got a fit of the giggles which proved contagious.

'*Out of the depths I have cried to you, O Lord; Lord hear my voice …*' Mother's low voice intoned.

'*Let thine ears be attentive to the voice of my supplication*,' the community of nuns answered. But by the time the prayer had ended, the two front pews of novices and postulants were shaking and gasping with laughter in full view of the older nuns.

They were called aside straight after Mass, admonished by Holy Angels, and afternoon recreation, which, if the weather was good, consisted of a half-hour stroll around the grounds after lunch, was cancelled .

'It was you that set me off!' Paula protested.

Me?' Cecilia protested. 'I merely made a mistake and the rest of you had to humiliate me!'

'A mistake!' Beatrice snorted. 'She pushes the candlesticks off the altar and then bulldozes her way through the flowers! What was your next trick going to be, Annunciata?'

All of them were now helpless with laughter.

'You looked mortified.'

'I was!'

'And by the way you were right off for the *Kyrie*,' Jane Francis declared.

'Was I?'

'Totally!' Jane was very musical. 'It starts on D and then goes to A-flat for the *Christe eleison.*' She began to sing it to demonstrate her point.

'Oh shut up, Jane,' Beatrice groaned. 'We don't want a lesson, thanks very much!'

'I was the bane of my mum's life,' Cecilia admitted ruefully when they'd all calmed down. 'She being so musical and me ... barely able to hold a tune.' Cecilia looked at Jane hopefully. 'Am I getting any better?'

'Nooo,' they all chorused. 'Worse!'

Staying with the same group for the whole hour of evening recreation was not encouraged. Sisters were meant to get up and change seats every now and then to sit with others they didn't know, so that special cliques and friendships wouldn't form. But the rule was often ignored.

Cecilia noticed a certain glint enter Breda's eyes when Mother made her way over to them and felt suddenly nervous.

'Good evening, Sisters!' Mother folded her thin hands easily in her lap as she settled herself in the middle of their little group. 'How are you all, my dears?'

'Good evening, Mother,' they all replied. 'Very well, thank you.'

'Sister Annunciata.' Mother Gabriel leant over and took Cecilia's hand briefly. 'Have you got over your cold?'

'Completely, Mother. Thank you. I'm fine now.'

In fact, she wasn't over it. She'd been quite ill for a few days, along with Jane Francis and a couple of the postulants, but it didn't do to tell Mother. The Provincial never got ill herself and became quite genuinely bewildered when anyone else did. When she'd come to see them in the infirmary the week before, they'd all felt as though getting sick had been their own fault. Good health was a prerequisite for entering the convent. If a postulant or novice proved to have a sickly disposition then she could be sent home for good, and they all knew it. So no one ever wanted to be sick.

'It's been a terrible winter.' The Reverend Mother shook her head. 'Mother Bernard tells me that three more of our girls in Sacred Heart have gone down with it.'

'That makes twelve, Mother.' Jane Francis frowned. 'Will there be room in the hospital?'

'We'll have to make room, Sister.' Mother shook her head impatiently. 'You'd think girls that age would be able to ward off a few germs. They get so miserable when they're ill.' She smiled around at them in a kindly way. 'So, my dears, you must look after yourselves. Eat well and keep warm.'

'Yes, Mother.'

The eating well was taken care of. It was mandatory to attend every meal and eat everything on their plates. As a consequence, most of the novices had put on weight. Keeping warm was more problematic, in spite of the layers of clothing, because the heating was so inadequate.

'Well well.' The Provincial pulled her little silver watch out from under her guimpe and checked the time. 'Almost time.' She smiled at them all. 'And some of you look very tired. Sister Beatrice, have you been getting enough rest?'

'Yes, Mother,' Beatrice admitted guardedly. Beatrice had come into the order having almost completed her degree, and she had special permission to finish it so long as it didn't interfere with any other activities. Which meant she had to study when everyone else was asleep.

'Nothing is worth your health, my dear,' the Provincial said severely.

'Yes, Mother.'

'Oh Mother, I was wondering,' Breda said suddenly, her face pink, 'if I might ... *ask* something?'

'Yes, Sister Perpetua.' Reverend Mother smiled warily.

'That old court down near St Mary's?'

'Yes, dear?'

Breda hesitated. 'I was wondering ...' She looked around at the rest of the group. '*We* were wondering if we might play tennis on it?'

There was a collective sigh of release and anticipation. It was out now.

'Tennis?' the Reverend Mother repeated, and everyone nodded enthusiastically.

'Yes, Mother.'

'You mean ... with *racquets*?'

'And a ball, Mother,' Breda said brightly, and Cecilia almost burst out laughing.

'But when would ...' The Provincial seemed mystified rather than dismissive, which was a good sign.

'Saturday afternoon before Benediction, Mother,' Breda chirped, quite as though it was a normal request. 'For an hour.'

'But, my dear,' the Reverend Mother smiled as though the silly idea could be put to rest quickly, '*clothing*?'

'We could tuck the outer layers up a little, Mother. Into our belts like this.' Breda stood up and demonstrated. The various petticoats were shorter than the outer garments. The Reverend Mother watched her, nodding thoughtfully.

'No one will see us, Mother.'

The Reverend Mother opened her mouth but nothing came out.

Breda went on excitedly. 'It would be *exercise*, Mother.'

'Exercise?'

'Exercise is good for our health, Mother.'

'Is it now?' Mother smiled. 'And have you spoken to your Novice Mistress about this?'

'No, Mother.' Breda hesitated and then grinned. 'We thought we'd have more luck with you!'

The other novices held their breath. Playing one of their superiors off against another would surely go against their cause. But Mother Superior seemed not to have heard. If she had, she pretended otherwise.

'Well,' she sighed, shaking her head as though in exasperation. 'I really don't see why not. As you say, it's exercise and a little enjoyment for you.'

'Oh thank you, Mother!' they chorused. 'Thank you.'

'With the exception of Lent, of course, or any other ...'

'Of course, Mother.'

The Provincial stood up. Her tall, angular frame was elegant in all the heavy robes. 'Besides, tennis might use up a little of the energy that was on display this morning.'

'Yes, Mother.' The novices tried to look ashamed, but they all noted that Mother's eyes were twinkling.

'Believe it or not, we were all young once,' she said suddenly. 'I remember being caught in a fit of giggling that had me going without supper for a week!'

They stared at her dumbfounded, trying to imagine it.

'Really, Mother?'

'Oh yes!' She was laughing. 'Good evening, and God bless you, my dears.'

'Good evening and God bless you, Mother.'

So every Saturday afternoon for an hour, except in Lent or on Holy Days, they would play tennis. The novices and postulants running around the court in their black lace-up shoes, voluminous skirts and veils, falling over, laughing and yelling as they tried to hit the ball over the frayed net, taking it in turns to join the onlookers on the sidelines, who would call out encouragement and keep a tally of the scores.

But now the bell rang and the Great Silence descended.

'Ask and you shall receive,' Breda whispered to Cecilia as they made their way to chapel behind the other sisters.

Breda now lived in a little house in Fitzroy North, right near the Merri Creek, in walking distance of St Georges Road. Inside, the house was as small and quirky as its owner. There were three bedrooms and a bathroom off a central hallway.

'The man of the house is out on business,' Breda said wryly, pointing at one half-open door. Cecilia grinned at the unmitigated adolescent mess.

She was shown into the bedroom opposite, a small, simply furnished room with an old wood-framed window looking out onto the street. She dumped her luggage and they made their way down to the kitchen.

The back of the house was lovely. It had been renovated into a light-filled kitchen and dining area leading onto a lounge with a built-in computer space and bookshelves along one wall. Glass doors led out onto a small back garden.

'You hungry?'

'I could eat something,' Cecilia admitted.

Breda pulled out cheese and bread and sliced a tomato and poured them both a wine. 'I'll let you sleep after this.'

'This is so nice, Breda. I can't tell you. I'm so grateful.'

'Be not grateful but be *glad*.' Breda laughed. 'I'm so glad you're here.'

'Oh Breda. So am I.'

'Did you sleep on the plane?'

'I never sleep on planes.' She was buzzing with excitement as well as exhaustion.

'So you'll go see your mum?' Breda asked, after they'd had a drink and a snack.

Cecilia nodded.

'You said you haven't had anything to do with her for years?'

'Nothing,' Cecilia said without emotion. 'I … I can't explain it. I hardly know why myself.'

'The brothers?'

'Nothing.' She looked at Breda, but there was no sign of judgement or shock.

'It's good you've come, then,' was all she said.

'What if she's dead?' Cecilia bit her lip.

'She's not,' Breda said. 'I made a few inquiries when you said you were coming home.'

'Is she … Is she still out on the farm?' How weird. She was asking the whereabouts of her own mother.

'No. The farm is sold. She's moved into Castlemaine. Don't worry, she doesn't know anything about you coming.' Breda grinned. 'I was very discreet in my inquiries. But maybe you should write first … let her know you're around before you just turn up.'

Cecilia nodded. She didn't have the energy to ask any more questions.

'You go have a shower and get into bed,' Breda ordered. 'I'll bring you a drink and one of my little pills for special occasions. We'll talk in the morning.'

'Okay,' Cecilia laughed.

There was such comfort in having someone else take charge and tell her what to do. When Cecilia had cleaned her teeth and showered, Breda came in with a mug of hot cocoa.

'I always have one of these to help me sleep.'

'I can't thank you enough.'

At the door Breda hesitated and turned.

'And the child?' she said quietly. 'Will you make contact with … the child?'

So Breda knew. But how?

Cecilia shrugged.

'Well, good night then. Sleep tight.'

'I will.'

Some time later Cecilia woke with a start, her heart galloping. *Where am I?* Then it came to her and the panic slowly abated. But in its place dread loomed. She'd been having the same dream that had plagued her night after night during the last winter in London. Oh the relief when it wore itself out and other dreams took over. Now it was back, the same and yet always so *raw* and fresh.

It started off so realistically. Here she is again on her first day in the convent, standing in the dormitory inside the calico curtain, feeling nervous, trying to work out what to do first. The Mistress of Novices has told them that they have ten minutes to wash themselves and change into the new clothes lying on their beds. Then they are to walk in silence down to the chapel. Cecilia isn't quite sure where the chapel is, and she isn't sure if she is to wash just her face and hands or … Warm water, a thin towel and washcloth have been left for her.

And so she climbs out of her street clothes and stands semi-naked, rubbing at herself, washing away the world and her former life. She puts on the ugly plain underpants, the cotton bodice thing, the petticoat and the black dress, the cape and the small veil with pleasure. Then, just as she is fitting the leather belt and cross around her waist it comes to her: *I've lost the baby.*

She pulls aside the curtains and runs down the long corridor towards the door screaming, *My baby! My baby!*

The other novices are filing out, backs to her, heads bowed. She screams for them to stop and wait, that they all must help her find her baby. But they don't turn around. One by one they disappear out the door. It slams shut, the heavy bolts slide into place, and she realises that she has been left behind, alone in the dormitory with no baby. She runs for the door and beats her fists on the wood. *Don't leave me. Please don't leave me.*

Cecilia looked at the little clock on Breda's side table. How amazing. She'd been asleep for six hours and it had felt like ten minutes. She lay in the dark thinking about the dream … and her baby.

1980

One more hurdle and it would be over. *Over.* Cecilia sat back in her chair and closed her eyes. She'd had enough! Enough of questions, and red tape, and people who knew best. She'd had enough of strangers, with their anxious looks and clichés. She'd had enough of 'working through the issues' and 'letting go of the grief '. Where did these people get off? If they bothered to read a good book, go to a concert or to the art gallery once in a while, they might realise that the tedious language they used had the *opposite* effect to what was intended. It made her want to run a thousand miles.

Why did she have to explain herself over and over again? She was perfectly sane, a thirty-six-year-old woman with a university education.

In a few weeks she'd be in London. She'd have a couple of weeks catching up with people and then it was over to Paris – forever, if she could wrangle a work visa out of someone. A whole new life was out there and she couldn't wait.

The door opened quietly and a nurse came in carrying the swaddled infant in her arms.

Cecilia stood quickly.

'Well, here we are then,' the nurse said breezily. 'How are you?'

'Very well, thank you,' Cecilia said.

The nurse handed her the baby. 'I'll leave you alone a while.'

'Just as you like.'

'Why don't I come back in half an hour?'

'Okay.' Cecilia read the name tag on the woman's chest. 'Thanks, Helen.'

'A pleasure.' The nurse smiled. 'She's just been fed and changed, so I doubt she'll wake.'

'Good.'

'I'll see you soon.'

The nurse was almost out of the room when Cecilia thought to ask, 'Have they come yet?'

'They'll be here within the hour.' The nurse hesitated and turned back. 'Would you like to meet them?'

'No no.' Cecilia shook her head. 'No, thank you ... I just wondered.'

The nurse came a few steps back into the room. 'They're very excited,' she said carefully.

'Are they?' Cecilia smiled.

'Absolutely over the moon. I saw them yesterday.'

'I'm so glad.' Cecilia looked down at the tiny, sweet face poking out of the pink blanket. 'So they've got to know her a little?'

'Oh yes, they have! They adore her. And they're such lovely people.'

'Yes.'

'I think you've chosen very wisely.'

Cecilia knew that Helen was probably referring to the parents and not to the larger decision of giving her child away, but she was touched nevertheless. It was one of the very few times during this whole business that anyone had been really positive.

'Thank you for saying that, Helen,' she said quietly.

The older woman nodded again before leaving the room.

Lovely people! They damned well ought to be, she'd gone to enough trouble picking them. Cecilia stood up with the baby lying in the crook of her arm, and went over to the window to look out at the big wild grey sky. It looked as if the rain had started already out in the distant Dandenong Hills. During the last three months of her pregnancy she'd gone into the adoption agency for hours at a time, looking at tapes, reading profiles, talking to caseworkers. She wanted to feel one hundred per cent sure and didn't care how long it took. The process was difficult and often very confusing. Many of the couples wanting to adopt were absolutely right in so many ways, and yet … she hadn't felt sure. It wasn't that she wanted highly successful or wealthy people. On the contrary, sometimes when couples wrote about their careers and 'secure homes and incomes', she'd shuddered with distaste. Money wasn't what she was after. Nor were good looks or 'breezy' personalities who 'got things done' or 'saw the glass half full' when times got tough. Those clichéd self-assessments put her teeth on edge.

So she decided to throw away all the criteria and trust her gut instinct. Recognising the true parents of her child would be akin to falling in love. She would *know* them when they came along.

And they did come along eventually in the persons of Bill and Elizabeth Manning, a Melbourne medical couple in their thirties. Cecilia had liked the look of them immediately and then, when she read the profile and watched the tape they'd made about themselves, she'd felt a simple, profound sense of relief. *Yes.* Of course she'd had to check references and manage the rest of the red tape, but everything she learnt about them reinforced her initial impression. These were the ones she'd been looking for all along.

For a start, they weren't as earnest and careful as some of the other applicants. Neither of them considered childlessness a tragedy, only saying that they would think a child or children a wonderful blessing.

Cecilia liked the wry, humorous way they spoke about themselves. *He's bad-tempered in the mornings. She doesn't know how to cook. Neither of us is very tidy.* Yet they were serious people with an outward-looking attitude to life that she liked. They'd both worked overseas with aid agencies. Elizabeth had gone straight into a war zone and worked for two years as soon as she'd finished her medical degree, and her surgeon husband had done similar work in Africa. Both of them did occasional stints in remote Aboriginal communities in Central Australia.

Cecilia liked the man's heavy, plain features, and all the wrinkles and creases around his dark eyes. His wife was younger and better-looking, with short fair hair and widely spaced cornflower-blue eyes. There was such honesty in her smile and gentleness in her manner. Cecilia found herself imagining her child with this woman. She was warm. She would know instinctively how to hold a baby. She would pick the child up when she needed to be picked up, and she would read stories and make good food. There was something else about her that made Cecilia feel completely confident. This woman knew how to love. There was something wholehearted, even recklessly loving, about her.

The final aspect that won her over was that they were upfront about not having any religious affiliations whatsoever. Most of the other applicants seemed to be churchgoers, or said they were. When Cecilia read *agnostic non-churchgoers* on the form she offered up a prayer of gratitude – *Oh praise be to God!* – clapped her hands and laughed aloud. *Bill and Elizabeth, you'll do!*

Cecilia was in a private room which looked out over a car park and a small square of green grass with a few straggling trees in the middle. Today there was only one group of people enjoying the grass and the trees. Lots of others crisscrossed around them on their way to somewhere else. Cecilia looked down at the sleeping babe in her arms and marvelled again at the perfection. To think that her own body had produced this lovely living creature! The eyelids fluttered every now and again like soft butterfly wings. Cecilia placed one finger on the soft little cheek and wondered if babies could dream.

'Goodbye, little one,' she whispered. 'May God bless you and keep you safe.'

But although the baby squirmed and yawned a couple of times her eyes remained tightly shut. One tiny fist appeared over the edge of the blanket and Cecilia tentatively put her index finger inside it. When the child's grip tightened, Cecilia smiled.

Still with her finger inside the baby's fist, Cecilia stared down at the cars and people and wondered if the couple had arrived yet.

Would they have an ordinary car? A Holden, maybe, or a Honda. Perhaps they'd have a fancy European car like a Saab or a BMW. After all, they were both doctors. Whatever it was, they'd have the baby capsule all set up in the back and probably one of those big colourful bags of baby things right next to it. Inside would be a little jumpsuit, maybe, booties, nappies and bottles and little jars of cream. Elizabeth wouldn't say much on the way in the car. But every now and again she'd look over at her husband who was driving; maybe she'd put her hand on his knee and they'd smile at each other. *Today is the day.* Cecilia could almost see them. *The day we become parents.* She could imagine their anticipation and their joy, just as she felt her own desolation.

It had been hard to recover from the horrible scene she'd had with one of the younger nurses the day after the baby was born. Bits and pieces of their conversation kept playing back in Cecilia's mind.

The nurse, in her late twenties, had come in to take the usual observations, but there was something odd about her manner. It was as if she was holding something back; her smile was uneasy and she never looked directly at Cecilia. When she finished taking her temperature and blood pressure and began packing everything back onto the trolley she turned.

'Do you mind if I ask you something?' she said, looking at Cecilia directly.

'Go ahead.'

'I know it's none of my business, but why are you giving your child away?'

'You're right; it's none of your business.'

The young woman flinched as though she'd been slapped. 'Sorry I asked, then,' she muttered, and then cleared her throat uneasily. 'Well, I'm done now. If you're okay?'

Cecilia nodded.

The nurse turned her back and wheeled the trolley towards the door.

The very last thing Cecilia wanted was to continue the conversation, but she couldn't help herself. 'I'm sorry I snapped at you,' she called. 'The answer to your question is that I don't want a baby.'

The nurse stopped abruptly by the door. 'But ... you went ahead and *had* a baby!' she said.

'Yes, but the pregnancy was a mistake.'

'So *why* did you?' There was a faint note of ridicule under the outrage. 'I mean, you're not a kid. You must know ... the options.'

'You're right. I'm thirty-six.'

'That's five years older than me.'

'Right.'

'How can you *not* love her?'

'Who says I don't love her?' Cecilia snapped.

The nurse stared back wonderingly, as though Cecilia was another species.

'But ... if you love her, then ...'

'I'm not married.'

'But, that man who comes in ...'

'My brother.'

'Does the father of the baby know about her?'

'No.'

'Why not?'

Cecilia stared at the nurse coldly and said nothing. Did this inquisitive stranger seriously expect her to explain her relationship with Peter?

The nurse seemed to read her mind, because her manner was suddenly apologetic. 'It's just that my husband and I want a baby so much,' she said hurriedly. 'We'd do anything for a baby and ... I'm really sorry, but it just seems so unfair that you've had a beautiful baby that you don't want.'

'Life isn't fair, though, is it?'

The nurse stared at her.

'You think it's *fair* that mothers all over the world have to see their children die of hunger?'

'We've been trying for eight years.'

'So do something else!' Cecilia snapped. 'Do something for children already born. Why is it that people think they have a right to children?'

'That's just heartless,' the nurse mumbled.

'Not heartless, actually,' Cecilia said. 'I've had a child and I'm going to give her to someone who really wants her. I don't think that is heartless at all. I think that it is rather *big*-hearted of me.'

The nurse walked out and let the door slam shut behind her.

Cecilia was so angry that she wanted to fly after her and give her a good shaking. *How dare she? How bloody dare she?* Cecilia's hands were trembling and it took her the rest of the day to get over it.

But now the compact beauty of the tiny face had transfixed Cecilia completely. *I will remember this,* she thought to herself. *I will make sure this image stays with me.* She had a sudden strong urge to undress the baby and look at her little limbs one last time, but she didn't dare.

On the farm she'd watched newborn lambs stumbling to stand, their mothers licking them all over. She would have liked to do the same, smell her, kiss her, lick her feet and the tiny limbs. Very gingerly she unwrapped some of the swaddling and then chickened out. It would be terrible to upset the poor little thing. But she did take off the booties and study the tiny feet. Then she lifted the sleeping child up to her face and wished she could cry.

The door opened and the older nurse came back. She smiled and walked over to where Cecilia was looking out the window, still holding the child close to her face.

'So how are we doing?' she said softly.

'Are they here?'

'Yes,' the nurse said, 'but no hurry. They're having a coffee.'

Something about the older woman's kind manner caught Cecilia unawares. Her throat suddenly ached with a million unshed tears.

'So I guess we should ... I should ...' Her voice petered out and she looked around the room in bewilderment. Where was she again? What exactly was happening? *Is this really me?*

'I guess I ... I should just ...'

'No *should* about any of this,' the nurse said firmly. 'You take all the time you need.'

'No no.' Cecilia held the baby out for the nurse to take. Then to her complete shock a terrible sob broke from her. It was followed by another and then another. The nurse stood there a few moments without taking the baby, then moved to put an arm around Cecilia's shoulders. 'You hold her a bit longer, love. There is no hurry.' The firm grip of the woman's hand on her shoulder felt like a lifeline. Tears splashed the front of the new pink-striped shirt she'd bought the week before.

'Oh, I'm sorry!' she gasped. 'I didn't expect that I would be like this ... Are there any tissues?'

The nurse pulled a wad from her pockets without letting go of Cecilia's shoulders. 'Don't be sorry.'

'But ... I don't understand it ... I really don't. I didn't expect to ... feel like this.'

The nurse smiled and gently took the baby.

Still gasping, Cecilia went right up to the window and put her hands on the sill. She was getting a headache, but in a way it was a relief to feel the grief rolling through her. It was inside and it wanted to get out.

Maybe ten minutes went by. When Cecilia turned around, the nurse was sitting in the chair holding the baby in the crook of her arm.

'I'm okay now.'

'You sure?'

'Yes.'

The nurse stood up and smiled. 'There is just one thing, Cecilia.'

'Yes?' *Please just go. Take the child and go.*

'They wanted to be very sure—'

'I'm absolutely sure,' Cecilia cut in. 'Please let them know that there is no question that I want anything else. Please, Helen, make that clear.' *Damn it. I have signed all the papers. Just go. Take the baby and go.*

'Are you still happy for them to name the child?'

'Well, of course ... She belongs to them now.'

'They were very clear that you must feel free to name her.'

'Oh, I see.' Cecilia was a little dumbfounded.

'Would you like a little more time with it?'

'No no ... well ... So they said that?'

'Definitely.' The nurse smiled. 'They were adamant.'

'Well then.' Cecilia had been thinking about her convent days a lot in the last months of pregnancy. She'd thought about herself as that girl of eighteen, and also Breda, who'd become Sister Perpetua on the day Cecilia had become Sister Annunciata.

'Well, if they don't mind, I have ... I *would* like to name her.'

'I think they'd be pleased.'

'Really?'

'Honestly, I do.'

'Then I'd like to call her Perpetua.'

Cecilia waited for the nurse to raise an eyebrow and maybe comment that it was old-fashioned and that maybe such a strange name wouldn't go down so well with the parents.

But she gave no such reaction. She simply smiled. 'Do you have a second name?'

'No no, let them choose that. Tell them if they hate Perpetua, they should feel free to change it. It's just that I ...' She looked away and said softly, 'I will always think of her as Perpetua.'

'I'll tell them that.'

Peach

Cassie is in a stink. She barely nods when I front up at exactly five to seven. No smile, no little chuckle when I try to make a joke. Nothing. Luckily Sam is there to take the ice off.

'Welcome.' He looks at the time and grins. 'Good start.'

I know what Cassie's mood is about, of course, but it still isn't pleasant, especially on my first day in a new job. Thankfully I'm so busy that it doesn't matter too much at first. I'm put to work on the coffee machine, and it takes all my concentration to remember how to hold the jug so the milk doesn't froth over and when exactly to start each coffee. Luckily there are not many customers until about half-past seven, but after that we're hit with a steady stream of people wanting coffees and pastries on their way to work. By eight, all the people working at the convent site are around too. Whenever I have to ask Cassie something about where things are, or tell her that a coffee is ready, she nods coldly and studiously avoids my eyes. After a while her coolness starts to get to me and I lose concentration.

'Where is the flat white?' she snaps.

I've just put six perfect lattes on the tray and forgotten the flat white. 'Oh God, sorry! I'll have it in a jiffy,' I say.

She sniffs as though I've made an unforgivable blunder. I'm being paid back for not coming along to tell Det what to do. Normally I'd be the one to broach the subject and we'd have it out in the open, but apart from not having the opportunity, I don't much feel like doing that.

Just when I start to feel like I'm going to snap, Nick walks in on the dot of nine o'clock.

'Hey hey hey!' He high-fives me as he comes behind the counter, 'The two babes!'

I smile in relief. 'You look wrecked.'

'Yeah, well,' he groans and starts piling the fresh bread into the baskets at the back of the counter. 'What about you, young Cass?'

'What about me?' she says curtly.

Nick takes a moment to look at her again, and then at me. 'Just asking if the universe is treating you kindly,' he says.

'Not particularly,' Cass snaps.

'What's with her?' he says under his breath when I next pass.

I shrug and smile. She might be driving me crazy, but there is no way I'm going to backbite her.

So we work on for another couple of hours and I begin to forget about her. I stay at the coffee machine, and Nick is right alongside taking the orders. Cass is serving the cakes and baguettes and running the coffees outside when she isn't busy.

'Two lattes and a weak long black, thanks.' The suited business-man is smiling at me.

'Okay.' I smile back. 'Where are you sitting?'

'Outside.'

So far so good. Four hours into the job and I've more or less got the hang of it. I'm starting to calm down.

There is a lull in proceedings, so I go outside and bring in two armfuls of dishes and pack them into the dishwasher.

Suddenly Cassie is standing over me with her hands on her hips, glowering.

'So you don't want to know what happened with Det?' she asks.

I look up. 'She wouldn't listen to me,' she says. 'Honestly, it didn't matter what I said, she just wouldn't listen.'

'Well, it's her decision,' I say calmly, trying to concentrate on getting as many cups and mugs into the washer as I can.

'But we'll be the ones doing everything!'

'How can you be so sure, Cass?' I say.

'Have you forgotten?'

'It was depression last time.'

'You think she's not going to get depressed with a *kid*?'

'Well, I don't know, do I?' I sigh. '*And nor do you.*'

'Yes, I *do* know!'

A sudden flare of anger catches alight in my head. How come she thinks she can tell everyone what to do? How come because her life is all set up with the perfect family and perfect boyfriend she thinks she has everything sewn up?

'No, you *don't* actually, Cass,' I say, straightening up. The dishwasher is full so I switch it on and look around for something else to do, because I sure don't want to stand here arguing with her. But Nick is serving the only two customers.

'So you're on her side?'

'I didn't realise there were sides,' I say.

'But it's so irresponsible,' she says furiously.

'When has Det ever been *responsible*?'

Cassie stares at me. The devil lands on my shoulder. All thought of reining myself in disappears. I want to pay Cassie back for the last couple of hours, when I needed a bit of help getting used to the job.

'I'm glad, actually,' I say angrily.

'What?'

'Yeah. I am. I'm glad she's having a baby.'

'*What?*' Cassie is looking at me as though I've gone crazy. 'She doesn't even want it. You heard her!'

'Words, Cassie, just words! Some part of her obviously *does* want it, don't you think?'

There is a stand-off for about five seconds. I pick up a dishcloth and start wiping down the benches; she stands there looking at me.

'Well, *I* think it's a disaster,' she says coldly, turning her back, 'for her and the kid.' I keep on wiping down the bench. 'And also for us.'

'Not everyone can live an ultra-neat life, Cassie,' I spit back.

She turns around and gives me a sharp look. She knows I'm having a shot at her. She has already confided to me that she thinks that she and Stephano will probably get married.

'Not everybody meets Mr Right and settles down in a big house full of stuff and has their kids at the perfect time,' I add for good measure. *Whoa!* I tell myself to pull back. I'm really twisting the knife now, and I'm ashamed even as I want to say more.

'Try to imagine not being wanted!' she shoots back. 'Imagine having a mother who doesn't want you! Could anything be worse than that?'

'*What?*' I say furiously. Did I hear right? *Could anything be worse than that?*

'I'm asking you to imagine what it would be like *not* to be wanted!'

'I heard you the first time!' I shoot back.

She stares at me uncomprehendingly and then the *click* moment happens. I see it. Her face falls. She knows she has trespassed into dangerous territory, and I see that she is sorry about the turn the conversation has taken, but I'm in no mood for forgiveness.

'Your birth mother is dead,' she says defensively, trying to climb out of the hole she's just dug herself. 'I remember you said once that your mother was probably dead.'

'I would, wouldn't I?'

'What is that supposed to mean?'

'Well,' I say viciously, 'since yesterday I know that my birth mother is alive and well, and that she gave me away because she didn't want me.'

'*How* … how do you know that?' Cassie's face has drained. She really looks as if she might be sick. But what do I care about that?

168

'I got a letter.'

'From who?'

'Her mother … my grandmother.' I laugh but it comes out hard, more like a bark. I feel like crying.

Cassie's mouth falls open. 'God! What did she say?'

I shrug, because a crowd of people have come in and are standing by the glass counter looking in at the cakes.

'Hey, that is big news. I'm sorry,' Cass says before turning away to serve them.

My shift is longer, so when Cassie finishes up at midday I still have a couple of hours to go.

Stephano arrives on the dot to pick her up. He stands by the door, smiling at both of us as he waits for Cassie to get her things together. She hesitates before walking out the door and comes back to face me. I'm behind the coffee machine making three lattes.

'Peach, I'm sorry about today.'

'Okay,' I say, 'me too.' But I'm not really. It's too raw.

'So when can I talk to you about all this?'

'Later … whenever.'

Cassie flushes. 'I'll ring you later.'

'Okay.' I shrug.

I take the coffees outside to the waiting people and watch Cassie and Stephano walking hand in hand out those huge gates, and a flash of bitterness unfurls inside me like a horrible worm. *How come she gets everything she wants?*

At the end of my shift I walk out along the path into the enclosure and look up; all those windows that used to be nuns' bedrooms are now little studios. I walk over to the big tree in the centre, wondering which one would have been hers. I shut my eyes and breathe in.

'Cecilia,' I say under my breath. 'Annunciata.'

It's ridiculous but I can't help it, so I say it again and again. It's as if I want to roll the name around in my mouth and sort of feel it. Cecilia Madden who became Sister Annunciata. *Where are you now?* What made her come here to lock herself away? All I've ever heard about the sixties is that it was a time of change and social upheaval and music. Nothing about ... *nuns!* Cecilia became a nun here while the rest of her generation were rocking out to the Stones, Jimi Hendrix and Janice Joplin and getting high on acid and grass. Why did she join and why did she leave? I close my eyes and try to imagine what it would be like to believe in God. What kind of God did *Annunciata* believe in?

But I can't get my head around it. I have no idea. The only image that I can summon is a solemn-faced old man with a long beard looking down through the clouds. What about Jesus? But my image of him is hardly any clearer and feels almost as crazy, the tortured body writhing on the cross. Why would you pray to *that*? He died and then came alive again. *Oh come on!* None of it makes any sense. But I'm intrigued anyway. Deeply intrigued.

'Hey, up here, fatso!'

I open my eyes and look up, and there is Det hanging out the window on the top floor waving her arms.

I laugh.

'What the hell are you doing?' she screams out for all to hear. 'I've been looking down at you standing there like a post for ages.'

'Contemplating my navel.' I laugh.

'Seriously, what were you thinking about?'

'My mother,' I say.

'She okay?'

'The other one,' I say.

Det takes a moment to process this. 'No shit?' she says more carefully.

'She was a nun here apparently,' I call up as though it's nothing. 'Her name was Mother Mary Annunciata.'

'*What?*' Det begins to laugh.

'I found out yesterday.'

'Goddammit girl, get up here!' she shouts.

I give Det the letter, slump down onto the unmade tangle of her bedclothes in the corner of the studio and close my eyes. She stands by the window, frowning as she reads. Finished at last, she drops the letter to the floor, sits down on her chair and props her legs up on the desk.

I look over at her for a sign of what's going through her head, but Det remains silent, her head thrown back, eyes closed, arms crossed over her chest.

'I know what you're thinking,' I say after a while.

'Oh yeah?' Det sighs without opening her eyes.

'That I've got to write back to her. Go see her. Make her my new best friend. Hold her hand when she's dying and tell her I'm so glad I found my *real* grandmother at last. Then they'll do a show about us on television. And then my *real* mother, the nun, will come on at the end and hug us and cry.'

Det smiles and raises an eyebrow. Then she gets up and plonks herself down next to me.

'Wrong.' She grins at me.

'Really?'

'Do nothing. Sit tight.'

'But...'

'Stuff like this can blow up and become completely shitty,' she says wryly, 'as we both know.'

'Yeah.'

We're both thinking of Stella.

'Any word from the *spiritual mother*?' Det asks sarcastically.

I shake my head.

'No one needs two mothers, Peach.'

'Couldn't agree more. So how should I proceed?'

'Don't,' Det says.

'You think I should just ignore it?'

'She doesn't even know where your mother is.' Det shrugs. 'So why bother?'

Hearing her say 'your mother' in relation to someone other than the mother who brought me up is sort of shocking. *My mother is in Paris.* I want to put her right but I don't.

Det gets up to make us both a coffee in the machine that she bought from the Salvos. She stretches and sighs and stares hard at her painting.

'She might die soon,' I say weakly, wanting her to keep her mind on my problems.

'Hopefully,' Det mumbles.

'Det!' I laugh.

'She's in her eighties and she wants to die, so ... let her die.'

'But not without seeing me.' I pick up the letter and put it carefully back in my bag. 'You can be very mean, you know.'

'Mean?' Det sniffs dismissively. 'Yeah well, mean works. Take it from me. *Mean* is exactly the way to go when families are involved.'

I remember her physical state. 'So, how are you?' I bluster. 'How you feeling?' She's so thin still.

'Good,' she says matter-of-factly.

Her casual attitude makes me wonder if she might be rethinking her decision to stay pregnant. I cross my fingers and secretly hope that some of what Cassie had to say has sunk in.

We sit there a while, Det frowning as she sips the coffee.

'Crazy that they were *both* here, though, isn't it?' she says softly. 'I mean, your grandmother as a kid and your mother as a fucking *nun*. And then you get a job here the very day you find that out. That's totally *weird* ... It's verging on spooky.'

The same thought had occurred to me. When I look at Det there is a gleam of mischief in her eyes.

'Why don't we see if we can find a photo of her?'

'Who?'

'The nun.' She smiles. 'Your birth mother.'

'How?'

'There is an archivist. He's got all kinds of stuff.'

'Really?'

'Yeah, I've met him. Nice guy. I'll call him up and ask for an appointment.'

'Can you do that?'

'Yeah. He'll be able to look her up. Do you know the years she was here?'

I'm suddenly nervous. I don't want to do it. But I don't want to *not* do it either, if that makes any sense.

'Sometime in the sixties, I guess.'

'Hmmm, it would be cool to see a photo of her, wouldn't it?'

'I dunno, Det.'

'Why not?'

'It's just that ...'

'We'd just be looking at a photo, if there is one,' Det says. 'That doesn't mean you have to get involved.'

'Okay.'

Within two minutes we have an appointment with the archivist for the following week.

'Stella is going to have a field day,' I sigh, getting up to go.

Det smiles. 'You told her yet?'

'I wanted to talk to you first,' I say. 'I'm dreading telling her.'

'Why?'

'It will affect her too.'

'Stella is okay.'

'She's not okay, Det. Look at the size of her!'

'She's fat. So what? She'll be okay. I'm going to ask her to sing at my launch.'

'Good luck,' I say.

'You don't think she will?'

I shrug and shake my head. I haven't heard Stella sing for a long time.

We could all tell things were tipping over into crazy when Stella started taking flowers to school for her music teacher, Ms Baums. She'd wait for her outside the staffroom after school to tell her about such and such concert or this and that problem. Then she dug up Ms Baums's mobile number and started leaving her heaps of messages. She'd developed this bizarre theory that because Mum didn't have a musical bone in her body somehow this woman had been sent by the gods or the universe to take Nana's place.

The Saturday of the auditions for the big school musical, Stella spent all afternoon getting ready and emerged from her room looking totally gorgeous in a fantastic long white tunic dress with beading around the neck and hem, a glowing, bubbly mess of insecurity. She was desperate to play the main role. Everyone, her friends and the other teachers, thought she was a shoo-in. She'd been practising the songs and they sounded wonderful.

Her hair was piled up at the back of her head and she had long dangling red earrings to match the beading. 'Do I look all right?' she giggled nervously.

'Fantastic,' I said, smiling, meaning it absolutely. 'I've never seen you look better.'

'You think Beatrice will approve?'

Det and Cass were there. Dad was going to drop Stella off first and then us off to see a film. None of us knew Ms Baums at that stage, but we all chorused our approval.

Det grabbed Stella's hand. 'Babe, she'll want to eat you,' she said seriously, 'but she'll have to fight me to do it.'

Stella had the best singing voice in the school, so when we pulled up outside school again later that day we were expecting to congratulate her.

After telling us she'd missed out, not just on the main role but on any role, she'd taken the front seat next to Dad and immediately wound down the window to put her face out.

'She told me my attitude was all wrong and I wasn't physically right for ... *any* part. In front of everyone. They all laughed.'

Cassie, Det and I were in the back and none of us knew what to say.

When Dad started the car I leant forward and squeezed Stella's shoulder, but she didn't turn around. We got every red light on the way home, but when we got there she just kept sitting in the car. So we all sat there too, waiting for her, not saying anything.

At last she turned around. 'Ms Baums is so right. I'm an idiot. Tomorrow I'm going on a serious diet. And I'm going to change my name to Beatrice,' she declared.

There was a moment's pause while the rest of us took it in. Then Det lunged over the front seat and grabbed Stella in a tight neck embrace.

'Please do *not* do that,' she said hoarsely.

'Why not?' Stella sounded startled.

'Because … you're … *Stella.*' Det hardly ever got emotional. But here she was flinging the car door open and shouting, 'And we all really love *Stella*!' She got out and slammed the door. 'And I for one absolutely *hate* the name Beatrice!' She marched off down the street, calling over her shoulder, 'Not in my wildest dreams will I ever call you that poxy fucking name. So forget it!'

A bewildered Stella turned around to look at Cassie and me.

'Det is crazy,' she whispered.

'Yep.' I grasped one of her hands and Cassie leant over the seat and took the other one.

'But she's right,' Cassie murmured.

'You think?'

'Oh yeah. Stella is your name, babe.'

We all got out then, and Stella never spoke again about changing her name.

But within a week she'd developed an appetite, a hunger that couldn't be sated. Stella stopped going out. Stella stopped seeing her friends. Stella stopped practising piano and caring about how she looked. Stella simply … *ate.*

Home now. My front-door key is already in the lock when I notice the bunch of flowers at my feet. A lovely full bunch of white roses within a mass of frothy green fern, bound up tight in bright red paper with a twine bow. I pick them up and open the tiny card pinned to the red paper.

Sorry, it reads, *Fluke x*.

I let the flowers drop to the ground, my face hot with shame because I'd been thinking of him. I push open the door, close it quickly behind me and stand in the hall, my back against the door, breathing hard. I can hear Stella watching TV so I tiptoe up the stairs.

I assumed that university would be the next step for Luke after he got his VCE, but instead he applied to the police force and was accepted. *The police force!* I didn't know any policemen, or anyone who thought of it as a career option.

'I want to be a detective,' he told me seriously when we were walking home one night. Then he grinned at me shyly. 'And running the fraud squad by the time I'm thirty-five.'

A detective! It took me a while to get my head around that one. He had a sharp brain for sure and was a genius with technology, and so I saw no reason to doubt it. But still ... *a detective?*

Stella took to Luke straight away but my other friends took longer. I think they were wary more than anything. But I didn't care. He was nothing like anyone else I knew. He was tall, well muscled from all the outdoor physical work. His face was square, his nose and chin sharply defined, and he loved listening to loud, hard music, like me.

Of course I *did* care. When Cassie declared her approval I was enormously relieved.

'He's great, Peach,' she said. 'Just what you need.'

'What do you mean?'

'Well, he's courageous.' She smiled. 'I like that.'

I knew she was referring to the way he'd managed to transcend his dismal background, and I both loved and hated her for it. Cassie is always so practical. But anyway ... I was pleased.

Det was more cautious and her approval meant more to me. Det can be very harsh and if she doesn't like someone, then she never holds back. We were in the kitchen of her grotty sharehouse, the grot piling up around us, the dog whining outside the back door, and Fluke was in the other room trying to fix her old computer.

'He's okay, you know,' she said thoughtfully, lighting a cigarette and giving me the thumbs-up at the same time. 'In fact, he just might be the real deal.'

The real deal? But I knew what she meant.

I get off my bed, go downstairs and retrieve the flowers. I find a big vase in the laundry, fill it with water and the flowers and set it on top of Stella's piano in the front room. I bury my face in them. *You are such a shit, Fluke. I wish. I just wish . . .*

I'm turning to leave when Stella pokes her head around the door. 'Hey,' she says, her face alive with anticipation, 'so?'

'What?'

'You ticked the box.'

'Oh.' I smile. *Here goes.*

So I tell her about the letter and the grandmother and the fact that my birth mother was a nun.

Stella's mouth falls open and her dark eyes become as wide as saucers as she listens. 'Can I read it?'

'Sure.' I race upstairs, get the letter out of my bag and bring it to her.

She sits on the couch and reads every word, twice, while I sit next to her, my arm around her shoulders. I look around the room trying not to look at the flowers, but my eyes can't seem to focus anywhere else. The fact that they're so beautiful makes the pain worse somehow.

After she's finished it the second time she is uncharacteristically quiet, so I twist myself around to see her face. I want to get some idea of what she's thinking.

'This is so absolutely *fantastic,*' she breathes at last, shutting her eyes. 'A *nun.* Your birth mother was a nun! That is so cool, Peach.'

'What is so cool about it?'

'It is *totally* cool,' she exclaims loudly. 'It explains everything!'

'What?' I have to laugh.

'So much,' she whispers, and her eyes fill with tears. She blinks them away and turns to stare at me as though seeing a whole lot more in my face than she did five minutes ago. I find this slightly unnerving.

'Stella, I'm me. The same person you've always known.'

'No,' she sighs, 'no, you're not.'

'She'd stopped being a nun when she had me!' I say impatiently.

'That doesn't matter.' Stella cups my face in her plump hands and stares into my eyes.

'It's where you get it from.'

'*What* are you talking about, Stella?' I sigh in exasperation, pull away and get up. 'I'm not religious. I'm—'

'What are you going to do?' she breaks in.

'Wait until Mum and Dad come home, I guess.' I walk towards the door.

'You know they'll say to write back!' she calls from the couch.

'Yeah … I suppose.'

'You don't have to wait.'

'Well, maybe not, but I …' I stop a moment by the door and close my eyes. I'm not really pissed off with Stella. She is just being herself. It's the questions, clawing at the edges of my mind like ants, that get to me.

'Oh, Peaches!' She hauls her body up off the couch and holds out her arms to me and before I can think, I run back over and fall into them, and burst into a flood of tears that comes from a part of me that I didn't even know existed. We fall down onto the couch together and I'm clinging to my sister as though she is the only connection I have left in the world.

'Oh, honey,' she croons as she rocks me, 'what is it?'

I shake my head.

'Come on,' she insists.

'I … I just wish.'

'What?'

'I wish I'd never even met Fluke,' I whisper. Believe me, she is the only person in the world I would risk sounding this pathetic with.

'Fluke?' I hear the disappointment in her voice, and I start laughing through my tears. She'd much prefer to keep talking about nuns.

'Yes.'

'But you did meet him.'

'And I can't get him out of my head even though he's ...'

'He's what?'

'A complete dickhead.'

She pushes me away, puts both hands on my shoulders and looks me fair in the face. 'So are you, Peach,' she says.

'No, I'm not.'

'Yes, you're a complete dickhead, but,' she tightens her grip on my shoulders and peers into my face, 'you are also the daughter of ... a holy woman!' she whispers hoarsely.

'She wasn't a saint, Stella! She left the convent. And she had me.'

'She was strong enough to withstand the temptations of the world,' Stella mumbles dreamily, looking off into the distance. 'A strong spirit.'

'Well, you can have her!'

'No, I can't. She's yours.'

'Will you *please* shut up about it?'

'But it is so totally cool.'

'What am I meant to do about *him*?'

She smiles and raises her eyes to heaven. 'Think about what attracted you to him in the first place.'

It was one of those wild freezing midwinter nights that Det thrives on and just about everyone else wishes away. We'd been invited down the coast to celebrate Dicko's birthday. His parents were loaded and he had access to what he described as 'an awesome pile of bricks' for the event.

I wish now that I'd taken heed of Stella's warning. She'd come outside while I was waiting on the front verandah in my warm coat and boots for Fluke to pick me up.

'Be careful, Peach,' she said, frowning at the apple she was eating.

'Why?'

'Clear sky, full moon, winter.'

'So?' I laughed.

'Be careful.'

'I'm always careful, Stella,' I said, jumping up to hug her goodbye as Fluke pulled up out the front. I picked up my waterproof and my overnight bag.

'Enjoy the concert!' I kissed her on the nose and hurried to the gate. 'And don't let Dad go to sleep!'

She and Dad are obsessive J.S. Bach fans. They had tickets for a special choral work that night at the Arts Centre in town. After a long day at the hospital, Dad has been known to go straight to sleep as soon as the concert starts, and then embarrass everyone around him by snoring.

She laughed and hugged me back. 'I'll take the hatpin.'

I was ready for a party. Mid-year exams were over. Fluke had a few days off from the pier. Heading down the coast together was going to be fantastic.

Fluke drove the car he shared with his mother and I sat next to him. Det, Nick and Walter, a really nice Canadian guy that Det had hooked up with the night before, were in the back. I could tell straight away that Det was still a bit *wired*. A few weeks before she'd had a nasty break-up with a guy she'd been crazy about, and it was still clouding her mood. She hadn't wanted to come but I'd insisted. Sitting home all weekend wasn't the answer to anything, I'd told her sternly. But now I wasn't so sure. Det often found big social occasions difficult. Maybe I should have let her stay at home to lick her wounds.

Walter was older than us – probably late twenties – and for most of the way down he entertained us with stories of growing up in sub-zero temperatures.

'So how do you take a piss in all that gear?' Nick wanted to know.

'Well, there are these little flaps and ...'

'What about sport?'

'Ever heard of ice hockey, Nick?'

Basically we gossiped and joked and blathered on about our lives all the way. Fluke and his mum were big fans of the blues. Underneath our chatter a succession of old gravelly songs moaned on about someone doing bad by someone else, until the rest of us couldn't take it any more.

'Jeez, mate,' said Nick good-naturedly, 'I'm aware that these guys are like the king daddies of everything and all but I'm ready to slit my wrists. You got any other kind of music?'

'Radio?' Fluke laughed.

'Yes please!' everyone chorused.

'So, what?'

'Bland and banal, please,' Nick moaned. 'Kylie would be better than this.'

We wasted a fair bit of time taking wrong turns and peering at maps. Dicko's instructions were not very accurate, but at last we found the dirt track turn-off and we knew we were right.

Most of the house was secluded behind a high fence and overhanging trees but the rest of it loomed up before us like an ocean liner. The second-storey windows blazed out into the surrounding darkness like the top deck.

'Oh shit!' Nick groaned. 'Don't you just hate rich people?'

'No,' Walter drawled coolly, 'I love them. Especially when you get to use their stuff!'

Within moments of us calling through the intercom, the gate slid open and we were driving up to the front of the house and parking alongside a number of other cars. We got out to stretch after the long drive, delighted to be there at last. Music was thumping out into the night all around us.

Dicko met us at the open door in a white dinner suit, silk tie and patent leather shoes.

'Shit, man, were we meant to dress up?' Nick tried to look concerned. He was in an old jumper and grimy jeans.

'Yeah.' Dicko threw an arm around his shoulders, and motioned us all inside. 'Feel bad, Nick. Feel really bad.'

We pulled off our coats and shoved them into one of the cupboards in the vast plush hallway.

I'd dressed up a bit, in tight black pants and red boots, my red silk shirt hidden under an awful long jumper that I planned to take off just as soon as I warmed up. Walter wasn't much better than Nick. Fluke was probably the best dressed in a nice charcoal jacket, jumper and clean jeans.

'Your parents actually *own* this place?' Fluke was looking around the spacious hallway incredulously.

'Not really.' Dicko shrugged dismissively.

'They stole it?'

'You got it.' We all laughed.

'From who?'

'Some poor deranged aunt.' He held the door at the end of the hall open for us. 'Welcome!'

We knew quite a few people and there was the usual shrieking and wild hugs as we all recognised each other. Trying to introduce Fluke over the music was pretty well impossible, but no one seemed to care much. Nick's three totally dolled-up Greek cousins descended, squealing their greetings, pointing out possible girlfriends for Nick.

And checking out Fluke as if he was some kind of prize at a raffle.

'Way to go, Peach!'

'He's cute!'

'Got a twin brother?'

Fluke grinned and put his arm around me.

Drinks were shoved into our hands, and Det, Fluke and I headed through the crowd to the glass doors at the back of the huge living space and peered out. The big fluorescent-blue square of the pool was surrounded by wooden decking and further out were paving stones heading down to a row of tall eucalypts along the back fence.

Det sidled out to join the smokers braving the cold, leaving Fluke and I inside, smiling at each other.

'You and me, Peach!'

I nodded happily and took his hand. 'You and me.'

When Dicko came over to refill our drinks I asked him if we could go upstairs for a look.

'By all means.' He waved us towards the stairs. 'Just hold off throwing yourselves over the balcony. I don't want any trouble with the police.'

Fluke and I made our way up the wide marble staircase, hand in hand. It was like being on a movie set. We poked our noses into bedrooms and bathrooms and studies, marvelling at the huge lights and luxurious carpets and nice paintings and knick-knacks. The master bedroom opened up onto a wide, tiled balcony.

Out there without our coats it was absolutely freezing, but the clear, bright night gave us such a fantastic view that neither of us wanted to go back inside. We laughed and yelled, pretending we were on the *Titanic* about to go down, clinging to each other in the bitter wind.

But after a while we grew silent.

The house was built out on a cliff and the ocean lay below like a huge, dark desert. The moon sat up high in the clear sky, sending an arch of light skidding across the shining surface of the water. The occasional flashing light from passing fishing boats in the distance enhanced the dreamlike feeling. I let my mind float out across the expanse of water, almost able to feel it against the bare skin of my face and arms.

Luke stood behind me. He put his hands under my jumper and shirt, encircling my bare waist, and turned me around so we were facing each other. Then he pulled me closer, caressing my back. I pulled his shirt out of his trousers and we stood there our bare bellies pressed against each other. I felt for the coarse dark hair of his chest and then followed the line of it down from his chest past his navel and into his jeans. He gasped in shock, but I laughed and kept touching him.

Desire licked up between us like a flame, getting hotter and hotter with each kiss. *Oh God, I could die now.* I let my head fall back, feeling his lips on my neck. *I could die and I wouldn't care.* Our bodies trembled and ached as we clutched each other in the biting wind, skin on skin, laughing through chattering teeth, swaying like reeds at the bottom of the ocean.

We pulled away eventually, tucked in our shirts and rearranged our clothes and hair.

'Just keeping things nice, bro,' I joked.

'Okay, sister.'

We both knew that later, after the party was over, we'd be alone in the dark, in the warmth of some borrowed bed or mattress on the floor, or maybe even in the double sleeping bag that I'd thrown into the boot just in case. That same desire would hold and devour us until we fell asleep in each other's arms. And when we woke it would be as if our lives had just begun.

'I will never leave you, Peach,' Fluke said seriously, doing up the buttons of his shirt, staring straight ahead.

'*What?*' It was such an odd thing to say.

'I will never leave you,' he said again.

I stared at his profile against the light streaming from the bedroom, trying to quell the sudden tears that had raced into my eyes. It was too much. Way too much. And yet ... my heart leapt towards those words like a parched person grabbing at a bottle of water, and my pulse quickened all over again with giddy gladness.

I hadn't told him anything about the dreams I used to have, but his words told me that on some instinctual level he knew anyway. It was as though he had seen right down into the very core of me and understood where my deepest fears lay.

'But what if we break up?' I said, trying to sound light, desperate not to give myself away.

'You're in my heart,' he said. Then he grinned. 'Nothing will change that. You are in my heart.'

I buried my face in his shoulder and wished that I could bottle what I was feeling right at that moment. *Imagine having a row of little glass bottles of this lined up in my room,* I thought. Whenever I woke feeling bleak, I'd just reach over and suck one down before I got up.

'Let's go inside,' I said at last. 'My face is turning numb.'

'As long as you know.'

'I know.'

We walked back down the stairs, hand in hand. Why do people say that love is hard? I was in love and it was the easiest thing that had ever happened to me.

The party had hotted up in our absence. More people had arrived and a lot of them were getting pretty smashed. The lights had been turned down and the music up, and people were laughing and screaming inanities at each other above the din. Raucous and crazy, but it was fun too. Doubly so because of what had happened on the balcony between Fluke and me. I was living on another planet to everyone else.

Nick, his face glowing with alcohol and pleasure, put his arm around my shoulders. 'Got to get the dancing going, Peach,' he declared, and prising me out from under Fluke's arm he hauled me out onto the polished floor near the speakers.

But I didn't need encouraging. I felt like dancing. I tried to pull Fluke in with us, but he laughed and waved me on and went over to get himself another drink.

Cassie and Stephano joined us and within a few minutes the square of polished floorboards was full. Then came a sequence of events that are impossible to remember with absolute accuracy. First up, I lost sight of Fluke for some time. After I'd danced myself to exhaustion I had a couple of drinks in quick succession – probably too quickly – and felt quite pissed for a while. So I went and got myself some water and found a seat next to a girl named Robin who I hadn't seen for ages. We had an interesting conversation about the time she'd spent working up in an Aboriginal community near Darwin the year before. We were interrupted by Dicko, who insisted that everyone had to stop talking and get into his Gatsby mood with some weird sort of conga dance that he'd worked out was all the rage in the roaring twenties. Dicko was known and loved for his eccentricities, so just about everyone put down their glasses and joined in. Even the smokers came inside for it.

In no time there were a couple of circles of inebriated dancers holding onto each other, laughing and screaming, falling over, weaving in and out and around the furniture. I saw Det and then Cassie and Stephano across the room from me and was really glad to see that Det seemed to be having a good time. I couldn't see Fluke, but assumed that he was somewhere in the mix. When it finished I was sweating and dry-mouthed. After getting more water I started for the bathroom. Det intercepted me at the door.

'A few of us are going down to the beach,' she said excitedly, 'want to come?'

'But how would we get down there?' I said, not liking the idea. 'This place is up high.'

'There's a track down to the beach,' Det said. 'I've checked it out.'

'It will be freezing, Det.'

'So? We've got coats.'

The reckless glint in her eye alarmed me. Det had two ways of getting over heartache. She either closed herself up in a room for weeks at a time and never went anywhere, or she went *wild*. Seeing as it was me who had talked her into coming to the party, I figured that I should keep an eye on her.

'Okay,' I agreed.

'So get your coat. We'll wait for you outside.'

'I'll just find Fluke and see if he wants to come.'

'Fluke's in the kitchen,' Nick said on his way into the toilet.

'You coming, Nicko?'

'No way.' He grinned at me. 'I'm not mad.'

They were the only two people in the kitchen. Fluke and this amazing-looking, sharp-faced girl, with very long, straight black hair and dark skin. They were holed up in a corner away from the buckets of ice and drinks, having some kind of deep conversation. She was covered in silver, rings on every finger, chains around her neck, silver combs keeping her hair back from her face. She was older than him, definitely, probably in her late twenties, and dressed in tight shimmering green pants and a very small, cropped green leather jacket with studs all over it. More than anything she reminded me of a praying mantis, all thin and spindly and green, but beautiful too in an oddly elegant way.

The way they were standing together, not actually touching but so very close, was disconcerting. He was leaning against the wall, bending over her and she was looking up into his face, her eyes glowing and animated. They were intent on each other in a way that didn't include anyone else. A spurt of jealousy rushed through me as I stood watching from the doorway. *What is going on here?*

She saw me first. Her eyes left his face and narrowed. *What do you want?* As though I had no right to be standing where I was. When Fluke turned around I swear it took him a few moments to place me. It was as though my sudden appearance had flummoxed him.

'Oh hi,' he said, as though suddenly remembering. He came over, put his arm around me and dragged me over to her. 'Come meet an old friend.'

'Is that what I am?' The girl's laugh was thick with suggestion and she barely looked at me as I mumbled hello.

Luke's face coloured with embarrassment. 'Ada, this is Peach.'

'*Peach*,' she mocked, 'as in the *fruit*?'

I nodded. 'Det and I are going down to the beach,' I said to Fluke. 'Do you want to come?'

Fluke didn't notice, or pretended not to notice, my consternation.

187

'Oh sure. Yeah. Let's go.' He turned to the girl and smiled. 'How about you, Ada?'

'No way!' She gave me a withering look. 'It will be freezing.'

There was a moment or two of awkward silence and I watched in shock as her eyes flitted flirtatiously over him. She placed one of her ringed hands briefly on his arm in a mocking gesture of supplication.

'Don't go yet,' she whispered. 'We've only just found each other again.'

'Listen,' Fluke said to me quietly, as though I was his kid sister or something. 'I'll be down in a little while, okay?'

'Sure,' I said stiffly, and turned my back, almost in tears. I went and found my coat, pulled my proper boots from my bag and joined Det and Walt and two others I didn't know who were waiting for me.

Det led us over to the track at the end of the garden. Thankfully Walt had thought to bring a torch, because halfway down the very steep track got really rough. Any one of us might have taken a tumble and broken our neck. Det was going faster than everyone else, screaming out instructions about tree roots and slippery bits, completely wired on the danger of what we were doing. I could hear it in her voice and I wanted to yell out for her to calm down. But I was too churned up by the scene in the kitchen.

Miraculously, the five of us got down to the beach in one piece. Once we hit the sand we all began to run to keep warm, because the wind was really sharp.

'Isn't this fantastic?' Det yelled as she passed by.

'Yeah,' I screamed into the wind, running after her. I told myself that Fluke would be down to join us any minute. He'd explain the scene in the kitchen and we'd laugh together about what had just happened.

But he didn't come. And after about twenty minutes every minute that passed had me feeling worse. I was running about, screaming into the wind, acting drunk, but really it was just a show. I suppose I still might have been a little drunk, but not so it mattered. I kept turning to scan the cliff face, my eyes raking up and down the beach trying to discern a lone figure making his way towards us. Surely any moment he'd be there. I knew the rough track down wouldn't stop him. *So where was he?*

The five of us linked arms and walked along the beach. *Who was that girl? What the hell was going on between them? Why had they been standing like that? Why hadn't he chosen to come with* me*?* It was as though the ground was giving way beneath me and I was clutching for anything to help me keep my balance. *Didn't he tell me just a couple of hours ago that*...Well, what did he say really? Maybe I imagined that too. *Maybe I've read him wrong all along*...*maybe he was*...

'Listen, I want to go back,' I said to the others.

'Just a bit longer.' Next to me Det threw her head back to look at the star-filled dome above us. 'This is *so so so* great.'

'No, Det.'

'Come on, Peach! It's magic.'

And it was. Some part of me could see that. Just the five of us on the lonely windswept beach, the stars flickering above, the dragging sound of the waves on one side of us and the rugged cliff face on the other. The moon. The brilliant round moon beaming white light down on us. I thought of Stella and the way she'd warned me off this night. *Oh Stella*...*I wish you were here.* I let myself be dragged along until Walter decided that he'd definitely had enough. The two others also wanted to go back, but something had got into Det. Or something that was always there had reared up and come to life. Just as we were heading back up the sand towards the track she stopped.

'Hang on,' she said.

We all turned around. 'What?'

'I've got an idea.'

A pause. The four of us looked at her.

'Let's go *in*!' she shouted.

'What?' Walt shouted into the wind.

'A swim,' she screamed.

My heart sank. She had to be off her head. It was either booze or grief or something else I didn't know about. 'Listen, Det, no!' I yelled.

'Oh, Peach!' She ran towards me, laughing, and threw both arms around me and lifted me in the air. 'Come on, let's do it. See if we're strong enough.'

'Det, it's freezing!'

But she was already taking off her coat.

'Come on!' she laughed. 'We're young and we're tough! We can do anything.'

Walt sighed and shook his head. So did the other two guys. 'Come on, Det, please. The cold will kill you.'

But Det already had her boots off. She unzipped her jeans and threw off her shirt and underclothes. Completely naked, her thin white limbs so childlike and utterly vulnerable in the moonlight, she ran into the waves, shouting and shrieking.

'Det,' I yelled after her, 'you can't!'

'Yes, I can,' she shouted. 'Watch me.'

And so we stood and watched her. Me and Walter and the other two guys on the sand, watching Det plunge naked into the icy cold of the Southern Ocean at midnight in July.

'Oh God!' she screamed again and again. 'I'm going to die. I swear it! I'm going to die!'

The three guys laughed and shook their heads in grudging admiration at her courage.

'Christ, she is nuts,' Walter groaned. 'You'd have to be totally and utterly nuts to do that.'

'I reckon!'

There was nothing for me to add to any of that. *She is nuts*. I watched her small head bobbing against the waves. She wasn't hanging about in the shallows. She was actually swimming out.

'Det,' I yelled into the wind, 'enough!'

'How long will she stay in for?' Walt asked me.

'How would I know?' I snapped.

'I think she's, like, swimming out,' one of the other guys murmured. 'Jeez, I hope she'll be able to get back.'

'Det,' I screamed, 'don't go too far.'

But she was too far out to hear me. I watched her head bobbing along and her white arms chopping through the water as if she had a destination in mind. And I thought of sharks and stingers and the terrors of the deep and waited for her to turn around. Then she disappeared.

At least, I couldn't see her anymore. I stood there on the edge of the water peering into the blackness for some sign but there was none. When I turned around the three guys were standing with arms crossed against their chests, edging away, mumbling again about wanting to get back to the party.

'You can't go now,' I yelled sharply.

'She'll be all right,' Walt said defensively.

'But what if she's not?'

The three of them looked at each other uncomfortably.

'Well, what do you want us to do?'

'I don't know!' I was on the point of tears. 'But we can't *leave* her.'

'Can you see her?'

'No, I can't.'

'She'll be okay,' Walter said, as if he knew something that the rest of us didn't. 'Det has a pretty good radar for danger.'

'And how long have you known her?' I screamed at him. 'All of about twenty hours!' I was the only one there who really knew Det. And what I knew was that there was always one part of her racing towards her own destruction.

'Listen, I'm sick of this,' the short guy said. 'It's up to her. She decided to go in. I'm not hanging about. I'm going back.' He turned on his heel and started up the sand again.

'Me too,' the other bloke said and walked off. So it was just Walter and me looking at each other waiting for the other to move or say something.

'Whatever happens, I'm not going in there,' he said awkwardly, 'I want to make that clear. I'm not a good swimmer.'

'That's comforting,' I snapped. *Fucking shit.*

'But I'll go and alert someone if you like?' he added.

We both turned back to the black water.

'Can you see any sign of her?' I mumbled desperately.

'No. I'll go back up and raise the alarm then?'

'Okay.'

It was while I was watching the three of them head back up the track that I felt it coming on, although I didn't immediately recognise it for what it was. It crossed my mind that someone might have dropped a slow-acting something in my drink, or that I was having some kind of heart attack. Anything other than being pulled backwards into no-man's-land. But it was dread filling me.

In my dreams I was always alone, abandoned on a railway platform, or an empty house, a shopping centre with everyone else moving slowly away from me. Mum and Dad and Stella. I call out, wave, scream, but no one hears me.

First Luke, then Det and now those three guys. *What is it about me?*

In my madness – because that's what it was, madness – I decided that if Det was going to drown, then so would I. I pulled off my coat, my jeans and jumper and ran down to the water in my underwear. The first icy wave across my feet took my breath away and the next one was even worse. *No. I can't do this.* Yet somehow the dread pushed me forward. *One step at a time,* I told myself when every instinct told me to retreat. *One step at a time.*

I did it. I actually made myself go in. Filled with blind terror I plunged under the freezing water, gasping, spluttering and shrieking, and then, like Det, I started swimming straight out. All thoughts of the dangerous creatures hiding under the waves faded. I swam and I swam and as my blood cooled so did the terrible racing panic. But I still couldn't see Det. I looked back to the beach, just able to see the three figures making their way up the track in the moonlight.

The first two were almost at the top of the cliff face and I guessed it was Walter about halfway up. *Cowards!* But it didn't matter so much anymore. I'd come back into myself and knew who I was again. Still treading water, I watched them.

Then I saw a figure stumbling out of the water and running along the beach. *Det.* Had to be. A shot of pure elation raced through me, but before I had a chance to savour it properly a wave out of nowhere picked me up and threw me back into the shallows. In the process I lost my pants, scraped my knee badly and took in a great mouthful of water, but I was able to stumble to my feet.

'Peach, you hero!' Det was screaming as she rushed into the water to help me out. 'You did it! I knew you would. We both did it! Wasn't it just so fucking *unbelievable?*'

I was numb with cold, half blind, there was water coming out of my nose and my eyes were stinging like crazy.

'Shut up!' I spluttered.

'You fucking little hero!' She screamed and put both arms around me and carried me back to where our clothes were. 'That was the biggest buzz I've ever had in my whole life. *Thank you*, sweet Peach, for making me come!' She was drying me off with her own clothes by this stage. The special shirt she bought for the party was soaking within a minute. I wanted to kill her. I did. Seriously. She was a maniac.

'Stop it!' I said, pushing her away. 'Fuck off!'

'Okay, okay!'

Teeth chattering, we put on our jeans and coats, picked up our boots and headed up the track.

It was hard going, but less stressful than coming down. In spite of being a smoker, Det led the way. By the time we reached the top we'd warmed up a bit and I was feeling more reasonable. We stood under the darkness of the trees and tried to tidy ourselves a bit. Det grinned at me in the moonlight, such delight in her face that I hadn't the heart to stay mad at her. We both looked like drowned rats but some of her exhilaration bounced onto me.

'We could have drowned,' I said.

'As if!' She poked me in the ribs, then looked past me towards the house and frowned. 'Is that your boyfriend over there?'

I looked up and saw Fluke and the girl looking into each other's faces, arms around each other. We were well hidden by the trees and they obviously hadn't seen us yet. They pulled apart and started walking hand in hand down through the garden towards us.

'Hey!' Det shouted. 'Over here!'

I watched him let go of her hand, take a few steps away and look around, trying to locate where the voice had come from.

'Who is she?' Det muttered.

I didn't answer. My heart was hammering in my chest, so loud I figured it could be heard.

He came towards us, smiling, with the girl close behind.

'What happened to you two?' He reached one hand out to touch my hair and my wet clothes but I ducked away. 'We were just on our way down to join you.' The horrible girl in green was staring from one to the other of us.

'Did you actually go in the water?' she asked incredulously.

Det laughed. Fluke shook his head and tried to touch me again but I moved away again.

Det must have picked up on the tension between us. She pulled away. 'I need to get dry,' she said, stumbling off towards the house. 'Going to see if I can snatch a shower,' she called back. 'You need to warm up too, Peach. Soon.'

'Okay.'

There was so much I wanted to say, but not with the green insect there so I said nothing. Fluke moved over to me again.

'Peach? We were ... I was just about to ...'

'Piss off,' I hissed furiously.

'Listen, it's not what you think.'

'How do you know what I think?' I was so furious I could have hit him.

194

I ran after Det and when I caught up I thrust my arm through hers and we marched off across the lawn.

'Hey,' she said as we reached the decking, 'who the hell is that chick?'

But I didn't answer. I went inside to look for Nick.

I found him standing inside the back porch talking with some other guy. 'Are you okay to drive? Can you take me home, Nick?'

'What, now?' He took in my bedraggled appearance.

'Yeah, now.'

He looked at his watch. Then back at me. 'Should be fine,' he said, after a pause. 'I'll ask Dicko for the Honda.'

'Thanks.'

Det was watching this, and I think she was really upset, but I didn't care.

'You want me to come with you?' she asked.

I shook my head. 'No, thanks.'

I slipped into one of the bathrooms to clean up a bit and wash the salty water from my face and hands and then stared at myself in the mirror above the sink. I looked so freaked-out that I shrank from my own image. My face was peaked and white. Bits of dirt, twig and seaweed had attached themselves to the clumps of soggy hair hanging about my neck. My blue eyes were the only things I fully recognised. Even so, the red rims and smudges of black mascara made me look half mad. I felt a bit like one of Shakespeare's witches.

Nick was waiting for me in the car when I got outside again. I saw Fluke standing nearby too, this time without the girl.

'Why are you going?' He tried to grab me, but I slipped under his arm. 'Come on, Peach!'

'Don't,' I snapped furiously as I got into the car.

Within moments we were sliding through the front gates. I turned at the last moment to see him standing there staring after us, and this incredible feeling of loss exploded inside me. Within a minute it had seeped out into all the outlying areas of my body, filling every nerve ending that only a few hours before had been tingling with excitement and joy.

I cried on and off most of the way back, and Nick was the best. He hardly said anything, just kept the music rolling, one CD after another, all of them beyond poxy. Dicko's mum surely had the worst musical taste in the universe, but I didn't care. Anything was better than silence. Every now and again Nick smacked my knee.

'Hey, Peach, you're going to *love* this one.' And it would be Sinatra or Rod Stewart or early Madonna. Then he found a little stash of old musicals. *Hair. Sweet Charity* and *The Sound of Music.*

And by the time we hit the city we were both singing along with the words, and although I was still crying I was laughing too.

It was after three when he pulled up outside my house.

'You got your key?'

'Yep.'

He got out and saw me to the door.

'I love you, Nick,' I said as we hugged each other.

'That's what they all say.' He pushed me inside. 'Listen, have a hot shower and go to bed. You'll feel better in the morning.'

'Okay.' So that's what I did.

Over the next few days Fluke rang and sent texts, then he called around. He spilt it out on our front doorstep. The girl had been his first girlfriend, they'd grown up together, both of them foster kids in the same house for a while. Both their mothers had bailed. He had deep feelings for her, but there was nothing between them anymore. Hadn't been anything between them for years. Yeah, of course he loved her. He would never lie to me.

He loved her. That was the part I heard.

I understand all this on one level, but every time I think about it, I am flung back to that night on the beach, the full moon, those two in the kitchen, the blank look, the terror, the icy water, the wanting to die and ... I just can't.

Fluke and me are finished.

Cecilia

Breda tapped on Cecilia's door. 'Tea before I hit the road for work?'

'Oh, yes please,' Cecilia called back. She lay there feeling a little groggy but luxuriating in the cosiness of the room and warmth of Breda's welcome. She sat up when Breda came in with two cups of tea and a thick slice of buttered toast.

'So, how did you sleep?'

'Good. Only woke once with my dream but then went straight back.'

'A man?' Breda grinned.

'I wish,' Cecilia smiled, 'always a baby.'

'Oh?' Breda sat on the end of the bed.

So Cecilia told her about the mixed-up dream of being back in the convent on the first day and being filled with anxiety about the baby.

Breda listened intently. 'Are you worried about your daughter?'

'You know, Breda, I can't even answer that question.' Cecilia sighed. 'I don't know the first thing about myself.'

'None of us do, kid.'

'You do.'

'I just muddle through each day,' Breda said, 'like most people.'

They sat for a while in silence.

'Do you think I'm crazy to want to find her?'

'Yeah. But that won't stop you will it?'

'You're a nurse, Breda. What do I do first? Is there some place I go? A form I have to fill out? I was so crazy when she was born that I didn't even want her to know my name. Imagine how she'll feel seeing that when she tries to find out about her origins.'

'*If* she does.'

'How do you mean?'

'She might not ... want to find out anything.'

Cecilia tried not to be shocked by this. 'I know she might not ever want to meet me, but she would probably still want to know basic stuff, even for health reasons.'

'Maybe.' Breda shrugged.

'So what do I do?'

Breda sighed and looked down at her mug of tea and then she looked at Cecilia.

'Think about doing nothing for a while,' she said quietly. 'Find your feet. Get a job. Catch up with your family and then ... see how you feel.'

'She *is* my family. She—'

'No, sweetheart.' Breda reached out and touched her hand, 'She's *not* your family.'

Cecilia looked away, the old familiar weight settling down into her chest, the awful heaviness of having failed at every important juncture of her life.

'You think that it is wrong of me to want ...?'

'Good God, no. Nothing is *wrong,* Nuncie!'

'So where do I start?'

Breda frowned and picked up her tea and took a couple of sips.

'I know where she is,' she said softly.

'What?'

'She's at the convent.'

'*What?*'

'Mad, isn't it?' Breda shook her head as though she couldn't believe it herself.

'Doing *what?*'

'She works there.'

'But last I heard it had been sold to developers.'

'No, no, it's all markets and artist studios and cafes now. Your daughter works in a cafe.' Breda stood up. 'I'm not sure if I should have told you that. You've got to promise me that you won't do anything silly. You've got to go through the right channels.'

Cecilia's heart felt like a tennis ball belting against a brick wall. 'What else can you tell me?'

'Nothing.'

'How do you know it's her, then?'

Breda looked at her watch.

'I have to go to work. Can we talk about this when I get home?'

'Of course.'

Breda bent to kiss the top of her head. 'See you around five, then.' When Breda was at the door she turned around.

'Relax. Go for a nice walk. Reacquaint yourself with your country.' She smiled. 'Have coffee in the little place around the corner and just try to ... enjoy yourself and ... go easy. I promise we'll talk.'

'What does she look like?' Cecilia whispered.

'Just like you.'

'Have you spoken to her?'

'No.'

'Do you ... do you know her name?'

'Perpetua.'

And they both smiled.

Then Breda disappeared out the door, closing it softly behind her. Cecilia lay in the warm bed listening to her friend running around before leaving. The front door closed and Cecilia was alone in the house. She sat up and picked up the cup of tea.

Of course she knew she could make no claim on the girl. Whatever her feelings, the child didn't belong to her and any connection had been broken the day she'd willingly given her away. *Except...*

It was Cecilia who'd carried her for nine months inside her own body. It was Cecilia who had pushed her out into the world. It was Cecilia who'd first held the tiny squirming body in her arms and watched in wonder as the child's eyes opened and she calmly surveyed her mother's face. No one else's. She was the child's mother. And so she had the most fundamental claim of all.

Over the next week Cecilia and Breda caught up properly.

'What about that girl, Ida?' Cecilia wanted to know. 'Did you really run away with her?'

Breda nodded. 'I knew I was going to have to leave or else I'd go insane. We planned it together.'

'But she was a laundry girl!' Cecilia said incredulously. 'How could you possibly have confided in her?'

'I don't know how it happened.' Breda shrugged. 'But she was bright and funny and so unhappy. One night I just took the risk and told her I was thinking of nicking off. I asked her if she wanted to come with me.'

'But how did you know you could trust her?'

'Gut instinct.'

'How old was she?'

'Twenty-three. She had no family or friends to look out for her. And none of us bothered to tell her that she was actually free to leave. Isn't that just so ... *incredible?*'

'She wouldn't have had anywhere to go.'

'True, but ... it was criminal what went on there, Cecilia. You know that, don't you?'

'At least she had a roof over her head and three meals a day,' Cecilia muttered. 'It beat being on the streets or being raped by your stepfather. So many of them came from that kind of thing.'

'I know, but she was a bright young girl and the only education she got was folding up clothes!'

'Yes.' Cecilia sighed and looked away. It seemed there were many ways to look at just about everything. 'So what happened when you got out?'

'We were lovers.' Breda was laughing. 'My first lover was a woman. I'm rather proud of that.'

Cecilia's mouth fell open in shock.

'It turned out that neither of us was particularly that way inclined in the end, but that didn't matter. We were lonely and confused and ... it was good, anyway. Don't look so damned stunned!'

'Do I? I'm sorry ... What *happened*?'

'After a couple of years we just grew apart and then I met my darling Mike, the love of my life, and I started having kids.'

'Do you ever feel angry about what we went through, Breda? All the wasted years?'

'No!' Breda laughed. 'I'm over the angry stage and the sad stage and the I-could-have-done-so-much-more-with-my-twenties stage. I'm actually incredibly grateful for those years.'

'Grateful?'

'How many people can say they had our experience, Nuncie? I was on a quest for holiness and so were you. It was a worthwhile quest. Don't you think?'

Cecilia could only stare at her.

'And I *did* get closer to God,' Breda said emphatically. 'And I've never lost that. How about you?'

Cecilia shook her head.

'Come on, Nuncie! You were so devout. What happened to you?'

Cecilia tried to explain how she didn't know what had happened to the Cecilia that Breda had known back then. She didn't know if there was much left of her at all. 'So, the child's father?' Breda asked mildly.

'Peter.'

'Are you going to tell me about him?'

'He was a priest,' Cecilia blurted out. 'My daughter's father was a Colombian priest.'

Breda sank her head into her hands.

'Oh jeez, Nuncie,' she groaned from behind her fingers. 'You poor darling. And you were in love?'

'Totally.'

'And him?'

'Yes. Yes. I believe he loved me too.'

'So … Is he still a priest?'

'As far as I know,' Cecilia nodded.

'Where?'

'The Philippines.' She waved one hand in exasperation. 'Breda, I'm a total adolescent next to you.'

'Nothing wrong with adolescents,' Breda shot back with one of her grins. 'I've had four and believe me, they're great!'

'What about middle-aged adolescents?'

'The best, kiddo.'

Cecilia had met all four of Breda's boys: Michael, Sean and James, and the youngest, Conner, who was still living with her. The fact that wiry little Breda had produced such great strapping lads – all of them were over six feet – was nothing short of amazing. The three who'd left home were constantly dropping by with their mates and their girlfriends, joking and arguing and making food for themselves. It was a close and lively family. All the boys were loud, good-natured and very accepting of Cecilia. Sometimes when she was in her room listening to their voices down in the kitchen she was transported back to her own childhood. It made her sad all over again to realise all she'd lost. *Suck it up*, the mean voice played in her head. *It's what you deserve.*

Breda suggested again that Cecilia begin the family reconnection with a letter to her mother. So Cecilia sat down and wrote a letter and then … didn't send it. Couldn't, somehow. Then she wrote another and another and when she found she couldn't quite find the courage to send even one of them she found Patrick's address and began to write to him.

But the same thing happened. In the end she couldn't bring herself to slip the stamped and addressed letter into the box.

Some days she was tempted to jump on a plane and go back to Europe. Why stay hanging out on the periphery of Breda's life, writing letters that she didn't post, thinking thoughts she knew were rubbish?

And yet something stopped her. It was too much like running away again.

Peach

A week after we'd made the appointment, Det and I are in the archivist's small office. Apart from a desk and a computer there's a central table and some chairs. The place is neat and ordered and the man polite and friendly. All kinds of memorabilia hang around the walls.

'Please sit down,' the archivist says, smiling at us. 'Now, which of you was wanting the information on Sister Annunciata?'

'Me,' I say nervously, 'and thanks for seeing us.'

'That's a pleasure,' he says, 'but please understand we don't have much on any of the Sisters, nor on the girls who passed through here.' He frowns. 'Things were different then. They didn't take many pictures and the records aren't very thorough. But I did have a quick look for you and have found a couple of items.'

My heart begins to race as he picks up a thin manila folder from near the computer. I'd agreed to this meeting without really considering what it would be like if I was shown ... anything.

'We're busy trying to computerise.' He shakes his head. 'I'm only employed here part-time, and it's a big job.'

I nod and try to return his smile.

He puts the folder on the table between us and draws out a piece of paper.

'Sister Mary Annunciata entered the noviciate in 1963. She supervised the girls in the laundry for a good part of her time here, but she also taught in the infants' school while attending university.'

'University?' Det is surprised.

'Yes, a lot of the Sisters went to university at that time. Would you like to see a photo of her?'

I nod mutely.

He opens the folder and brings out a couple of black-and-white photos. One is a group shot of rows and rows of nuns, all of them dressed identically in heavy dark robes, most with black veils and some with white.

'So many,' I mutter in awe.

'Over a hundred.' The archivist smiles. 'Looking after over a thousand girls.' He points to a nun standing tall in the middle of the back row. She is looking directly at the camera and smiling, her head turned slightly to the side. 'That's her.'

I stare hard at the face but the image isn't sharp. The closer I look the less able I am to discern anything distinctive.

'This is better,' he says, pulling out the next photo.

I gasp involuntarily. It's *much* better. Not only is the image clearer, but it is a close-up by comparison. The camera snapped three of the Sisters in the middle of work. They are standing in some kind of garden – vegetable patch, maybe – with their overskirts and aprons pinned up behind. It looks as if one of them has just said something funny and they are stopping a moment to laugh.

The archivist points to the thin one in the middle. 'That's her.'

But I'd recognised her already. My birth mother is leaning on a work shovel in the attitude of a workman, which is sort of funny considering all that elaborate headgear she's wearing. Her leather belt is pulled in tight to reveal a small waist, and the white starched material around her face encases bright eyes and a wide mouth with even teeth. The nun on her left is quite a bit older. She has thick glasses and a wide girth, and the other one has a round and jolly face. They all look happy and relaxed.

Det leans down closer and chuckles softly.

'You look like her! The mouth, the eyes!'

I shake my head awkwardly and pull at my mouth. 'No …'

'You do!'

I feel self-conscious staring at this photo. As if I've been caught preening in front of a mirror.

'Can we have a copy?' Det asks.

'I can have one made for you.' He smiles at her enthusiasm.

'No!' I say quite loudly, surprising myself as well as them. 'I don't think so. I don't really want a copy.' I laugh off the anxiety so evident in my voice. 'Thank you for showing us and everything, but …'

'Of course,' the man says kindly. 'So this Sister is a close relative of yours?'

I open my mouth and then look to Det for help.

'Her mother,' Det explains, which makes me want to cry, because just the word immediately makes me think of my real mother. The one who bathed my knees when I had a fall, and made me hot drinks in the winter after school. The one who sat on the floor between Stella's and my twin beds and read to us every single night.

'Oh, I see.' The man seems slightly taken aback. He slides the photos into the folder. 'Yes, well, people often find this kind of thing confronting.'

This kind of thing? I want to ask how many times he's had people coming in wanting to see photos of their birth mothers. He must be able to read my mind.

'I have people coming in all the time wanting all kinds of information,' he says. 'I do have another item of interest, but you might rather wait for another day?'

I stare back at him.

Det looks at me eagerly.

I nod. 'What is it?'

'We have a letter she wrote to one of the laundry girls. The woman who received it gave it back to us. She'd heard we were interested in such documents and so …' He looks directly at me. 'Please feel free to say if you would rather I simply kept it here with the other material for another time, perhaps.'

'I would like to see it now.'

The man nods, takes out a page of lined paper and puts it down on the table in front of me. 'You see here.' He points to the date. '1970.'

'Yes,' I whisper. *Ten years before I was born.*

My dear Faye,

Thank you for your letter. It made me sad to read of your distress since leaving us. I can only pray your bitter feelings will fade in time and that you can find it in your heart to forgive us our mistakes. The laundry work was very hard and relentless. Especially in summer and, well, you're absolutely right, it hardly seems fair to put young girls to such hard work, especially, as you say, when there was no way out.

You write about me being the 'only kind one', but, Faye, if you think hard you'll remember that isn't true. What about old Mother Paula? And Mother Aloysius, with her cordial on the hot days and the sweets she'd pass out to keep everyone going when spirits got low? So many of the Sisters loved you. We still love you! It is true that we are not good at showing it. With so many girls to care for, and with so much work to get through every day, individual needs did get lost sometimes. But I promise you things are slowly improving. You might be interested to know that the Sacred Heart girls don't work such long hours now. They are now divided up into smaller family-type groups, and they're learning all kinds of different skills. I remember how you hated needlework. These days you wouldn't have to do it! So that is something, isn't it? We have a lady coming in once a week teaching leather work and another basic accounting. And we've got some deportment classes too. I'm sure the smaller, family groups work a lot better.

Mother Madonna leaving you on 'the Cross' until midnight that evening as punishment for using bad language was most unfortunate. That it was in winter and you were without a coat would have made it doubly awful. But, my dear, please believe that Mother would not have meant to do that. As you know, she was very strict but she was never deliberately cruel. Still ... it was very hard for you.

I can only say again how sorry I am and that I will remember always your lovely bright restless spirit. You will always be in my prayers.

Yours faithfully in Christ,
Sr M. Annunciata

'Faye was one of the laundry girls,' the man explains. 'You've been over to the far part of the convent?'

We shake our heads.

'There is a whole section over there that was pretty much cut off from the rest of the convent. Over the years, thousands of women and girls worked in the Magdalen laundries both here and in other cities around the world. The Sisters took in linen from outside, a lot of it from the hotels and the ships. It was the way the convent kept afloat financially.'

'Were the girls paid?'

The man shook his head. 'There are many written testimonies on the net and elsewhere as to the harshness of the work, but I thought seeing it was your ... mother who wrote the note, you'd be interested.'

'Thank you,' I whisper.

'It's a very nice note,' the man says encouragingly. 'A note you can be proud of.'

'Yes.' But I can't work out what kind of note it is. I feel numb.

'Not such a nice note.' Det decides for me.

'Well ...' The man looks uncomfortable. 'We have to remember that it was some time ago.'

'So they worked in the laundry for no pay?' Det is determined.

'Many were in trouble with the law. The nuns would take them from the courts; instead of going to jail they did their time here. But others too. Destitute women, women and girls with nowhere else to go.'

'I see.'

'It's important not to judge by today's standards. There was no government help for single mothers then or for wives fleeing abusive husbands with nowhere to live. It was a different world altogether.'

'Hmmm.' Det frowns and looks at me. 'You had enough?'

'Yeah.'

We thank the man and Det leads the way out.

At the door I turn back. 'The Cross?' I ask. 'What was that?'

'Not quite as bad as it sounds.' The man smiles. 'Up the far end of the Sacred Heart enclosure there was a big crucifix and sometimes girls had to stand beneath it as punishment.'

'Sounds like fun,' Det says.

We are quiet as we make our way out onto the street.

Cecilia 1968

'Mother and Sisters, I humbly accuse myself of breaking the Great Silence twice during the last week and …' Cecilia hesitated, feeling her face grow hot, 'and also of being negligent in my work with the girls.'

It was Friday night and the Chapter of Faults was progressing slowly. Cecilia had come forward to kneel at Mother Holy Angels's feet. Behind her the novices and postulants shifted on their knees wearily. She'd been dreading this all day and still held out hope that she might be spared having to go into details.

'In what way negligent, Sister?' *No such luck.* Mother was sitting upright in her large chair in front of the whole community, her eyes bright and alert in the soft light coming in through the windows, her right hand playing with her rosary.

Cecilia hesitated. There was no way out of this. Knowing that Mother Bernard, the nun in charge of the laundry, would have already told Mother Holy Angels the gist of what happened was making her feel sick.

'There was an altercation in the laundry, Mother, and I forgot my prime responsibility.'

'Forgot?'

Cecilia heard the sympathetic intake of breath from the novices behind.

'A fight broke out between two girls in the laundry, Mother. It quickly escalated with the others taking sides.'

'So a dangerous situation?'

'Yes, Mother.'

'What was the fight about?' Mother asked.

She knows what happened, but she wants to make it hard for me so I'll give up the poetry group.

'It was about the little poetry group, Mother.'

'The poetry group?'

'Yes, Mother.'

'What about it, Sister?'

'The roles, Mother.'

'The roles?'

The Sacred Heart girls worked in the laundry all day, five days a week, as well as Saturday mornings. They had a few hours on Saturday afternoons for leisure activities like needlework or cooking classes or basketball. Many girls were not interested in any of the activities and spent the time mooching around aimlessly in the few hours before Benediction. In that atmosphere, gangs often formed, gossip was traded and vendettas were carried out over trifling offences. To counter this, Cecilia had sought permission to start a little poetry group with some of the girls. There was no library, nor access to one, but she'd spied *The Complete Works of Shakespeare* getting dusty sitting up on the shelf in the recreation room amid the many volumes of pious literature. And so she asked if she might borrow it and write some of the famous speeches on the board for the girls to copy and learn off by heart. Initially the small group of eight or ten girls had not been enthusiastic, but when she began to tell them about *Romeo and Juliet* – the play she'd studied in matriculation – they became excited. It was about love and they were interested in love even if the language was impenetrable. One of them suggested they learn some of it, dress up and 'play' it at the end-of-year concert.

Mother Holy Angels had been most unenthusiastic. 'That kind of thing is too difficult for these girls,' she told Cecilia. 'Remember, most of them can't manage even the simple things in life. Some nice songs for the end of the year would make more sense.'

But when Cecilia confessed her lack of any musical aptitude, Mother Holy Angels reluctantly relented. 'Well, one can only hope it might improve their language,' she'd said tartly.

'And so, Sister? What happened?'

'Mavis Banes badly wanted the main male role of Romeo, but I gave it to Faye Slattery who looks more the part of a boy and Mavis took offence.'

'That child would take offence at anything,' Mother muttered.

That child? Cecilia felt like reminding the nun that the girl was twenty-four, older than Cecilia herself. Mavis was heavy and clumsy and, it had to be said, rather slow. She'd not done well at the family placement she'd been assigned to earlier that year – the mother of thirteen children had sent her home early, reporting that Mavis had been worse than useless. But having no interest in little children was hardly a crime.

'Go on, Sister.'

'Unfortunately they were both allotted to the ironing room on Wednesday morning. They used the opportunity to snipe and to rouse each other up.'

'Which is why we have prayers throughout the working day, Sister!' the Mistress of Novices cut in sharply. 'Prayers and hymns to keep the girls focused on their work.'

'Yes, Mother.' Cecilia felt her jaw tighten. 'But it is sometimes hard to keep the girls praying *all* day, especially in the hot weather.'

'Be that as it may, Sister,' Mother sighed. 'It works to quell frustration and rebelliousness.'

'Yes, Mother.'

'Then what, Sister?'

'Well, Mavis kept calling Faye names, implying that she was a ... well, that she had loose morals and the like.' Cecilia flushed. The dreadful words the girls had used were simply unrepeatable. 'Then they began to slap and pull at each other, and I was afraid that—'

'As well you might be!' the Mistress of Novices said indignantly. 'The hot presses are very dangerous and all the irons would have been on. Something terrible could have happened, Sister. You and I both know there is *always* someone nearby for just such occurrences. You only had to ring the bell.'

'Yes, Mother.' Cecilia hung her head. She loathed calling in reinforcements.

'And then?'

Cecilia felt weary. *How long was this going to take? Why so much detail?* 'They were rolling around the floor clawing at each other,' she whispered, 'so I went over and ... I sat on Mavis.'

A sudden soft ripple of mirth broke out behind her. Cecilia looked up hopefully, but Mother Holy Angels was not amused.

'You *sat* on her?'

'Yes, Mother.'

'It is against our Rule to touch the girls, Sister,' she said severely, 'much less *sit* on them!'

'It was very remiss of me, Mother.' *But was it?* In fact, sitting on Mavis had worked beautifully. The tough girls had Cecilia sussed out as a softie very early on, and when she supervised them at meals or at work in the laundry their scorn was barely disguised. She was a nun, yes, and so she got surface respect, but as soon as her eyes moved or she turned her back they returned to their tricks.

When she'd panicked and sat on Mavis to try to stop the fight, the rest of the girls who'd gathered around to cheer on the two combatants pulled back in complete amazement. There was a few seconds of silence as they took in the sight of Cecilia, in full habit, her white veil awry and her legs poking out the end of her voluminous dress, sitting on the toughest girl among them, who was sprawled out on the floor. Then everyone had burst out laughing. Even Mavis.

'You okay, Mother?'

'Need a hand up, Mother?'

It had been one of the sweetest moments in Cecilia's life until she realised that Mother Bernard had been watching the whole incident from the doorway. Her face like thunder, the older nun had come pounding over, pulled both girls roughly to their feet by the hair and virtually thrown them back at the ironing presses.

'We have two hotels to get through before the end of the day!' she'd shrieked.

Faces dark and sour, the girls did as they were told.

'Where is your gratitude for all that has been done for you?' The old nun walked up and down between the lines of ironing girls. 'Do any of you ever wonder why you are here? No? Well, let me enlighten you. Because no one else will have you! No surprise to me that your families don't want you. No decent man would ever want to marry the likes of most of you.'

When she finally came to the end of her rant, red-faced and puffing with indignation, she began a decade of the rosary.

In the name of the Father and of the Son and of the Holy Ghost...

Most of the girls answered mechanically, just as they worked, in unison, folding the freshly laundered sheets and pillowcases into the presses, checking the lists from the hotels and carting the finished piles into the packing room.

Holy Mary, Mother of God.

Their voices murmured under the clanking of the machines like the low, monotonous sound of a well-oiled engine.

But once Mother Bernard had gone, the girls turned one by one to give Cecilia their shy smiles. On their way out to lunch, Mavis had apologised.

'Sorry, Mother,' she said as if she really meant it.

Then a few others muttered the same. 'God bless you, Mother. God bless you.'

'God bless you, girls.' Cecilia's eyes had filled with tears. 'God bless you all.'

When everyone was gone, Mother Aloysius had come in from the mangle room to walk out with Cecilia.

'I heard all that,' the sweet-faced Irish nun chortled, raising her eyes to heaven. 'Mother Bernard must have got out on the wrong side this morning.' She smiled at Cecilia and took her arm.

'You did well, dearie,' she whispered.

'Oh Mother.' Cecilia shook her head in consternation. 'I wish I had your knack.'

The girls all loved the cheery Mother Aloysius. She was able to keep full control and get the work done without ever raising her voice or getting angry.

'Have the girls in question been corrected?' Mother Holy Angels was asking now.

'Mavis said she was very sorry, Mother,' Cecilia said. 'I decided to leave it at that.'

'And the other girl?'

'Well, the other one was Faye, Mother.' Cecilia hesitated, unsure if Mother remembered that Faye had only been back from St Joseph's in Broadmeadows a few weeks. 'Faye Slattery. She said she was very sorry too,' she added quickly.

Mother Holy Angels gave a deep sigh, closed her eyes and shook her head.

With dismay Cecilia realised that she'd just *lied* to the Mistress of Novices. *Oh dear Lord!* The girl hadn't apologised at all.

Faye had been only fourteen years old when she first came to live at the convent some months before. Her parents had asked the Sisters to take her in because she kept running away from home and had been expelled from two schools and was now completely unmanageable. No one knew she was pregnant. She was so very young, so quiet and watchful. Something about her had made Cecilia warm to her straight away.

When her pregnancy became obvious nothing was said, but she was put on lighter duties in the packing room until her time came. Then she was taken to Broadmeadows by ambulance to have her baby. Ten days later she was back again, working in the laundry. In the three weeks she'd been back she hadn't caused any trouble at all until the fight with Mavis.

But Cecilia had noticed the heavy dark rings under the girl's eyes, and the fact that she barely spoke now. At break times she lurked around the canteen or sat alone on the steps leading into the little chapel, just staring into space.

It was strictly forbidden for the girls to talk about their pasts to each other or anyone else. Situations that couldn't be changed should be forgotten. Indeed, the girls were given new names to help them forget their old selves.

Cecilia knew the rules, but Faye was so friendless. None of the other girls liked her. Even those who'd had to give up babies themselves had no sympathy. She'd heard them complaining about her crying at night.

'*What's with her?*'

'*I'm going to gag her tonight.*'

'*She acts like it's never happened to anyone else before!*'

'Faye needs a little time, Mother,' Cecilia said desperately.

'I see.' Mother Holy Angels shook her head. 'And yet she wants to recite Shakespeare?' A smile played around her mouth.

'She does, Mother.'

'Well well.' The old nun sighed again.

Cecilia had given Faye the role of Romeo because she was tall and thin, but it was more than that. There was a fierce intelligence in her pale, solemn face, and such gravity in the deep grey eyes. Cecilia found herself thinking of the girl at odd times, wondering how she might be able to help her and saw again the sudden flush of pleasure on the sad girl's face when told she would make a good Romeo.

'Would you like to do it, Faye?'

The girl had nodded quickly and then lowered her eyes as though she might be going to cry.

'You think you can learn all those lines?'

'Yes, Mother.'

'You will spend some time in quiet meditation, Sister Annunciata,' the Mistress of Novices was saying, 'paying particular attention to the rule of obedience.'

'Yes, Mother.'

And then, as though she could read the anguish in Cecilia's heart, 'And let me remind you again that we do *not* become familiar with the girls in our care, nor single one girl out for special attention. It is *not* what we are here for.'

'Yes, Mother. Thank you, Mother.'

The novices stayed on their knees until Mother Holy Angels had swept out of the room.

'So what *are* we here for?' Sister Jane Francis said, loud enough for them all to hear.

Peach

Every time Mum and Dad ring I'm on the point of telling them about the letter and the photos and everything, but then I chicken out and tell myself it can all wait until they get home. I do tell them about Det's pregnancy, though, and after the shock they become immediately supportive. When they ask all about her living arrangements and what plans she's made I feel foolish because I don't know much at all. When they suggest she move in with us I try to buy time by thinking up excuses.

'But ... there isn't room.'

'Nana's room isn't being used,' Mum says.

'But I don't think she'd want to. I mean, she's so—'

'Try her,' Dad cuts in dryly.

'If she won't move into Nana's room, then suggest the bungalow,' Mum persists.

'But it's full of junk.' I've never even imagined living with Det, much less wanted to. The bungalow consists of two small rooms. One is a basic kitchen with a sink and a funny little stove, the other is a bedroom with a small shower recess and toilet off it. 'Where would we put all that crap?'

'In the garage,' Dad says patiently. 'It's only a few boxes and cases. When I get home we can chuck most of it out. You will have to clean it out though. It's pretty grimy.'

'But there's no heating,' I protest.

'So we get her a heater for the winter,' Dad laughs. 'Come on, Peach.'

'Okay,' I say slowly. Det probably won't come at the idea, but still … it's a good suggestion.

'It won't be forever, darling,' Mum says gently. She can read my thoughts from all those miles away and it makes me sick with shame. 'But she needs a secure base from which to make plans. Don't you think?'

'Okay,' I say, 'yeah, of course.'

'It's coming up to Christmas, too.'

Oh jeez.

I put the phone down. Trust my parents to suggest the obvious solution. Why wasn't it me who came up with the idea?

In my defence, it is pretty easy to forget about Det's pregnancy. She never talks about it and although she must be getting bigger, no one would guess because she wears these huge oversized shirts.

But two days after talking to Mum I go up to her studio after my morning shift at the cafe and knock on her door.

'Hey, Peach,' she says when I push the door open. She's working at her desk.

'Move in with us,' I say without any preliminaries.

'What?' She stares at me.

'Mum and Dad rang.' I try to make it sound as if it's no big deal. 'And they want you to move in with us and … I do too.'

Her face screws up further into a deep frown. She gets up and walks to the window, and stands staring out a while, then moves back to the painting that she's working on.

'I'd be in the way,' she mumbles.

'No. You won't.'

She picks up a knife and starts scraping the paint from one corner of the picture, still frowning hard.

'Where would I sleep?'

'The bungalow. We'll clean it out.'

'Hmm.' She throws down her palette knife, flops down onto the desk chair and closes her eyes.

'What about Stella?'

'She loves the idea. She's head-over-heels excited.'

Det draws her knees up and wraps both skinny arms around her legs and buries her face.

'Okay,' she says softly.

It's at that moment I understand she is terrified. That the frantic work pace is all about keeping the terror at bay as much as preparing for her exhibition. I want to grab those thin shoulders and tell her *everything is going to be fine*. But I hold back. Det doesn't take kindly to sympathy, and if I'm being honest ... I'm not sure things will be fine. In fact, there is a lot to worry about. This is a gamble that might well not pay off.

As soon as I tell Cassie the plan she moves straight into action mode as only Cass can. Det has to go to a landscape painting class in the country for five days, but Cassie comes straight around with piles of cleaning equipment and all sorts of plans about how we'll do the place out. I stand there listening to her, amazed by her energy and focus. *Hang on ...* I want to remind her, *this is just the bungalow, a place where we dump stuff.*

But over the course of few days, Cassie transforms the two little rooms. I help, of course, but she is the brains behind it. First off, we move all the boxes into the garage, then we roll up our sleeves and get stuck into the cleaning. It takes the two of us about three hours. Stella, who never gets her hands dirty if she can help it, brings out drinks and makes us food and acts like she's got all kinds of important things happening inside the house when there is anything serious to do. Still, she's helpful in her own way.

I'm at work when Cassie and Stephano paint the place with some white paint his father had left over in his garage. When I come home the two coats are already finished. The next day Cassie brings around bits and pieces of furniture and household stuff that she's begged and borrowed from her relatives. There is a good bed, a small table and chairs, a desk, even a small sideboard, curtains, table linen and a few vases. Most of it arrives courtesy of a trailer hooked to Stephano's car, but one little bookcase comes on the back of a mate's motorbike, and a little table is walked around on a trolley by someone who lives nearby.

By the time Cassie is finished, our little junk room looks fantastic.

When Det arrives a few days later, with a couple of battered suitcases, a mini fridge that doesn't shut properly and a box of household stuff, she is totally amazed. She stands in the doorway and looks around.

'Who did this?' she mutters suspiciously.

Cassie and I laugh, and I point at Cass. 'She did.'

'She helped me!' She points back at me.

Det flops down on the rug, and lies out flat on her back.

'What do you think, Detto?'

She moans, putting both hands up over her eyes. She sits up to take another look, then buries her face in her knees, wrapping her arms around her legs.

'It's totally fucking brilliant. You two are the best mates anyone could have. I mean it. The best.'

She holds out her arms and Cassie and I lie down on either side of her on the rug.

'I thought I was going to move in on top of a heap of dusty boxes!' she whispers hoarsely. I hear the tears in her voice but pretend I don't. She hates nothing quite as much as she hates gush.

'We couldn't have that,' Cassie says crisply.

Det and I laugh.

From the very start it works perfectly, almost as though Det has always lived with us. Three in a house works better than two. Somehow Det's bluntness and brand of dry humour evens Stella and me out. We're not under each other's skins as much.

And I rediscover my love of cooking. With Mum and Dad away and Stella being such an erratic eater, I'd stopped cooking proper meals. But with Det here, shopping for food and cooking suddenly becomes something I want to do again. Det doesn't cook herself but she is very appreciative of anything I manage to pull together, and she always cleans up, *and* insists that Stella do her share too, which is nothing short of a miracle.

Cassie drops in all the time, sometimes with Stephano – more often than not with delicious leftovers from his mother's kitchen. Nick and Dicko are regular visitors and even old Screwloose comes every now and again with baguettes he buys on his way home from the city.

Suddenly Christmas is on us. Stella and I try to talk Det into coming with us to our aunt's for the day, but she flatly refuses.

'Det, you can't be alone on Christmas Day,' Stella protests. 'We can't have it.'

'Why not?'

'Christmas is … serious.'

'Is it?'

'Yes.'

'Then I want to be serious by myself.'

We're not a religious family, but Christmas is special and we always spend it together. So when I wake early on Christmas morning it all feels a bit sad not to have my parents around.

I lie in my bed watching the light flickering through the blinds, thinking of them and Christmases past, and then Fluke wanders into my head. Instead of immediately shutting the door on him I let him stay. Maybe Christmas is the time to … to *do what?* What would I say?

I lean over and grab my phone and then remember that I

deliberately wiped his number weeks ago. No problem. I know it off by heart. How tragic is that? After six months I still remember his phone number. I tap in the numbers just for the hell of it and stare at them, marvelling that I am just one small movement away from hearing his voice. *Do I dare?* My finger hovers over the buttons, but before I can do anything, the phone starts ringing and I almost drop it in surprise. It's an unknown number. What if he's at his mother's place and thinking of me too? Against my better judgement the idea of him remembering me at Christmas makes me feel mushy.

'Hello?' I say tentatively, my heart pounding.

'Peach! Happy Christmas!' Mum's voice crackles down the line and I'm both glad and deeply disappointed. 'Happy Christmas, darling.'

'Thanks, Mum,' I reply, more heartily than I feel. 'Happy Christmas to you too! Where are you?'

'Waiting for our flight to London.'

'So you'll be with Dad's mum, I mean Grandma, for Christmas Day?'

'That's the plan.' Mum pauses. 'You sound a bit . . .'

'I'm fine, Mum. It's early here. Your call startled me.'

'I knew my early bird would be awake,' she says warmly. 'Was I wrong?'

'No.'

'So did you both go to the carols?'

'No.'

'Oh.'

I can tell she's disappointed. The four of us always go to the local park and sing carols with Mum's sister Claire and her kids. We take a picnic, light our candles and sing. We always enjoy it and I suddenly can't believe that I forgot all about even ringing Claire back to arrange it.

'Oh well, tell Stella I'll ring later. I knew she wouldn't be awake yet.'

'Okay ... so tell me about Paris.'

'I spent yesterday walking around my old university, and it was so wonderful, but I want to know how it's all going at home,' Mum says. 'I mean with Stella?'

'Still the same,' I say quickly.

'What time do you think she might rise?'

'Around noon,' I say, and we both laugh.

We chatter on a bit and then she puts on Dad and we go through the same Christmas palaver.

'Send Grandma our love,' I say when we're saying goodbye. But I'm only going through the motions.

Dad's mum came out to visit when I was about twelve and stayed for a month and that was the last time I saw her. We were so excited to be meeting our other grandmother. But she was nothing like Nana. Everything was wrong from the beginning. The new bed that Dad had bought especially for her was too hard, the heat and the flies were unbearable and the Aussie accents indecipherable, and Stella and I were way too noisy. After she'd gone, Stella and I confessed to each other that we were glad she'd gone. We felt bad about saying anything to Dad until he confessed he'd come to Australia to get away from his uptight parents. And fifteen years on he still reckoned it was the best decision he'd ever made.

Det strolls into the kitchen at around ten with two gifts under her arm wrapped up in brown paper and tied with bright string.

'Happy Christmas.' She kisses me briefly, plonks herself on a stool and puts her two presents to the side.

I get down another cup and go on making the tea. 'For me?' I point at a present.

'Yeah.' She looks around. 'So where is mine?'

'Wait!' I pour the tea and hand her one. 'How are you?'

She cups her belly and nods. 'Okay ... I guess.'

'Merry Christmas!' Stella enters with an armful of presents.

Det gives me a really nice framed drawing of Stella sitting cross-legged on the floor eating an apple. And for Stella there is one of me looking thoughtfully out the window. Stella immediately hangs them both on the wall and wraps tinsel around them, which looks totally awful, but anyway …

My present for Det is two bright cushions for the bungalow that I thought looked really fantastic in the shop. Once I see them in our kitchen I see that they're totally *not* in the least way fantastic.

'Hey thanks, Peach.' Det grins and puts one under her bum and the other one under her shirt. 'They're really nice.'

I groan and get myself a block of chocolate from the fridge. I'm known for this. I take forever to choose a present and it's always wrong.

'Oh wow!' Stella tries to sound pleased as she slips the combs I bought for her into her hair. 'Really great, Peach. Thanks!'

'Do you really want a couple of bunches of rotten grapes in your hair?' Det is suddenly helpless with laughter. 'Or some old geezer's haemorrhoids!'

I throw a screwed-up ball of wrapping paper at her, but I have to laugh. She's right. They're awful.

That night, Mum and Dad ring us again to say that Dad's mother's health is a lot worse than they thought, and that they'll probably have to extend their stay.

'How long?' I ask in alarm.

'Well, love …' Dad says guardedly 'I don't think your grandmother is going to get better … so we'll have to see.'

My grandmother? *No.* My grandmother is an old lady living in an Australian country town.

Cecilia 1972

'Whose side are you on?' The young priest looked around at the packed lecture hall and smiled. 'My friends, that is a question some of us have to ask ourselves every day.'

Unlike the other speakers during the week-long Church Conference, he didn't use the lectern but strode up and down in front of them, cracking jokes and gesticulating with his hands and occasionally laughing at himself. It was very different to anything Cecilia had heard before.

She'd known nothing about poor sugar farmers in the Philippines, but he made them come alive for her. His descriptions and anecdotes let her feel what it would be like to be in the sweltering heat of Manila, amid the open drains and mosquitoes.

'Being on the side of the poor is not only dangerous,' the priest went on, 'but it is beset with all kinds of contradictions. Is it right to baptise the landowner's child and officiate at his daughter's wedding when we know that he is behind the disappearance and death of a local union organiser? What do *you* think?' he asked the audience.

What do I *think?* Cecilia stopped breathing.

'We are sometimes the only ones standing between the peasants and those who rule over their lives, and believe me, it's fraught and sometimes gets dangerous.'

A very old nun down the front, only a few seats from Cecilia, tentatively raised her hand.

'Sister?' The priest broke off from what he was saying.

'In what way dangerous, Father?'

'Well, our lives are threatened sometimes.'

There was a gasp as the audience took this in.

'You must get some support, though, Father, from the bishops?'

'The only contact we get is to tell us to stop what we're doing. It's not surprising,' he added with a dry laugh. 'The wealthy have lived off the backs of the poor for centuries. They've got very good at intimidating people who ask questions. After all, a priest's only role is to save souls,' he added.

Cecilia leant forward in amazement.

'Last time I looked that *was* our role,' a male voice came from the back of the audience. 'Render unto Caesar what is Caesar's and to God what is God's.'

'And what if Caesar demands your children don't eat and don't go to school?' the priest asked mildly. 'Rich countries – France, England, the USA, Australia – also have poor and marginalised. Isn't it time to speak on behalf of the indigent, the dispossessed and the poor?'

There was an uneasy silence for a few moments before a young nun in the middle of the room raised her hand.

'With respect, Father, that is exactly who most of us are serving,' she said quietly, 'in our hospitals and schools and outback missions.'

'Yes, Sister,' the young priest cut in, 'that is what most of our religious orders were originally set up to do. But things have changed and we haven't. Governments have stepped in with money and know-how. So what is the Church's role now? And let's ask ourselves, why is it so often on the side of the conservative and repressive?'

Whose side are you on? When the lecture finished, Cecilia had a lump in her throat and she was hardly able to speak for the rest of the day. *Whose side was she on?*

Ideas spun and danced in her head. After the last speaker, late in the afternoon she sought the priest out.

'Father, I need to know something.'

'Yes, Sister?' He turned away from the men he was talking to and indicated that she should sit down at the table.

'Your talk confused me.'

'Well, that is a good start.' He smiled, and she saw that he was older than she'd first thought – well into his thirties – and that his eyes were warm.

She relaxed a little. 'Did you baptise the corrupt landowner's child?' she asked and when he sighed deeply and nodded, she went on awkwardly, 'I would like to know *how* you decided to do that.'

'Why?' His eyes twinkled with laughter. 'Has Rome come through at last?'

She looked at him, not understanding.

'With the ordination of women, I mean?' He laughed at her shock. 'Of course women should be ordained,' he went on, smacking one hand down on the table for emphasis.

'But ...?' Cecilia was suddenly hot with confusion because she had the feeling that he was actually serious. What could she say? The very idea was preposterous.

'Well, you tell me why not.' He leant forward, his brown eyes gently mocking her. 'What makes me better than you?' He stuck a finger down his dog collar and rolled his eyes.

She laughed at that and he motioned at all her garb – the stiff white casing around her face, her voluminous dress, the cape and long veil – and shrugged as though it was a whole lot of nothing very important.

'In fact, probably the opposite is true. The nuns we work with in Manila are much better than most of us. Men have such big egos, Sister!' He laughed at her confusion again. 'You might not know that, but it's true. Why shouldn't the Sisters baptise children, say Mass and hear confessions? Tell me, please?'

Cecilia was dumbfounded. She had never heard anyone, much less a priest, talk like this. When he understood that she was truly shocked he smiled.

'Anyway, Sister, to answer your question: How do we decide what to do in difficult situations? Well, there are ten of us in the house: six priests and four lay brothers. We decide together how to go about things.' He smiled again. 'There are a lot of arguments because everyone has a different view, but in the end we always come back to the same thing.'

'Which is?' she asked curiously.

'What else is there?' He shrugged, then smiled disarmingly. 'There is only the Jesus of the Gospels. So we ask ourselves, *Where is Jesus in all this*? Whose side would *He* be on?'

Cecilia got up. 'I see,' she said slowly, 'thank you, Father.'

'You're welcome, Sister.'

Whose side was she on?

Finally Cecilia decided she must at least *see* her daughter. Just that. See her. She would not try to talk to her or make any other kind of contact.

So she found herself walking the bike path along the river towards the convent, dressed in a long dress and big sunglasses with a scarf covering her hair.

To Cecilia's incredible surprise, when she entered through the big convent gates she was overcome with a deep flood of joy. It flowed through her like soft rain on parched ground, and was so unexpected that her first instinct was to sit down on the grass and cry. Instead she leant up against one of the gateposts to steady herself and stared around. There were people everywhere, ordinary people, walking around as if they had a perfect right. She almost burst out laughing. There they were, sitting at wooden tables, eating, drinking and talking.

Along with the gladness came an unfamiliar tenderness towards her own younger self. That girl who'd come so willingly through these gates to embark on the biggest adventure of her life. *Where was she now?* And the others who'd entered with her. *Where were they all?*

Cecilia forgot her initial reason for coming and wandered around, staring at everything, peering into rooms, walking up stairs and along corridors, intrigued and amused by how the place had changed, and at times utterly moved by the way every room was somehow just as she remembered it. Memories bubbled up only to be replaced by more. Here was an ATM in exactly the place where she'd lost her veil that day in the high wind and had been reprimanded by Mother Agnes as a scatterbrain. *A scatterbrain!* She was the least scatterbrained person she knew. As a young novice she'd been so serious and methodical, way too much so in fact. If only she'd been more like Breda, easily distracted, quick to laugh at the ridiculous and respond from the gut.

But the smell of coffee was new. Yes, she would have one of those in a little while. She would sit in that little cafe and remember sweet Mother Our Lady of Fatima O'Reilly who worked with the old Italian gentleman whose name she couldn't remember, making the bread every day for over a thousand Sisters, girls and women.

She walked up the front steps and stood in the lobby outside the Bishop's Parlour and saw herself on her first day, feeling grown up and worldly in her sleeveless red dress with the black high-heeled sandals, her hair tied back with a clip-on bow.

Except for Dominic, her whole family had come. Patrick was dressed in stovepipe pants and a daring black cotton shirt, his hair slicked back in rocker style. Brendan was wearing the pink-striped shirt that Mum had begged him not to wear because it would 'shock the nuns'. The twins were eyeing everything warily as if they might have landed in jail.

Mother Gabriel had come out of a side room in full regal splendour, tall and straight, her fine Gallic features on display inside the stiff white bandeau encasing her face. She raised her chin as she greeted them, holding out her hand like a queen deigning to greet her subjects.

'Ah, the Maddens!' she said. 'You are all so very welcome. Was the drive long? And in such heat. Well, you must be ready for afternoon tea.'

They'd traipsed meekly after the Reverend Mother through the vast building, out along the path and into a large high-ceilinged room, which was cool despite the heat outside. There was a big polished-wood table in the middle laid with fine china and silver spoons and tiny cakes and stiff white table napkins, and already a couple of family groups were sitting at the table, all looking uncomfortable as at least a dozen smiling nuns hovered over them offering more tea and hot water.

'Now I'm going to leave you in the capable hands of our Mistress of Novices.' The Reverend Mother gave one of her high musical laughs and motioned with a slight lifting of one hand for Mother Mary of the Holy Angels, who was speaking to a very anxious-looking older couple. 'So nice to meet you, Mr and Mrs Madden.'

Cecilia's family, even her father, had chorused humbly, 'Thank you, Mother Gabriel. So nice to meet you too. *Thank you.*'

But her father had muttered, 'I can't stand these places,' as soon as the Reverend Mother was at a safe distance. 'If Cecilia left tomorrow it would be a day too late.'

The boys had all laughed, but her mother had said, *Hush, they'll hear you!*

Now Cecilia peered through the old refectory window, hardly seeing the artwork on the walls or the new coffee machine and modern chairs. Instead, she was wishing Breda was with her. *And here is where we ate,* they would say to each other. *This very spot was where I lay in disgrace after keeping that photo. Do you remember? Where have all the long tables gone? Do you remember?*

She wandered up the stairs to where they'd slept, to the long corridors with the cells on either side. Things seemed very quiet, and a little musty and worn. But she loved it that the old paintwork was still there even if the polished boards had been replaced with fraying carpet. There were names on the doors now, notes stuck on with sticky tape, jokes and posters. A couple of young arty types ignored her as they passed, talking animatedly. A little redhead in jeans smiled before disappearing into one of the rooms, and she could see a few people at the end of the corridor standing right where the Sacred Heart statue used to be, drinking coffee. *My God*. Cecilia was filled with a mad impulse to run over and tell them to stop. She wanted to ring the bell, knock on the doors, call everyone to order and tell them … *what?* That they must never forget that the rooms did not belong to them, but to the hundreds of women who'd gone before, to those who'd willingly sacrificed their young lives to silence and ritual and prayer in a quest for holiness?

She passed the cell that had become hers after her final Profession, but the door was closed and she didn't dare knock although she stood outside for a full minute and thought about it. Instead she headed back downstairs again.

How many times had she rushed across that bit of ground from the Sacred Heart enclosure, worried that she'd be late for lunch, the day's dramas and the girls' sad stories swirling around her brain?

Would Leanne ever learn to iron properly? Why was that girl Sonia so quiet? Would they get the Windsor Hotel laundry done by the end of the day? If not, she'd have to stay up with some other Sisters and get it done, and there was her university work to complete.

The memories were flooding in so fast now that she had to sit down. She didn't know whether to laugh or cry, but found a stone seat outside the refectory and made herself take some deep breaths. Then she went and stood under Breda's tree again, and looking up she laughed aloud.

After wandering through the front gardens she walked back

towards the cafe the other way, noticing that the high iron gates which used to lead into the Sacred Heart section were now leaning up against one of the walls. They must have only recently been pulled down. A shiver of disquiet went through her when she saw the heavy hot water pipe along the top. At least one girl had been badly burnt trying to escape over that gate.

Cecilia hesitated a moment, then walked straight into the enclosure and stared at the bleak grey cement buildings that surrounded her on every side. She'd seen it first as a nineteen-year-old postulant, but now the miserable reality of the place stunned her. With no women and girls to break the monotony, the main purpose of the ugly buildings was so … obvious. She took hold of the iron balustrade and stared at the high walls, the barbed wire. It was a prison.

No, it wasn't.

Yes, it was.

The huge laundry complex was up one end and the little chapel down the other, and only one tree to relieve the drabness.

She saw herself in her early twenties, not yet fully professed, locking the gates on the girls when it was time to go to her own lunch. How relieved she'd been to get away from the clank of the machines, the never-ending baskets of sheets and tablecloths and shirts, the sullen faces of the girls working in the heat, the smell of their sweat and their periods. That room where they changed their rags!

Why hadn't she ever suggested painting the wooden window frames a bright colour or insisted that there be some pot plants for the girls to tend? Why hadn't she demanded the younger girls go to school for at least part of the day? To be put to such hard work in the laundry at age fourteen, fifteen or sixteen for a full day was cruel. *Anything!* If she'd just said … anything.

When had she ever asked a question? Cecilia leant by the wall, memories gnawing at the edges of her brain. Because to ask *why* was always wrong. It meant you hadn't learnt the first thing about the life you had freely chosen. She closed her eyes, overcome with an odd sensation that her whole self was being sucked down a long grey pipe and out into an empty nothingness.

1966

'Why are you a nun, Mother?' Lizzie asked. She was such a pretty girl with a long childish plait of blonde hair down her back and blue mischievous eyes that sparkled when she spoke. Cecilia could discern a real inquiry underneath the bold question from the girl not much younger than herself.

'Well, a vocation is like a calling, Lizzie.'

'But you're pretty,' the girl interrupted with a smile, 'you could get a bloke.'

Cecilia had been about to answer that prettiness had nothing to do with it and nor did 'blokes' for that matter, when they were interrupted by Mother Michael the Archangel, who'd sidled up behind them without either of them noticing.

'Off you go now,' the older nun had snapped at the girl.

'Mother, I was just—'

'I know what you were just doing, and if you don't want to miss out on the film on Sunday night you'll do as you're told!'

The girl trudged off to join her friends and Cecilia was left looking after her.

'Remember, Sister, it is a mistake to fraternise with the girls.'

'Mother, she was only asking—'

'It is not our job to answer their questions, Sister.'

Cecilia had seethed for the next hour. Why hadn't she been able to answer the girl's question? It just didn't make sense.

But by the Saturday night Cecilia had convinced herself that she was in the wrong. To question her Superior's wisdom was tantamount to disobedience. And so when her turn came she confessed the incident to the rest of the congregation. *'I want to confess that I questioned Mother Michael's advice and I solemnly ask forgiveness and I ask that you pray for me.'*

But the incident had left her feeling rattled. Was there no end to this daily struggle with herself? True, some days were better. She'd go through the whole day in a state of placid indifference to such petty things as whether the food was to her liking or that her body felt grimy and unclean. At the end of such days she was buoyed by the fact that she was getting on top of it all, moving closer to the goal of true holiness.

But the bad days. *Oh, the bad days.* The days when her personality asserted itself were torture. At the end of such days she was overcome with a weary pessimism. Back to square one, just like the man in the Greek myth who was destined to pull his heavy boulder up the mountain forever. Such effort, only to have to repeat that effort again and again and again. On such days outrage would rise in her, uninvited and without warning, over some silly thing, like being chastised for being late when Mother had asked her to do something that made her late. *It's not fair.* She'd been on the point of screaming at the Novice Mistress. *You know why I'm late. You made me late. Why are you doing this to me?*

On the bad days she was riddled with longings she couldn't seem to subdue. Longings for impossible things like fresh oranges or the feel of sunshine on her limbs, for a swim on a hot day, or for throwaway pads instead of the rags they were issued when their monthly periods came around. On good days she joyfully accepted the humiliation of having to convey the small bag of bloody rags down to the laundry in front of everyone. It was nothing, a small cross to bear, and if she approached it with an open heart it would bring her nearer to the divine sufferings of her Saviour.

Other days she could barely bring herself to pick up the bag. Only the fetid smell of the dried blood getting stronger could make her do it. And when the bag of rags was in the hands of the old women whose job it was to boil them clean, the overwhelming relief sent her into a fresh spin of angst. In truth she had no right to feel such gladness at being out of that sweltering, stinking room, away from that semi-daft fat woman who took her bag of rags with a knowing imbecilic grin. Oh, this relief was more akin to pagan ecstasy than to the quiet inner joy that St Augustine described as befitting a true Christian.

On such days she couldn't win. She was a cat turning around and around in circles chasing her own tail. What was the purpose?

If her soul was a garden to be tended and cultivated with the fresh water of daily prayer and sacrifice, then it took monumental effort to keep the weeds at bay.

Cecilia wandered over to the stairs at the northern end of the old laundries and climbed as far as she could. A bundle of barbed wire at the top was still there. She thought of the girl who'd tried to jump over and broken both her feet, and the other one who'd torn her hands trying to get past it. *Trish ... Patricia ... or maybe it was Nola*. But the name eluded her. Trish or Nola's bid for freedom had surprised them all because although she was bright and cheeky, the small sharp-faced girl had never caused any real trouble.

Cecilia sat for a while halfway up the iron stairs, resting her back against the banister, and thought of the desperation the girl must have felt.

On her way out towards the cafe, Cecilia noticed a hunched-up figure tucked away between the chapel wall and the old hall. The woman's face was hidden in her hands. Cecilia hesitated and then walked over and stood for a moment a few feet from the woman.

'Can I help you?' she asked quietly.

The woman flinched at the sound of a voice so near. She looked up and tried to smile.

'No, but thanks anyway.'

The crying had made her eyes puffy and red and her face blotchy, but Cecilia could see that the woman, probably about fifty, had once been lovely looking. The good skin and the large hazel eyes were still there, under the nicely dyed red hair that was pulled back with pins. Her slim frame was dressed for the warm day in a cotton dress, tucked tightly around her knees.

'Let me at least go and buy you a cup of coffee.' Cecilia suggested. 'It would be no trouble. I'll bring it back.'

But the woman shook her head again.

Not wanting to intrude, Cecilia turned away.

'It's my first time back,' the woman blurted out. 'I suppose I'm in shock.'

'Oh ... really?' Cecilia waited.

'This place stole my childhood,' she said, her voice low. 'I was here from the age of thirteen until I was twenty-four.'

'What years?'

'1961 to 1973.'

Cecilia gulped in surprise and sat down next to the woman. 'Where were you before?' she asked, a dull roar of dread beginning in her head.

'St Joseph's in Ballarat, which was even worse than here, if that's possible.'

'And before that?'

'My mum died when I was eight and my brother was six, and there was no one to take us. Dad drank and ... it was all hopeless.'

'So it was hard for you here?' Cecilia murmured.

'I was bashed by the older girls because I was pretty and they were jealous of me, and I was belted a few times by those auxiliary monsters too. You know about those nuns that weren't really nuns?'

'Yes.'

The woman threw her head back and laughed.

'The foot soldiers, we used to call them.'

'Yes.'

'But I reserve my real hatred for the *proper* nuns.'

'Really?' Cecilia gulped.

'This was a jail,' the woman spat angrily, 'and what had I

done to deserve jail? What had most of us done? *Nothing*. I just ended up here because I had nowhere to go.' She looked hard at Cecilia. 'I came here at thirteen and never even saw a book or had a pen in my hand! No school. Just work. That is just criminal.'

'Yes,' Cecilia sighed.

'Just work and ... bloody prayers all day, every day!' The woman's mouth was tight with fury. 'We couldn't move but we had to pray about it. Fat lot of good it did us. Or them, for that matter. I would like someone to pay for what went on here. I really would.'

Cecilia nodded.

'There might be some compensation ...'

'I don't want money!' the woman cried. 'I want someone to admit what happened to me!'

Cecilia nodded and said nothing.

'It wasn't just the work. It was the horrible way they treated us. The lack of any ...' But the woman couldn't go on. Tears were gushing from her eyes, but she was wiping them away angrily. She had things to say and she was going to say them whether Cecilia wanted to hear it or not. 'I was a young girl with no one, and the lack of any understanding or kindness was just unbelievable.'

'Tell me,' Cecilia whispered. *Don't tell me. I don't want to know about it. It's over now. What good can come from going over this stuff?*

The woman stood up abruptly and Cecilia suddenly recognised her. That same oval face *had* once been extraordinarily beautiful. She saw her again as that gutsy sixteen-year-old who'd stood up to Sister Bernard in the dormitory that night.

'You worked in the mangle room,' Cecilia said quietly. 'I remember you.'

The woman stared at Cecilia in surprise, her eyes narrowed slowly. 'Yes.'

They stared at each other.

The woman was the first to turn away. She sat back down as

though her outburst had depleted her of everything. She put her face in her hands and leant her elbows on her knees, shuddered a few times and was still.

'Marie?' Cecilia said.

'Yvonne, actually,' the woman whispered. 'I wasn't even allowed my own name.'

'It was about having a new start,' Cecilia murmured.

'We were *children*,' the woman said dully. 'So many of us had had terrible things happen to us before we even got here. But we weren't allowed to talk about it.' She was staring at her shaking hands. 'We were just kids and we needed to tell somebody.'

'Yes.'

'I know your face too,' the woman said after a while. 'You were one of the young Sisters, weren't you? Forgive me. Some of the nuns … were kind enough. They did their best, anyway. It's just the shock of being here and remembering it all.'

Cecilia took her hand and held it. 'Don't apologise.'

'It is just that all the horrible stuff stands out,' the woman whispered, 'the hard work and the lack of love. No schooling. That's what you remember.'

'Yes.'

'You know that lovely garden out the front?'

Cecilia nodded.

'We never saw it. We never even knew it was there!' The women gave a loud harsh laugh. 'Can you believe that?' She stared intently at Cecilia. 'Did any of the nuns ever talk about why we weren't allowed to go and walk around in the lovely garden?'

Cecilia shook her head.

'Remember Mother Bernard?'

'Yes.'

'She cut off my hair … that bitch.'

'I remember,' Cecilia sighed.

1965

Cecilia knew something was up when the girls were called together before breakfast. All two hundred and forty of them lined up in rows, sullen and silent.

Mother Mary Bernard was out the front.

'Someone brought these items into Sacred Heart, and I want to know who it was,' she huffed, holding up a cheap compact, some rouge, two lipsticks and some black mascara. 'This was found in the dormitory, and I want to know who brought it in. Right now.'

No one spoke. No one said a word. The auxiliaries walked around the edges of the group looking out for any note of insubordination.

'It would do you all well to remember that you weren't asked to come here. You were put here because no one else would have you. And so you will abide by the rules. If I don't have an answer by the end of the day, then every single one of you will be punished.'

The day went on. Mass and then work and then prayers, and Cecilia forgot about the incident. It wasn't her night on dormitory duty, so it was quite by accident that she came upon the scene.

She'd been asked by Mother Holy Angels to find Mother Bernard to ask about something completely unrelated, and she planned to catch the nun before she retired to her quarters. But when she got to the dormitory she stopped in the doorway. All the girls were standing mute, watching three girls who were kneeling on the floor in front of Mother Bernard, who was walking up and down in front of them.

'At last!' Particles of spit were flying from the woman's mouth. 'At long last you've seen fit to own up –' she looked dramatically at her watch, '– twelve hours later!' She grabbed the nearest girl by the scruff of the neck. 'And what have you to say to the rest of us who have been waiting all day for your confession?'

'Sorry, Mother,' the girl whimpered.

'Are you sure now?'

'Yes, Mother.'

'You do realise that you're going to have to learn a lesson, don't you?'

'Yes, Mother.'

The nun motioned to the two nearest auxiliaries, who came forward with the scissors. One held the girl tightly by the shoulders while the other chopped off her hair. Mother Bernard moved along to the next kneeling girl.

'And what do you have to say for yourself?'

'Sorry, Mother.'

Many of the onlooking girls sobbed as the auxiliaries methodically chopped off the hair of the next girl. The hair piled up on the polished floorboards, massing like clouds, all shades of brown, clumps of it, tumbling soft and curly, some of it dead straight, all around the kneeling girls.

'There are consequences when we deliberately flout rules.' Mother Bernard was puffing, two bright spots burning like angry flames on her cheeks by the time she got to the third girl, who was *not crying*.

'And what do you have to say for yourself?' the nun huffed.

The pretty girl said nothing.

'Well?'

The girl looked up slowly, straight up at the nun and ... *laughed*.

Sister Bernard reared back in shock for a couple of moments and everyone, including Cecilia, stopped breathing. The crying stopped. Not one of them was brave enough to smile, but it was there in their eyes anyway, a sort of pride that one of their number had dared to be so outrageous. *To laugh in Mother Bernard's face ... Oh that was ...* That sudden laugh had opened a skylight inside every head, bringing with it a sudden gust of elation. Hope crackled recklessly about the dormitory. *One day ... one day ... one day this would be over. One day they would be free.*

That kind of laughter was dangerous. Along with the pride came a new level of dread. *What would happen now?*

'I'll ask again,' Mother Bernard said very quietly. 'What do you have to say for yourself?'

'Nothing,' the girl said.

'I beg your pardon.' Mother Bernard was incredulous.

'Nothing,' she said again.

'You still have nothing to say?' The nun's voice was quieter now. The girl nodded.

'Then we'd better help you find your voice.'

The nun's hand shot out and grabbed the girl by the ponytail. She pulled her roughly to her feet, then motioned to one of the auxiliaries who immediately went to work with her thick leather belt. The girl's dressing-gown flew open and her nightie became tangled up around her knees and thighs as time after time the leather cracked sharply on the soft skin of her legs and bottom. She screamed and cried and then collapsed to the floor as the other girls looked on, terrified. But the beating went on. Cecilia, too, watched in horror.

'Have you anything to say now?' The nun pulled the girl up to her feet again by the ponytail.

The girl's eyes were wide with pain and terror, but she shook her head defiantly. 'No,' she said loudly in her deep voice.

It was at that point that the older nun caught sight of Cecilia watching from the doorway. 'Sister?'

Cecilia gulped and hurried forward with the note.

'Thank you, Sister.' Mother Bernard's heavy face was red with exertion as she read the note. She handed it back without looking at Cecilia. 'Tell Mother I'll be there when I'm finished here.'

'Yes, Mother.' Cecilia looked over to where Marie was now kneeling alongside the other two, shuddering and shocked.

'Open defiance cannot be tolerated, Sister,' Mother Bernard muttered.

'Yes, Mother.'

Peach

Unlike the rest of us, Cassie has never been one for side-stepping issues. There's just the four of us – Stella, Det, Cassie and me – and we're not long into the meal, which I have to say is fantastic even though I cooked it, but I can feel that Cassie is on the verge.

'Okay, I have something to say.' Cassie puts down her knife and fork and waits for the rest of us to go quiet. 'All three of you have me deeply concerned.'

I laugh and wait for the blast.

'So lay it on the line then.' Det serves herself a third helping of potatoes. 'By the way, Peach,' she raises one eyebrow at me, 'these potatoes are awesome. What's on the top?'

'Just parmesan.' I grin back. 'Glad you like them.'

'You, for starters,' Cassie cuts in sharply, looking hard at Det.

'What about me?'

'You have done nothing about finding the father of this … kid you are about to have.'

Everyone stops and waits for Det to say something.

'Well, have you?'

'No,' Det says.

'Also, you have no … long-term plans for housing.'

'She does!' Stella snaps. 'Here.'

'I mean *long* term.'

'My name is on the list for—'

'Get real, Det! People are on those housing lists for years!'

'So she stays here,' I bluster nervously, wondering how long Mum and Dad meant her to go on living in the bungalow.

Cassie ignores me. 'And Stella, you know I think you're fantastic, but you've got to do something about your weight. You don't want to go into Year Twelve looking like an elephant.'

'I know.' Stella squirms.

'And Peach,' Cassie hardly hesitates, 'you've got to deal with the mother issue. I can tell it's eating you up.'

'I couldn't agree more,' Stella says quietly.

'For both of your information.' I try to sound dry and worldly but it comes out more defensive than anything. 'My mother is overseas looking after her dying mother-in-law.'

'You know what I mean!' Cassie is exasperated. 'All right, so let's consider each situation in turn.'

'Hey, let's *not*,' Det cuts in through a mouthful of potatoes. She swings a fork in Cassie's direction. 'We really appreciate your insightful analysis on how fucked up we are, Cass. But I, for one, don't feel like hearing it right now. Chill out and enjoy the food, eh?'

'*Chill out?*' Cassie counters furiously. 'That's all you can say these days, Det. Well, I can tell you that in a few months' time you won't be *chilling out*!'

'Everything is under control.'

'I know for a fact it isn't.'

'Listen, Cassie, just …'

'Have you organised *anything* yet?'

'What do you mean?'

'Any clothes, for example?'

'What?'

Det looks genuinely perplexed and I have this weird flash – which, if true, is too scary to be funny – that she might have actually forgotten about being pregnant.

'For the kid!'

'Well ... er ... not really?'

'So what is it going to wear?' Cassie snaps.

'Well ...'

'You have to dress a baby, Det. In clean clothes. Every day. Sometimes a few times a day because it vomits and shits *all the time.*'

'I know that.'

'And where's it going to sleep?'

Det looks uncharacteristically flustered. 'Once the paintings for my show are finished I'll get onto all that ... kind of stuff. Shouldn't be too difficult.'

'Oh, right,' Cassie sings sarcastically. 'So easy to get a million difficult things sorted in about two days. So very easy.'

'Listen, don't worry,' Det mumbles. 'I'm going to be okay.'

'And if it comes early?'

'Shit! I don't know, Cass.'

'You've got to get sensible before then or ...'

'Or what?'

Cassie gives a deep sigh and shakes her head. 'You should contact your family. Your mother in particular.'

'*What?*'

'Your mother.'

'Cass!' I say warningly. *Please don't go there.*

Det is staring down at her plate looking totally mutinous. Det's family in Mildura has barely ever been mentioned, much less been on the agenda for a round-table discussion.

'You're having a baby, Det,' Cassie continues in a softer tone. 'You should have someone with experience to help you.'

'I've got you guys,' Det mumbles, her eyes still downcast.

Stella and I both nod vigorously.

'But none of us knows about babies,' Cassie persists. 'You need your family.'

'I need my fucking family like a hole in the head,' Det seethes. 'Can we please talk about something else?'

After dinner, I walk Cassie out to her car.

'I know you think I'm being hard,' she begins defensively. 'I am pushy. I'm a bull in a china shop, but it's because I'm worried and . . . I love you all.'

'Yeah, I know.' I smile at her.

'Someone has got to be practical.'

'If it makes you feel any better, Cassie, I did write to. . . to the old woman in the country.'

'Your grandmother?' Cassie's eyes light up. 'Why didn't you say so?'

'I dunno.' I shrug. 'I just don't want to make it into a big deal.'

'Has she written back?'

'Not yet. I don't care if she doesn't.'

'She will.'

'Maybe.'

Cassie is unlocking the car door now, throwing her bag in. She turns to me seriously. 'None of you seem to realise how huge these things are. This baby of Det's . . .'

'That's why we need you, Cassie,' I say.

And I mean it.

Cecilia

'And have you seen your daughter?' Breda asked.

'No one who looks even remotely like they could be her,' Cecilia replied truthfully.

'It might have been a holiday job,' Breda said thoughtfully. 'If she's a student she'd be back studying now.'

'Yes.'

'But you're still hoping to see her?'

'Well…' Cecilia didn't know how to explain that there was something else about the convent itself that kept drawing her back. Most days she walked down there and stayed about an hour. Somehow it helped with the feelings of dislocation. The past was beginning to unlock itself.

And then, the day after her conversation with Breda, the girl appeared, seemingly out of nowhere. Cecilia had already placed her coffee order with a young man at the counter when a gorgeous blonde girl with pale skin and bright blue eyes like her own bounced out from the door leading to the kitchen. Some of her curly blonde hair was falling out of the red band she'd tied it up with.

Cecilia knew her straight away because she used to look exactly like that herself. *My daughter.*

'Have you been served?' The girl was smiling straight at her now.

Cecilia had a mad impulse to lean across the glass and place one hand on the girl's soft cheek, to run a thumb softly over her eyelids, just as she'd done when they'd put her tiny daughter, still sticky with blood and muck, into her arms. But instead she merely adjusted her sunglasses.

'Yes,' she gulped. 'Thank you.'

There was a momentary flicker of curiosity before the bright eyes moved on to someone else.

The man behind the coffee machine was holding out a paper cup to Cecilia. 'Long black to take away!' he said, without looking up.

Cecilia took the coffee and headed outside. The jangling feeling inside made her unsteady. She needed to sit down. She found a seat and tried to calm herself. She knew now that somehow or other she would have to speak to the girl. With shaking hands, Cecilia pulled out her book.

When she next looked up, the girl was standing near the cafe door having an animated discussion with a heavy, dark-skinned girl with thick, coal-black hair. Hidden as she was in the busy weekend crowd, Cecilia was able to observe her properly. She held back a smile as she watched both girls' hands flying around in all directions as they talked. How lovely the girl was in her tight jeans, with the black square apron tied to her slim waist, big round silver earrings swinging down to her shoulders.

The two girls stepped away from each other before doubling up with laughter. Then they both held out their arms at exactly the same time, and the sudden fierce hug that followed made Cecilia's throat jam with longing.

My daughter.

Peach

Dearest Perpetua,

I can't tell you the joy your letter brought me. And don't you go worrying about the photo not being so good. To me it is just beautiful. You look just like your mother did at your age. It was just lovely to hear that you're alive, that you're with good people and that before I die we might meet.

But all those questions! They've caught me on the hop. But I'll do my best because I can tell you are genuinely interested in an old woman's struggles.

Yes I do still have my faith but I must be honest, it took a battering when Dominic died. And it never really recovered.

Not so much that he is dead. Many a poor mother has had to see her child dead. But that his death was so very unnecessary! At least that is my opinion. I have never forgiven my husband for it. And that is where my problems lie, Perpetua. He is long dead and yet I still just can't forgive him. Our Lord tells us that we must forgive. Our lives are useless if we can't forgive. And yet I can't do it.

The boy was one of those difficult, cranky, contrary kids. He

249

wasn't often able to be cheerful or helpful or even kind, although he could be all those things when the mood took him. But my husband thought that the way to deal with a difficult boy was to beat it out of him. He thought that because the boy liked fashion, smoked and drank and preferred mucking about with horses to farm work, that it meant he was hopeless.

I tried to protect the boy as much as I could. But I wasn't always there and I was so often expecting the next child. Oh, Perpetua, I should have done more.

Kev was a good man in many ways. A good provider, loyal and true but his harshness drove that boy to drink and from there, as we all know, it is a rough slide down.

When he died so did I. And so did your mother. Cecilia never got over Dominic's death. I believe that is why she left the convent and I believe it is why she has nothing to do with us. I believe it is why she thought she couldn't manage a baby. His death took the stuffing out of every one of us.

That Kev had the gall to cry at his funeral and shake hands with people solemnly was particularly irksome to me. 'Tragic,' he kept saying when people came up to shake his hand. 'Yes, the poor boy had a tragic life.'

It was a bleak day in the middle of winter, Perpetua. I stood watching him accepting condolences from the few brave souls who'd showed up, and I was overwhelmed with hatred and vengefulness, and I'm ashamed to say it has never really left me. I could have shot him that day if I'd had a gun. The way I saw it then was that he put the bullet through his own son's head.

Because that is the way my Dom died, Perpetua, all alone in a room. He put the shotgun in his mouth and pressed the trigger and blew his own head off. How can a mother get over that?

We rang to tell the Mother Superior that her brother was dead and she told Cecilia before we got there. As soon as I saw your mother that day I knew the extent of her lonely suffering. She'd lost weight and her eyes were ringed with tiredness and grief.

She neither kissed us nor let us hug her. All through that twenty-minute visit after Dominic's death her hands clung to her rosary. We were strangers to her. Your mother left the convent a couple of years later and it was like she'd decided she'd had enough of everything.

As to my life, the convent days, Perpetua . . . I hardly know where to start.

Living in the girls' hostel in Rathdowne Street and working in Treasury Place were the happiest years. The country was in the grip of the Great Depression so we were glad to have jobs to go to even if we could barely keep ourselves on the money we got. I'm ashamed to say that having a job didn't mean that I worked hard. No one got sacked from a government job in those days. I remember when the supervisor would go out I'd often stop typing and read my book or do knitting under the desk!

Every morning hail or shine I was at six o'clock Mass at St George's just up the road. Not just me. Most days there were at least a dozen girls from St Anne's. The parish priest was a young fellow named Father O'Rourke and we all loved him. He arranged the tennis club and came with us often for trips to the country for picnics.

Every Saturday morning I practised violin in the Parish orchestra. We were often asked to play evening concerts, weddings and the like. I was the leading violinist for the two years before I got married. We all revered the nun who ran the orchestra. When she saw me showing off my engagement ring to the other members of the orchestra, she just glowered at me sourly and turned her back. Oh that hurt! Her refusal to congratulate me had me in tears. But she lived for the orchestra and I was letting them down by getting married.

The other thing I lived for was horses. I was a city girl – with no real home, much less a spare paddock to keep a horse – but my friend Anne's Uncle Len took a shine to me. When I came up to stay with them in Marysville he always gave me the same horse and I thought of her as my own. Pearl. She was a big, dark-grey mare with one white sock and a lovely splash of white on her *forehead in the exact shape of a drop pearl. While I was working all week in the tax office at the Treasury buildings up the top of Melbourne I would be thinking about Pearl and those dirt tracks around Marysville and Healesville, riding that horse amidst the tall trees and the smell of eucalyptus.*

I am lucky enough to be able to say that I have always had good food. Sometimes there wasn't much for anything else, but I could feed my children well and for that a mother must always be grateful. A word of advice from an old girl, Perpetua, don't ever scrimp on good food! It's more important than anything. Simple good food. And some light in your house too. Never rent a house where you don't get plenty of daylight coming in. The meat doesn't have to be the best cut and you don't need a lot of vegetables. If you've got any sort of garden at all then you can grow tomatoes and silverbeet and, depending on the soil, spuds. For years I had nothing but the vegetables I grew myself in the backyard, along with the eggs from the chooks and milk and butter from the cow. I suppose it wasn't very interesting but the children went to bed with full bellies and for that I was always grateful.

I never saw a banana when I was a child and oranges were hard to come by too, but my kids often had them, along with plums and cherries from our trees in the summers. I have always loved oranges and so did your mother. Sometimes my friend Evelyn and I would get a box sent down from Mildura on the train, and we'd share them out. Cecilia would stand by me while I peeled one for her.

Up until two years ago I went to Mass every morning. I got a ride with Evelyn, who was also a widow. Every day, rain, hail or shine, I was on the footpath in front of my house at six-fifteen a.m. in Bellrose Street waiting for Evelyn. Sundays was our sleep-in. We would go to the nine o'clock with Father Mannix. (No relation to the Archbishop!) But old Father Duffy said Mass during the week and he was just the most wonderful man. Evelyn and I loved him and I think we were his favourite parishioners. Sometimes in the winter he'd invite all the early weekday Mass attendees up to the presbytery for a cuppa before we went home. Sometimes he had biscuits and once he cooked toast for everyone because he'd had a win at the races! Oh that was a day. We stayed for over two hours, laughing and talking over old times. But old Duffy got arthritic a few years back and had to retire. I don't think he's dead yet.

Up until last year there were usually only a dozen or so at six-thirty a.m. mass during the week, but I don't know who is left now because I don't get there anymore. No one to take me! On the 26th Dec the year before last, Evelyn didn't come to pick me up. (That's right, the day after Christmas!) Oh Lord, the things that went through my mind that day! Perhaps she'd had an accident or she was caught out in the highway in her car? I don't know why I was so surprised to find out that she'd died overnight; she was actually older than me. But I do miss her dreadfully. She was my dearest friend for close on sixty years. She grew up in Abbotsford Convent, too, but we didn't know each other there as girls because she was in a different section to me. I had my father, you see, who would come and take me out and pay for the extras that I needed, but Evelyn had no one at all, so she did it very tough when she was young. She worked the laundry from the time she was thirteen up to twenty-six and it was hard work. No pay either, and some of the nuns were very strict, but Evelyn was never bitter.

Poor Evelyn. Seven kids and thirty-two grandchildren and she died alone. No priest to give her the last rites and hear her last confession; no one to hold her hand either. I suppose that is the way I'll go too. I just wish we could have said goodbye. Anyway, I still talk to her in my dreams; she's never dead there.

When I first came to this district as a young wife we became close. Neither of us had families yet, but we knew the same nuns back at the Abbotsford Convent, so we had a lot to talk about. There was a nun back at Abbotsford called Mother Peter. Oh she was a character! Very pretty with a wonderful light laugh and just the most joyous nature. You wouldn't believe this but if there was *a priest around she'd have perfume on. God knows where she got it! She was as prissy and vain as a film star!*

There was a lot of work running a family in those days. None of the mod cons like now. Every day that blasted copper had to be lit and the nappies boiled. It's wash day every day when you've got a lot of kids. My hands were raw with all that scrubbing! And the midday meal had to be on the table on the dot of twelve for Kev and his father.

Men. Oh don't let me get onto them, Perpetua, or I'll be here all day!

So much work! And then the dread of finding out that you were expecting again when you'd hardly got over the last one! But we were young then and when you're young you find ways to look on the bright side and have a bit of fun. Evelyn and me did anyway. Lord we laughed! We'd be doubled up over the table in the kitchen or the ironing board on a Saturday, me getting the kids' best shirts ready for Mass in the morning and Evelyn telling me stories about everything.

Especially after the first three months with the sickness over and before I got too heavy, we laughed a lot. I think we learnt how to laugh in the convent. You get a whole lot of girls together and they're either laughing or crying. Evelyn had seven kids and I ended up with nine. I had five miscarriages as well; a couple of them were around three, four months but I didn't mind too much. There wasn't time to be sorry. You just buried the poor little mite and said a prayer over the ground and hoped they'd be welcome in heaven.

Another would be along soon enough. There was no help for mothers then. We just did the best we could.

You think you'll never cope with another baby but somehow you do.

So don't you let anyone tell you that life is getting worse! As far as I can see it's getting better all the time. I'd like to be young now. I think I'd still have a big family but I'd space them out so the work didn't get too much. I'd do a lot of things differently if I had my time again.

I have stopped to read this through and I am ashamed that I sound so ungrateful. When I think of all the poor people all over the world with the famines and earthquakes and wars, all the mothers having to see their children die.

So as a finishing note I must tell you that there has been much good in my life too. Kev was a good man in his own way. He took his responsibilities very seriously but every now and again he eased up and became the lovely shy young fellow I married all those years ago. I got to know his moods. He came from a hard background himself and I saw how he suffered.

We rubbed along together for over fifty years and I don't think I would have been able to do that if I didn't love him. And so that is what all these years have taught me, Perpetua, that you can go on loving someone even when part of you hates them. That probably doesn't make much sense to a young person ... yet it is true.

Even now when any of the grandchildren drop by I remember what happiness is. Declan's girl, Eva, is a darling. She tries to keep me with it. Oh Granny, she says, get rid of that dress. It's so old-fashioned. So I do. Then she tells me what radio station I should be listening to for the music I like, and she helps me fix little things around the house. She is a sweet girl with a lovely smile. But they all had to move away and get their education. And I'm glad for that. I wouldn't wish my life on any of them, Perpetua. Believe me, it's so much better now. Evie wrote last week and told me that she is going to teach me how to work a computer. She's going to bring an old one when she comes up next so that I don't have to wait until I feel strong enough to walk the extra distance to post my letters! She tells me that on the computer, which is more or less like a typewriter, the letters you write just get to their destination straight away with just a click of a button or something. Well, that is hard for me to believe, but I told her that I'd try to learn anything she wanted to teach me.

Kev thought your mother was choosing an unnatural way of life, all right for others but he didn't want it for his daughter. Well, he was proved right in the end because she didn't stay. Some would say that she wasted ten years of her life. But at the time I was so proud. I knew a lot of those older nuns, you see. To be bringing my daughter back to enter the convent and be one of them was a real feather in my cap!

I hope you can make head and tail of this, Perpetua.

My love to you, darling girl,
Ellen

Cecilia

Two weeks later Cecilia saw the girl again.

Cecilia had been sitting outside in the sun for over an hour and was on her second cup of coffee.

'Hey, Peach.'

'Det!' The girl looked up from the table she was clearing. 'What's up?'

'Nothing.' The pregnant girl's voice was droll. 'Thought I'd come down and check out the poor slaves in the salt mines.'

'You want tea?'

'No, I want strong coffee, but yeah, I'll have tea.'

Cecilia had noticed the pregnant girl before. She always sat in the same place, the table nearest the door. Her head was usually bowed over one of the big fat notebooks she always had with her. She always had a pot of tea in front of her, and sometimes she smoked.

A couple of times the girl had looked up and their eyes had locked. It had been Cecilia who turned away first, but she'd felt safe enough in her sunglasses and hat, and until now she'd not thought anything of it.

'Anything to eat, Det?' the girl called as she moved away.

'Yeah.' Her voice was low now and raspy. 'One of those muffin thingos.'

'Take-away?'

'Nah.' After Perpetua had disappeared inside, the pregnant girl looked at Cecilia. 'Mind if I sit here?'

'Please do.' Cecilia had a moment of foreboding. The girl's usual place was empty and there were a lot of other unused tables. She found herself being coolly scrutinised by the pregnant girl, who was now sitting opposite.

'So when is the happy event?' Cecilia forced a lightness she didn't feel.

'Eight weeks.' The girl's tone was cold.

'You looking forward to it?'

The girl shrugged and looked away.

They said nothing while one of the young men from inside put the tea and a big muffin in front of her. She heaped the spoon with sugar and began to stir.

'Great place this, isn't it?' Cecilia began. 'Are you a local?'

'I live with her.' Det indicated with her head back to the cafe entrance.

'Oh.' Cecilia was beginning to feel claustrophobic, which didn't make sense as there was plenty of air. She drained her cup and packed her book into her bag.

'Her parents are away and so I live in a bungalow.'

'Sounds … good.' Cecilia tried to smile but panic was gripping her internal organs. Had she given anything away over the days she'd been coming to the convent? Occasionally she'd taken the dark glasses off and refitted her hat. *Oh God*. 'So, just the two of you?' she asked lightly, on the point of standing up.

'Her sister, too.'

'Oh?' She couldn't help herself, she was greedy for details. 'How old is the sister?'

But the pregnant girl didn't reply. She just sighed as though she couldn't be bothered conversing anymore and they both turned to watch Perpetua rush by to collect another tray of used crockery before disappearing inside again. When Cecilia turned back the pregnant girl was still staring at her.

'I know who you are,' the girl said in a low voice. 'So don't fuck around with me.'

Stunned by the tone as much as what the girl had said, Cecilia could do nothing but sit and wait for what would come next. Her head was filled with a mass of impossible knots. *Breda had warned her. And now ... caught out! Snooping.* When she looked up again the girl's gaze had moved to Cecilia's hands, to the flat gold ring with the one small deep ruby that Peter had given her. She wore it on her middle finger of her right hand, and she'd never taken it off, except for once when she'd tried to give it back to him.

'Does she know?' Cecilia asked.

'Not yet.'

Cecilia nodded. Well, that was something. She stood up, her face hot now with embarrassment. 'I'm sorry, you must think that I'm ...' But she didn't know how to finish the sentence. She would go now before things got worse. Breda was right – if she wanted to contact her daughter, then she had to do it through the right channels and be patient.

'Why did you give her away?' the girl asked coldly.

'*What?*'

'I'm interested.' The girl pointed at her belly. 'I need to hear something apart from *This will be the happiest event of your life*,' she laughed dryly.

Cecilia nodded and sat down again.

'Well ... I'd been a nun,' she said and then immediately regretted it. *What did that have to do with anything?*

'I know that.'

'Does she know?'

The pregnant girl nodded and Cecilia laughed to hide her utter dismay.

'So, no man?'

'Not really.'

'What do you mean, *not really*?' the girl barked.

Cecilia would have got up again right there and walked off if it had been anyone else. But the girl was her daughter's friend and her sharp tone was weirdly hypnotic.

'No man I could count on,' she managed at last, wishing she smoked too so she'd have something to do. 'I'm sorry, but ... even after all this time it's very difficult to talk about.'

The girl nodded slowly.

'What about family?'

Cecilia bit her lip. 'I had a family.'

'But not close?'

Cecilia sighed and closed her eyes and wished that she could be somewhere, anywhere, else.

'I could have kept her if I'd wanted to,' she whispered. 'My family would have helped. I just couldn't ...'

'You didn't want her?'

'I ... couldn't see myself with a child.'

The strange girl nodded and looked away, and there was probably a full minute of silence between them where Cecilia felt herself teetering on the edge of some kind of emotional precipice. *Do I jump now?*

'So now you think I'm a monster?' she ventured softly, trying to keep her voice light.

'I don't think you're a monster,' the girl said coolly before taking another sip of tea. 'But *she* might.'

'Yes.'

Of course she would. Cecilia was filled with despair, coupled with a sudden need to explain herself. 'I first fell in love with him, her father, when I was still a nun, but of course nothing happened between us until I'd left.'

'Of course not,' the girl mocked.

'Please understand the whole business of falling in love with him wasn't what made me want to leave the convent. I know it will sound so ridiculous to someone your age, but I fully intended to stay a nun after meeting him.' The words sounded ridiculous even to herself, but they were true and they'd rushed out of her before she'd had time to think. 'We'd never been lovers. I would have got over it … him. '

'Oh you don't need to convince me of that!' The girl smiled for the first time. 'We excel at that kind of stuff.'

'*We?* What do you mean?' Cecilia asked weakly.

'Catholics. Sacrifice and misery and *not* having what we want.' The strange girl was chuckling now as she sipped her tea, her long dirty fingers circling the cup. 'Both of my parents were full of that shit and look where it got them!'

Cecilia sat back in stunned silence. *So what did happen to your parents?* was what she wanted to ask but didn't dare. This girl was too sharp, too blunt and too much in control for her liking.

'So you didn't get pregnant while you were a nun, but you met him then?' she asked.

'Yes.'

'I thought it was an enclosed order.'

'Yes … it was.'

'So how did you meet him?'

'I was in France. I was studying over there.'

'They sent you to *France*?'

'There was a big international Church conference.' Cecilia smiled as she remembered her own excitement just to be there.

'So who was he?' the girl said, staring her down through narrowed eyes.

'I … can't say,' Cecilia stammered. She knew she'd said way too much already.

'Whatever.' The girl shrugged.

How odd this girl was with her grimy hair and world-weary manner. She couldn't be more than early twenties. Cecilia was reminded of some of the laundry girls she'd dealt with over the years; belligerent, gutsy and tough, they had no use for niceties.

Dealing with them was often a battle and in the end, as much as she tried, it was not one she was particularly well cut out for.

'Are you still a Catholic?' Cecilia asked shyly.

'No, I'm a visual artist, which is worse.'

'Ah … what kind of stuff do you do?'

'Painting. Montage with some photo work.'

'You work here?'

'I have a studio up there.' She pointed to the west wing of the convent. 'Which reminds me that I'd better get back to it. I've got an exhibition happening in a couple of months and there is a lot of work to get done.'

Cecilia watched her stand up, collect her shoulder bag and check her pens. She was frowning as she did up her coat.

'I … I worked as a photographer for years.' Cecilia was suddenly desperate to keep this girl talking to her. 'I had an exhibition once in London.'

'Really?' The girl stopped to look at her again. 'How did it go?'

'Most of it sold,' Cecilia said proudly. 'It was such a good time in my life …' She hesitated.

'So you still working?'

'No. But I'd love to see your stuff.'

The girl's pale face suddenly tightened into a scowl. 'Do your own dirty work,' she said sharply.

'*What?*'

'Don't think for a minute you can get to her through me. I'm not going to play the go-between.'

Cecilia took a deep breath and tried to stay calm. 'I'd still like to see your work.'

'I'm on the second floor of the west wing, room 207.'

'Right.' Cecilia tried to smile.

'And let's get something else clear,' the girl continued sourly. 'As far as I'm concerned, parents who bail out on their kids and then turn up twenty years later have to cop *whatever* happens, okay?'

Cecilia nodded, numb with humiliation. 'I understand what you're saying,' she managed.

'Good.' The girl gave her a brusque nod. About to walk off with her bag over her shoulder, she stopped. 'I'm Det, by the way.'

Cecilia stood up and held out her hand. 'Cecilia. Pleased to meet you, Det.'

Peach

I forgot to shut the blind properly and a shaft of golden light in my face wakes me early. I push off the bedclothes, get up and walk across the hall to my parents' room. Their neat, empty bed sends a shiver down my spine. Dad rang last night to say that his mother is back in hospital.

I push open the doors onto their little balcony and go out and stand there, breathing in the cool early-morning air. A sharp gust of wind sends a smattering of last night's summer shower from the leaves of the big peppermint gum straight into my face. I look over at the white moon resting in folds of mauve early-morning light above the trees and think of Stella.

She has been at her new school now for a few weeks. She doesn't say a lot about it, but I know I'd be hearing about it if things were really bad.

I look down and catch sight of her in her white nightdress moving about in the garden below, mucking around with the hose. It's six-thirty on Sunday morning. Why the hell would she be up?

I resist the tempatation to spy on her, and call down, 'Hey, Stella?'

'Wondered when you'd see me,' she yells back. 'I've been up for ages. Want to go for a ride?'

'Yep.'

I pull on my jeans and runners and a T-shirt, gladness filling the empty spaces inside me.

We unlock our bikes and pull them out of the shed.

'So where to?' I ask.

'You'll see.'

Instead of turning right at Dights Falls we go straight ahead across the bridge and along a dirt path to the vast green expanse of the Yarra Bend golf course. We pass a couple of speed walkers and then another bike rider going really fast, head down and dressed in bright green lycra. After that, apart from a stray white dog, we have the track to ourselves. Stella takes the lead and once we're over a rough patch she picks up speed. I have to pedal hard to keep a few yards behind. Her broad back is encased in a long red shirt, and her black hair blowing out behind her in the wind makes her look like a pirate ship in full sail.

'Where do witches keep their magic?' she yells back at me.

'Under their toenails, of course!' I reply without hesitation.

'Do spiders go to school?'

'Of course,' I reply. This was a game we used to play when we were younger. She'd come to me with these crazy questions and I'd have to try to answer them.

'Where?'

But I am drinking in the early sunlight falling on the grass. The way it rolls away over the hills and between the trees like new carpet. I love the sharp breeze in my face. My feet push hard against the pedals and my fingers grip the handlebars tightly.

'Peach?'

'Under leaves?' I say hopefully.

'No!' she yells. 'How could you have forgotten?'

'So where?'

'In little girls' shoes at night!'

'Oh yeah, of course. How could I have forgotten that?'

She snorts with laughter. 'And what do kids do *before* they get born?'

'Play on top of the clouds.'

'Okay.'

She stops suddenly next to a huge gum, its branches splayed out against the sky like an arterial roadmap. We drop our bikes, and Stella beckons me over to the river.

'This is a special place,' she whispers.

She is right. At this time in the morning the high cliff face opposite looks ancient against the sky. Rocks jut out and recede, making a moonscape surface, full of cracks and crevices and smooth patches of oranges and rust red and yellow. At the top a tracery of black trees stand like lonely skeletons waiting for their chance to jump. All of it, the trees, the rocks and crevices, are reflected in the still brown river below.

She crouches down as near as she is able to the river and dips her hand in dreamily.

'I come here sometimes,' she says as though reading my mind.

'When I'm at work?'

She nods and my gladness intensifies. We sit together, the morning sun on our backs, and when I catch a whiff of her hair I feel giddy with hope.

'Cecilia would have seen this.'

'They weren't allowed out,' I say quickly.

'By the seventies they were,' she counters. 'Groups of them sometimes went for walks along the river.'

'How do you know?'

'I've been reading about them. I know all kinds of stuff.'

I look at her bent head, and her plump hand drawing in the dirt with a stick, knowing she is dying to tell me more. But I can't bring myself to ask what else she knows. I stand up and throw a stone into the water, trying to imagine a group of nuns walking along the path. The soft plopping sound of the stone is full and final in the silence. Already the cliff face opposite us is changing as the sun rises higher in the sky.

'Have to get going,' I say. 'Work.'

We ride back along the beautiful river track. At Hoddle Street we stand together waiting for the lights to change.

'Do you think that one soul is worth the whole world?' Stella asks seriously.

What a stupid question, I am about to say. *What does it even mean?* But I close my mouth and search around my brain for the answer I know she wants. 'Yes,' I manage to say firmly, 'definitely.'

She turns around and gives me one of her dazzling smiles, making me feel as if I've just passed a very difficult exam.

The lights change and we cross the road together.

Cecilia 1970

'Sister, may I please be excused?'

Cecilia turned around and sighed. It was Margaret Hurley again, the poor, skinny, snivelling little thing. She'd come to them at fifteen, was twenty-three now and still looked about twelve. She had some kind of trouble with her periods that had her running to the lavatory all day for the best part of two weeks of every month. Only the night before Cecilia had suggested to Mother Bernard that the girl be shifted to the sorting room because she wasn't strong enough for the mangle, and neither of them wanted a replay of the fainting scene of earlier in the year.

But Mother seemed to have forgotten that drama. She told Cecilia firmly that the sorting room was full to bursting and that the girl couldn't be trusted to keep the baskets from the different hotels separate, and that if she really couldn't manage then she could be given a try in the ironing room.

'Yes, Mother.'

Why Mother Bernard had been put in charge of the laundry was a mystery to everyone. She hadn't the first idea how to deal with troublesome girls.

It was summer, and sometimes the temperature in the ironing room got to forty degrees. Poor little dithering Margaret wouldn't have the concentration to stand at an ironing board for eight hours a day.

'Are you still taking the iron tablets, Margaret?' Cecilia asked cautiously, knowing that any such question was likely to bring on a barrage of information from the girl about the blood clots that were the size of plums, and cramps that felt like 'claws in her belly'.

'Yes, Sister.'

'And?'

'Same, Sister,' she said, eyes swivelling this way and that. 'Got to go now or there will be a … flood.'

Oh, if only you could look whoever you're speaking to in the face, girl! Your life would become so much easier. 'Yes, of course, dear. Off you go then.'

The girl reminded Cecilia of a badly treated dog they'd had at home on the farm. Old Gunner would cringe and crawl on his belly as soon as her father came anywhere near. It always upset her to see it, further proof that her father was a bully.

The Angelus bell went for lunch, and the noise of the machines gradually died away as the girls slipped off their aprons and knelt down where they were, in front of the machines. Cecilia sighed her relief as she began the prayer. There would be lunch and an hour-long break from the noise.

There were four big ships in dock, and along with their usual hotels there was a lot of work on. The laundry had been operating since eight-thirty that morning. The girls had been working in the heat for a four-hour stretch with only a fifteen-minute mid-morning break. They all looked exhausted, with slumped shoulders and sweat patches under the arms of their dresses.

'No chatter, please, until you're outside,' Cecilia said sharply.

There was a sudden scream from the back of the room. She craned forward to see what was happening. Josie Dalton, of course, making trouble for someone. Cecilia walked towards the lumpy, tiresome girl, trying to hide her distaste. She had light, pink-rimmed, protruding eyes, a small mean mouth, and her hair hung like damp straw about her face.

'What is it, dear?'

'She took my comb, Mother!' Leanne Harris whined, another misfit who always managed to wheedle some sympathy from somewhere.

'You are not meant to bring combs into the laundry, Leanne.'

'I know, Sister, but … I forgot.'

'Please try to act your age!' Cecilia was unable to hide the exasperation in her voice. 'You are both over sixteen and you behave like primary school girls!'

'But we get treated like children, Mother,' some cheeky voice muttered behind her. The comment was followed by a ripple of agreement, but Cecilia didn't turn around. It was too hot and she needed to be gone. Anyway, it was the truth. Half of them were over twenty and they had no personal autonomy at all.

'But I want my comb back!' the girl wailed.

Josie threw the comb hard at the window and then let out a shout of nasty laughter.

A sudden flare of rage suffused Cecilia. She imagined grabbing that great lump of a girl by the back of the neck with both hands and drowning her in the nearby sink of dirty, soapy water.

'Pick that up, Josie!' she hissed. 'At once!'

'But, Mother!' The girl was enjoying herself now. 'She said I was a *fat bitch*!'

The rest of the room stilled. Swearing in front of a nun was defiance on another level altogether.

'I will not have that language in here!' Cecilia sounded rattled even to herself and that wouldn't do. Unlike Margaret, Josie was clever in her own sly way, with an unpleasant cruel streak that made her unpopular with just about everyone.

'Josie,' she lowered her voice to an ominous whisper, 'do you want to stay in here over lunch?'

Josie smirked. She could tell Cecilia's heart wasn't in the threat. 'Not really,' the girl shrugged.

'I beg your pardon!'

'Not really, *Mother*,' Josie sighed insolently, and began to tap a rhythm with her feet, as though she was bored. There were titters of laughter from the other girls.

'Not really?' Cecilia repeated warningly.

'No, Mother.'

'Then pick up the comb, please, and give it back.'

Josie looked around and saw that all the other girls were tired of her antics. She lumbered over to the window, picked up the comb.

'Here.' She smirked as she handed it over.

'Thank you, Josie,' Cecilia said.

'That's okay, Mother,' the girl replied.

This too is one of God's precious creatures! Cecilia reminded herself. *And yet ... I loathe her. I loathe her and this terrible laundry and the fact I have to be here and ...*

The patches of sweat under the girl's heavy arms had fanned out onto her back and chest and Cecilia's heart softened even as she shuddered in revulsion. 'Please go and change your dress before lunch, Josie.'

'Haven't got another one, Mother,' the girl sang as though it was a big joke.

If it had been any other day, Cecilia would have let the others go and tried to talk to her. Her insolence was getting worse. Something must be happening with that wayward father who brought a new woman with him every time he came to visit. But after lunch was the meeting with Mother Mary of the Archangels, and she didn't have time.

'Then go to Mother Bridget and say I sent you for a clean dress from the spare linen closet.'

'Nothing there will fit me, Mother!'

'She'll find you something, Josie.' Cecilia clapped her hands. 'All right, girls! Is everyone ready?'

'Yes, Mother,' they all chorused.

Cecilia peered into the centre of the room at two girls who were having a heated discussion under their breaths. Sandra and Janice were a little older than the rest of the group and had to be watched. The small, dark-haired Sandra slipped an envelope into the front pocket of Janice's pinny.

'When you're ready,' Cecilia said icily.

They both looked up when they realised that everyone was waiting for them. Sandra went red with fright.

'Sorry, Mother,' they said in unison.

Cecilia made no comment. 'In the name of the Father and of the Son and of the Holy Ghost...'

At the end of the prayer Cecilia told the girls that they could all go except for Sandra and Janice. They came over reluctantly, eyes downcast.

'Thank you, Janice.' She held out her hand for the envelope.

'But, Mother, I—'

'I'll have it, thank you. Then you can go.'

With a sigh of relief Cecilia locked the door behind them.

The next day she was searching for a hanky when she saw Sandra's letter, fallen behind the pile of singlets and petticoats. She'd dumped it there and forgotten it. The Rule demanded that she give it immediately to Mother Bernard, but a perverse sense of justice made her open it.

Breda had gone and so too Jane and Monica. She was unsure now ... about the Rule, about everything.

Ricky,

You gotta help me get out of here. It is way worse than jail, I swear! I wish I was in a proper jail; they'd leave you alone sometimes there. Everything about this place is hell. We get up at six, go to boring church, eat some shit and then work in this hot steamy laundry from half-past eight until five. One hour off for lunch. The bloody crows are on our backs the whole fuckin time! We're unpaid slaves

*and that is the truth of it. If we're not working, we're on our knees.
Mass every day. Rosary after work and prayers before everything
we do! No let up. 'Yes, Sister! No, Sister!' Every day! It never
ends. Working and praying! That's it. If I can't get out of here
soon, then I'm going to do myself in. I mean it. I'll neck myself or
I'll jump from the roof, so help me. You gotta help me!*

*The old one in charge hates me. So what? I hate her too. The
ugly old cow! All their bullshit prayers and boring singing. It's so
creepy some of that stuff that I actually feel sick half the time. I
can't stop thinking about how I'd like to get into the Church at
night and chuck stuff everywhere. I'd like to spit and piss on the
altar and smash everything. Seriously. Get those gold candlesticks
and shove them through a window. And the only thing stopping
me is that if I get caught they'll make it even worse.*

*Why should I love God? He hates me. Why else would he
have taken my mum when I was only four? And make my dad a
dirty old geezer? Answer me that!*

*Am I still your Princess, Ricko? If I am then stick by me, please.
Help me get out of here. I got a plan. (Read this next part carefully.)*

*On the 23rd of this month I'm going to try to cut loose. Some
of these morons are putting on a play. The costumes and sets are
kept down under the stage. They leave the windows open down
there. Everyone will be in there watching the play. At interval I'm
going to get in there, and climb through the window, run down
to the river and swim across. You gotta be waiting for me on the
other side. Please Ricky. If it's the last thing you do. Don't forget
me. The 23rd of this month is opening night. Interval will be
around nine o'clock.*

Love and a million kisses to you,
Sandra (Sandy, to you)

Cecilia put the letter back in her pocket. She would give the
letter to Mother Bernard at second sitting. The boy, whoever he
was, would have to be chased up, threatened with the police if

he so much as showed his face. And the girl would have to be hauled up too. How old was she? Seventeen or eighteen? Cecilia couldn't remember her family background except that the father did sometimes turn up to see the girl and there was something shifty about him. Did he really abuse his daughter? She shuddered. Impossible to believe, and yet some of them had been forced into sex with uncles and stepfathers and brothers if the whispers and the innuendos were to be believed. But when she'd spoken of her fears about the whole murky world that many of these girls had come from to Mother Bernard, she'd been told that it was preposterous, that the girls exaggerated and shouldn't be believed. Sisters should refrain from listening to such talk; it only encouraged the girls' wild imaginings. At the door, Cecilia stopped and pulled the letter out again. Then, hardly knowing what she was doing, she ripped it up into little pieces. No, she would not give it to Mother Bernard. The girl was right, the woman was an old cow!

Oh God, what is happening to me that I can think that?

'Well, that didn't take you long.' Det was in bare feet and wearing a paint-splattered man's shirt, which almost but not quite hid her pregnant belly.

'Am I interrupting?'

'Come in.'

Cecilia walked into the room and stopped. She gasped as she looked around at the dozen or so paintings, big and small, lining the walls. She forgot to be nervous, forgot, too, about her previous connection to the room. 'Are these all *yours?* I mean, you did them?' she added stupidly.

'To the best of my knowledge,' Det said.

'God, they're so strong, Det! And ... beautiful.'

'They hold up okay?'

'They certainly do.'

The smaller canvases were hung in a line around the room at

about eye level, with the bigger canvases above them. The images were of rivers and lakes, children, people, trees and foliage. All of the paintings, even the smaller playful ones, were painted in oils, the layered colours giving each surface a rich glow of hidden light. But there was a dark side to every image as well, a wild, urgent strain running through the highly realistic pools of flat water, the night skies, the rampantly growing succulents and the blank faces on the people. Each one had a kind of weird underhand humour that was not immediately obvious. Small monsters lay in wait under bushes, ladders ran out of windows to nowhere and teenage girls preened in front of mirrors with their hair on fire. The paintings spoke of the quirkiness of life, the caprice and mystery lurking under the everyday. Cecilia was awestruck.

She particularly loved a series of four small paintings hanging side by side, with the same figure in each, a thin lone ghost of a man who was either smoking or just standing by himself in a surreal landscape. In one he was in the middle of the red outback with only one tired acacia tree to keep him company. In another he was surrounded by a crowd of city shoppers, all busy and harried-looking. He stood by himself at the edge of the painting, his face averted, staring down at a photo of a little child. In the next he had assumed an ominous sneering presence under a blistering sky with a collection of cans crushed at his feet. Cecilia could almost smell the beer in that one, the lush rainforest and river in another, the searing heat in a third.

'They belong together,' she muttered, 'in spite of being so different. That man holds them together.'

'Yes.'

'I hope you can sell them like that.'

'I doubt it.'

'Who is he?'

'Him? My father. Dead now.'

'Oh.' Cecilia moved around the room to look at each painting. 'They are going to look so brilliant hung properly,' she said softly.

'Hmmmm.' Det was screwing on the paint tube tops. 'Yeah, I'm looking forward to that.'

'When's the exhibition?'

'Six weeks.'

'You excited?' She turned around and saw that Det was sitting in a chair with her feet up on the little desk, scrutinising her dispassionately.

'The work is wonderful, Det,' she said.

'Thanks.' The girl shrugged.

'So April exhibition?'

'End of March it opens.'

'The baby?'

'About the same time.' Det looked at her and they both laughed.

'Well, with a bit of luck . . .'

'Yeah.' Det got up, went to the kettle and switched it on. 'With a bit of luck it won't come while I'm handing out the champagne on opening night. Tea?'

'Thanks.' Cecilia sat down in the funny worn old armchair in the corner. 'Do you have help with the organisation and publicity?'

'Yep. Cassie. She's in charge.'

'A friend?'

'Yeah. Cassie, Peach and me are best mates.'

'Oh.' Cecilia smiled weakly. Mention of her daughter had brought all her nerves back.

Det brought her over the tea.

'Are you normally a coffee drinker?' Cecilia asked, politely taking the mug.

'Yeah . . . and a heavy smoker and a junk-food addict.' Det grinned. 'And an intermittent drug taker.'

'You smoke much now?'

Det hunched her shoulders and sighed. 'I've got it down to three a day,' she said, 'never more than that now. It's . . . it's the best I can do.'

'What does the doctor say?'

276

'They say everything looks fine, but … I dunno.' Det sat down at the desk and closed her eyes.

Cecilia took another look around at the extraordinary work. 'Do you have a partner, Det? To help with the baby, I mean?'

'No.' The girl shook her head and doodled on her notepad.

'Does he know about the baby?'

'No.'

'I see.'

Cecilia was overwhelmed with a sense of the girl's vulnerability. She wanted to wrap her arms around her, to shield her in some way. 'So you'll go on living in the bungalow?'

'I have my name down for public housing.'

'Have you got someone to take you to hospital?'

'I'll get myself to hospital.'

'But what about someone to be there … during?'

'I want to be alone.'

They were quiet for a moment, staring at each other over the table.

'Did you have someone?' Det asked.

'No.' Cecilia shook her head. 'But that was a long time ago and I wouldn't recommend it.'

'I want to be alone,' Det said again.

'What about your friends?' Cecilia said softly.

'Cassie thinks I'm crazy, and Peach … your daughter … well, I don't want to put her through it.'

'Why is that?' Cecilia gulped.

Det shrugged and took a long sip of tea and stared out the window. Then she suddenly smiled and put both hands on her stomach. 'I'm growing quite fond of the little critter, to tell you the truth, but that doesn't necessarily mean the whole thing is … viable.'

Cecilia nodded.

'I don't need a whole lot of other people there telling me how fantastic it is and how beautiful and all the rest of it. I want to see for myself and then … decide.'

'I understand what you mean.'

'Yep. I guess you do.' Det got up. 'I guess you do.'

'But it is a mistake to think that—'

'Sorry to cut you off, Cecilia, but if you've finished your tea. I have to keep working.'

She was being dismissed just when things were getting interesting. Cecilia stumbled to her feet.

'Are you going to contact your daughter?' Det asked bluntly when they got to the door.

'I want to,' Cecilia said. 'Do you think it's a good idea?'

Det made no reaction as she pulled the door open. Cecilia waited in the doorway.

'You should know that *this*,' Det pointed at her belly, 'is confronting for her.'

'Confronting?'

'She's shoved the whole thing of being adopted away for most of her life, but now she's having to think about it. Me having this baby has made it real for her.'

'Are you thinking of…' Cecilia began and then thought better of it. 'Thanks for showing me your work.'

'Pleasure. But listen, don't come here again,' Det said grimly. 'Peach is my best friend. I don't want to go behind her back.'

Cecilia nodded and bit her lip as a hot wave of humiliation coursed through her chest and up to her face and neck.

'Of course,' she managed, before turning to go. 'I'm sorry.'

She stumbled down the corridor towards the stairs, already half blinded by tears. What had possessed her to think that she'd set up a friendship with her daughter's best friend? She must be out of her mind.

What have I done?

It was the same panic that had beset her that first night in the convent when she felt her shorn head.

And that last night in Paris.

What have I done?

Peach

'Hey, stranger, can I come in?'

I'm up early for my Saturday double shift, so when I hear the shower going in the bungalow I decide to pay Det a visit. We haven't seen each other properly for ages. She's working hard towards her exhibition and often stays overnight in her studio.

'Yeah, of course.'

I walk in and look around. Nothing has changed since the day she moved in. Everything is neat and in its place. Det comes out of the shower cubicle with one towel around her head and another big one around her body. The bulge is huge now. It juts out as round as a ball because the rest of her is still so thin.

And it hits me hard. I can feel tears starting in my eyes.

'I'm sorry, Peach,' Det says quietly.

'For what?'

She pulls on a singlet and then one of her outsized shirts over the cheap maternity jeans she bought from Target. Her back is as thin and white as ever.

'For what?' I say again.

'For being here.'

'Det,' I say too loudly, 'you're my best friend. I'm glad you're here!'

Her body becomes still, but she doesn't turn around to face me.

'And if it weren't for you, I'd have to deal with Stella on my own.'

She turns around then and we both laugh a bit. 'You have your own stuff,' she says. 'I can see that.'

'I know—'

'And my being pregnant sort of makes it worse.'

'No ... no,' I say bravely, 'it doesn't. Det, you are my best friend.'

'I know that.'

But she's not dumb. There's no point lying. It's true that her being pregnant is somehow making all the stuff about my birth mother harder to deal with.

'It's just that I can't stop thinking about her,' I admit carefully. 'It's driving me nuts. All the time working at the convent I'm thinking about her. What will I say if I ever meet her?'

'You could always try *hello,*' Det says, and goes on buttoning up her shirt.

'Hello,' I repeat softly. '*Hello.*'

'You could also try contacting her through the adoption agency. She's probably nice enough, Peach.'

'How could it be fucking *nice* to give your own kid away?'

Det stops what she is doing and looks straight at me. 'Easy,' she says.

'How do you mean?'

'It would be easy ... not to want a baby.'

The words bounce against my skull like little stones. 'But I thought ...'

'Yeah, well ... you thought wrong,' she says.

'So ... what?' I have no idea how to formulate the question I want to ask. Anyway, there is no point asking Det anything. If she's got anything to say she'll say it.

'Even if you want it, it's about whether you can do it or not.'

'*Do* it?'

'Yeah.'

I look at Det, but she is still staring out the window.

She must be thinking about giving her child away. The thought makes me go cold.

'But you've got us,' I whisper. 'You can stay here. It's all set up for you.'

'I know that, but ...'

'But what?'

'I reckon you've got to be cut out for it.'

I open my mouth to speak but close it again. I have this weird feeling that I'm not living in the present at all anymore. The past is rolling in like a tsunami, and pulling me along with it.

Ellen

Ellen woke to the sound of the magpies on her lawn and smiled to herself. The best sound! She'd always loved it. But why was Kev taking so long with the tea? They'd had a bit of rain overnight. Maybe the wood had got wet. Every morning after lighting the fire he brought her a cuppa on a saucer, just as she liked it, not weak but not too strong either, with a few grains of sugar and a half-piece of toast and vegemite on the side. The clock on her bedside table struck seven and she remembered with a start that Kev had been dead for more than a decade.

The girl had written again and asked a whole lot of new questions. Ellen felt tired even thinking about them. It was natural enough that she wanted to know about her mother as a little girl, but she didn't seem to understand how mixed up things could get. Of course some events stood out very clearly, but others were so hazy as to be almost unreal. Whole years collapsed into thin streaks of time, like eels in a bucket, too slippery to catch. Still, she would try. She'd do her best. As soon as she was up and dressed she'd sit down to write. It was best not to plan these letters, best by far to let the pen fly along on its own.

Ellen pushed off the bedclothes and with both her feet down on the cold floor she reached for her dressing-gown and began the slow process of dressing. Out on the kitchen table the biro and writing pad waited.

1945

After two weeks of hospital rest she was brought into the four-bed labour ward at three a.m. She was relieved to see there was only one other bed occupied. She hoped to deliver quickly and be back in the ward before they brought anyone else in. Having a baby was hard enough without listening to another poor woman's shrieks and groans. The only privacy was drawn curtains around the bed.

She put on the white robe and let the young nurse help her onto the bed, then lay there passively as the gloved hands began to wash her belly and private parts in preparation for shaving. She closed her eyes and began to pray the rosary under her breath. With Our Lady's help it would be well and truly over before the morning and she'd be able to go back to the ward and sleep to regain her strength. She worried about leaving the boys alone for too long.

'So what number is this?' the nurse chirped as she swabbed her belly.

'Seven,' Ellen groaned through another contraction.

'You'll have a football team soon,' the girl giggled. 'So who is looking after the others?'

Ellen felt like slapping her. *What business is it of yours?* 'The youngest two have gone to their grandmother.'

'Oh, that's nice. Your mum?'

'No.'

'She good with them?'

'No.'

Ellen gasped as the contraction hit its peak, and tried not to think of poor little three-year-old Michael and baby Brendan with Kevin's mother, Eileen. How was that hard-faced, nervy old bat going to cope with two babies? Even Kev hadn't liked the idea but... there was no one else. It was a busy time of the year with everyone doing their shearing. The four older boys would be all right at home as long as they did their father's bidding and kept out of his way.

'So... your mum couldn't do it?'

'No.'

'Pity.'

'Yes.'

'You're a friend of Sister Patrice,' the chatty little nurse said, drying her hands on the towel.

'Yes.'

'She told me to tell you she'd be coming by soon.'

Ellen closed her eyes. Sister Patrice had been the nun in charge of the maternity section of the hospital since Ellen had come in to have her first child thirteen years before. *Hail, Holy Queen, Mother of mercy! Hail, our life, our sweetness and our hope!*

The pains were coming fast now, but it was bearable. She'd managed the last three labours well enough. They'd all come in under three hours and with luck this one would be the same.

'So where do you know Sister Patrice from?'

'Her sister taught me at the Abbotsford Convent.'

'A nun too?'

'Yes.'

Ellen gasped and grabbed the edge of the steel bed to ride out the wave of pain as it came straight for her, wishing the nurse would finish her business and leave.

'What did she teach?'

'Music... piano.'

The grunts and groans from the young woman opposite suddenly changed to sharp yelps of terror and she began to cry out.

'Do you play?' the girl said, surprised.

'I did. Yes.'

'Oh, I need help, nurse. Sister! I need help,' the young voice opposite screamed, 'or I'll die!'

'You won't die,' the little nurse called back heartlessly, 'you're doing fine.'

'But I'm not! I'm … this is … terrible … I can't … bear this!' The girl began to sob through her loud shrieks. 'Please … oh please.'

'First-timer,' the young nurse explained to Ellen.

'Give her something,' Ellen snapped.

'I'll have to ask the Sister-in-charge.'

'Then ask her!'

The girl sounded so young. Ellen was filled with pity. She sounded like a rabbit caught in one of those terrible steel traps that Kev laid all around the creek beds, except magnified a hundred times. Ellen could well remember her own first time. The total shock of it. Left in agony for hours on her own with no one to utter a comforting word and then, when the waters broke, they'd all descended like crows. It was horrible, lying there being poked and prodded as her body split apart. Even the second and third births were hell. But after that it had become much easier. It was as if her body had become accustomed to the whole business. She wished she could hold the poor girl's hand and give her some comfort.

'She'll forget as soon as she's got the baby,' the young nurse said airily. 'They all do.'

You wait, Ellen thought darkly. *You just wait!*

'So how are we going here, Ellen?' The curtains parted and Sister Patrice poked her head in and smiled.

The young nurse stood back as the senior woman stepped into the sheeted enclosure. Sister Patrice was as neat as a pin in her starched white wimple and robes, the big black rosary and crucifix stuck into the waist of her leather belt. 'Thank you, nurse,' she said curtly, waving her away, 'I'll see to Mrs Madden now.'

'Yes, Sister,' the girl said meekly and disappeared.

The nun lifted the sheet, put one cool hand on Ellen's belly, then parted her knees and very matter-of-factly took a look.

'Shouldn't be too long now.' She smiled, and Ellen was reminded of Sister Seraphina. Such sweet faces on both of them.

The woman opposite began to scream again.

'Help me. Oh, please help me!'

'Hush, dear!' Sister Patrice called out in a firm voice. 'Don't upset yourself now.'

'Can't she have some help?' Ellen asked.

'I'll go see to her in a minute.' The nun frowned as she wrapped the pressure band around Ellen's upper arm. 'These girls get themselves into trouble and think it's all going to be easy.' She shook her head disapprovingly.

Ellen knew this was code for saying that the girl wasn't married.

'Will she give the baby away?' she whispered.

The nun nodded, still frowning.

'I suppose it's for the best,' Ellen sighed.

'Of course.' Sister Patrice took off the blood pressure band. 'She'll be right as rain. A few months and she'll have forgotten all about it.'

The girl gave another long, terrified scream.

'I'll be right with you, dear,' Sister Patrice called again, 'just as soon as I've finished here.'

She put both her cool, capable hands on Ellen's raging belly.

'You've got another strong little fellow in here, Ellen,' she smiled. 'That's my bet.'

Ellen nodded wearily.

'It won't be long now,' Sister Patrice said kindly. 'This will be over before you know it.'

Until next time! Ellen suddenly wanted to scream, not with pain but with ... she didn't know, sorrow maybe. She was thirty-six years old but already so *old*. There had been four miscarriages in the years she hadn't produced a child. The change of life came around forty-five or fifty. That gave her time to have another six or seven children. A loud, bleak sob broke from her before she had a chance to pull it back.

'What is it, Ellen?' the nun said softly. 'Is something worrying you?'

Ellen grimaced as a sudden tight spasm wrapped itself around her groin like a huge squeezing snake. Did this woman have any idea? Did any of them have any idea about... *anything?*

'How will I cope?' she muttered hoarsely.

'You always cope,' the nun said encouragingly. 'You do a wonderful job.'

'Seven children!'

'Seven precious little souls and a good husband. You've said yourself that Kevin is a wonderful provider. He's not a drinker or a gambler. There is plenty of food on the table for those boys ... and he's keen for them to do well in life.'

'Have you any idea of how much work it is?' Ellen shouted. 'The washing alone is a full-time job! Then there is the feeding of them and the ... house and ...'

'You wanted a family,' the nun reminded her gently.

It was true. Ellen had wanted a family above all. At the convent as a little girl she'd sometimes take some stones from the garden and make herself a circle and sit inside and pretend it was her own house, the stones her children. She'd never known what other people meant when they said they went home to family and loved ones. The convent had been her only home and she'd left there with a deep longing to have her own home and family.

And until this last pregnancy, she'd had all the energy in the world for what she'd chosen. As hard and disappointing as it so often was, with God's help, most days she could do it with a loving heart. The children were what mattered. She loved them unequivocally. Those six boys were her own flesh and blood. She knew that she would die without hesitation for each and every one of them if she had to, without a second thought.

For years she'd been able to steer Kev's bad temper away from the two older boys and stop a lot of beatings, as well as give the kids a semblance of happiness with her storytelling and songs. Once the older ones were at school she'd get the littlies up on the horse in the afternoon and take them down to play in the creek.

But this time, as the pregnancy went on she had to close her ears to the sharpness of his tone when he ordered them around and nagged them ceaselessly. There was no knowing when it would happen or for what reason, only that when it burst into life it was important to get out of his way – and more importantly, get those kids out of his way too. She was the only thing between them and his foul temper and heavy hands and it grieved her terribly not to have the physical energy to defend them properly.

'Marriage is hard, Sister,' she whispered. It was as much as she could say, but oh she needed to say it and this nun was safe. It didn't do to blather to anyone else about it.

'It's been ever thus,' the nun smiled down at her, 'but remember that God is with you always, Ellen. No burden is so great that God will not share it with you.'

Suddenly and without warning that didn't seem enough any more. Ellen's life rolled out in front of her like a dry, rutted track leading nowhere. Where was the lightness? Where was the joy? Desperation welled up in her like vomit. *Oh dearest God! Oh Blessed Virgin Mary, help me!* She reached for the nun's hand.

'Pray I'm not here again next year.' She kept her voice as low as she could because she knew what she was asking was a terrible sin. 'God will listen to you!'

'Ellen!' The nun was genuinely shocked. 'I can't pray for *that*! God has a plan for each and every one of us. We all must accept the burdens that we are given.'

'But it is too hard,' Ellen gasped. 'It is just too … hard.'

'It just seems that way sometimes, dear!'

'No … it is … too hard.'

'I will pray for you,' the nun said gently, 'and I'll ask all the other sisters to keep you in their prayers too.'

'No more children …' Ellen groaned, closing her eyes. 'Please pray I have no more children.'

'Now, come on, Ellen,' the nun said sternly, 'you don't know what you're saying. Concentrate on what you're doing here now. Remember Our Blessed Lord never sends us a burden that we can't carry. And you know better than I do that a dear little child is not burden but a blessing. There is always a way.'

Ellen turned her face to the wall and began to sob quietly to herself. The labour pains were strong, but they weren't registering. The *core* of her wasn't even present. The pains simply went on without her.

'Pray, Ellen,' the nun whispered kindly.

'For what?' She grabbed hold of the cool, small, soft hand with her own rough one. 'What do I pray for?'

'For grace, dear,' Sister Patrice said softly, 'to accept the things we cannot change.'

Ellen let the tears run down her cheeks. She thought of Dominic, the eldest and her darling, and consequently the one Kev picked on most. His lively young face pulled so often into a frown now, his shoulders getting more hunched every day. He was becoming a little old man before he'd even begun to grow up. Oh … she knew she had to hang on for him!

Ellen gasped as a flood of water streamed out of her.

'It's coming! The waters have broken.'

'Good,' Sister Patrice said calmly, 'I'll call Doctor.' She squeezed Ellen's hand. 'And we'll have a lovely new babe here before too long.'

Oh this was the worst part! The pain didn't let up at all. And that poor girl still screaming and groaning opposite. Ellen could hear Patrice's soothing voice over there helping her use the gas. *Breathe deeply now, dear. That's right.*

Think of something else! Something good and nice! Feast days in the big hall back at the convent. The special food; how they loved the lollies and cordial. She'd won the elocution prize three years in a row and still had two of the little gold medallions with her name inscribed on the back. How proud she'd felt heading up in front of all the girls and the nuns. There were so many feast days and concerts and special Masses and so much beautiful music to look back on.

She hardly ever even heard music anymore, much less played any, and the worst thing was that she was so busy that she barely missed it. But sometimes, after feeding a baby in the dead of night or in those precious few minutes with her morning cuppa, she'd become aware of the empty space inside herself, a space that used to be filled with notes, rhythm and songs.

By the time Sister Patrice was back with the doctor the second stage was over and Ellen had the familiar urge to push. Relief set in. It was downhill from here. The waves of pain and the need to push out the child became one and she felt well able to do it. She imagined herself in a ship on the ocean, roiling about in stormy seas. How frightening it would be and yet she wished she were there on that ship and not where she was, on her back with her legs up in stirrups.

'Only a few more and we'll be finished,' the doctor murmured, one cool hand on her stomach.

We'll be finished? An intense stab of hatred for him and for all men filled her. There she was naked from the waist down, grunting like a farm animal, her body bursting with all she had to expel, blood, muck, water and a child. There was no dignity in it. None whatsoever. Why hadn't someone told her? If she'd known she would have become a nun herself. She longed suddenly to be the one standing coolly by watching someone else suffer!

'I think we have another big one here, Mrs Madden!'

Ellen was suddenly too exhausted to care. The next urge came and she simply lay back and looked at the three of them, the doctor, the nun and the nurse, standing by waiting for her.

'Ellen?'

'I'm too tired,' she whispered.

'Come on now, Mrs Madden,' the doctor said sternly. 'This is the easy bit now.'

'So why don't you do it,' Ellen yelled, 'if it's so bloody easy?'

'Ellen.' Sister Patrice was leaning low, whispering into her ear. 'Come on now, dear. This little one is ready to be born.'

'But I don't *want* another baby!' Ellen shouted. 'I don't! I can hardly deal with the poor mites that I have already!'

'Come on now, dear,' Sister said soothingly. 'One push now.'

But how could she tell them how afraid she was of going back to the farm, of being lost there, smothered under the blanket of work. No friends. No time. No music. Of being subject to Kevin's sour tempers and hot needs. No rest. No rest even in bed! To the waves of terrible exhaustion that had her going to bed each night wishing she wouldn't wake up.

'Ellen! Concentrate!' the nun said severely, taking her hand.

'I don't want to!'

'But you must!'

Ellen sighed and gathered up her energy and pushed with all her might.

'Yes yes yes.' The nurse bent down and smiled into her face. 'It's crowned now. Good girl. Good girl! You're doing well. Just one or two more.'

'But I can't.'

'You can! You must!'

And she did. She pushed the little body out into the hands of the doctor. All she saw was the top of the bloodied head before she fell back and closed her eyes.

'There you are!' the nun chortled, putting a hand on her shoulder. 'See, you did it.'

'Yes indeed,' the doctor mumbled approvingly, 'and a good weight too.'

Leave me alone.

Then she heard a shrill, hard, newborn baby's cry. It was hers, she supposed, but she still didn't open her eyes. *Let someone else deal with it.* They were whispering together, cooing over the baby, but Ellen didn't really care. It was over. She vaguely knew she should be thanking God for the healthy child, but all she could feel was a profound and bitter relief. It was over ... *over, over, over.*

Until next time.

'Aren't you going to look at your baby?' Sister Patrice asked gently.

Ellen shook her head. Someone else came in and there were whispers and the clink of instruments on steel dishes. She supposed they were cutting and tying the cord. She felt the doctor's hands on her stomach again and felt him push down firmly and then there were a couple of tugs as the afterbirth was pulled from her.

'Mrs Madden?'

'What?' Ellen moaned.

'Ellen, dear.'

'Leave me be, please.'

'Ellen, there is a surprise for you,' Sister said. 'Come on now, dear. Open your eyes.'

It was the word *surprise* that did it. Slowly, slowly she opened her eyes. The nun was holding the baby right up next to her. Its little face had been washed of the blood and gunk and she could see the jaw working, the eyes tight shut and one tiny hand poking out of the blanket.

'See.' Sister Patrice opened up the little flannelette blanket, and Ellen's mouth fell open. 'See!' Sister Patrice laughed. But Ellen didn't laugh. She sat up a little on the pillows and simply stared at the child.

'You have a girl,' the nun whispered softly. 'A lovely healthy little girl.'

'But is it ... Is she mine?' Ellen croaked. She thought they might be playing some kind of trick on her. Either that or maybe she was dreaming.

But the nun and the doctor were both smiling. 'Yes,' they said in unison.

'Mine?'

Ellen saw the tears in the nun's eyes and it touched her. This old woman had told her once that although she'd presided over hundreds of births she always considered it a privilege and a joy.

'Your first girl, Ellen,' Sister Patrice said joyfully.

'Oh!' Ellen held out her arms for the baby.

'What will you call her?'

But Ellen couldn't speak.

A girl! The child's eyes were closed tight and her little fist clutched the blanket. She held the baby close, noting the hair and the prettiness of her features and wishing suddenly that all her boys, especially Dominic, were there to see their new sister. Ah well, they'd see her soon enough. She'd be home soon enough.

Could there be any better place than resting in a quiet ward of new mothers? Could there be a better feeling than being put into a bed that someone else had made with clean, fresh sheets? Could there be anything more welcome than that first cup of hot, sweet tea?

Ellen sipped her tea and returned the smile of the woman in the bed alongside hers.

'What did you have?' the woman asked.

'A girl. A girl after six boys.'

The woman laughed. 'Well done!'

Ellen lay and watched the light change through the three long windows at the end of the ward. And when the nurse brought the baby back for nursing, she felt a fresh spurt of joy as she held out her arms for the pink-blanketed bundle.

It was while she sat there with the babe in her arms that the music began to play. She looked around. Where was it coming from? Oh, but Ellen knew this music so well. It was Bach's *St Matthew Passion* and she hadn't heard it in years. The woman in the bed next to her had a little radio.

'Not bothering you?' she asked.

'Oh no no.' Ellen smiled. 'No, not at all.'

Just at that moment the child's eyes opened and Ellen laughed with delight. The little girl had lovely blue eyes like her brothers, and she seemed to be listening to the music too.

Ellen closed her eyes and tried to conjure up the mother she'd never known. She imagined her coming in through the door of the ward to see her granddaughter. How would they greet each other? What would they say?

Oh, St Cecilia, she prayed, *patron saint of music, let goodness flow through this little girl like the sweetest song! Let her voice rise up to the heavens every single day! Keep her away from men and marriage and babies and manual work. Take her into a life of holiness with you and all the other saints.*

When Sister Patrice dropped by later that night with a pair of booties knitted by one of the old nuns, she found Ellen lying quite still staring into space.

'So do we have a name yet?' the nun asked.

'Cecilia,' Ellen said with a tired smile.

The nun nodded approvingly. 'Let's hope she will sing.'

Ellen put the biro down. Even if that granddaughter of hers never found out about the circumstances of her own birth, at least she'd know how much her own mother was wanted that first day on earth.

Cecilia 1972

It was her last night in Paris, and they walked back to the convent together along a winding narrow street. People stood respectfully aside for them to pass. After all, she was a nun in the full habit and he was a priest and they were in one of the most Catholic countries in the world.

Cecilia was very aware of being alive, of walking through that soft dark evening in the most beautiful of cities.

'I believe you have eight brothers, no less?'

'Yes,' she laughed.

'I'm an only child,' he told her.

'Then we'll never see eye to eye,' Cecilia said quickly, and then wanted to bite out her tongue. Why had she said such a stupid thing?

He was silent for a while. Then he turned to her with a soft smile. 'I think we see eye to eye, Sister.'

'Yes.' Cecilia felt her face grow hot.

'After the seminar the other day, I noticed when someone came up to you and said something, and you started laughing, and you bent from the middle like you really meant it. You were really laughing and I thought ... Well, after that, I was unconsciously looking around for the Sister who knew how to laugh.'

Cecilia took a deep breath. This was not an appropriate conversation to be having. 'You're going back to the Philippines tomorrow?'

He smiled. 'I am.' He slowed his pace and sighed. 'And you?'

'I'm going home.'

'Do you think you'll stick it?'

'What do you mean?'

'The convent?'

Cecilia opened her mouth but nothing came out. She clasped the silver heart in her hands and thought of the solemn vows rolled up inside, how dear they were to her.

'Why do you ask?'

'Because I have my doubts that you will,' he said simply.

'Why do you say that?' Cecilia was stunned.

'There is too much going on in here.' He pointed to her head. 'There is only so much bullshit a smart person can take.'

She was shocked, completely unused to anyone swearing in her presence, much less a priest. But she was flattered too, in an odd way. He was treating her like an equal. No one had called her smart for a long time.

'What about you?' she managed.

'I'm in the right place.'

Cecilia laughed nervously. 'And I'm not?'

He shrugged. 'Far be it from me to tell anyone where their place is.'

She said nothing, just walked along stiffly beside him, but tears came to her eyes. He was right. And yet ... he wasn't. The convent was changing. It was more inclusive and more open. The Magdalen laundry was going to be phased out. When Cecilia got home she'd be part of all that. Things were changing. 'How do you know you are in the right place?' she asked suddenly.

'You know, Sister, I thought when I was first ordained that

I knew something.' He stopped and touched her hand briefly before going on. 'I had a couple of degrees under my belt, and I was ready to take on the world. Then I got sent first to that little remote mountain parish and I consoled myself with the idea that I would be bringing God's word to the ignorant poor, the illiterates. But ... I was so wrong.'

'How so?'

'They taught me.'

'What did they teach you?'

'That I knew *nothing* ...'

Her skin was burning from the brief touch of his hand.

'My first job as a priest was to bury a newborn baby. The young couple didn't have money for a coffin, so they decorated an old shoebox with Christmas paper that someone else had found and the whole village came to that Mass. We carried that tiny box three miles up the mountain to where the hole had been dug in the hard soil, and as I looked around at those patient, weathered faces who'd known nothing but injustice all their lives ... I don't know how to explain it, but I knew I was in the right place.'

'Because they needed you.'

'They needed someone on their side. Why should their lives be blighted by sorrow and hardship for want of food and medicines and all kinds of rights that we take for granted?'

She shook her head and sighed and wished that she could sink down onto the pavement. That they both might just sit there all night and talk, talk through it all so that she would understand and by morning ... by morning she'd have it all worked out.

He put his hand up to ring the bell but stopped and turned back to her.

'I'm going to miss you, Sister,' he said quietly.

Cecilia was glad for the dark night, because her face was hot with a rush of conflicting emotion.

'I'll miss you too, Father.'

'I'll pray for you,' he said seriously.

They shook hands formally.

'Good luck with all your work, Father,' Cecilia said.

'Thank you, Sister. You get home safely now.'

'I will. Thank you.'

That night Cecilia hardly slept. The turmoil inside felt like some kind of build-up to an explosion. At three a.m. she took a small torch from out of the broom cupboard, and although it was against the rules to read at night, pulled the Holy Bible from the shelf near her bed. She closed her eyes and let the book open anywhere. It fell open at St Matthew's Gospel.

> *Enter by the narrow gate, since the gate that leads to perdition is wide, and the road spacious, and many take it. But it is a narrow gate and a hard road that leads to life, and only a few find it. Matthew 7:13-14*

She had her answer; had known it all along.

There would be no easy way for her.

Peach

'What a complete and total piss off,' Det snarls under her breath, walking into the kitchen where I'm at the stove cooking paella. She has paint all over her hands, and her boots are completely inappropriate for the summer and her belly is protruding like a beach ball, but she looks well, better than I've ever seen her, in fact. The pink in her cheeks makes her look pretty, but if I told her that she'd probably tell me to go stand under a cold shower.

'Well, hello, Det,' I say. 'How come you're so happy?'

She leans up against the fridge and looks at me. 'It's just plain shit behaviour,' she spits out, glowering across the room at Cassie, who's sitting at the dining-room table looking fabulous in red with dangling gold earrings, watching Nick and Dicko making up the granita.

'Are we still going to go?'

'How can we go now?'

'Do you *want* to go?'

'I dunno,' I mutter.

Det groans, wanders over to the small sofa under the window and slumps down to watch the others make the drink.

I've never made paella before so I thought I'd give it a go and invite Cassie and Stephano along with Nick and Dicko and Screwloose to come try it out. I suppose I was imagining a nice relaxed night, kicking back before the visit with the old lady in the country the next day. Nick and Dicko volunteered to make granitas and Det offered to grab a big tub of the best ice-cream from Carlton on her way home from the city. Cass has brought guacamole and bread. Screwloose said he was definitely coming but wasn't bringing anything because he was broke.

I'd gone to the market in the morning and bought up big. Seafood and greens and spices. Then Cassie rang to say that she had to pull out of the trip to my grandmother's tomorrow because Stephano wanted her at some big family do for his grandparents. She's the only one with a car, and from the beginning the plan had been that she drive us up there. It was extra annoying given that she'd been the one to convince me to finally see my birth grandmother. *Peach, if we all go together it will be fine.* All along Cassie was much keener than Det about the whole enterprise and now she'd decided to pike out the day before we're due to go.

'Sorry, kiddo,' she'd said, 'you're going to have to find someone else with a car.'

'But who?'

'Well ... if you can't find someone to drive you, then you'll have to go by train.'

'She lives too far out.'

'You can catch a local taxi out to where she lives.'

'I'm not going by train,' I said.

'Why not?'

'I don't want to be caught there.'

'What do you mean, *caught* there?'

'I mean hanging around for hours waiting for the train back.'

Cassie gave a deep sigh as though I was being obdurate and childish. 'Then you're going to have to hire a car.'

'I need a full licence for that, Cass.'

'Det has a licence.'

'Okay, but … she is almost eight months pregnant.'

'Pregnant women still drive,' Cassie snapped.

But it turned out that Det only had a P-plate licence, too, so neither of us could legally hire a car anyway.

Without a driver or a car I figured I was going to have to call the visit off, and I was not looking forward to ringing that poor old lady with the news. She'd already written twice to say how much she was looking forward to it. Apart from that, underneath I was curious to meet her too.

As I shelled the prawns, made the stock and chopped up vegetables I racked my brains trying to come up with some way of getting there. But neither Stella nor I could think of anyone.

By the time everyone had arrived for dinner and the food preparations were more or less done I was in a bit of a state, furious with Cassie and wishing like crazy that I'd never agreed to go see the old lady in the first place. The whole enterprise had become one big headache.

'You feeling okay, Det?' Cassie calls, but the edge in her voice gives her away. She knows we're both pissed off with her.

'Fine,' Det calls back coldly. She puts her feet up and, with both hands on her belly, closes her eyes. The edginess between them tells me that this dinner that I have been working on all bloody afternoon is going to self-destruct. Probably within the next ten minutes.

'So where's the boyfriend?' Screwloose asks Cassie.

'Can't come,' she explains defensively. 'He's got a big job on.'

'Cooking this meal was a big job, too,' Det yells from the couch without opening her eyes. 'Ask Peach.'

Cassie ignores Det and looks at me. 'He's really sorry to miss this dinner, Peach. I told you that.'

'So you speak *for* him now, do you?' Det says belligerently. 'The way he does for you?'

'Meaning?' Cassie replies coldly.

'Just a question.'

'No. I don't speak for him.'

'So how come he can't ring Peach himself and give his own apologies?'

I come out of the kitchen and see that Det is on a roll and she won't let up until there is a showdown.

'I didn't know this was a *formal* occasion,' Cass says in her best *I-am-being-reasonable* tone, 'otherwise he would have.'

'It's *not* a formal occasion,' I interject. 'Come on, for Christ's sake, cool it. It's just bad luck. Stephano's got this thing on and ...'

'So how come you were so keen for her to go meet the old duck,' Det shoots over at Cassie, 'and now you can't even get it together to come and support her?'

'But *you* can! And I've already said I'm terribly sorry that I have to pull out,' Cassie counters passionately. 'I'd rather come with you guys, believe me, but ...'

'But what?'

'Stephano's parents insisted I be there and—'

'So not just the boyfriend now but his fucking parents as well! Listen to yourself, Cassie!'

'Det,' I say warningly, 'cool it.'

'Well, she sounds like his fucking *wife!*'

There is a stand-off for a while, a moment between the three of us that excludes the guys.

'I'm happy to have a boyfriend, Det!'

'Great! Does it mean he has to rule your life?'

'Stephano doesn't rule my life!'

'No?'

'He is my partner.'

'Jeez, I hate that fucking word!' Det sneers. '*Partner.*'

'Oh, I forgot,' Cassie says, 'you're just way too cool for a *partner*, aren't you? Way too cool.'

'Whoa!' Det shouts and jumps up from the couch. 'Implication being that I *should* have one?'

'It just *might* be handy in your condition, Det!'

Det prances around the room laughing as she holds her belly out for everyone to notice.

'Do I look like I care that I don't have a fucking *partner*?'

'You might in a month.'

'You know something, Cass?' Det is coming in for the kill now. '*I don't think so.* I'm fucking glad I *don't* have a partner who insists on dragging me along to his *grandparents'* place!'

'Well, good, but—'

So it goes on. It never ceases to amaze me how they ever manage to pull back from these arguments. The nastiness is *palpable.* But, believe it or not, they actually do love each other. Amazing, really. They should be giving classes to world leaders. Meanwhile, there is this dinner to get through.

'Come on, you two,' I say quietly. 'I've cooked this nice food. Let's at least try to enjoy eating it.'

'Yes, let's do that,' Cassie says.

'Start acting like a real friend, then,' Det fumes.

'I beg your pardon, Det?' Cassie says coldly.

'A friend doesn't pull out at the last moment.'

For a minute it looks like Cassie is about to storm off, but she is merely turning up the knob a notch or two. Mesmerised, we all watch as she goes to her bag, kneels down, unzips it and pulls out a pile of brochures instead.

'Don't you dare lecture me about *friendship*!' she hisses in a barely controlled whisper, 'I have been working my bum off for you all week organising *your* exhibition!' She throws the brochures down next to Det's feet. 'I have been traipsing around the city for weeks getting these into every appropriate venue I can. I have made a million phone calls to all kinds of people. I have personal acceptances to your opening from people from the NGV, and from Extra Blue Galleries, and you and I both know if they come then everyone else will too. Not only that, I have *Art Review* promising a leading article in the September issue and *Flair* are giving you top billing for their piece on hot new emerging artists.'

I only have a vague idea who these people are, but it sounds very impressive.

Det holds up both hands in surrender. 'Okay, okay,' she sighs, 'righto.'

'And all of it *unpaid,* I might remind you!'

'I know.' Det shrugs. 'Thanks.'

Cassie's eyes flash furiously around at the rest of us. 'Not one person in this room would have the first idea about how to organise a proper exhibition. I'm way better than any of the agencies and I'm doing it *gratis!*'

'Okay!' Det is still sour. 'I'm the dick. I admit it. I'm *grovelling.*'

'Just don't question my commitment to you or to Peach. I may not be perfect, but …'

Det kneels awkwardly on the floor in front of Cassie. She starts bowing and scraping and then tries to lick Cassie's shoes. Everyone else finds this funny but Cassie doesn't even smile.

'I swear you are too much sometimes, Det.'

'Listen, I'm on the floor licking your feet. What else do you want from me?

'Oh both of you just shut up! Please,' I yell.

There are a few moments of quiet, then Det, still on her knees, looks up. 'Really, I am sorry,' she says seriously.

Casssie gives a tight nod and bends to pick up the brochures.

'Okay, you two chicks!' Nick shouts. 'Time for some rocket fuel! We need glasses and more ice.' He holds up the jug of deep pink liquid, slices of lemon and chopped mint floating on the surface. 'Where are the glasses, Peaches?'

'Over there.' I point to the side cabinet and take over more ice in a jug.

Nick and Dicko pour it into the glasses.

'Is it very strong?' I ask.

'Is the Pope Catholic?' Nick mutters. 'Does a one-legged duck swim in circles?'

'What about Det?' I say, worried. In times past after such a nasty fight Det would make it her business to get completely plastered.

'Bambino special.' Nick hands Det a separate glass. 'No rocket fuel in this one, kid, sorry.'

Det takes the drink, slurps a bit down and grimaces. 'Did you ever think you'd see the day, Nicko?'

'Never.' He grins.

She takes another gulp and pats her stomach. 'The things I do for you, kid.'

'So where is Stella?' Dicko wants to know.

'I dunno,' I say.

'Have you rung her?'

'No.'

'Are you going to?'

'Why should I?' I grumble. 'She knows tonight is on.'

I'm totally pissed off with Stella. She volunteered to clean up the room and set the table with flowers. None of it has been done and she's nowhere to be seen.

Everyone moves over to the easy chairs with their drinks while I clear the table of newspapers and old letters and half-finished mugs of coffee, and set out cutlery and paper napkins. Then I run back to the messy kitchen and give the huge dish of paella a last stir through.

'Hey, how many more weeks you got, Det?' Dicko asks, lying back against the back of the couch.

'A few.'

'So it's still … *alive*?' he asks quite seriously.

'Bloody hope so,' Det replies, and we all start laughing again.

'Can I feel it?' Nick asks shyly.

'Yeah sure.' Det smiles and pushes her bulge out.

He kneels down in front of Det and puts his head close to her round belly. Det takes his hand and places it on one side. His face is still with concentration, eyes closed, and then he breaks into a delighted smile.

'It's sort of ticking!' he declares. 'I can feel it. Is that the heart-beat?'

'I dunno. Probably.'

'Shit. It's really moving now.' He motions the rest of us over. 'Come and feel it. It's starting to go crazy.'

'Get them off me!' Det laughs.

'It's going berserk!' Nick has his hands wrapped around her belly now and his brown eyes are wide with wonder. 'I reckon he can feel us all out here.'

'Maybe.'

'Is it a boy or a girl?'

'Dunno.'

He looks up at Det seriously. 'Must be weird. Is it? Like … having it inside you?'

'Yeah,' Det sighs. 'It is pretty weird.'

'Peach,' Cassie calls me over excitedly, 'come and have a feel.'

But I just laugh and turn back to the kitchen. The paella is ready and in spite of Stella not being around I'm not going to ruin it by waiting any longer.

After we eat I'm going to have to make a call to the old lady to tell her I'm not coming, and I'm kind of dreading that. But the bewildering truth is that also I find Det's baby a bit of a freak-out. She still doesn't talk about it much except in the most abstract way, and I guess I've got pretty good at putting it out of my mind too. But it's there anyway, in the background, *a baby*. I look around at the six of us and wonder what the future holds for us all. Maybe our tight friendship group is already skidding off the rails and none of us wants to admit it. Cassie made it pretty plain this very morning that her boyfriend comes first.

And my other best friend is going to be a mother very soon. *A mother.* I try to imagine what a friendship with Det *and* a baby will be like, but it's beyond me. Where will I fit in? Things will never be the same again and that's for sure.

We have just settled down at the table when the front door bursts open and Stella comes bounding in, dressed in bright red

Indian cotton, her hair massing around her shoulders and down her back like a black cloak. She actually looks fantastic, but I don't tell her because I'm so pissed off.

'Where have you been?'

'I've got a car and driver for tomorrow!' She throws her bag into the corner and slumps down into a spare chair at the table. 'We're being picked up at ten tomorrow morning. So be ready.'

'See.' Cassie looks around at us all triumphantly as though she's organised the whole thing herself. 'Not that hard! It's worked out. I thought it would.'

'So, who?' I ask, smiling at my sister's bright, enthusiastic face, glad that I don't have to make the phone call and disappoint the old lady.

Stella squares her shoulders and pauses a moment.

'Fluke,' she says defiantly.

'*What?*'

'Fluke said he'd drive us.'

I literally can't believe I'm hearing this. It has to be a bad dream. Of all the people on this earth!

'Stella, what possessed you?' Det can see how shocked I am. 'You know how Peach feels about him.'

'I didn't *ask* him,' Stella says defensively. 'I met him in the street and one thing led to another. He offered.'

Everyone at the table turns to me, but I'm beyond words. All I really know is that I'm ready to kill my sister.

One thing led to another...?

'What exactly led to what, Stella?' I say through gritted teeth.

But she just shrugs and smiles as if she is the cleverest person on earth.

'Well, then,' Det says slowly. I see after the initial shock she is warming to the idea. 'What do you say, Peach?'

'You told Fluke all about the letter?' I stare at Stella incredulously.

'No!' She tries to look apologetic, but having won Det around I see she is actually feeling quite secure. 'Well, only a little bit.'

'But I've broken up with him!' I wail. 'Don't you understand that? I don't want him to know. It's nothing to do with him.'

'I know, but—'

'So what made you think—'

'Breaking up doesn't mean you can't speak to someone,' she says defensively. 'Or that he can't … help out.'

'Stella!'

'No one is suggesting you get back with him!' Cassie contributes.

'And he offered!' Dicko says with a laugh.

'Hey, cool it,' Nick cuts in. 'Have some respect. Remember the baby.'

Like complete idiots we all stop and frown and look around the room as if a baby is suddenly going to appear from under the table or behind the door.

'What are you on about?' Det says, and then as soon as she says it, she realises what he means and bursts out laughing. She picks up a cushion and chucks it hard at his head. 'You are such a dick!'

My fury breaks and I have a few moments of thinking that I love them all, which is a bit strange seeing as I still very much want to kill Stella.

'You don't have to talk to him,' Stella whispers through a mouthful of food a few minutes later, 'he told me that.'

'He said *what*?'

'He said, *Tell Peach I won't talk to her if she doesn't want me to.*'

I sigh and pick up my fork again.

'You and Det can sit in the back,' Stella carries on blithely, 'and I'll go in the front with him.'

'I don't want him to meet my … my … the old lady.' I flush with embarrassment, because if Ellen is *my* grandmother then … what is she to Stella?

'He's not going to. Said he'd drop us off and then clear out until we ring him.'

'But I don't want to travel in his car!'

'Why not?'

'Memories.'

I can't see that I've said anything funny, but they all start hooting and sniggering. Det puts two fingers in her mouth and gives a loud wolf whistle.

'*Oh, memories!*'

'Memories . . .' Nick starts to sing the song from *Cats*.

'Oh, shut the fuck up.'

'Come on, Peach!' Det puts an arm around my shoulders. 'We're not suggesting you *marry* the dick. Why not just *use* him?'

When we've finished eating, Stella goes out into the hallway and comes back with a big bag. She pulls out skeins of brightly coloured wool and a pattern book.

'The other thing I did today,' she explains. 'None of you is going to believe this.'

'Knitting?' Cassie picks up a couple of skeins, staring at them as if they might come alive. 'What are you going to knit?'

Stella pulls out the front half of a tiny multi-coloured baby's jumper.

'I've already started . . . see, I'm almost ready to start the back.'

We all crowd around for a better look.

'How did you know how to do it?' I ask.

'Ruby's mum showed me.'

'When?'

'Today.' Stella smiles. 'She said I was a natural.' She looks at Det. 'For your baby,' she adds casually.

Det nods slowly and we all look on in awe as Stella fires up the needles and begins clacking away as if she was born doing it.

'Oh, I forgot to say that my old girl is collecting stuff for you, Det,' Nick says casually.

'Your mum?'

'You mention the word *baby* and she goes into automatic drive.' He clicks his fingers and grins. 'She said to tell you that she's got all kinds of things from my sister. There is a lot of shit you gotta have.'

'What kind of shit?' I ask curiously.

'Oh, you know, *baby* shit,' he laughs. 'There's this cool little plastic bath with ducks around the edges that I sort of didn't want to let go! And one of those high chairs and heaps of clothes, a million of those playsuit things. They're yours if you want 'em.'

Det gives him that edgy smile that I find so hard to read.

'Okay, tell her thanks. That'd be good.'

No one is talking much. Fluke and I haven't exchanged a word apart from *hello*. I purposely chose the seat behind him so that I wouldn't have to see his face, but that hasn't worked out quite as I planned it. We've only just passed the airport and I've already caught his eye twice in the rear-vision mirror.

Stella is still prattling on about knitting. Det is trying to seem interested, but she's looking out the window most of the time and mumbling 'hmmm' a lot.

I wish I could get as distracted myself. I want to look out the window and muse about nothing in particular, but I keep staring at the back of his head, at that squared-off copper's cut, and I think about the way I used to touch him there. I'm also thinking of his skin, and the mole on his shoulder that he had to get cut out. There was a whole day waiting for the results. I think of sitting out on the back steps listening to him joking bleakly about what should go on his gravestone if it proved to be a fatal melanoma.

Here lies a magnificent hero was his first suggestion. So of course I started getting into it and before long we were laughing like hyenas.

He tried hard, but failed miserably in all he did was my final suggestion before Fluke picked me up and dumped me under the sprinkler, holding us both there until we were completely soaked. After we dried off we swore to each other that if he was let off this time we would never sunbake again. Ever.

But there are no shenanigans today. Fluke is playing Mr Responsible, both hands on the wheel, looking straight ahead.

I know him well enough to know that he is trying to tell me that there is nothing at all strange about driving his ex-girlfriend (who at last meeting told him she never wanted to speak to him again) up to the country to see her birth mother's mother – when she'd always been adamant that she neither wanted, or needed, to have anything to do with her birth family.

I want to tell him that nothing has changed, that I'm really only going for the old woman. But that would mean talking to him, and I am determined not to do that.

'How's the new school, Stella?' I hear him ask my sister.

'Okay,' she says, the needles still clicking away.

'Just okay?'

'Look at me! Only the losers bother to talk to me.'

'So,' he asks casually, 'what you gonna do about it?'

I immediately see red. Just as if her problem is something that can be fixed there and then.

'I dunno,' she sighs miserably.

If he weren't doing us the *huge heroic good deed of the century*, I'd tell him to shut the fuck up and leave her alone.

'You think it's about your nana?' he asks Stella, and our eyes lock for a second in the rear-vision mirror before I turn away. 'I know Peach thinks it is,' he adds, 'and the teacher.'

'Not really,' she says, 'but maybe.'

He must be getting the vibe from me because he pretty much shuts up after that. In fact, we're all so quiet for some time that it begins to feel a little eerie. The radio plays quietly underneath the hum of the car, and we're all lost in our thoughts, I guess. I look at Det and then at my sister and finally end up staring at the back of Fluke's head again.

The countryside unwinds on either side of the freeway as we speed north, but I don't really see it. Fluke is gunning the beast along, only just keeping to the speed limit most of the way. We surge past huge semitrailers and signs leading off to different towns, and I have a strong feeling that I'm hurtling off into the unknown.

After half an hour, Det asks Fluke about his car, where he got it and how much it costs to run, which breaks up the silence. But the conversation peters out pretty quickly.

I'd like to ask her if she's thinking about ditching her beloved motorbike but that would mean joining in the conversation, so I lean my head against the window and close my eyes instead.

'I can help,' I hear Fluke say softly to Stella.

'How?' Stella replies.

'Why don't we get out together in the mornings?'

'How do you mean?'

'I'll drop by, and we'll do an hour's training before school.'

You think I haven't tried that? I want to scream.

'You mean ... running?' she asks. 'I hate—'

'No,' he cuts in easily, 'we'll start off with a few easy exercises, then a fast walk. Build up. That's the whole idea. Go at your own pace.'

I get the feeling that the back seat isn't meant to be listening to this conversation, so I look out the window even as I'm straining to hear. Stella suddenly turns around to me.

'How would you feel about that, Peach?' she asks tentatively.

'What?'

'Me and Fluke training in the mornings.'

'What's it got to do with me?' I snap. Her face immediately crumples, so I mutter, 'Whatever. Okay.'

She nods and looks hopefully at Fluke again. 'I could try, I guess.'

'So, is that a yes?' He grins.

'Okay,' Stella smiles back, 'yes.'

'So when will we start?'

'What about tomorrow?'

'You're on.'

The Castlemaine turn-off comes into view. We exit the freeway onto a narrow road that winds west. It dips and turns over hills and through clumps of overhanging trees, lush rolling pastures on either side. What a shame I feel like throwing up.

'How are you feeling, Peach?' Det turns to me.

'I'm okay,' I say guardedly, and Det grins and digs me in the ribs.

'Aren't you a bit nervous?' Stella turns around.

'Maybe ... a bit.' I smile at her.

'How do you want to work this visit?' Fluke asks, eyeing me in the mirror. It's the first thing he's said to me in the two hours we've been on the road. Then again, I haven't been exactly garrulous.

'What do you mean?'

'I'm obviously going to get lost, but are Stella and Det going to stay?' I panic slightly. *Of course* they're going to stay!

'I've been thinking about that,' Det cuts in. 'You should have time on your own with her.'

'I agree,' Fluke says.

'I don't think so.' I'm feeling a bit desperate. 'The whole idea of you both coming was so that ... you'd be there in case ...'

'In case what?' Fluke says lightly, and I turn away.

'It's not like we're going to drop you and never come back,' Det laughs. 'We'll be here.'

'Why don't I drop the three of you off first, and then I'll come back for Det and Stella after half an hour or so?'

'But what will we do?' I can tell Stella doesn't like the idea either.

'Go check out the shops.' Fluke shrugs. 'Or the gardens? It's a nice town.'

'Well,' Stella looks at me, 'whatever Peach wants.'

I shrug as if I couldn't care less, but it's a complete act. I don't want Fluke to see that I am terrified to be so close to meeting this old woman. And I feel stupid. Why would anyone be scared of an old lady? It doesn't make sense, and yet that is what I feel. Blind terror. What if she tells me stuff I can't handle? What if she brainwashes me and I come out of there thinking that I'm someone other than who I am?

'What am I going to say to her?' I mutter.

'If you want my opinion, she'll do the talking!' Fluke quips.

But no one asked for your opinion.

313

'Come on, kiddo,' Det says. 'You've got your phone. If things get really awkward then you only have to call us.'

'Okay.'

I look out the window at the town's outskirts. It's an old goldmining town and many of the houses are really pretty. We come to the statue of the digger and turn right into the main street as directed. Stella is first to see the big landmark church on our right.

'St Mary's,' she says. 'We've got to turn here. Straight up the hill.'

Number 57 is a tiny house. A cottage, I suppose, but well kept. It is well back from the road with a small iron gate opening to a straight concrete path up to the verandah, which is virtually covered in pot plants. She must have been watching out for us, because the door opens before the three of us have even reached the verandah.

'Perpetua!' She is old, stooped and frail, dressed in a blue summer dress with a white collar and black lace-up shoes. She holds out both arms. 'Thanks be to God!' Her voice is strong for someone so slight. The others stand back as I awkwardly move forward. She grabs me and kisses me fiercely on one cheek and then the other.

'You're an exact replica of your mother.'

'Am I?'

She stands back and holds me at arms-length and turns to the others and then back to me, smiling. Her weathered face is wreathed in wrinkles and both hands are stiff and swollen with arthritis and yet ... yet there is something youthful about her. Lively, anyway. Tears glisten in the blue eyes and she blinks them away. 'This could well be my little Cecilia standing here,' she says softly. 'The spitting image.'

'Really?'

'Oh yes.'

My fixed smile starts to feel as if it's set in concrete while she looks me up and down all over again as if I'm some kind of prize. I pull away from her and grab Stella's hand and drag her forward.

'And this is my sister, Stella.'

'Stella,' the old woman breathes the name as she takes in the physical differences between us. 'Your sister?'

'I know.' Stella smiles tentatively, almost apologetically. 'I'm the younger one.'

I take Det's arm then and pull her forward. 'And my best friend, Det.'

'Bernadette?' The old lady smiles.

Det gives a wry laugh. 'Everyone calls me Det.'

She glances down at Det's protruding belly and then back up into her face. 'And you're expecting, dear?'

'Yes.' Det nods.

'You keeping well?'

'Yes, thanks.'

'Well then,' Ellen whispers, 'a child is a blessing.' She holds open the door. 'Come in. Everything is ready!'

Everything?

We go into a dark hallway and she shows us into what is probably the best room in the house, but it's dark and smells a little musty as though it hasn't been aired for some time. It's crowded with old-fashioned furniture and strange little bits and pieces. Small vases and china animals, strange little bunches of artificial flowers. On the walls are a few badly painted pictures of vases of flowers and young girls looking into the distance.

'I have a grandchild who is very artistic,' Ellen says proudly, pointing to the paintings. We all nod and murmur appropriately.

There is a three-piece lounge suite in the same green as the heavy drapes guarding the windows. The wooden arms on the chairs are polished and so too is the wooden piano in the corner and the small side tables and glass cabinet where all the best plates and glasses are displayed. Cups have been set out on the top of an old autotray near the piano along with some plates covered in bright tea towels.

'Sit down, girls, please.'

We do as we're told and she sits herself in the one straight-backed chair and simply surveys us.

'Bernadette and Stella,' she says quietly to herself, her eyes moving from one to the other as though trying to work out something. Then she turns to me with a smile. 'And Perpetua, of course.'

I try to smile. We all do. We smile and smile and wait for what will come next. I fold my arms over my chest to stop my hands shaking. I have this feeling that there is some strict protocol here – that I should be doing something – but I have no idea what it is.

'Let me give you this comfy chair,' Stella says suddenly, very politely, to Ellen. 'I'll have that one.'

'No, I have to sit on this chair,' Ellen explains. 'I can't get up from the couch.'

'Oh really?' I smile nervously. 'Why not?'

'No strength in my arms,' she laughs. 'Too old.'

'Oh.' My face floods with embarrassment and I look around at the others for help. But they too sit stiffly, knees pressed together and hands joined on laps, waiting to see what will happen. Now we're here, what are we going to talk about?

'Well,' Ellen jolts, 'how about tea?'

'Thank you,' we chorus like primary school kids on an excursion. Anything but just sitting here.

She gets up and goes for the door.

'I'll help,' I say, getting up too.

'No,' she says firmly, 'I can manage.' She disappears out the door and the three of us are left looking at each other.

'She seems really nice,' Stella says encouragingly.

'Yeah,' Det concurs, 'pretty sprightly for nearly ninety.'

'And she's so glad you're here.'

They're trying to be kind.

'It's too weird,' I mutter darkly.

Ellen brings in the tea and milk on a tray and begins to pour it out into the delicate cups. Then she fusses around serving the homemade cake and scones waiting for us on the autotray, telling us about the recipes and how she manages her old stove.

Although I'm not in the least hungry, I get stuck into the food along with the others just for something to do. My nerves calm down a bit.

But the conversation is still really all about the trip up, the weather, how old we all are and what courses we're doing. I'm finishing off my second cup of tea, wondering how much longer we're going to have to stay, when Stella points to a black-and-white photo sitting on the piano.

'Is that … your daughter?' she asks shyly.

'Yes.' Ellen gets up and hands Stella the photo, and we all crowd around. It's a full-length black-and-white shot of a girl who looks a lot like me but in 1960s clothing, leaning on a verandah post, smiling into the camera. She is dressed in a sleeveless dress and high-heeled sandals. She carries a large white handbag and her hair is tied back with a bow.

'How old is she here?' I ask.

'It was taken the day she entered the convent. So, eighteen,' Ellen says softly. 'Eighteen years and three months.'

'Wow!'

'Younger than you are now,' Ellen says to me with a smile.

'Have you any more?' Stella asks.

'Of course, dear.' Ellen gets up, throwing a tentative glance at me. 'But … I didn't want to crowd you.' She goes to the piano stool, opens the seat and pulls out a few more framed black-and-white prints. 'Evie told me, "Gran, you mustn't overdo the photos!" So I put them in here in case you felt it was too much.' She's holding the photos close to her chest. 'Evie is Declan's girl. You might meet her one day.'

'Yes,' I say, taking a photo.

There are nine children standing in a line up against a fence. The eldest boy is about fourteen, the first of six boys, all of them sturdy and nice-looking, dressed in long shirts and boots. Then one little girl in a cotton dress with her hair in pigtails. After her come two young boys.

'So this is …'

'Your mother, with all her brothers.'

'Wow!' Stella exclaims. 'What are their names, Ellen?'

'Dominic, Brendan, Patrick, Rory, Michael and James.' Ellen points to them one at a time. 'Your mother. Isn't she a darling? And the twins, Declan and Sean.'

'Your uncles!' Stella digs me in the ribs.

'That's right,' Ellen smiles at her, 'and every one of them wanted to come today to see you.'

'Really?' I gulp.

'Yes, especially Pat. He's down from Darwin, and he was so keen. They all wanted to come and see their sister's girl, but I put my foot down. Not today, I said. It wouldn't be fair. It would be too much.' She looks at me anxiously. 'I hope that was right, Perpetua? Evie was the one to tell me. She said not to frighten you off or you'll never come back.'

I nod and try to smile, staring down at that row of boys, my mother in the middle of them all. How innocent that little girl looks with her bright smile and pigtails. Yet she grew up and gave her child away ... And all those sturdy handsome brothers will be middle-aged men now.

'This one is ... Dominic?' I point to the eldest boy.

'Yes,' she says stiffly. She reaches out and takes my hand in her old rough one, and squeezes it and lowers her head and closes her eyes. 'Your mother loved Dom.'

For a few moments she stays like that, quiet, with her eyes closed, both hands now holding my hand. Disconnected thoughts surge and swell inside my head until my skull feels ready to crack open. The air around us is heavy, holding its breath with all the unspoken things. I have a weird impulse to spread both hands over my head to hold everything in place. *Oh God, why did I come here?*

I look around at Det and Stella for help, but they seem struck with the same dull sense of blank helplessness. None of us knows if we should speak or not.

Det eventually reaches out and touches my other hand. 'You okay?' she whispers. I nod.

Eventually Ellen seems to pull herself from her slide backwards into the past.

'Would you like to see a few more of your mother?'

Not really.

'Okay, thanks, Ellen.' What I'd really like is to get up from this couch, say a few quick goodbyes and go home.

The first one is Cecilia in her postulant's dress, black and simple with a very white collar. She has a small veil on her head, but her neck and ears are visible, and a belt holds in the dress at her slim waist. She is laughing, pretty and young.

'Her entry into the noviciate,' Ellen says, pointing to the next photo, where her head and face are encased in white. The dress is voluminous with wide sleeves. Her hands are hidden under a long apron-like thing hanging down from the shoulders at the front and back. In spite of having seen her in a similar dress in a photo in the archivist's office, I find it strangely shocking.

'Is that thing an apron?'

'No ... it was part of the habit. A scapular.'

'Did they wear all this in the summer?' Det asks.

Ellen nods. 'So hot and impractical,' she mutters and hands me another photo. It's of Cecilia sitting next to a couple of women in ordinary dress, looking down at something. This time her veil is black and she has a ring of flowers on her head.

'She made her final vows that day,' Ellen says. 'The ring of flowers was put on their heads during the ceremony. Of course it all changed not long after this ...'

'When did it change?'

She frowns and gives a deep sigh. 'I'm not much good with dates, love, but it wasn't long after she made her final vows that they changed the habit.' She hands me another photo. There is Ellen alongside her daughter the nun. Both of them looking cheerful.

'She's lovely, isn't she?' Ellen says, looking at me shyly.

'She looks happy,' I say.

'She was happy.'

'So what happened?'

But Ellen just smiles and hands over a picture of a closed door set into a black granite wall.

'See this gate? It was the only way into the convent. Cecilia asked me to take that picture when she'd been a novice for a couple of years. See, here is the grille. You had to ring the bell and someone would open this and talk to you.'

'Checking you out?'

'Yes.'

'Like a jail?'

Ellen smiles again.

'She asked you to take a picture of *the gate*?' Det asks. 'Why?'

'Because for three years she never went outside the walls of the convent,' Ellen laughs. 'She said she'd forgotten what it looked like!'

Oh God. There is a pause. I think they're all waiting for me to say something, but I can't. It's too weird. I'm thinking about this young girl, younger than me, *willingly* putting all this stuff on. Willingly shutting herself off from the world, behind a big thick wall. There are so many questions that I want to ask. So much I want to know. Det and Stella are hunched over the photos, smiling and intrigued. All very well for them, but this girl was ... *my mother.*

'Have you heard from your mother, Perpetua?'

The question jolts me into the present. I look at this old woman and know that of course she is talking about her own daughter, not the mother that I spoke to on the phone last night. 'No, I haven't,' I say.

'So you have no idea if she is in the country?'

'No.'

And that is when Det makes her move. 'Stella and I are going to go now. We'll find Fluke,' she says firmly, 'and give you and Ellen some time.'

Det is digging Stella in the ribs, making her get off the couch. I can see Stella is reluctant to leave me, and I love her for it.

They turn in the doorway. 'Thanks for the delicious tea, Ellen. See you later.'

Ellen closes the door behind them and we are left looking at each other. It is only politeness that stops me from running out after them.

'You can help me clear up the cups,' she says.

The kitchen is a small yellow room at the back of the house, freshly painted, bright and cheerful, full of things like the other room, but much nicer. I go to the window and stare out onto the small back garden. There is a lemon tree in the middle and a plum in the corner. Two rows of tomatoes line the fence.

'You said in your letter that you never knew your own mother, Ellen?' I say, putting the cups in the sink and turning the water tap. Washing up will give me something to do. 'Why was that?'

'I was put in the convent by my father.'

'Why?'

'We didn't ask questions in those days,' she says.

'And you never saw your mother again?'

Ellen sits down at the little table. 'Only the once,' she whispers. 'My memory is very faint, but they told me what happened.'

'Who told you?'

'One of the nuns who was there that day told me years later, and I've felt guilty ever since.'

Guilty?

'Silly, isn't it? I was only four years old.'

An eighty-eight-year-old woman feels *guilty* about something she did when she was four? I sit down on the opposite side of the table and take her hand.

'Tell me what happened,' I say.

Sadie 1916

All the way home Sadie thought about how much easier it was working with men. They might pinch you and touch you and put their dirty hands where they shouldn't, but most of them knew how to have a laugh, which was more than you could say for the sniping old bats she was working for now. Men didn't trick you with smiles that meant the exact opposite of what was coming out their mouths. Bar work was better pay too. Give out a bit and you got it back in tips. Simple.

But Sadie had good reason not to go back to any of that. She was making hats now and proving not too bad at it. She was determined to stick it out for as long as she could.

Today, old Dolly Simpson had kept her back out of spite. Sadie had had to go to the dental hospital and have a tooth pulled. It was Friday and she wanted to go home early to deal with her aching face, but when she got back to work her boss hadn't even looked up from her machine when Sadie asked if she could make up the hours the next week.

'You'll stay back tonight or your wages will be docked,' the old biddy had snapped, as if she was pleased to have a chance to say it. 'There is a war on, in case you haven't noticed.'

Sadie had gone back to her table and picked up the red felt that she'd been working on for two days. It didn't have to be done until the next week. *The war!* Couldn't they talk about anything else? People made it an excuse for everything. But those lists of the dead every Monday morning were enough to sicken a saint.

Anyway, she was home now. Bone tired and alone, her eyes sore from a day of close needlework, one side of her face swollen and throbbing where the rotten tooth had been. She flipped open the letterbox and fumbled for her key at the same time, expecting nothing. But there was a slim envelope with her name in extravagantly beautiful letters on the front. She pulled it out and stood still a moment, trying to guess who might have written. She pushed open the door and hurried down the hallway.

There was only one thing on her mind these days. One thing. If it meant working hard for terrible money and putting up with sour old biddies who used any power they had to make life hell for her, then so be it. There would be no more pub work. No more booze and no more men either until…

Stan had given her the idea. Stanley Kindred, a forest cutter from Gippsland down for a few days in the big smoke. She'd met him at a dance in the Collingwood town hall and they'd got on well. Poor eyesight had saved Stan from the war. He told Sadie it was the best bit of luck he'd had in his life. All these bloody war-mongers needed their heads read. There was no reason to fight. None at all. He had nice hands and a gentle way with him, too, and so she'd ended up telling him about the way her little girl had been taken from her.

For the first few weeks she hadn't been able to stay away. She'd walked to the convent every day and simply stood there on the street next to the high walls, for hours, in the hope that some kind of miracle might be granted to her, that if she longed hard enough the child would materialise out of thin air.

If she heard children's voices she'd press herself up against the bricks and close her eyes and pray that her child was on the other side, pressing her little plump body up against those same thick walls. *Ellen*, she whispered, *my little one.*

Most days she heard nothing except her own ragged breathing, but just occasionally she thought she heard the child whispering back.

Mumma. Come and get me. I'm waiting for you to take me home.

Those were the good days.

The bad days were when she heard only her own dull heartbeat. At such times she searched the walls for small cracks in the cement to peer through. She half knew she was going crazy when she found herself imagining getting hold of some kind of small shovel or knife and scraping the cement away, making it wide enough for her to slip her hand through at first and then one by one pulling the bricks out. Not too many, but enough for her to be able to edge her body through. She'd wait until dark and then crawl inside and find where her daughter was sleeping. She'd pull her from her bed and wrap her in a nice cosy rug and sneak away with her without anyone seeing. They'd get on a train. Head off somewhere and never be found. Oh, if only, even for a little while. Just to have her on her knee, wrapped in a towel after her bath, to hold her there and smell her neck and hair. Kiss the rosy cheeks, the fat knees and dark curls.

Ellen had been gone fifteen months now, and it still wasn't real.

Once, a junior nun came out and told her to go away. That if she didn't stop loitering outside the premises the police would be called and she'd be locked up. Fearful and ashamed, Sadie had gone away and she'd stayed away until...

She began to turn up again, after work and between shifts, usually with a few drinks inside her. She would stand banging her head softly against that convent door, crying. *Give me back my child. I want my little girl.*

Once there'd been movement on the other side and a small square panel had slid across, creating a tiny window in the door. Sadie stopped crying. Eyes were staring out at her.

'What do you want?' a disembodied voice asked.

'My child,' Sadie gasped, 'I want my baby.'

The door creaked open and she was brought inside

Within a few moments she was being ushered into a huge room with very high ceilings. The young nun, who couldn't have been more than seventeen, left her there to stew as she hurried off to get the one in charge. Afraid, Sadie began to shake as she looked around at all the polished wood, the tables and chairs and windows, the sombre religious paintings.

As soon as the old nun swept in, done up in all her white starch and fancy long robes, Sadie's heart fell.

'What did you want, dear?' The nun didn't bother to soften her voice.

'My child,' Sadie said, too desperately.

'Name of child?'

'Ellen Reynolds,' Sadie whispered.

'And you are …?'

'Mrs Sadie Reynolds. Her mother, Sister.'

'Please rest assured, Mrs Reynolds, the little girl is perfectly well.'

'I'm her mother,' Sadie began to sob.

'I am well aware of that.' The iciness in the woman's voice made Sadie stop crying. 'But you have no claim to her.'

'I'm her mother,' Sadie said again hopelessly.

'Mrs Reynolds.' The Sister took Sadie's elbow and sat her down in one of the straight-backed chairs and then sat down herself in a similar one a couple of feet away. 'It usually takes mothers some time to adjust, and that is why we've shown you leniency up to now. But this loitering outside our gate has got to stop. If it happens again, the police will be called.' Her eyes bored into Sadie's, not letting up for even an instant. 'Do I make myself clear?'

Sadie nodded. Such was the older woman's power that within a few minutes Sadie was allowing herself to be led to the door, her elbow held in a vice-like grip.

She nodded meekly when the nun said that she should be grateful that her child was well and happy, and no, she would not make a nuisance of herself again. But at the doorway she suddenly realised that she was being dismissed, got rid of, thrown aside like a piece of rubbish, and that made her forget about the formality of the situation. The high ceilings, the paintings, the polished wood and the formidable woman herself ceased to exist.

'Give me back my baby!' she yelled. 'Give her back, you heartless *bitch*! You have no right!'

It ended badly, of course. She was dragged kicking and screaming onto the street and the police were called and she was locked up for two hours until she calmed down.

But then here was Stan telling her that he knew of a woman who had got her kid back from the babies' home in Broadmeadows, and Sadie was all ears. It was a matter of 'cleaning up her act', he told her. She needed to put a bit of gloss on things. First off, she'd better give up the pub work and take on something more respectable. Chuck away the make-up and wear dowdy clothes and make damn sure no male ever darkened the door of her house because they'd have the spies out. Then she should write to the kid's father. Tell him that she'd turned a new leaf, beg him to meet with her so he could see for himself. Then she should write to those nuns, whoever they were, apologise for all the trouble, tell them she'd seen the light and changed her ways. If Sadie couldn't write the letter then he had a sister who'd help.

Sadie decided that she'd give it a go. She would do all Stan told her and more. She'd become a paragon of virtue. She'd write to Frank, tell him she'd changed her ways, beg his humble forgiveness for whatever it was that she'd done wrong.

She was a month into her new life, with the job making hats and the loneliness every night, when she got the letter. To save power she lit the fire with the matches that she always kept in her coat and laboriously read her letter by the red, flickering light.

Dear Mrs Reynolds,

After the last unfortunate visit we contacted the child's father and

*told him of your distress. He has agreed for you to see the child.
Please be at the convent at two o'clock sharp on Sunday the 30th.*

Yours sincerely in Christ,
Mother Mary Help of Christians

Sadie stared at the letter and read it again and again. Finally she dared believe that what she had in her hand was real. It had come by post, hadn't it? It wasn't some trick. And look, there was that woman's signature. Sunday was Sadie's birthday. That meant something, didn't it? Maybe Frank had remembered and relented. She'd begged him enough. Begged him and those sisters of his to have mercy. So ... maybe it had come to pass.

But how would she ever be able to wait till then?

On Sunday morning she was up at six, dressed and bathed by seven and walking the streets trying to fill in time by nine.

Midday came and went and then she was waiting in a little sitting room in the convent. She could hear children's voices, chattering and crying, and it made her edgy. How long were they going to make her wait? How long before she could gather her little one up in her arms?

The door opened and there she was – her own wee girl – wearing a little dress with a blue pinny over it, held in the arms of a young nun. Just behind came the older nun who Sadie had met in the night. Sadie stood nervously and watched as the young nun set Ellen down on the floor. Tears rushed into her eyes and her throat jammed as she knelt down and held out her arms.

'Come to me,' she said. 'It's your mumma.'

But the little girl only stared at her and clung tightly to the young nun's skirts. When Sadie spoke again Ellen hid her face in the nun's apron.

'As you see, Mrs Reynolds, the child is well.'

Sadie could barely breathe. She edged a little closer and the child edged back.

'Does she look neglected in any way?'

'No, but—'

'She loves her food.' The young nun smiled kindly at Sadie. 'And she's growing well.'

There was a pause while they all looked at the child, who was coming back out from the nun's dress and staring hard at Sadie.

'Come to Mumma,' Sadie coaxed, trying not to sound as desperate as she knew she looked, with her hat askew and her face still swollen where the tooth had been. 'Come to Mumma.' Oh if only she hadn't worn her good clothes. The silly new hat and the gloves and the special suit made her look like someone else. 'Ellen, darling.'

But the child slunk further into the nun's skirts.

'Ellen is quite happy where she is, Mrs Reynolds,' said the older nun. 'Aren't you, Ellen?'

The child stared out at them both, her deep eyes as round as little blue plates.

'All the Sisters tell me you're a very happy little girl.' The older nun smiled. The little girl put her thumb in her mouth. '*Are* you a happy girl, Ellen?'

The child's big blue eyes moved over to the nun. She nodded.

The two nuns looked at each other and then at Sadie.

'You see, she is happy with us.'

Sadie stared at the nun in shock. Whatever was happening, it was happening too fast. She couldn't keep up.

'Do you want to go with this lady?' the nun asked the little girl. *This lady?*

Ellen shook her head slowly.

'No. You see?' The nun gave the younger nun a dismissive wave. 'Thank you, Sister.' The young one nodded and took Ellen's hand, leading her out the door.

'No!' Sadie clambered to her feet. 'Please don't take her.'

The young nun stopped and looked at her Superior for directions.

'I've got a new job now,' Sadie babbled desperately. 'I make hats with a Mrs Simpson in Pigdon Street, Carlton. Mrs Simpson and Miss Valerie Wilson. Just the two of them, and they're very reputable women. It's above a shop. Number 507. She has written me a reference.' Sadie fumbled in her bag for the envelope. 'Please, Sister, you can check. I'm never out at night now. I lead a very quiet life.'

'My dear,' the nun cut in, a faint smile wavering on the edge of her mouth, 'on the child's father's advice she is now a ward of the state. As such, she will continue to reside here.'

Sadie gulped and knelt down at the Reverend Mother's feet.

'Please.' She reached for the edge of the nun's habit, and bowed to the floor. 'I'll do anything.'

When she looked up they were alone. She was on her knees in front of the senior nun and the young nun had slipped out with her little girl.

'We must act in the best interests of the child, Mrs Reynolds,' the nun said in her quiet, cool manner. 'You have seen for yourself that she is well. Come now, dear.' Pale hands came out from under the habit and fluttered abstractedly in the air. 'Get up now.'

Once Sadie had stumbled to her feet, the nun went to the door and opened it.

'Now I'll get Mother Sebastian to see you out.' Her face moved into the shape of a smile. 'God bless you, dear.'

Sadie watched mesmerised as the figure in black glided out of the room. She thought of the spiders crawling up the walls of the outhouse at home. So big and black it didn't matter that everyone said they were harmless. They terrified her.

Very soon another nun appeared, older and more kindly. When Sadie slumped forward as though about to faint the nun took her arm to help her stay upright and held it all the way out to the gate.

'Now now, dear, take heart,' she murmured in her thick Irish brogue. 'All is not lost. Our Lord is with you.'

Sadie let herself be led out the way she'd come, a weird rushing sound in her ears. Almost as if someone had left a tap on full bore.

The old nun saw her out on the street. 'Now you're not to be coming back, dear,' she said gently. 'It's over now, you understand? Over.'

'Yes, Mother.'

Peach

'Will you have another cup of tea, Perpetua?' Ellen digs in the pocket of her dress and wipes her eyes.

'Yes, please. But I'll make it.' I get up and switch on the kettle and then get the cups out again. The yellow kitchen is darkening in the late afternoon.

'What happened to her after that?' I ask.

'I don't know.' Her voice is tired now. 'But I would like to see where she is buried before I die.'

'Do you know where that is? I can try to find that out for you, Ellen.'

'Would you do that?'

'We could go there together.'

Her face breaks into a warm smile; her weathered hand sneaks across the table towards mine.

'I'm just a sentimental old fool, Perpetua, but I'd like to tell her I'm sorry I didn't rush into her arms that day.'

'And your father?'

'Every Sunday, hail or shine, he came to take me out.' Ellen smiles. 'I was devastated when he died. He was all the family I had in the world, you understand, except for his sisters, but … they didn't accept me.'

'Didn't you ask him about your mother?'

'We didn't ask questions in those days, love,' she says for the second time, shaking her head as though the truth of it is baffling to her as well. 'Not like now. People didn't talk about such things. He just gave me to believe that there was something not right about her, and as much as I longed to know, I couldn't ask.'

We are silent on the way home, sitting in our allotted seats. I stare at the back of Fluke's head again.

'Are you glad you came, Peach?' Stella asks.

'Oh, I dunno,' I say, trying to sound normal, 'suppose so.'

'Did she tell you stuff?'

'Yeah,' I smile, 'a bit.'

'Are you going to see her again?'

'Yeah, I think so.'

'When?' Fluke's voice.

I thought you said you weren't going to talk to me, dickhead!

'First, I'm going to try and find her mother's grave,' I say, looking out the window, 'then I'll take her there.' I don't turn around, but I have the feeling that they are a little shocked by what I just said.

'*Why?*' Det groans.

'Shut up, Det,' from Stella.

'What do people expect to find at gravesites?'

I am on the point of reminding Det that she'd told me once that when her father died she used to hitch rides to the local cemetery where he was buried and stay there for hours.

'She's nearly ninety,' I say instead, 'and she wants to see her mother's grave before she dies. There is nothing wrong with that. Where do I start looking for it?'

'Have you got her full name?'

'No,' I say, feeling stupid, 'but I will.'

'She should be easy enough to trace.'

'I really wish that your birth mum would go and see her before she dies,' Stella moans. 'Doesn't anyone know where she is?'

'Nope,' I say, 'none of the brothers know.'

'Can we stop soon, Fluke?' Det asks sharply. 'I mean, when it's safe?'

'You need a wee?'

'And a cigarette.' She turns to me defensively. 'I haven't had one all day.'

'Don't look at me,' I say irritably. 'I'm not your conscience.'

'Ah,' she laughs softly, 'but you are, Peach.'

Fluke pulls over and Det jumps out and disappears down the slope to pee. The rest of us get out and lean against the car. Fluke goes up the front and leans against the bonnet, leaving Stella and me at the side. When Det gets back she plonks herself next to Fluke and starts rolling the smoke. The day is closing down around us. We're out in the country, and despite it being the freeway with cars roaring past, it's kind of nice.

Det drags hard on her smoke and doesn't say anything for a while. I wish I knew what she was thinking. Finally she butts out the smoke with her boot and opens the car door.

'Thanks for that.' Then she pats her tummy. 'Sorry, kid.'

We climb in again and Fluke puts the key into the ignition.

'I've met her,' Det says suddenly, and then looks at me. 'Your birth mother, I mean. I've met her.'

There is stillness. We wait for Fluke to start the engine. My head flips into reverse gear and I replay the last few moments.

'What did you say, Det?' Fluke says, turning around to face her. *Oh good, I can relax. It isn't just me. He heard wrong too.*

'I've met Cecilia,' Det says. 'Peach's mother.'

She winds down the window on her side and puts her head out like she might need air. 'She's back from overseas and has been hanging around the convent a bit. Anyway, I recognised her. She came up to my room and had a look at the paintings.' Det brings her head back in and faces me. 'I told her not to come back.'

I start to move, slowly at first, ever so slowly. I just breathe in and out a few times and then I reach for the doorhandle and lift it. I make sure I've got my bag on my shoulder and then I make a dash for it, slamming the door behind me. I run back along the highway the way we've come, remembering the huge petrol station not too far back. I'll be able to get a ride back home or ... I don't rightly know what I'm going to do, but I'm in full control and being quite sensible. I just can't handle any of this anymore. I know I will not be able to be in that car with those people for the rest of the trip. If needs be, I'll go back to Castlemaine and catch the train back to the city.

I hear footsteps behind me. I quicken my pace. Det won't be able to catch me. Tears are stinging my eyes. Fuck! I wish things weren't such a mess. I feel a hand grasping my elbow, pulling me around and I wrench myself away. It's not that I blame Det for this. I never can blame Det for anything. But I have to tell her to leave me alone. Only that ... I have to be left alone.

Leave me alone ... please.

But it's Fluke. Fluke. Pulling me towards him. The bastard. Part of me thinks he was waiting for something like this to happen. That's why he offered to take us. But it feels so good to have his arms around me.

It's just him and me on the side of the highway. And all the big trucks have their lights on and one of them sounds a loud horn as he passes.

'This is dangerous,' I say. I'm shuddering and crying too, I think, my hands over my face.

'I know,' he says and keeps hugging me.

Then he grabs me tighter and kisses me, first on one cheek and then on the other and then on the mouth. And this I can't explain. I give myself over to it. It only last a few moments but I haven't kissed anyone for so long and it feels so wonderful, as if I've come home to something I thought I'd never feel again.

A kiss is just a kiss. It can be as sweet as a bunch of freshly cut mint, or as stale as week-old bread. But even a small kiss can take you on a ride that you never come back from. A kiss can mean everything in the world, or it can mean absolutely nothing …

'This means nothing,' I say sharply.

'Okay,' he says.

We pull apart and stand there not touching, looking out at the trucks passing, both awkward, slightly ashamed … and totally amazed at what has just happened.

Then he grabs my hand. I resist until I hear him speak.

'Peach.'

His voice is so ragged that I fall into his arms and we kiss again, for longer. He is first to pull away this time.

'Nothing,' I say again firmly. 'Absolutely fucking zero. So don't get any ideas.'

'Believe me, I haven't,' he snaps.

'What?'

'Ideas.'

'Don't lie!'

I turn away and try to walk off towards the petrol station, but he puts one arm around my shoulders and steers me back towards the car.

'I want to be alone,' I say.

'I know that,' he says quietly, 'but there is no way except by road.'

'I'll get the train.'

But we're back at the car now, and he is opening the door. I get in warily, all ready to flee again as if I'm some kind of shy animal caught in the headlights. One sly grin or smart comment from Stella or Det, who would have seen us kissing, and I swear I will take off again and not allow myself to be diverted.

But no one jokes or says anything for that matter. Det and Stella don't even look at me.

When Fluke has the car out on the road again, Det mutters under her breath, 'I'm sorry. I should have told you.'

'It's okay, but just don't talk to me now, okay?'

'Okay.'

Cecilia 1968

She was four days into the six-day retreat. Apart from prayer and what was absolutely necessary she'd not spoken at all during that time. But one of the very old Sisters was motioning her into the front parlour.

Two visitors had arrived unexpectedly and the old nun didn't know what to do with them. It was five o'clock in the afternoon and the whole community was at prayer. Cecilia recognised Mr and Mrs Bryant immediately. Nice people, the parents of one of the six new postulants who'd entered eight months before. Cecilia had met them during last month's visit.

But they stood nervously now, trying to smile at her.

'Mr and Mrs Bryant from South Australia.' Cecilia smiled and held out her hand in greeting, her own voice sounding strange after such a long time of not speaking. 'How are you both?'

But she could see for herself that something was wrong. They looked exhausted. Their clothing was grimy and dishevelled. She guessed that they'd been travelling all night.

'How can I help you?' she said.

'There has been ... news, I'm afraid, Sister,' Mr Bryant said quietly. 'And we have to ... We want to tell Monica ourselves.'

'I see.' Cecilia hesitated. Was it up to her to tell them that there could be no visits during retreat? This rule was adhered to very strictly.

'I'll go and find Reverend Mother,' Cecilia said carefully, 'and ask if that will be possible.'

'Thank you, Sister. We'd be most grateful.'

Cecilia slipped out of the room wondering what had brought them such a long distance. Someone must have died ... She shuddered and tried not to remember the Reverend Mother breaking the news to her that Dominic was dead. Reverend Mother had begrudgingly allowed her a quarter of an hour with her parents before they were ushered out again. *Fifteen minutes for my brother's life and no relaxation of the Rule to attend the funeral.* She doubted Monica would be allowed to see her parents at all.

She found Reverend Mother coming out of the chapel, her head bowed.

'Excuse me, Mother.'

The older woman stopped and stared at her blankly.

Cecilia's resolve to speak wavered as the steel eyes met her own. *This better be important* was what the nun was telling her.

'Mother, Monica Bryant's parents have arrived.'

'*Pardon?*'

'I'm afraid old Mother Seraphina showed them in, Mother.'

'Did she now.' The nun frowned. 'And what do they want?'

'They want to see Monica, Mother.'

'Did you tell them that that is impossible?'

'No, I didn't, Mother.'

The older nun frowned in exasperation and then spoke quietly. 'Sister, we are on retreat. Visitors are not allowed. Please go and tell them that.'

'They've come all the way from Adelaide, Mother.' Cecilia was looking at the ground. 'They seem very upset and worried. I think ... there might have been some terrible thing happen. Some death in the family.' Cecilia felt her Superior's whole stance still

336

in the momentary silence between them. *She remembers my brother.*

'Sister Annunciata, would you please go and tell the Bryants that their daughter is on retreat and that it will therefore be impossible to see her,' the Reverend Mother said.

Cecilia found she couldn't move. And with each passing second it seemed more unlikely that she ever would. Her eyes were on the ground, but she could feel the air rushing around them both. It was thick with tension. *Go now. Right now.* Still she couldn't move. Cecilia edged one black shoe back a fraction so it was in line with the other one and saw again the faces of the old couple. How tired and worn and sad they'd been.

'I can't do that, Mother,' she said softly.

The five simple words swung in the space between them. *I can't do that, Mother …*

There must have been something in Cecilia's tone that convinced Mother Gabriel. Her own expression didn't change but she took a breath, turned on her heel and strode off, leaving Cecilia standing by herself in the small courtyard.

Cecilia stared around in a state of shock, half expecting the buildings to crumble down around her or the sky to cave in. *Oh, what have I done?* But the sky didn't cave in and no buildings crumbled. In fact, everything remained remarkably as it had been three minutes before. She looked at her watch and began to walk back to the chapel. It was time for Vespers.

At the chapel steps such a wave of feeling swept over her that she had to hold the door to steady herself. She could not have said if it was happiness or fear or astonishment. But by the time she took her place between Sister Marie Claire and Sister Jane Francis she was quite calm. She picked up her breviary and began to sing.

Deus in adjutorium meum intende,
Domine ad adjuvandum me festina
O God, come to my assistance,
O Lord, make haste to help me

Peach

I'm in a lecture when I hear the ping of my phone and see that it's Det. A shiver of apprehension galvanises me. Det doesn't 'do' text messages. So this means it's something serious. She told me that she doesn't want anyone to come to the hospital with her, but I've told her that I'm not turning off my phone for the next few weeks, just in case. She didn't say anything but I could tell she was sort of in agreement that it might be a good idea.

She's here.

I want to ask who, but I don't because I know.

Where?

Cafe. Ride down if you want to see her.

I'm in a lecture!

Okay then don't.

The lecturer is explaining the way drugs work in the blood.

My best friend is sitting drinking a coffee with my birth mother. Are they talking? What about? Me? This doesn't feel right.

Are you talking to her?

No.

Ignoring her?

Moi?

So what gives?

She cuts out at that point, leaving me hanging, and of course that pisses me off. Part of me wants to jump up and ride down there and check her out for myself. I imagine introducing myself. Holding out my hand. '*Oh hi there, I'm Perpetua and you must be …*' '*Cecilia,*' she'll say, looking me up and down as if I'm kind of interesting but maybe a bit disappointing too.

Why am I thinking this rubbish? There is no need for introductions. She already knows my name. Anyway, I'm in a lecture, a very interesting lecture, so why should I go running after her?

Except the lecture isn't interesting. So far this year I've found university totally boring. I have to drag myself to the lectures and make myself do the reading. I've always been such an enthusiastic and industrious student, I can't get used to the idea of myself as one of the plodders.

I manage to push aside all thoughts of my mother and am concentrating on what the guy up the front is saying when there is another ping. Fluke's name comes up. A rush of excitement hurtles down into my gut. *At least wait until the end of the lecture,* I tell myself. *At least do that, you weak idiot!*

But there has been nothing between us since the trip home from Castlemaine last week. So I read the message.

You okay?

Why shouldn't I be? I write back before I even think.

Drink?

No.

I look up. The lecturer is telling us about spinal cord fluid and how it works.

Where is he? What is he doing? Why does he want to see me? Did he mean a drink now or … some other time? What makes him think he can text me out of the blue? How come I'm behaving like such a jerk? Against all my better instincts I pull out my phone again.

Maybe, I write, *when?*

He doesn't write back and I'm left hanging again.

How do you catch the moment when things shift up a notch or two? Or down? Something changed after Fluke and I kissed on the highway.

But it isn't just him that's making me toey. I keep thinking about Sadie, about Ellen and my birth mother. Cecilia. Any day now, a woman who looks a lot like me is going to stand in front of me and tell me her name is Cecilia and then ... *what?* Maybe unconsciously I want it to happen, but I'm also dreading it.

When my shifts in the cafe are over I've been wandering through the place thinking about where things might have happened and trying to imagine them. I walk in and out of the gate where Sadie would have come to petition for her child back, and I stand in the chapel where Ellen would have sung, and where my own mother made her vows.

I wander through the corridors of Det's floor trying to imagine Cecilia coming out of one of those rooms. It feels pretty close to crazy. And sometimes I find myself crying without knowing why.

Cecilia 1973

Courage, Cecilia, she told herself as she walked up and down between the rows of girls. *Take courage.* She'd taken to calling herself her old baptismal name again without making a deliberate decision to do so. Strange, the way for close on ten years she'd learnt to forget that she'd even had another name. Almost. Thinking of herself as Cecilia again felt reckless.

After lunch, Cecilia went back to her cell and changed the bandeau under her black veil, which was damp with sweat, and checked her shoes were clean. Mirrors were forbidden, but she peered at her reflection in the glass vase on the pedestal at the end of the corridor. Just as well too. There was a tiny spot on her guimpe. On her way downstairs she ran to the basins and rubbed it off with a hand towel.

Feeling almost as if she wasn't walking on her own two legs but on someone else's younger, lighter ones, she hurried out towards Mother Gabriel's office. It was happening. She was doing it. She knew if she waited even one more day she would lose her courage.

She took a deep breath, threw her shoulders back and knocked on the shiny wood.

There was a pause and Cecilia thought she'd better knock again, but just as she raised her hand, the door opened and Mother Mary Gabriel the Archangel was there, opening the door in person, smiling at her.

'My dear Sister Annunciata!' the older woman exclaimed, ushering her in with one hand. 'Do come in, my dear!'

'Thank you, Mother.'

Cecilia stood in the middle of the beautiful room as the Prioress carefully closed the door. The ceiling was high and two long windows were partially draped in heavy curtains to keep out the heat. The carpet was a muted green and all the furniture was polished wood. Cecilia longed suddenly to lie down on the floor. She would have liked to close her eyes, breathe in the cool, calm air and listen to the small sounds of a big empty room. *Tick tick tick* as the hands of the big clock on the wall slowly shifted. The roar and clank of the laundry only barely discernable. She would lie ever so still and wait for ... whatever was going to happen next. The longing for peace was suddenly so intense that she wanted to cry.

The Reverend Mother stopped a few feet from Cecilia and, still with the faint smile, looked her up and down.

'Please sit down, my dear,' she said, pointing to the two identical green armchairs near the window. 'You do look tired and thin!'

Cecilia would have much preferred a hard straight-backed chair with the desk between her and the Superior, but she did what she was told.

'Are you quite well?'

'Yes, Mother.' Cecilia was taken off-guard by the concern in her Superior's voice. 'Perfectly well, thank you.'

'You were on laundry before lunch?'

'Yes, Mother.'

'And ... the girls?'

'Oh well,' Cecilia said, 'it was very hot.'

'They do tend to act up when it gets hot,' Mother Gabriel sighed. 'It makes everything more difficult.'

'Yes.'

'Well, now.' Mother Gabriel smiled coolly and then turned to the window. A breeze was making the blind rattle slightly. 'Dratted thing,' she murmured and got up to fiddle with it.

When she slammed down the window Cecilia jumped, then had the strange sensation that her Superior was locking her in.

Mother Gabriel would have been a good-looking woman in her day. Even now, although her face was lined and she was in her early seventies, her bone structure held firm under the fine pale skin. She was tall, with blue eyes and a small nose. Her figure was upright and neat with not an ounce of extra fat.

'Now, where were we?' The older woman sat down again. 'You do look very tired,' she said, peering at Cecilia closely. 'We do notice such things, my dear.'

'Yes, Mother.'

She knows! Cecilia thought. *I have told no one, and yet she knows. But how could she?* Cecilia had seen this strategy at work before. The display of concern was intended to upset the balance of Cecilia's inner resolve. Of course Mother knew. This nun knew her better than she knew herself. Knew all her faults and inner angst. Nothing was hidden. Cecilia had been fully professed now for close on five years, and every week they had to confess their shortcomings in front of the whole congregation. Not that Cecilia had given even a hint of the momentous decision she'd come to.

Cecilia averted her eyes as the nun continued to look at her.

'Have you been eating well, dear?'

'I've come to speak of something very important, Mother,' Cecilia said desperately. 'Something I can no longer remain silent about.'

The Superior nodded. 'I assumed as much, seeing as we've hardly spoken since last year.'

Cecilia flushed. This was a rebuke for her lack of acceptance of the nun's decision to refuse permission for her brother to visit before he went overseas. Michael had written to Reverend Mother well in advance, telling her of his decision to move to Italy with his Italian wife and children, and *most humbly requesting special permission to visit Cecilia outside visiting hours to say goodbye*. The request had been *sorrowfully denied* on the grounds that they were an enclosed order and that if exceptions were made to the rule then they would have to be made for everyone.

But Cecilia had made the mistake of asking the nun to reconsider the decision on the grounds that she might never see him again. That earlier exchange played out in her head as she watched the older woman settle herself back down in her chair and arrange her hands on her lap. Beautiful hands they were, with fine long fingers and oval nails.

'I'm sorry that you have seen fit to question my decision, Annunciata.' The cold fury behind the words had been terrifying.

'It's just that . . .' Cecilia had stammered.

'Just that *what*, dear?'

'That I think that—'

'What *you* think is beside the point!' The Superior had cut across her like a sharp blade slicing into soft cake.

The shock of her anger had made breathing difficult. Cecilia could do nothing but hang her head.

'Do I make myself clear?'

'Yes, Mother.'

'Then let us hear no more about it.'

'Thank you, Mother.' But what was the point of dwelling on it? They *were* an enclosed order. By committing herself to this way of life she had willingly agreed to forgo all the normal relationships with family and friends. The visiting rule was two hours every first Sunday of the month. No exceptions. None. She knew it.

Concentrate on now, she told herself sternly, *just say what you've practised*. She knew if she didn't keep focused then she'd be likely to lose her nerve completely.

'Mother, I've come to humbly ask that you write to the Holy Father in Rome asking that I might be released from my vows.'

Her voice cracked and she thought for one dreadful moment that she might burst into tears. 'I ... have thought and prayed long and hard about this, and I am absolutely sure that *I ... must ... leave*,' she stammered wretchedly, and looked up to see the older woman still smiling at her.

Nothing was said for close on a minute. Cecilia watched the second hand making its steady progress, and even noted the short click of the minute hand. Every now and again she allowed her eyes to flicker to the nun who was continuing to stare straight at her, still with the fixed smile. Cecilia had geared herself up for this, but it was hard to withstand. Her throat jammed with tears when she thought of how she hadn't been allowed to go to her father's funeral ... Instead of admonishing herself for her bitterness as she would have done in the past, she purposefully dwelt on it and let it grow. The anger would keep her focused and give her strength. On the face of it, her father had been a tyrant and a bully, and yet she'd loved him beyond all reasoning and she was his only daughter. She had wanted so much to see him buried and to pray over his grave.

'Well ...' The older nun sighed. 'And here I was thinking that our dear Sister Annunciata had dealt with her demons at last. That she might be coming here today to express some kind of explanation for her attitude over the last few months.'

Cecilia was speechless. *My attitude?* Hadn't she done everything expected of her? And more? She was supervising the laundry most days, working late into the night sometimes, well after the girls had gone to bed if there was a big job to finish and they were running behind. She went to the university two afternoons a week and was on the Sacred Heart dorm five nights out of seven, and only after that was finished could she even look at her university work, which would take her to midnight most nights. Then she was up again at five-thirty for Lauds. She was worked to the bone and yet it wasn't enough. *Nothing is ever enough.*

'You have been so reticent of late.' The Superior smiled grimly.

'I began to wonder if our Sister Annunciata was going to sulk forever about not being able to farewell her father.'

Had she sulked? Cecilia swallowed desperately. If she was to stay on track, then it wouldn't do for her to be waylaid by this woman's sly innuendos and accusations. 'You usually run the Christmas concert, and last year you had nothing to do with it.'

'I've no voice, but I sang and—'

'But you're usually the one in charge.'

'It was time for someone else to have a turn.'

'Hmm…' The older woman was leaning in towards her. The glittering blue of her eyes pierced Cecilia's resolve, making her doubt everything about herself, making her forget what it was she'd come in to say. 'So, what are these black rings under your eyes about, my dear?'

'I have trouble sleeping, Mother.'

'But that is terrible.'

'Yes, Mother.'

'No one can function without sleep.'

'No, Mother.'

The Superior leant in closer and smiled gently. 'And no one can decide anything without sleep either.'

'No, Mother.'

'You've been with us for … how many years, dear?'

'Nearly ten years, Mother.' *As you well know.*

Reverend Mother shook her head thoughtfully. 'And you made your final profession five years ago?'

'Yes … it is a long time,' Cecilia whispered.

'And you are … how old?'

'Almost thirty, Mother.'

'And you've been happy with us for much of that time?'

'Very happy, Mother.'

'Listen to me, child. Your father and your dear brother are dead. Another beloved brother has gone abroad, perhaps forever, and you're worried about your mother up there on the farm alone.'

'Yes—'

The nun held up one hand to silence her.

'Life *has* been very hard for you of late and that will affect the way you see things. The work here is difficult and you've found it so, haven't you?'

Cecilia gulped and looked away.

'Am I right?'

'Yes, Mother.'

'Some of the girls are very difficult.'

'Yes ... I've had cause to think about a lot of other things.'

'And that is how it should be!' the nun said firmly.

'I mean our girls,' Cecilia said. 'Most of them are just poor. Why should they be punished so?'

'Punished?' The older woman looked amused. 'What on earth do you mean?'

'They have no say over their lives.'

'Everyone has a say over her life, Sister,' the Prioress cut in coldly. 'May I remind you that the Magdalen girls have been sent to us because they have either transgressed society's laws or have been found to be in grave moral danger?'

'By getting drunk with some boy and stealing a pair of shoes?' Cecilia said angrily. 'Or not having a family to take care of them?'

'Yes, all that!' The Prioress stood up and went to the window. There was silence for a while. 'And you more than anyone know that our girls and women are cared for here. Because you are so very good at it.'

'I don't think that I'm special in any way. I—'

'Yes, you are. The girls love you.'

It's true. I'm good with those girls.

'We need bright young women like you, Sister Annunciata,' Mother Gabriel went on relentlessly. 'That you see fit to question some of our practices is a good thing!'

Cecilia stared at her. *A good thing?* She thought bitterly of her noviciate when to question *anything* was considered sacrilege.

The older woman smiled as though she could read her mind.

'Why do you think *you* were chosen for university when others were passed over?'

Cecilia shook her head. She honestly didn't know. Only that she'd been so pleased.

'Because even five years ago we realised that the order was at a crossroads. Our community needs Sisters with education and ideas.'

Cecilia lowered her head. *This woman will kill me.*

'We saw your potential. All of us, Mother Leonard Sebastian along with Help of Christians, we've all noticed your abilities. When the time comes, my dear, you may well be the one to bring our whole community forward into an exciting new era.'

Cecilia's mouth fell open. *When the time comes? What was she saying?*

'Yes, my dear.' The older woman gave one of her musical laughs. 'I would like to see you sitting behind this desk one day. You think and learn quickly. You have a good head for figures, and, most importantly, an ability to combine your compassionate nature with a rigorous, practical attitude. Rare indeed! From the start you saw that the break-up of the girls into family groups was a positive move. So much of our progress over the last few years has involved you.'

Cecilia was suddenly terrified. 'But, Mother, I feel—'

'Please, dear, put your feelings aside for the moment and listen carefully.'

'Yes, Mother.'

'All I ask is that you wait a little while and that you pray.'

'I have prayed about it!' Cecilia protested before she could think. 'For weeks, months!'

The Prioress held up one hand and lowered her voice to a confidential whisper. 'Pray deeply with an open heart for Our Lord's guidance, my dear.'

'Yes, Mother.' Cecilia felt slightly dazed. The woman's eyes were boring into her own.

'As you know, others of your group have left. Paula and Jane Francis to name just two. I was sorry to see them go, but I accepted that it was probably the right decision for them. But for you, Sister Annunciata, I feel deeply that you have been called by God to this way of life. I felt it strongly at your reception and I feel it now.'

'Please, Mother—'

'Of course you can leave whenever you like, dear.' She waved her arm at the door. 'You can walk out of this room and onto the street right now should you so desire.'

'Mother, I don't want to do that.'

'Of course you don't.' Mother Gabriel shook her head. 'No one would want that. To leave as Perpetua did would be completely ... *unnecessary*.'

Cecilia stared at her. This was the first time Breda had been mentioned by any of them. But remembering her friend's hasty departure had the opposite effect to what was intended. It brought Cecilia back to her former resolve with a whoosh. Everything became clear again.

Breda. How she missed her. That tinny little radio that she kept hidden under her mattress! The pictures of football stars she slotted into her missal. The way she taught the laundry girls to dance rock-and-roll on Saturday nights. *Okay, divide into pairs. Tall girls are the blokes.* Breda had the sourest of those girls laughing with a flick of her fingers.

Mother Gabriel was smiling, waiting for a response, but Cecilia was already gone. There were formalities to be got through, that was all, and it was remembering Breda that did it. Remembering her wilfulness, her passionate and impatient spirit. How repugnant to her would be a meeting like this one. She was always one for getting things done fast and furiously.

Just leave. Cecilia could almost hear her. *Too bad if they want you to stay. You don't have to. And you don't have to be polite either. Just go! Piss off, kid!*

Cecilia stood up.

'I have made up my mind, Mother,' she said firmly. 'I am formally asking you to write to the Holy Father in Rome to humbly request that I might be relieved of my solemn vows. My life as a nun in this convent is no longer possible.'

'I see,' Mother Gabriel said coldly, and stood up too. 'Very well.'

They stood looking at each other for a few moments and then, quite suddenly, all tension, enmity and suspicion was gone. It simply faded away, like heat leaving through an opened window at the end of a hot day. A wave of sadness broke inside Cecilia, bringing a rush of tears to her eyes. This proud, intelligent woman had been her Mother, Sister, Teacher and Friend for more than a decade. Cecilia wanted to grab both of those beautiful hands in her own and kiss them. She wanted to thank her, beg forgiveness and ask her blessing.

'Until then I shall speak no word of it to anyone and will endeavour to fulfil all my duties and responsibilities.'

'Very well, my dear.' The Reverend Mother squeezed Cecilia's hand briefly. 'May God be with you all the days of your life.'

'Thank you, Mother.'

Peach

When I look out the window, Stella is on the back verandah doing push-ups. There has to be a first for everything, I guess.

For the last three weeks she has been getting up every morning at six to run with Fluke before he goes to work and she goes to school. I make damned sure I'm in the shower by the time they get back, just in case we run into each other. Not much chance, because he never comes inside.

Of course it's fantastic. She might fall off the wagon any day now, but so far so good. Every three days she weighs herself and the weight is starting to move. I can even see a hint of the old Stella's cheekbones. It's so good to see that it's making her happy too. I just wish it wasn't *him* helping her.

The table is covered with packets of Coco Pops, biscuits, chips, jars of peanut butter and chocolate bars. I turn on the kettle and get a cup.

'I'm getting rid of all that stuff,' she says, coming back inside, puffing slightly, 'so I'm not tempted.' She points at the wall. 'See! We've resurrected the Rules!'

'But I like peanut butter,' I say, rescuing a jar that is almost full. I look over to where she is pointing. The fifteen points of dos and don'ts that we'd worked out months before is now pinned to the wall again. I'm happy about this until I move closer and see Fluke's handwriting scrawled over my neatly printed points.

Under *Think positive about yourself*, he's written, *when you've made some changes!*

Under *Don't weigh yourself too often,* he's written, *Do weigh yourself every few days. It's the only way you can tell how you're doing.*

Where I'd written, *Eat what you like but in small amounts*, he's added, *No! Don't eat what you like. No sweets at all. That goes for fatty stuff. And only small amounts of bread and rice and potatoes too.*

'Has he been in here?' I snipe.

Stella is wandering around the kitchen looking for something. 'He's not an idiot.'

'What is that meant to mean?'

'Well, if someone was waiting for you behind a door with an axe, would you walk through the door?'

I have to laugh. 'Stella, he doesn't know anything about food and diets!' I'm trying to sound rational. 'I did a whole unit on diet and obesity and weight-loss methods at university, and I can tell you now there is no point in dieting.'

'Stop lecturing me,' she says mildly.

'It's just that you'll only put the weight on again. It's got to be a lifestyle change and that means—'

'I'm *not* dieting,' she snaps, 'and this *is* a lifestyle change, so shut up!' She pulls a skipping rope out from under a pile of papers, throws it around her neck, and heads outside again.

'Where did you get the rope?' I follow her out.

'None of your business! I've got to skip for ten minutes now without stopping.' She begins slowly. 'Will you time me, please?'

So I sit down on the top step and time her. At the end of the ten minutes she is puffing but seems happy. She flops down next to me.

'I need rules, Peach,' she puffs.

'I gave you rules!'

But Stella shakes her head. 'Not proper ones,' she sighs.

Loud male voices and laughter suddenly sound around the side of the house. It's the three guys, Nick, Dicko and Screwloose, carrying a wooden cot into the bungalow. 'Hi, you guys.'

'Hi, Stella. Hi, Peach.'

'Is the artist around?' Nick asks.

'Nope.'

'When will she be in?'

'No idea.'

Det comes in late and leaves early, working like a maniac to get her paintings ready for the exhibition before the baby comes.

After dumping the cot into the bungalow the boys come inside and I make them coffee and they end up eating most of the stuff that Stella has put out to throw away.

'So when do your mum and dad get home?' Nick asks, chomping on chips dipped in some kind of relish.

'Next week,' Stella replies, biting into an apple. 'I can't wait. It's been sooo long.' She pulls the chips away from Nick. 'Just think what that crap is doing to your body,' she says seriously, and when we catch eyes none of us can stop laughing for the next ten minutes.

'Oh, my darlings!' Mum grabs first Stella and then me into a huge bear hug. By the time we pull apart the three of us are crying. 'I can't believe how wonderful it is to see you. I've been longing for this so much! Tell me. Tell me everything! Stella, you look fantastic. Tell me, what has been going on? Peach, that colour is lovely on you!'

Cassie hovers near the coffee stand watching the crazy welcome.

'Cassie!' Mum gushes, calling her over for a hug. 'Great to see you, too, gorgeous girl! So good of you to drive us!'

'I'm the original saint.' Cassie laughs and hugs Mum. 'So how come you're so thin?'

Mum is so very thin. The circles under her eyes are big and dark and her clothes are literally falling off her. All the way to the luggage carousel she has to constantly hitch up her jeans. I suppose looking wrecked after a twenty-hour flight is to be expected, but the thinness is something else.

'I was sick for a while,' she says when she sees me and Stella looking at her.

'Why didn't you tell us?'

She shrugs. 'I'm a lot better now.'

'Mum!'

'Tell us.'

'Later. Dad misses you so much,' she says, taking hold of her battered case. 'I just hated leaving him but . . . he has to see his poor old mum out. There is no one else. And I needed to get home to my girls.'

We head out into the fresh blue day, and Cassie leads us towards the car.

'What a job you've done with Stella,' Mum whispers in my ear when we're getting in the car to drive home.

I have to shake my head. 'It's all her doing, Mum, honestly.'

In the car, Mum begins the usual after-flight babble.

'Is the house still standing?'

'Yes, Mum.'

'Is the garden still alive?'

'Yes, Mum.'

'Was Christmas *really* okay?'

'Yes, Mum!'

She tells us in a jumbled way about the trip, the people she met, and the fun they were having, and then about Dad's mother. And the months they've spent at her bedside, expecting her to die every day, and the amazing way she rallied when her only son was with her.

'It's like she's hanging on so they can have a bit of uninterrupted time together at last.'

'How old is she now?'

'Nearly ninety.' Mum sighs and winds down the window. 'Oh, this fresh air is making me drunk! You know, I really wish you girls could have known her.'

'Hmmm.'

'Such a lively woman! Tough too, of course, except she can hardly speak now.'

'Not as nice as your mum, though?' Stella says innocently.

'No way!' Mum says, and we all laugh.

Mum and me are in the back seat and Stella is with Cassie in the front.

'How is Stephano?' Mum calls to Cass, and I listen to them talking about Stephano's latest magnificent achievements, thinking of my other grandmother, Ellen, in the country.

Then Mum begins to cough and cough and cough. It just goes on and on. It's the worst cough I've ever heard, and in the end she has to ask Cassie to stop so she can get some medicine out of her case.

'Look at you!' Mum exclaims as Det opens the door for us when we get home. 'Just look at you!' There are tears in her eyes and her hands go straight to Det's huge belly.

'Get a grip, Elizabeth,' Det says, but she turns side-on so Mum can get a better look at her bulge.

'How are you feeling?'

'Pretty good.'

'So, boy or girl?'

'Don't know.' Det shrugs.

'You care?'

'Nope.'

'Long as it's healthy,' we all chorus together.

Det's one culinary skill is scones, and she's made mountains of them to welcome Mum home. The smell is absolutely wonderful. Bowls of cream and jam sit on the table. Cups are out and everything looks festive.

'Why do this to me?' Stella moans.

'It's a special occasion,' I say tentatively, 'maybe you can have one or—'

'No!'

'I'll give you a dispensation.' Det flicks Stella with her tea towel. Mum pats Stella. 'Just a little bit won't hurt, will it?'

'Fluke has got me new scales,' Stella wails, 'and there's a weigh-in tomorrow morning!'

'Fluke?' Mum looks at me.

'Ask *her*.'

'Fluke is my weight-loss guru,' Stella says.

'You mean Fluke Robinson?'

'The very one,' I say dryly.

'He's fantastic!' Stella sits up.

'But what does he know about losing weight?'

'Exactly,' I say.

'Peach's nose is way out of joint,' Det sings.

'It's working,' Stella snaps defensively.

'Well, if you're happy, that's wonderful,' Mum soothes. She looks at Det. 'How did you know I've been dreaming about your scones?'

We sit down and Det serves the tea and describes the feelings of tiredness and aching legs she's been having and how she wishes it was over. And Mum goes into doctor mode explaining what is happening, feeling Det's tummy this way and that, and asking questions.

I sit back and listen, trying not to be offended because Det has said more to my mum in the past minute or two about being pregnant than she has in the last eight and a half months to me.

Stella sits eyeing off the food like a hungry lioness. I can tell it's killing her to see some of the scones left begging on the plate. Her eyes keep edging back to the table. When everyone is more or less finished she dips her finger in the cream and brings it to her mouth, and when she thinks no one will notice she casually does the same with the jam.

'Stella,' Cassie says warningly, 'no.'

'Have a friggin' scone, Stella,' Det growls and pops one on her plate.

This is too much for Stella. She picks it up and breaks it in two.

'Don't undermine her, Det,' Cassie says sharply and smacks the scone right out of Stella's hand before it reaches her mouth. It rolls under the table.

'Let her eat it!' Det orders.

'No!'

Stella dives under the table and has already stuffed the scone into her mouth by the time she is sitting up in her chair again.

I don't really know why we all start laughing, but when I get up to clear the dishes I fall over and drop two cups on the kitchen floor. That only makes us laugh harder.

'I've got appendicitis,' Cassie groans after a while, holding her belly. 'I'll die if this doesn't stop soon.'

'And I've got a baby.' Det leans against the wall, holding onto her belly too. 'Which is worse.'

'And I'm starving, which is much worse,' Stella shouts.

'Please stop laughing, Det. *Please!*'

'Why me?' Det sounds as if she is choking.

'The baby...'

'What if she has it here?' Stella squeals.

'Go on, Det!' We shriek with laughter. 'Have it here. Now!'

When we come to our senses I look across at my mother only to find her looking at me, and there is such love in her eyes it makes me want to fall on the floor and bawl my eyes out.

But we just smile at each other and look away.

When I come out from my shower the next morning, Stella, Det and Mum are sitting at the table drinking tea and I ... I just know that she knows what has been going on. Mum looks more frazzled and worn out than she did the night before, and it makes me frightened to see her so. I look at the others.

'Tea?'

'Thanks.'

I pour my tea and get the milk and sit down.

No one speaks.

'I've just heard about the trip up to ... Castlemaine,' Mum begins. I nod and concentrate on my tea. They are all looking at me and so I get up and put in some toast.

'And Det has met her. Your ... birth mother?'

'Yes.'

'Are you okay about it all?' she asks tentatively and when I look up I suddenly see the fear in her eyes, and I know what I've always known to be true, although nothing was ever said – this stuff is actually huge for her. I'm overcome with guilt. She has come home, sick, only to find that she has to start being brave about one of her deepest fears.

'I don't know.' I shrug. 'I suppose.'

Mum gets up and stands looking out the window.

When I go to her I see that her face is ashen and drawn. 'What is it, Mum?'

'Sorry, but ... I just hate her now,' Mum whispers.

What? This is so *not* Mum. What happened to the idea of being appreciative of my birth mother? The idea that she'd given Mum the most precious gift in the world?

'Mum, what do you mean?'

'Of course you've got to meet her.' Mum is wringing her hands wildly. 'But if she thinks she can muscle in on your life and upset you and the rest of us ... If she thinks she can somehow be part of this family, then she has another think coming!'

'She won't, Mum! I promise. I won't let her!'

Mum bursts into tears and I take her in my arms and she feels as thin and fragile as a tiny bird, all skin and bone. 'You'll always be my mum,' I tell her. 'You told me that and I believed you.'

'But you were little then!' she cries desperately. 'Now you're an adult!'

'What difference does that make?'

'When you see her you might feel differently.'

'I won't, Mum.'

'But you don't know!' she sobs. 'None of us knows.'

It turns out that Mum is really sick. It takes a while for the doctors to work out that she has picked up a very nasty parasite, and by the time they do she is worse. Her immune system is run down and the drugs she has to take are very strong. Basically she has to stay in bed to let them do their work. You would think her being a doctor would make her understand what she has to do to get well, but the opposite seems to be true. She is the worst patient. As soon as she regains a little energy she is up wanting to get on with everything. Within an hour or two of rushing around ringing people up and organising things she collapses in a heap, unable to even get up to her feet. In the end Stella takes over and starts bossing her around.

I write to Ellen to tell her that my mother is home and sick and that the trip to the cemetery must be postponed. She writes a nice letter back. But even in the few months since I got that first letter her handwriting has gone downhill. The words on the envelope have taken on a shaky, fragile quality that wasn't there before. What if she dies? I will never forgive myself. I so very much want to take her to her mother's grave. I owe her that much.

It is an astonishing thing to admit, but ... *I love that old woman.* A few letters and a visit and she feels part of me in some weird way.

Cecilia 1979

It was more out of curiosity than anything else that Cecilia went along to hear the priest speak at a seminar called The Church in the Third World. He turned out to be just as mesmerising as the first time she'd heard him all those years before. It pleased her so much to see that the fire was still in his belly.

She was wearing a long red skirt with boots and a fitted black jumper. Her hair had grown and was blonde and curly, spilling all over the place. When the talk was over she decided not to approach him. Apart from the fact that he probably wouldn't recognise her out of the nun's habit, she was nervous. Her life had begun to ever-so-gradually come together. She was living on her own in the city, she had a job and a plan to go overseas as soon as she could.

But on her way out of the room she met a couple of older women she recognised and stopped to talk. After ten minutes of chitchat she was at the point of saying goodbye to them when she felt a hand on her arm. She turned around to find him standing there smiling at her, and it was as if someone had pulled open a blind in a dark room and let a flood of bright sunlight in.

'Annunciata,' he grinned, 'so you did leave!'

'Yes. And it's Cecilia now.'

'I couldn't believe it when I looked down and saw you.' His eyes had the same warmth, and so did his smile.

'Here I am.'

'So, you're working?'

'Yes. Teaching.'

'What are your plans?'

'I want to go overseas.'

'Good.'

They went for a cup of coffee and exchanged information. There was so much to talk about and not enough time and so they agreed to meet again the following day.

Cecilia made tea and they sat on the floor of her tiny apartment. Did it begin with hands touching? Maybe just a thumb stroking the inside of her wrist as they jabbered on about ... *What did they talk about?* A lot of the talk was about God. God and Mission and Life and Politics. They were two idealists in love with the grand order, wanting to put things right, wanting to find the right way to live. They wanted all the good in their hearts to connect up with the way they lived their lives in the world.

But in the end they were just two bodies gravitating towards each other as nature intended. Cecilia was thirty-five and had never been with a man before. Peter was nearly forty and had entered the seminary at twenty-three, living a celibate life since. But what they lacked in expertise they made up for in desire and, yes, love. It was love-making in the truest sense of the word and it was wonderful. He wasn't a handsome man exactly, his features were too roughly hewn, his nose and chin too big, his brows too heavy and yet ... his eyes were so warm and bright, and his mouth was moving all the time, smiling, laughing and screwing up with concentration, trying to understand things. The dark, coarse hair springing from his head reminded Cecilia of a horse's mane. When she wasn't with him she yearned to feel it in her hands, up against her arm, rubbing like a soft brush against the skin of her breasts.

What saved them, or perhaps doomed them depending on how you wanted to look at it, was the fact that he was due back at his mission in the Philippines in a few weeks.

'So, do you make a habit of this, Peter?' Cecilia asked.

'What?' he said dreamily.

'Sleeping with women?'

'No!' he said, shocked, sitting up. 'Why would you think that?'

They were lying on her narrow bed with bodies still entwined. Cecilia was high on the warmth of him and the hair on his arms and the fact that his face was pressed up against her ear.

'Why not? You're handsome. There would be plenty of opportunity ... everywhere you go.'

'I'm a priest,' he said, as though that was adequate.

'And yet here you are,' she said.

He said nothing for a while. Then he spoke quietly into her ear. 'Some priests can live dual lives, Cecilia, but not me. I've got to be able to look the people in the face. I owe it to them to be who I say I am.'

'And so?'

'Marry me.'

'What?' It was Cecilia's turn to sit up.

'I'll leave the priesthood if you'll marry me.'

She was overwhelmed, terrified because she could see he meant it.

And she almost said yes. *Let's buy a house together and have a family. Let's go on picnics and barrack for the Bombers.*

But in the end she couldn't. She knew his heart was with his work, and she didn't want to stop him being able to do the tough, great things he was doing. Wasn't it bad enough that she'd broken her own solemn vows? The idea of being the cause of someone else doing the same would have been too much to bear.

The right to personal happiness was not something she'd ever taken all that seriously. It was more important to live with integrity, and that was proving difficult enough. *To take the hard road through the narrow gate. The road that leads to Life.*

And so they'd parted without any agreement to meet up again or even to write.

It was over.

He would confess his fall from grace to his brothers in Christ and get on with his work. She would finish her Diploma of Education and get a job overseas.

Neither of them had any idea then that there was a child involved.

Peach

Sometimes the most extraordinary days begin in such an ordinary way. I wake on the morning of Det's launch to the now-familiar sound of Stella coming in from her run with Fluke. She barges around the kitchen whistling and singing, getting the coffee. Mum must be downstairs too, because I can hear both their voices.

I watch the light playing across the top of my bed and wonder idly how many will turn up to the launch. We all want Det to do well out of it financially. Apart from two paintings which are still not completely dry, all the work was hung two days ago and the final two go up this afternoon.

I go downstairs and find Mum and Stella sitting at the table, and Cassie, dressed uncharacteristically in old stretch pants, is at the door on her way out and looking agitated.

'Cassie?'

'Mild pains on and off yesterday.'

'What?'

'Have a guess!'

'But … it isn't due yet!'

'False alarms happen all the time.' Mum shrugs. 'Stop panicking.'

'She can't have it today,' Cassie declares. 'Elizabeth, is there something we can give her to stop it?' Mum and Stella and me raise our eyebrows at each other. 'I don't mean anything drastic!'

'Some little pill, Mum?' I laugh.

'I only mean something to see her through the launch.'

'Not really, Cass,' Mum says mildly. 'Odds on it will all be fine, though. First babies are usually late, not early.'

After uni I go down to the convent, where they are hanging the final two paintings. Det's in the middle of the room yelling at some guy that one painting should be higher and that another isn't in the right spot and that another isn't straight.

'Are you okay?'

'Yeah.' She looks at me like I'm stupid.

'You ... having pains or something?'

'No ...'

'So?'

'How is your mum feeling?' Det asks.

'Bit better.'

'I want her here tonight.'

'She's planning to come.'

But when I get home Mum says even though she feels so much better she won't be able to manage the launch. She'll go see the paintings during the week when she feels stronger.

'Will you be okay here tonight on your own?'

'Of course.'

I run my eye over the list of guests. Apart from our friends, most of the names are unknown to me except for ... *Fluke.* I consider garrotting Stella, but decide that it's not worth the effort.

'Who asked him?' I say. As though I don't know.

'Me.' Stella is completely easy about it.

'Why?'

'He's my friend now.'

'Really?'

'Yep.'

He and I haven't set eyes on each other since the Castlemaine incident, even though he and Stella have been running almost every day. He never responded to my phone message, which is humiliating. And Cassie has told me privately that she's seen him twice eating Saturday breakfast with some girl in a Fitzroy cafe. Of course I'm desperate to know who the girl is. Cassie didn't know, but said she'd find out. When I pressed her she admitted that the girl was very good-looking.

'How good-looking?' I asked stupidly. *As good-looking as me?*

'Pretty damned gorgeous, actually,' Cassie said sharply. 'What do you think? He's a nice-looking guy. If you want him, then do something about it.'

'As though I do!'

'Well... why the questions?'

'I'm interested is all!'

'Right!'

And so... the question of what to wear to the launch takes on a new importance. I want to look *hot*, of course, but in a cool, edgy way, like I've moved on in my life too.

I try a hundred combinations and by the time I end up in a flouncy black silk skirt with bright pink tights and some high-heeled ankle boots of Mum's, every single thing I own is strewn over my room and the green top isn't right but I don't know what to do about it and my heart is still jangling. To give myself an edge I tease my hair up into a kind of bun with this wax stuff that I find in the bathroom. Then I fit a big green sixties satin bow around my waist, wondering if I might have lost it completely. Is this edgy and cool, or is it just weird?

Stella comes downstairs an hour before the launch is due to start to find me tottering around the kitchen in my ultra-high heels at the same time waxing small strands of hair so they stand out at odd angles. She stops in the doorway when she sees me.

'God!' she whispers, her mouth falling open.

'Well?' I look at her hopefully.

'You look completely *ridiculous*,' she says.

I shrug as if I don't care.

'Sorry ... but someone has to tell you, Peach!'

I resist the temptation to turn nasty. After all, this is my sister talking.

'It's just all *wrong*,' she declares impassively.

'In what way?'

'Weird, Peach, and *not* in a good way!'

'Stella!'

'Well ...'

'I'm just trying something different.'

'It's not you. Are you trying to look like one of those princesses at a royal wedding or something?'

'No!'

Of course I care. Stella has always had a better sense of style than me. I pull the stupid bow off angrily and chuck it on the floor, and then I grab a comb from the table and drag it through all the teased-up knots. 'Well ... what *do* I wear?'

She shakes her head as if she is already thinking of something much more interesting.

'How come you and Det are allowed to look wacky and sharp when you dress up but I'm not?' I wail.

'Because we *are* wacky and sharp!' Stella laughs. She takes the comb from me and starts pulling it through the knots at a kinder pace. 'And you're not.'

'I'm boring, in other words?'

'Yep,' she giggles. 'Got it in one. Ask anyone.'

I snatch the comb back and go over to the window.

'Where's Mum?'

'In bed watching TV.'

We have less than an hour to get there and Stella is still in her jeans and old T-shirt and rubber thongs.

'Aren't you going to dress up?'

She makes a face and shrugs.

'Why not?'

'I've got a weird feeling,' she says.

Oh God, here we go.

'What kind of feeling?' I say, and when she doesn't answer I ask, 'About what?'

She sighs dramatically, as if it's me who is being deliberately obtuse, and walks out of the room. 'If you want to impress him, wear that short red dress,' she shouts from the hallway, 'with the black tights. Those high heels are good, but the pink legs aren't.'

'*Who? What do you mean?*' I shoot back.

'Just comb your hair out and leave it alone!'

About an hour into the launch I start to get a weird feeling, too, in spite of the fact that the whole thing seems to be working brilliantly.

Nick and Dicko and Stella have set themselves up in the corner with a double bass and an electric violin and keyboard. The fact that Stella has agreed to sing is ... well, it means a lot. The gypsy jazz stuff that Cassie specifically ordered for the evening works a treat in this space. Even before people begin to arrive, the room is alive with the warmth and gaiety of their music.

I stand and watch those three in awe as the room gradually fills up. They slip so easily from gypsy to jazz to waltzes to swing and back again, just as if they've been born doing it together. The reality is they've only had one proper practice the previous weekend, and yet with a little smile or a flick of the hands they all seem to understand that a change of rhythm is called for, or it's time to move on to something else. It's like a separate language. I really envy my sister this. Whatever happens to her in life she has this ...

I recognise the guy from the Arts Show, along with some semi-famous comedians. How did Cassie get onto these people? Within minutes, it seems half of Melbourne has followed them and the place turns from a quiet, contemplative space into a large room crammed with people, loud voices, chinking glasses, laughter and music.

Cassie is working the room like a pro, whizzing around from one group to the next, introducing everyone to everyone else. She looks fantastic in a black sequined dress with her dark hair pulled back under an old-fashioned velvet net thing covered in sparkles. I have a flash of her at fifty doing exactly the same sort of thing as she's doing right now, looking more or less the same, too, except for a wrinkle or two, and the sparkles in her ears and around her throat will be real diamonds, and she'll be doing it on the world stage. New York or London or Madrid.

She is literally crowing as she sidles up to me in the kitchen where I've gone to replenish the plate of glasses I'm carting around.

'Can you believe this?' she breathes into my ear, as I grab myself a slurp of wine. 'Eight paintings have gone already!'

'Fantastic!' I agree. 'You genius, you!'

'Det is the genius,' Cassie says quickly, 'but she needs people like us.'

'*You.*'

She grins at me. 'Okay, *me* then!'

On every wall, Det's extraordinary paintings hang like a collection of lovely shining dreams, some deep and dark and moody, others bizarre and even a bit ghoulish. There are a couple of portraits that I have to avoid looking at, because every time I do shivers shoot up my spine. It's as if some stranger has come up unexpectedly to whisper some devastating bit of news in my ear.

Even the four small, very beautiful and seemingly simple still-life canvases depicting roses have an eerie side to them. When you move in close you can see that most of the flowers are beset with grubs and ants; a few smaller puny buds have been eaten away and are on the verge of death. *Det!* I want to grab her and say, *Don't do this to me!*

'That whole series has gone already,' Cassie says triumphantly.

I nod and smile at her. Cass is on cloud nine; her eyes are sparkling like stars and her wonderful olive skin glows with excitement.

'Who bought it?'

'Some guy called Wishful Lee.'

'*What?*'

We both start giggling.

'True,' she says. 'I thought they'd made a mistake, but no.'

'Imagine calling your baby *Wishful*.'

'I know. Totally.'

'Maybe his parents were wishing he was someone else. Has everyone come?'

She grins and squeezes my wrist until it hurts. 'Owen Morrissey is running a little late,' she says triumphantly.

By now I know that Owen Morrissey is some crusty old bigwig with huge international credentials who is going to open the exhibition. More importantly, he loves Det's work. Getting him is a major coup, according to Cassie, because he hardly ever gets out anymore to look at the work of young artists.

She has gauged the evening perfectly. After work and before dinner on a Thursday night just before the long weekend seems to be the right time for everyone. The buzz is positive, excited. We walk out into the general throng again.

'See that guy she's talking to?' She points to where Det stands in one corner with a short man with a grey beard. I nod. 'Morris Blackwood from Becks, Blackwood and Westfield.'

I know I'm meant to be impressed by this, but I honestly have no idea. 'Who are they?'

'Peach! Only the biggest law firm in the city, and ... *they buy art*.' Cass relishes enlightening me.

'Oh. Have they bought anything yet?'

'Not yet. I just hope Det is not saying anything stupid.'

Det looks good in the deep red dress embroidered in black around the wide neck and sleeves that Cassie found for her in a quality samples shop in Johnston Street. It manages to diminish the size of her belly without actually hiding it. Her long red hair is clean and shining and pinned up with Stella's combs, and although Det doesn't smile a lot, every now and again her face lights up and that does me in. Det is happy.

'He's a really big collector!' Cassie whispers in awe. 'And I didn't even invite him.'

'How come he's here then?'

'Believe me, Peach, that doesn't matter. The fact that he's here is very good.'

'If you say so,' I laugh.

'Go check out the red dots,' she says gleefully.

'What do they mean?'

'Sold.' She looks at me. 'We've broken even and there is still an hour to go.' Cassie looks at her watch. 'Can you tell Det that speeches will be in twenty?'

'Okay.'

I set off in the vague direction of the corner where Det was standing with the short man. But I get caught up a few times, mainly with people I haven't seen for a while, and then by a couple of paintings that I hadn't see before.

I stand for a while in front of the one of her father that she did all those months ago. The kids playing, the man's uneasy smile, the crushed can under his feet... I can smell the grass and feel the heat from the sun. I see the desperation in the man's eyes. I suddenly have this mad urge to reach into the painting, grab him, shake him up and tell him to come back. *Marty.* I shudder because my birth mother had a brother who at roughly the same age decided to check out too. How bad would you have to feel to do that?

'If my baby is a boy I'm going to call him Paul or Marty,' Det told me a few weeks ago, 'maybe both.' I didn't like the idea at all although I didn't say it. *Too much for one kid,* was what I wanted to say. *Way too much.*

'Do you hope it's a boy?'

'I don't care,' she shrugged.

Then I notice that the painting is part of a series, four paintings in all, different sizes but thematically joined by the title *Blood Ties,* written in large black letters next to each one.

Down the creek is the first of the series, depicting three young boys playing in water under a harsh sun, surrounded by brown dirt. The father stands to the side with a shotgun, staring at crows crowded onto a branch of a nearby dead tree.

One sore head is another of her father with his head in his hands staring bleakly at a giant television screen where girls are dancing with old men in tuxedos. My heart skips a beat. So this is … *the family.* Her father features in every painting, along with various combinations of brothers as little kids and then as gangling youths. Det herself doesn't feature at all, of course.

The last one in *Blood Ties* is titled *Oh Mother!* and it is a nude - an older woman with long red hair. She sits near a window, looking out; her breasts are large and saggy, her skin pale, nails painted bright garish pink. Smoke from her half-finished cigarette wafts out the window into the silky blue sky outside. An ornate mirror hangs on a nearby wall, and in it the reflection of her husband's scowling face. It's a very beautiful painting. The red of the woman's hair ricochets off the deep slashes of red and orange around the edges of the cold blue and green tones of her pale flesh. Bold and careless, there is also an exquisite delicacy under the surface garishness. The knowingness in the woman's defiant expression makes it difficult to look at her for long. One thing is certain, she is not about to apologise for anything. *Oh Mother!* And yet she is heartbreaking, and I know this is crazy and I don't know how I know it but … I suddenly know … *Det loves her!* I can tell.

This angry, lost woman trapped inside a sagging body reaches right into the core of me and I can't turn away. *Blood Ties …*

A gasp escapes before I can swallow it down. Then a weird kind of fury creeps up on me like a sly thief who's been watching for his opportunity to pounce. Without warning, he is on me, hands around my throat, gripping like a vice, and there is nothing I can do but flail around like a sick bird trying to ward off the attack. *Blood Ties …* I don't even know my father's name! What if I have his smile or his gait, the way I have her hair and eyes? The thought half blinds me, races around my head like a kid made crazy on too much sugar.

The crowd mingles around me, warm, noisy and good-humoured, soaking up the music and the food and alcohol. But a thin coat of insulating ice covers my skin. I stand in a trance in front of the painting of the red-haired woman and the lost man in the mirror, unable to move. An image of the grimy abandoned Sacred Heart dormitories appears in my head, the way I first saw them with Stella. She said she could smell the girls, but I know now what it was she was smelling. After more than three decades it was still hanging about there in the wood and dust and empty spaces. *Loneliness.* I can feel it fluttering down through the decades, like kapok flung from an old mattress. On and on and on it goes.

I stand in front of the painting, feeling it settle inside me.

The trance lifts and the guilt, when it hits, is nothing short of astonishing. It rushes into my mouth and eyes, my gut and lungs, like poisonous air, stinging and foul, making me want to gag, double over and retch it up.

I rush outside and pull out my phone.

'Mum, are you okay?'

'Of course I am, sweetheart! I'm watching telly in bed. How is the launch going?'

'Good.' My voice wavers. 'Lots . . . lots of people.'

'I can hear! Wish I was there.'

'Are you . . . comfy, Mum?'

'Yes, just enjoy yourself.'

'I love you, Mum.'

I watch the party through the open doorway as I try Dad's number in England.

'Dad?'

'Peach!'

'How is going it over there? Your mum and . . . everything?'

'Very slowly, love. Poor old Mum.' He gives one of his laughs. 'They say she might leave us tonight, but who knows . . . What is that noise?'

'Det's launch.'

'Oh. Fantastic. Going well?'

'Yep.'

There is a pause. My throat jams. I can't speak.

'What is it, darlin'?'

'I just …'

'What, sweetheart?'

'I miss you, Dad,' I say, my voice catching. 'So much.'

'Oh I miss you too, love! All of you, so much. I reckon I'll be home in a week. Ten days tops.'

'Do you?'

'I'll catch the first plane back … after, I promise.'

I go back inside and join the party. This room was where the nuns ate their meals in silence. How strange all this chatter and noise would seem to them now. My own mother was here at my age, sitting at a table in this room, listening to readings in silence and praying … *What did her prayers sound like?*

For the first time in my life I seriously wish I could pray. I circle the room again, thinking of the way I've seen it done in the movies, kneeling down with closed eyes and clasped hands and then … *what?* Maybe something happens if you do all that? Maybe God is out there somewhere waiting for me to kneel down, clasp my hands and close my eyes? But I doubt it.

'Did you tell Det?' Cassie snaps at me.

'I can't find her.'

'What's up?' Cassie's narrowed eyes search my face. 'Are you okay?'

'Yeah.'

'You look as if you've seen a ghost.'

'It's nothing,' I sigh.

'We've got to have the speeches in a minute.'

Stella breaks in between us. 'She'll be taking a breather outside.'

'She'll be having a fag, you mean.'

In retrospect, it should have been obvious, but at the time we didn't really seriously consider the possibility.

As we predicted, all the chatter, the crowd and the general pressure had got a bit much for Det, so she decided to slip out and have a few minutes to herself in the dark, sitting on the stone steps leading into the Bishop's Parlour, rolling herself a cigarette. Then she remembered that the precious notebook where she'd made a few notes for the speech she planned to give was up in her studio. She put the unlit cigarette back in the pouch and made her way inside towards the huge dark staircase.

She got to the first floor okay and stood for a while on the landing between the two floors to catch her breath before beginning the second flight. It was after seven o'clock by this stage and no one was about. The corridor lights were very dim but she was able to make her way to her studio.

She tried the door, thinking that she'd have to go down again for the key, but it was in fact unlocked.

Det pushed the door open and turned on the light and to her dismay, suddenly and with no warning, a rush of water began to course down her legs. It took her some time to twig what was happening.

But within minutes she was swamped with gripping pains that had her crouching on the floor.

'Fuck this!' she said loudly for no one to hear. 'This can't be happening!' She fumbled around in her little bag for her phone to ring Cassie for help, but all she had with her was a packet of tobacco, her credit card and about fifteen business cards that people had given her that night. Even at that stage she was still thinking that it would pass and how she must get down to give her speech.

Of course, we knew nothing of this until much later.

Stella and I are wandering around outside calling her name and asking if anyone knows where she is.

375

We don't find her amid the small cohort of smokers standing about in the courtyard directly outside the exhibition space, so we check the ground-floor toilets.

When they prove empty we rush off around to the front of the convent into the lovely garden leading down to the river. When we come back round to the door of the reception room, Cassie is waiting for us.

'You found her yet?'

We shake our heads. Stella suddenly takes a few steps away from us, her strange expression illuminated by the yellow outside light.

'*What?*'

'Oh God.' Ever the drama queen, Stella's mouth falls open.

'What?' Cassie asks.

'I've got this feeling,' she says.

'What kind of feeling?' Cassie stares at Stella, who has this I've-just-seen-a-ghost sort of look on her face. 'She can't!' Cassie wails. 'Not *now!*'

'I'll go check her room,' Stella offers.

Cassie raises her eyes to heaven and then pushes back through the crowd to where the microphone is. I'm caught between her and Stella. I know I probably should try to help Cassie out, but instead I follow Stella. We look up, and sure enough, a yellow light is shining through the window on the second-floor room that is Det's studio. We turn to each other.

Stella is off, running towards the side door of the building that leads up into Det's wing. I begin to follow but a familiar voice makes me stop.

'Hey, Peach.'

I turn around to see Fluke standing there looking so very cool that I actually stop a moment to take him in. He's wearing jeans, and both his hands are tucked into the pockets of a really nice leather jacket.

'What's the hurry?' he says, not smiling.

I hesitate only a moment, and then on a mad impulse I rush

over to him. He steps back in surprise as though I might be going to strike him, and we stare into each other's eyes, our faces only inches apart.

'I miss you,' I say quickly.

His eyes drop to his feet as he considers how to respond to this piece of news, but I don't wait.

'Where are you going?' he yells after me.

'Got to find Det.'

It crosses my mind that all that exercise in the morning has been doing a lot for Stella, because I'm finding it pretty hard keeping up with her as she pounds up the stairs. Both of us are breathing hard by the time we get to the dim corridor of the second floor.

Without knocking we simply push the door open to find Det kneeling on the floor, her bum resting on her heels, one hand cradling her belly and the other hanging tightly onto the leg of her desk. There is a shiny film of perspiration over her face, but she manages a wry smile.

'I'd better go to hospital,' she says.

'Okay. I'll call an ambulance.' I try to sound reassuring. Then I realise that after talking to Dad, I put my phone in my bag and stashed it with Cassie's stuff at the back of the gallery. I look at Stella, who stares back blankly and shrugs. *Unbelievable.*

Det suddenly begins to groan, and that makes us both panic.

'Peach,' she gasps, 'I need to go to hospital!'

'Okay,' I say, still trying to sound like I'm in charge. 'I'll just go down and find a phone and we'll get you there, okay?'

Det reaches up and clutches my hand really tightly as though she is suddenly very scared.

'No, don't leave me here.'

I look at Stella, who nods. But Det grabs her too.

'No, please don't go. Not now, I need both of you!' She is groaning, sitting on the floor with her back against the wall, her knees up, whimpering with pain.

Stella and I look at each other. I'm suddenly in complete

panic. Everything I've ever learnt about birthing has just flown straight out of my head. I really have no idea if the birth is imminent or the level of pain has simply intensified or ... there is no way I'll be able to cope with this. None. I have no idea what we should do.

'Det, one of us has got to leave and get help,' Stella says softly into her ear.

'No no.' She is sweating and groaning and hanging onto both of us tightly. 'Please don't go yet. Just ring for an ambulance.'

'But we don't have—' I pull myself away from her clammy hands and go to the window. The launch is still in full swing down there inside the brightly lit room, and there are maybe a couple of dozen people milling around out on the lawn. I spot Fluke walking towards them. I pull up the sash and the talk and laughter drift up in through the open window.

'Call an ambulance!' I yell down.

No one hears, or if they do they don't take any notice and so I try again, this time louder. 'Fluke!' I scream down. 'Up here!'

He looks up to where I'm hanging half out the window and changes course towards me.

'Call an ambulance!' I shout.

'What?' He comes nearer.

'Call a fucking ambulance. Now!'

'Why? Are you okay?'

'Just do it!' I scream. 'It's the baby! Hurry. Tell them it's an emergency!'

He gives me the okay sign and pulls his phone from his pocket.

When I turn back to the room I see that Stella and Det are laughing, but I don't ask why because by the time I'm kneeling down on the other side of her, Det is beset with another long excruciating contraction that has her gasping and grabbing me so hard that the bones in my hand feel as if they might break.

'Ambulance on its way, Detto,' I whisper. 'Fluke will show them where to come. Try to stay calm.'

She snorts, as though staying calm might be beside the point, and continues groaning.

'Is it terrible, Det?' Stella asks simply.

'Yep,' Det says through gritted teeth. 'It's pretty bad.'

Unlike me, Stella seems to know instinctively what to do. She grabs a couple of cushions, puts them behind Det, and then, kneeling on one side of her, puts an arm of support around her back and the other under Det's knees.

'Get on the other side,' she orders me. 'Its okay, Det,' Stella says calmly. 'You're doing good and you'll be in hospital really soon.'

It goes on like this for a few minutes. I'm trying to keep time but I've forgotten why. All I know is that the contractions are coming really fast on each other. Det is sweating and groaning.

At almost exactly the time we hear the ambulance siren, Det give a really loud scream.

'Something is happening,' she shouts loudly, her eyes wide with fear. 'Oh sweet Jesus! Oh shit ... Oh this is fucking crazy! Help me!'

I go to the window and look out. Behind me I hear Stella telling Det softly, 'It's okay, baby. They're here now. We can see them. And you're going to be okay.'

'I don't think so,' Det is half screaming now. 'This is too much for me! I can't do this. This is terrible.'

'Yes, you can!' says my magnificent sister. 'Come on, baby, lie on your side a bit, that's right, curl up your legs and look at me, hold my hand. That's right. And we're going to breathe in and out together. Okay?'

'Okay,' Det sobs.

From the second floor I look down to see that the ambulance with all its flashing lights has arrived. Luke will tell them where to go. Relief fills my whole body and I start to shake.

'Hold on, Det. They'll be here any minute.'

'I can't hold on!' Det screams at me. 'I can't.'

'Okay. Okay.'

There is the sound of feet thudding along the corridor outside. I fly across the room to let them in. But it's Cassie, looking dishevelled.

'Oh God! God!' Det yells again. And begins to gasp and strain.

Two ambulance officers follow Cassie though the doorway, holding a stretcher, blankets and a black case of equipment.

'Well, well, well!' the middle-aged woman smiles as she comes into the room. 'So what have we here?'

'Hospital, immediately,' I snap.

'I'm Penny and this is Tony,' the woman says, ignoring me.

We all just look at her as though she's completely mad. What do we care what their names are when Det is lying here ... *dying!*

'Please,. I'm sobbing now myself, and I grip Det's hand again.

'It's okay, love,' the woman says calmly and I ... just want to slap her.

'And now who is our patient?' the woman asks mildly as she kneels down next to Det.

'Det,' the rest of us roar. 'But hurry! Please take her. Get her out of here.'

But the woman doesn't hurry. All her movements are assured, and I suppose that has the effect of calming the rest of us down. She kneels and gently checks over Det's belly.

'Hi there, Det,' she says. 'How are you feeling, darlin'?'

Between moans, Det answers her as best she can.

The woman asks a few more questions as she times the pains, and then the guy kneels on the other side and they both listen with the stethoscope and confer quietly, all the while murmuring reassuringly to Det.

The rest of us watch apprehensively, longing for the moment when they're going to hoist her onto that stretcher. But when they look under Det's dress I see the surprise on their faces.

'Oh.' The woman smiles.

'Please get her to hospital,' Cassie says desperately.

'No time, love. This baby is ready now.'

Oh God. Stella and I look at each other and we start to move away at the same time, but the ambulance woman motions us back.

'Stay where you are, girls,' she says calmly. 'I just need to ring back to base. Just stay holding hands with her, will you?' She smiles at us. 'You're all doing so well.'

And so we hold Det's sweaty hands as the young man lifts her onto a couple of sterile sheets and puts more pillows behind her. She grunts and moans and continues to grip our hands.

'You're doing well, love,' the young man says, so kindly. 'Really good.'

'Fantastic,' the woman interrupts her phone call to agree.

'I never knew having a baby would be so noisy,' Stella whispers to me.

Minutes tick by slowly. The grunts and groans, the puffing and shrieking are so visceral that it feels a bit like hell. When there is a knock on the door Cassie gets up.

The woman calls to her from where she is kneeling next to Det on the floor. 'We don't need any more people in here, sweetie,' she says calmly. 'Perhaps you can tell whoever it is there that we'll be done soon?'

'Okay.' Cassie's face is the colour of chalk. 'I'll just stand guard outside, okay?'

Cassie wants to be as far from the action as is politely possible and I have to say that I feel the same. As I'm thinking about scrambling to my feet to join Cassie, the pace suddenly changes.

Det begins to pant as if she is running hard, rocking back and forward, and the woman pulls Det's dress up to her chest and…

I see it.

I see the head come out first. Then along with a lot of sobbing and grimacing, and gasping and pushing from Det, the whole body sort of plops out into the waiting arms of the paramedic! It sounds like a wet foot being extracted from a rubber boot.

Stella and I hang onto Det and each other, watching spellbound, our mouths hanging open. The little one has struggled free, all bloody, gasping and mewing like a cat, covered in all kinds of mucky stuff, and doesn't seem to be all that impressed with the surrounds. But there is thick black hair on the head and fingernails on every finger and with the first cry I realise the truth of what I've just seen...

How amazing to think that every single person on the earth started this way! How could it be that all of us were this small and bloody and helpless? It doesn't seem possible. I'm so stunned I can't speak.

'A boy, Det,' Stella whispers. 'You've got a boy.' She is right. Along with the amazing little round head covered in the black fluffy hair, the arms, tiny hands and feet and legs and round belly, there are testicles and a tiny penis.

Stella and I are both crying as we plant tearful congratulatory kisses on Det's brow. Down the other end the woman and the young man do what they have to; cutting the cord I suppose, and helping to expel the rest of what has to come out.

Det is lying back, completely out of it. The young man, Tony, lifts the squirming baby up onto her tummy and whispers encouragingly. Det takes hold of the babe, cradling the little bottom, the other hand around his head, but she doesn't open her eyes.

Cass comes back into the room along with Nick, who was outside. The two of them stand by the door looking on in awe.

'Baby is fine,' the woman says softly, wiping Det's forehead with a sponge. 'Breathing well and a good weight. You've done so well, Det.'

At last, Det opens her eyes and looks down at the baby, but she doesn't smile or laugh. In fact, she frowns as she examines the tiny hands and feet and then she tips the baby to the side a certain way so she can see his face, and then, after checking him all over, holds him out for the woman to take.

'Keep holding him, love.'

'No, no thanks,' Det whispers. The woman takes the baby and sponges him down a little and then wraps him in a couple of little white blankets. She puts an encouraging arm around Det's shoulders and urges her again to take the baby.

'Such a little beauty.' The woman's tone is very gentle. 'Isn't he?'

'Yes.' Det leans forward and runs her thumbs over the baby's closed eyes.

'You want him back?'

'No.' Det lolls back again and closes her eyes.

I realise then that even up to the last ten minutes the whole idea of this baby was just a dream, plainly ridiculous. From the time she first told me she was pregnant I was secretly hoping that something might happen so she wouldn't have to go through with it. But he is here now. No longer just an idea or a vague notion or a plan; he's here and he's as real as the desk in the corner. In fact, this is the most real thing I think I've ever seen. I am beside myself, desperate for her to hold this little being she has just produced.

Come on, Det. Come on.

Nick comes forward and kneels down next to Det and holds out his arms for the baby. The nurse places the swaddled infant carefully into the crook of his arm and the rest of us crowd around Nick shyly for a better look. I can see that the two ambulance officers have become a little perturbed about Det's seeming disinterest in the baby. They smile as they watch us touching the baby's head, and then when Stella insists on a hold they help Nick pass the baby over, but I can see they're waiting for Det to return from wherever she is behind her eyes to claim him back.

Two more paramedics arrive with a special wheelchair.

'Time we moved,' Penny says after it has all been set up. 'Time to get you two to hospital. What about you hold baby on the way down?'

Det takes her baby then. She doesn't gush or cry or even smile, but she holds the baby firmly as she is shifted onto the wheelchair and then she seems to close her eyes again as they wrap blankets around her.

'Will you hold him for me, Stella?'

Stella looks at the woman, who gives her the nod, and Stella takes the baby.

'Okay.' Penny smiles at Det as she tucks in the blankets and packs up her things. She waves around at us all. 'You've got brilliant friends, Det.'

Det opens her eyes and stares at her, then looks around at us as though she can't quite remember where she is or how she got there.

Once she is in the lift with the paramedics and Stella, who is holding the baby, the rest of us rush for the stairs outside to watch her being put into the back of the ambulance.

The ambulance officer takes the baby from Stella and puts him back in Det's arms.

'You want anyone with you, love?' Tony asks.

'I'll come, Det,' I say immediately, 'if you want. Stella and me?'

'That's a great idea.' Penny smiles at us.

Det shakes her head. 'No,' she whispers.

'You sure?' I take her hand.

Det nods closes her eyes. I motion to the woman that I want a minute with Det. She moves out of the way and I climb all the way into the ambulance.

'Det,' I say softly, squeezing her hand, 'will you be okay being admitted to hospital on your own?'

She nods and squeezes back.

Stella climbs in on the other side of her.

'Thanks, Peach, but...'

'But...'

'But what?'

'I'd better warn you,' she whispers, 'that I'm probably going to bow out pretty soon.'

'You mean?' This is unthinkable now. Panic grips me. I shake my head, lost for words. *She can't do this! Not now... Not now we've seen him.* I look at Stella.

'I'll only fuck it up,' Det mumbles.

'You won't, Det,' Stella says calmly.

'I'm a head case.'

'You're a fantastic person.'

Det opens her eyes and grins at us both and it's like the old Det has come back for a moment.

'I don't think so.' She smiles and closes her eyes. 'Not so fantastic.'

By this stage some of the launch guests are crowding around, most of them half-pissed, shouting out congratulations and best wishes. Stella and I climb out of the ambulance.

'Have you got a name?' someone shouts as the ambulance doors are about to close.

Det shakes her head sadly.

The doors slam shut and the ambulance reverses out through the gate. Cassie, Nick, Stella and I rush out onto the street to wave her off.

Once the ambulance disappears, Cassie rushes back to the launch to take care of things. So it's just us three left, Nick, Stella and me, walking slowly back towards the convent. None of us speak.

'If she doesn't want him, I do!' Stella suddenly yells before bursting into a flood of tears.

'You'll have to fight me for him,' Nick says, his voice hoarse with emotion, and puts his arm around Stella.

'And me,' I say quietly. They don't hear me. But it's true. I mean it. That baby is ours now. He belongs to us all.

'You go home,' I say when Stella clicks off the phone from telling Mum what has happened. 'I'll just go up and make sure Det's studio is locked.'

'You want us to wait?'

'No thanks.'

I don't turn the light on immediately but stand against the door and breathe in the faint smells of sweat and blood that are still there in spite of the half-opened window.

How strange to be in this quiet room now when less than half an hour ago it was filled with people, and the noise and drama of someone being born. I walk over to the window and look out.

I can just see Stella in the dim light standing near the gate with Nick, along with some other figure I can't make out. Three dark shapes in the strange light. Remnants of the launch crowd trickle past them, chattering and laughing and calling their goodbyes as they make their way towards the big gates.

Across from me is the other wing of the convent, so pretty with the few yellow lights blazing, and above it the spires and roofline against the big, bright, star-filled sky.

Did she come tonight, I wonder. The launch was well advertised. Did my mother sneak in to look at Det's paintings? Did she see *Blood Ties* too?

A baby has been born in this very room and it fills me with an odd kind of wonder. I know it happens a million times every day in every country, yet I feel as though I have just witnessed a miracle.

Tonight I need God and ... not just any God. I don't want some vengeful old man in the sky, or some self-proclaimed prophet hanging on a cross. I don't want Zeus or Buddha or Shiva.

I want someone or something bigger than me to care about this child. Not only that, I need that same being to be prepared to put in motion all that needs to happen for that little boy to be safe. I'm not saying I believe this will happen, only that I must at least ask. So where do I find God?

It's not my father or my mother, but it's me, O Lord, standing in the need of prayer ...

Not my father or my mother but ... me.

The old spiritual that we sang at my last school speech night comes to mind. I remember liking it at the time, all the the sadness and the longing in it. I had no idea what it was about then, but I do now.

That's what I need. Prayer. But how do you do it? I don't kneel down. That would be too much. But I stand with my elbows on the windowsill. I close my eyes and try to conjure up something that feels like God. It shouldn't be that difficult, I tell myself; after all, my own mother presumably did this *every single day* at my age in a room just like this one. And my grandmother is still doing it.

But it turns out I'm no good at praying. I only get as far as a star-spangled sky with galaxies gliding grandly through space, our little planet so tiny and helpless, spinning around the outside of the sun, and a sort of cosmic breath blowing through it all and ... I lose focus. The whole edifice crumbles away.

I have come into this room to find God and ... *he isn't here.*

I pull down the window, lock Det's room and walk downstairs into the night. I let myself out the side door and through the main gate.

Passing the big bluestone church, I see that the door is open and I walk into its gloomy interior. There is some kind of ceremony going on. I don't know what it is, but an old priest is tottering around mumbling something; there are only a few other lonely souls in the pews.

I walk up the aisle and park myself in one of the pews and stare up at the mural above the altar.

Mary is ascending through the clouds towards heaven, with a legion of angels accompanying her on either side. Hands joined in prayer, she is on her way to some better place. Her expression is serene rather than happy, as though she might be holding a great secret. My grandmother would have seen this image every morning at Mass and likewise my mother.

And now ... here I am.

But my knowledge of Mary is as scant as my knowledge of her son. Jewish and poor, she had a baby in a stable and then had to watch that same child get horribly murdered thirty-three years later. And now, two thousand years after the event, here she is caught mid-flight on her way to the next life.

We have all fallen in love with a baby, I tell the floating woman swathed in veils and soft drapery as she glides through the clouds. *Please help her. Let her find a way to keep him.*

When I open my eyes, the woman is still drifting peacefully upwards through the clouds. Around me the polished wood shines in the light of the small lamps, and the low mumbled prayers of the old ones continue. It is easy for me to forget who I am and where I belong.

When I come out of the church I see just one dark figure waiting by the gate, and my heart skips a beat.

I hope it is who I think it is, and ... I hope he is waiting for me.

Fluke is driving. Here we are, travelling east out of Melbourne towards Springvale and I'm so damned nervous I can't sit still.

In spite of a few downpours over the summer, the state is still very dry. For the third year in a row there are water restrictions and bushfire warnings in place. But now the bright autumn afternoon is closing over right in front us. The blue has all but gone, leaving the air dank and grey. Colours take on an unnatural, almost spooky, intensity in that dim light. It is going to pour. Good news.

I ask Fluke if he minds if we have the radio off. But the silence is too much so I turn it on again. He puts a hand on my knee and I flinch like a horse.

'It will be okay,' he says. We pull up at the entrance. 'You've got the map?'

I nod and take it from my coat pocket.

He bends over my shoulder and points to our position and then traces the route I have to take with his finger. 'Just walk through the gates, turn right and follow this path,' he says. The smell of him makes me heady for a second, until I remember that I am here on another mission altogether.

'What if they're not here?' I say.

'They'll be here,' he says. 'I'll wait.' He pulls a book with a picture of the ocean on the front out of the glove box. 'Take as long as you like, Peach.'

I walk past rows and rows of straight, neat rose bushes with plaques underneath. Part of me wishes I was lost, but every signpost corresponds exactly to the map. What sort of person would want to meet you for the first time in a cemetery?

You're nineteen years old. You can handle this.

I come to a patch of ground with trees and a few old-fashioned gravestones lying about in no particular order. They look odd in this straitlaced place, like a group of old-timers sitting hunched over the bar in their local pub staring at the newcomers who are too well dressed and neat and making too much noise. I see a couple of women standing on a slight incline looking at me.

This is it. One foot in front of the other or ... you could still run.

'Perpetua.' Ellen comes towards me, smiling, both arms out-stretched.

'Hello, Ellen,' I hug her back. She grabs me by both wrists and looks me up and down a few times, staring right into my face, and I see that she has aged even since I last saw her. She is more stooped under her navy-blue winter coat, and her faded grey hair seems thinner. But her eyes are still bright. She turns around to the other woman.

'And this is your ...' She stops, flustered, but I'm not in any position to help.

'I'm Cecilia,' the other woman says.

I nod, biting my lip, hardly daring to look at her face. When I do, I want to laugh. We are exactly the same height, both fine-boned with bright blue eyes and fair, curly shoulder-length hair pulled up at the back in exactly the same way. She is wearing a red coat, and so am I. The deep red lipstick and gold rings in her ears make her look quite glamorous and I have a moment to think, *Wow! So this is how I'm going to end up when I'm in my fifties!*

I'm not wearing make-up, but I've got jeans on and so does she. Hers are tucked into classy red-leather high-heeled boots; mine are black and flat, but we've both got small feet.

She gives me a shaky smile and holds out both hands. I give mine to her.

'So good to meet you,' she says. Her eyes are full of tears, but she makes no move towards me. We stand there staring at each other. Her voice is vaguely familiar.

'I feel as if I have met you already,' I say.

'We spoke at the convent one day.'

'Oh.'

'I was in disguise.' She smiles. 'Sunglasses and a hat.'

'Oh.'

'I overheard you telling someone you didn't like your name,' she blurts out nervously, 'one day when I was having coffee and you were collecting the plates.'

'Really?' I say. 'I have no recollection.'

'Well, it wasn't... important.'

'I tend to go onto autopilot at work,' I mumble by way of explanation.

'Did your friend have her baby?'

'Yes. A boy.'

'What did she call him?'

'Gabriel.'

We all smile at that.

'And is she well?'

'Yes. Det is fine.'

'And the baby?'

'Yes.' I smile, remembering Gabriel that morning in his pram in our kitchen, his black hair sticking up like a punk, so solemn and thoughtful, watching us watching him. Nick calls him Buddha because he seems to know so much already. When he smiles for no reason and kicks his feet like he is having the best time, I swear that the whole world is smiling too.

'And this is *my* mother.' Ellen points down at the brass plaque on the ground beside us. '*Was* my mother, I should say. I wanted you both to see it before... I go.'

'Go?'

'Well, I am nearly eighty-nine,' she says.

Sarah Reynolds (Sadie). Much loved.
1889 – 1935.

Cecilia squats down and runs her hand over the edges of the plaque.

'This is really something, Mum,' she says without looking up. 'Thanks for bringing us here.'

'Thank your daughter. I mean ...' Ellen flounders with embarrassment, 'Perpetua is the one who found the site.'

'It's okay, Ellen,' I say gently.

'I just thought ...' Her voice trails away in confusion. 'She belongs to you both as well.'

The situation is thick with tension. Poor old Ellen is fiddling nervously with the buttons on her coat. A family group passes. A man holding a little girl, and his wife holding the hands of two nicely dressed boys. Ellen looks at them longingly as if she'd like to be part of *their* group. I don't blame her. She bends down to rub one foot where her shoes are cutting into her.

'You feel like a cup of tea?' I say.

'Oh!' Relief fills her old face. 'Do I what?'

'There is a cafe right near the entrance.' I look at Cecilia who nods.

'Let's go then, before the rain starts.'

We walk along the well-kept paths and I breathe in the stillness of the place. All the rose bushes. All the dead people. All the lives already over.

Dark clouds hover low, and it seems as though the whole world is on the brink, waiting for the right moment to lay itself bare and spill out its furious secrets.

'*Send it down, Hughie,*' I whisper, and think of Dad, the way he always says that before rain. I think of the creases around his eyes and how one side of his mouth goes up higher than the other when he smiles. Almost on cue there is a loud crack of thunder and the first hard bite of rain hits the skin of my face.

Ellen gasps and begins to hurry.

I take her arm and Cecilia takes the other.

'Not far now,' I say, thinking that just to be alive is probably enough. I mean, here and now and *alive*. I think of the many millions already gone and think of those that never got a chance to live, and when we reach the cafe I open the door and smile.

'We made it,' I say, ushering them inside first.

'We did,' Cecilia laughs.

Ellen hurries over to the nearest table, shakes off her coat and sits down.

We made it.

Sadie, Ellen, Cecilia and me.

AUTHOR'S NOTE

This book was on my mind well before I put pen to paper. Recently I found a note to myself dated November 1991:

Must look closer into where Mum grew up! How come she ended up in the Abbotsford Convent? Why won't she ever talk about that? What actually happened to her mother, I wonder? Who was her father? Why did he put her in that place at three years old when he lived so nearby? He came to see her every Sunday but ... who was he? Feel strongly about all this for some reason. Might make an interesting story. Too close to the bone maybe?

So the essential starting point was there, twenty-one years ago.

My mother lived as a ward of the state at the Abbotsford Convent in the 1920s, from the age of three to fifteen, and I heard many vivid stories of life behind those high walls – about the eccentricities of the nuns and other girls, the special feast days, the end-of-year concerts, the violin classes held under the broad branches of the Separation Tree in summer, the annual elocution competition and poetry prize, along with Archbishop Mannix's weekly visits to take tea with the Reverend Mother. My mother was a positive woman and so her stories were mainly positive. At the Convent she learned to play violin and piano well, and passed her exams with flying colours. But why she was made a ward of the state when both her parents were still alive was never open for discussion. When pressed, she'd resort to clichés to fob us off. 'No point raking over dead coals,' she'd say. 'We didn't ask questions then' or 'Why wash dirty linen in public?'

Living in an age when everything is spoken about, it is hard for us to remember that things used to be so radically different. The shame of my mother's illegitimacy and her ignorance about her early life was a pain that sat deep within her for the rest of her life. I believe she was barely able to think about it, much less talk openly of it.

A few things coincided over the last few years to firm my resolve to tackle this project. Mum died, and so I felt free to pursue the story without stepping on her toes. Then my elder sister, who in a previous life had been a nun for twelve years, moved back to Victoria. Talking with her about why she'd chosen the religious life all those years ago further ignited my interest. I was living in Collingwood by then – only a short walk from the Convent – and so the place and its magnificent surrounds, the cafes and former nuns' cells transformed into rented studios, were now part of my neighborhood. Each time I visited the place, the stronger became my sense of proprietorship. This is my place and ... I'm going to write a book about it!

By the time I did get around to actually beginning the book, my focus had widened. I decided that my mother's story should be told in the context of a bigger exploration of some of the Convent's history and so, some time later, armed with an Australia Council grant and a publishing contract, I hired one of those studios as my new workspace and set to work.

Most of the research involved meeting with people whose lives had intersected with the Convent at various points in its history: nuns and ex-nuns, pupils and of course the 'fallen' women whose young lives had been spent working the huge commercial laundry. Some of these latter were bitter about the way their lives had been stolen from them. Others spoke warmly of individual nuns even as they described the harshness of the daily routine and laundry work. The pathos and poignancy of their stories were as compelling as the nun's stories.

History is so often told from the male point of view, with the female experience either ignored or trivialised. The Convent was home to an enclosed community of hundreds of Good Shepherd nuns for more than a century, along with the thousands of girls and women in their care. Behind the high walls and with the varied communal spaces of dormitories and refectories, gardens, schools and kitchens they lived lives very different to our own. And so it was from a strong personal connection and a desire to explore some of that untold female history that I set out to research and write this novel.

Once I decided on the basic structure of four generations within the one family, everything just seemed to fall into place. I suppose because so much of it was there in my own background. I had the relinquishing mother (my grandmother), the orphan (my mother), the nun (my sister) and the present-day student (my friend's daughter) working a summer job in one of the Convent cafes: they were all there, in my own life. Many of the deeper issues to do with religious faith and family tension were based on what I'd seen and heard, felt and believed. The ceremonies, the music, the prayers and ways of thinking were so familiar to me that writing the book felt a bit like coming home after a long time away.

Like no other book I've written, *The Convent* feels like mine!

ACKNOWLEDGEMENTS

Writing a novel can be a fraught and lonely business at times. And losing heart is just part of the game. I want to thank so many people who helped me to the finishing line.

In particular, Erica Wagner and Susannah Chambers from Allen & Unwin. Your enthusiasm and support of my work over the last few years has been unwavering. That you both managed to turn it up a notch or two for *The Convent* says a lot about what fine publishers you are. Thanks for all your hard work.

My very sincere gratitude to the Literature Board of the Australia Council and Arts Victoria for grants enabling me to complete this project on time.

My sincere thanks go to members of the Good Shepherd Community, who agreed to meet and talk with me. Special thanks to Sister Bernadette Fox, who, in spite of ill health, was kind enough to see me a number of times, to answer questions as well as write a letter of support on my behalf. (And thanks to Mary Dalmau from Reader's Feast for putting me in touch with Sister Bernadette.) Thanks to Sister Monica Walsh, for showing me around the Convent, giving me a sense of when and where things happened, along with some lovely memories of being a young novice at Abbotsford back in the sixties. Thanks to Suzanne Gardiner who was a member of the Good Shepherd Community at Abbotsford for fifteen years. I really hope that some of her warmth and humour have managed to seep into the pages of my book. Thanks to Sue Gorden as well, who took the time to talk to me at length about her motivation and experiences as a Good Shepherd sister for around five years in the late sixties.

A very special thanks to four Presentation Sisters: Sister Paula Bourke; Sister Rose Derrick, who took me through some of the elaborate religious ceremonies of the sixties in great detail; and to Sister Kathleen O'Neil and Sister Rosaleen McCaffrey, who were kind enough to write about the feelings they'd had as young women when they were received into the convent all those years ago. Warm thanks to my sister Michaela for setting up the meeting with these women as well as her own intriguing stories and anecdotes about 1960s Convent life. And to Monica and John Murphy both ex religious of many years, thank you both.

Catherine Kovesi's historical work *Pitch Your Tents on Distant Shores – a History of the Sisters of The Good Shepherd in Australia, Aotearoa/New Zealand and Tahaiti* (Playright Publishing, 2006) was a wonderful reference. I thank her for being so open and enthusiastic about sharing all that she knew about the topic when we met on a couple of occasions.

My gratitude to Marjorie O'Dwyer (recently deceased) who talked with me at length about the years she lived in the Sacred Heart Section of the Convent from the age of thirteen until she was twenty-four, in 1970. Her first-hand account of what it was like working long hours in the laundry, the relationships between the older women and girls, the nuns and the auxiliary nuns, sleeping in the dormitories, playing basket ball on Saturdays etcetera was priceless. The day we spent together wandering the Abbotsford site, with her telling one story after another about her time there, is one I'll never forget.

Thanks to Fran Jenkins for her help in putting me in touch with some of the residents in the Good Shepherd nursing home. In particular Mary Murren and Jeanette Manley whose stories I found very touching. Thanks to Wendy McNamara, Kerrin Harvey and Dianne Heard, Sue Munckhof and Jenny Flynn, along with other former residents of the Sacred Heart Class.

A number of women, nuns, ex-nuns and former pupils and residents of the Convent I spoke to wanted to remain anonymous. I respect their wishes and thank them for their contributions.

Thanks too to Christine Carolyn and Jamie Edwards, Jenny Glare, Janey Keene and Dr Madonna Grehan for their insights and information. Thanks to Eleanor and Jasmina Davies for telling me their personal stories about being adopted. And to their parents and my good friends, Mary Ellen and Dave, I thank you too.

Thanks to members of the Abbotsford Convent Foundation, Maggie Maguire, Brenton Geyer and Andrew Evans, for your practical help, interest and enthusiasm.

Lastly, thanks to my three sons, Tom, Joe and Paddy, who throw light into my life in so many ways.

Also by Maureen McCarthy

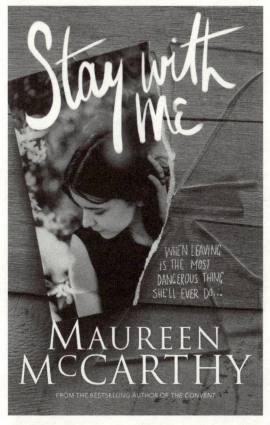

'The portrayal of abuse is sensitive and thoughtful, and Tess's escape is often thrilling. The characters are vividly real, and there is a beautiful sense of place ... *Stay with Me* is a powerful and sympathetic story that will speak to many older YA readers.'   *Books & Publishing*

An extract from *Stay With Me*

LUNACY ACT, 1915 - SCHEDULE FIFTEEN.
MEDICAL CERTIFICATE TO ACCOMPANY ORDER OR REQUEST
FOR RECEPTION OF A PERSON AS A PATIENT
INTO A RECEIVING HOUSE OR WARD.

Dated this 21st day of November, 1928,
in Melbourne in the state of Victoria

Name of the patient with Christian name at length:
Therese Mary Josephine Kavanagh
Sex and age: Female, 32 years
Married, single or widowed: Married
Number of children: 5
Age of youngest child: 14 months
Previous occupation: Home duties
Habits of life: Clean
Previous place of abode: Mayfield near Leongatha
Whether first attack: Yes
When and where previous under treatment: No
Whether subject to epilepsy: No
Whether suicidal: No
Whether a danger to others: No
Supposed cause of attack: Shock

Facts observed by myself:
On admission she was very violent and required
restraining. She was constantly calling to Jesus
Christ to spare her and thought the devil was
persecuting her. She now thinks she is insane and
is frequently out of bed praying. She claims she is
a very wicked woman.

Signed *Charles Mc ...*

Bruises on back and arms.

My great-grandmother was an ordinary woman, married to an ordinary poor farmer. She had no one to speak for her. Her husband was the only person who could have helped her, and he was the one who'd decided she was mad enough to be put away. No one in her life thought they might know better. Not her mother or father, or her two brothers, or any of her four sisters, three of them alive and living nearby.

She died in the Kew Asylum two years later, aged thirty-four, without ever seeing any of her five children again. The youngest was only three.

You can be old when you're still young. Even at thirteen you can feel like life has not just passed you by, but that it has nothing more to offer and never will. The threads holding you to the earth seem as thin and delicate as gossamer, so utterly arbitrary that they might as well not be there.

I'm twenty-one now, and everything that has happened to me seems completely random, and yet at the same time as inevitable as if I'd planned it all myself.

How could I have known while I was lying in that hospital bed with beeping monitors and drips in both arms that within only a few short days I would wake with a fierce desire to live?

It was my great-grandmother Therese, I'm sure now, hovering over me for those first twenty-four hours as I cruised between life and death. Standing behind my left shoulder keeping her eye on the plastic tubes and glass bottles, the beeping machines that kept me in the land of the living. It might have been the drugs they'd pumped into me, but I'm sure I felt her lean in close at one point.

Keep breathing, she whispered. *Stay with me.*

one

It's around three a.m. I can't be sure exactly, because I'm hiding under a house, ten minutes' drive out of Byron Bay, off the Old Bangalow Road. If you wanted to find us you'd turn off the main road and go over the railway line, then take a right into Cemetery Road and follow that road past the cemetery into the hills where it becomes a dirt track. We're right at the end, halfway down the hill in a small wooden cottage on stilts, hidden in among heavy palm-tree foliage.

I'm scared of snakes, and I hate crawling insects, but it's the smell that really gets to me. The dank dark smell that makes me feel as though I'm already in the ground, waiting for dirt to be shovelled in on top of me.

I'm not cold. It's still summer – just. Still the season for tourists, and surfers, and girls my age in skimpy halter dresses walking up and down the streets licking ice-creams, their shoulders pink from the sun and their voices careless with hilarity and boredom. I see them sometimes when we go into town, and it's as if I'm watching a movie about a different species. It's hard to remember that I used to be one of them.

I hear the soft sound of a radio playing old rock classics directly above me, then footsteps going down the hall. A door creaks open. He'll be checking his email for news of that container which has failed to arrive. The footsteps come back and I hear coughing and then the creak of bedsprings. It won't be long now.

Time passes in chunks of stale sponge cake, then stretches out in sticky grey lines, like chewing gum. The radio is switched off eventually, and under all the other night noises around me, the scratching wombat and the scurrying mice, I hear that low even rumble. He doesn't usually snore, except when he drinks, which is what he was doing earlier with his brothers.

I crawl out from under the house and go back inside. I go to the bathroom, clean my teeth, take off my clothes, then creep through to the bedroom and slip under the covers beside him.

He puts one hand on my hip and buries his face into the back of my neck and mumbles something like, 'You good now, babe?'

'Sure,' I murmur. 'I'm good now.'

But I'm not good. I'm so far from good it doesn't matter. Every cell in my body is on stand-by, a red-hot alert signal is swinging before my eyes like a neon strobe-light at a fairground. On and off it goes, and I'm half-blinded by its brightness.

He runs his hands up and down my legs a couple of times, turns me around and breathes his sharp vodka-fuelled breath in my face, squeezes my breasts, then he's on top of me, parting my legs with both hands, pushing himself in roughly like he has every right. It hurts like crazy. But I'm glad. Really glad, because sometimes when he's been drinking he is too tired. Then he wakes after a few hours, thirsty and discontented. Now his sleep will be deep and trouble-free and that's exactly what I need.

Try and leave and I'll find you. No woman messes with me, babe. I mean it.

But you say you love me.

I do love you.

He does mean it. There would be all kinds of ways of disposing of a body on this property. No one in town knows me anymore. His mother and two brothers would die rather than snitch on him. For all I know he might mean the loving bit as well.

I lie quietly beside him and before long he is breathing deeply again, not snoring now but taking deep even breaths. *So far so good.*

I can hardly believe what I am about to do. It feels as unreal as if someone else has moved their bits and pieces of machinery into my head and pushed the green button on the wall. Red and orange lights flicker as the pistons and levers slowly come to life.

I ease my body out of bed, pick up the pile of clothes I left carefully on the floor – jeans, T-shirt, pullover and jacket – and tiptoe out. Once I'm dressed, I creep down the hall to the end room.

She is lying on her back, arms spread out in her little bed as though she has only just finished playing. Barry, the homemade orange-tartan bear with two odd brown-button eyes, a small peaky snout and a sewn-on yellow hat is lying alongside her. He is a cumbersome, ugly thing, probably the worst-looking kids' toy I've ever seen, but Nellie loves him. She picked him from a table of other used toys at a street stall last year, and he rarely leaves her side. My daughter is three years old, speaks as clearly and precisely as a grown woman, and can already write her name and read a bit. I lean down and whisper her name now and she lifts one plump arm to my neck and mutters something about a green frog. She is tall for her age, sturdy too, with masses of wild black curls and a face sweet enough to break your heart. Just this morning she told me that she planned to marry our dog Streak one day. When I asked why, she said, 'Because I'll be able to go on long runs with him at night.'

'Okay,' I said, 'but what if you get tired?'

She had to think about that one for a while. 'If I get tired I'll climb on his back and tell him to bring me home.'

I have to get her away.

Her arm pulls me nearer, her other pudgy hand is wandering dreamily over my face and hair as she mumbles more about the frog. She puts three fingers into my mouth and when I suck them she giggles in her sleep as though she knows exactly what game I'm playing. I pick her up and settle her heavy head on my shoulder, reasonably confident that she won't kick up, because I slipped a bit of a pill that I saved from hospital into her drink. I grab Barry by one of his fat legs and make for the door.

My things – the stroller and the canvas backpack containing two hundred and forty-three dollars stolen from his jacket, spare clothes for her, a light dress, jeans, two T-shirts, a cotton jumper, underpants, a packet of tampons – are already waiting under a tree nearby.

I settle her into the stroller, wrapping the bunny rug tightly around her, and throw Barry across the handles. It's only then that I remember the old journal hidden under Nellie's mattress, and my breath drops away. *How could I have forgotten it?* The battered black book from my previous life, every page filled with close teenage scrawl. There's my father's Django Reinhardt CD tucked inside the front cover and a few photos stuck in the back. A head shot of my great-grandmother aged fifteen that my mother gave me before she left, one or two of my parents and another not-very-clear one of my brother and two sisters. I purposefully left it until the last minute, thinking that if he caught me leaving then at least he wouldn't get that. It's the one thing I've managed to keep hidden.

I stand still a moment, my heart thumping with the enormity of what it would mean to leave that book behind. He'd find it eventually. I imagine him pulling the room apart looking for clues, and then those long, strong, guitar-playing fingers picking it up and slowly turning the pages, studying the photos, reading every last word of my ramblings. He has the rest of me in place, and now the final piece of the jigsaw. Once he finished he'd turn it over to his mother and brothers. *You were right, mate. One crazy little bitch!*

I was seventeen when I came up here with a couple of friends for a good time. Had some part of me known that I would not be going back? Why else would I have brought that book and those photos?

One crazy little bitch. That's who I am now.

I leave Nellie sleeping in the stroller under a tree, creep back inside into her bedroom that smells of her, and lift up the mattress. When my fingers touch that hard shape, my soul floats above my body for a few seconds. I tiptoe out again through the back door, the lightness still bouncing around my head as I make my way back into the darkness and to Nellie.

Keep breathing. That soft voice in my head steadies me a bit. *Stay with me …* It's so easy to lose sight of what I've got to do.

I make my way gingerly through our front garden of ferns and trees, towards the track leading down to the main road. I can hardly think, I'm so afraid. Every noise, every rustle in the dark makes me more aware of what I'm doing.

The stroller wheels crunch loudly on the rough gravel. I consider folding up the stroller and carrying Nellie in my arms, but with the bursting backpack I know she would quickly get too heavy. There is no other way but this. Every time I hit a stone or a rut the extra noise jolts me to the bone, makes me stop and turn around. Would that one have woken him? I'm expecting him to appear, to hear his voice calling me. And once he catches sight of the stroller and backpack it will be all over. My heart races with the enormity of what that would mean. *Over.* I picture the look on his face as the pieces slot into gear in his head. Will he strangle me here in front of Nellie? No. I don't think so. He'll lock me in the shed and break me to bits first, and then he'll call his brother over; they'll finish me off together.

Think of now. Only now. One foot in front of the other … Or I will freeze to death with fear.

In the distance, the goods train thunders by, making its way down towards Sydney. That means it must be close to five a.m.

I close my eyes and imagine the might of all that iron and steel roaring through the night.

For the last five mornings, that same train has jolted me awake, the loud lonely whistle cutting through my sleep like a blade, making my blood rush in panic, scared that I've said something in my sleep, or that he will see by my face that something is going on.

Before long I am over the track. I edge my way to the smoother part on the side and begin the downward slope at a faster pace. There are hanging branches and deep shadows on both sides, but I know I'm not safe yet. If he were to look long enough through the front window he would be able to see my moving figure, and he might … he just might be doing that right now. A terrible fear grips my insides and I feel light-headed, as though I'm not getting enough oxygen. The air surrounding me is thick and dark, heavy with the scent of bush. I can't really breathe properly until I am over the small dip in the track. Then at least I'm not visible from the house.

Even then he only has to wake and realise I'm not there and it won't be long before he comes looking, and the more I think about that, the more I believe it might be happening. The drinking and the sex give me the best chance I can realistically hope for; even so, I am running now. *I will get there*, I tell myself, over and over. *I'll get there and those people will be waiting for me.* I have to believe it.

But I don't know them! I can't even remember their names. It was five days ago. Why would they put themselves into a potentially dangerous situation for a stranger? Turn back now. Put Nellie back to bed. You have time. If he wakes, tell him that she had a bad dream.

I keep on, one step after another. It's as though my legs and feet don't know how to go any other way. Under all my fear, I know that this might be my last hour on earth, so I drink in the surrounding night. I think of my dead father, my missing mother, my elder sisters and my shy sweet brother. Yesterday evening rushes at me, Nellie and I together on the verandah, with Barry between us, watching the shell-pink and pale gold sky before the sun finally sank. The brilliant mornings here, first light on the leaves and wet grass, birds chirping away in the trees – my love for it all sings alongside the low strident buzz of dread eating at my insides, slow and constant as a hungry rat gnawing through a wall. *Nothing good can come of this … How could it? A massive blunder that will cost … your life … Go back!* The bright morning sun, the frosts and fogs, the wind and the rain – I will die thinking of them. While he is killing me I will think of them. I will die free.

Keep breathing. Stay with me.

Normally, he never lets me out of his sight when we go into town. But something has been going on with the avocado farm he runs with his mother and two brothers. For the last couple of weeks there have been a lot of phone calls and low-level anger directed at the youngest brother, Travis. Just a few days ago, on the steps leading up to the front door of the library, he waved me inside because there was someone coming out he needed to talk to, and he didn't want me to hear the conversation. Whatever they're doing is dodgy. They keep buying more land. The farm brought in virtually no income last year, so where is the money coming from?

I noticed the girl first. She was dressed in a mauve shirt with torn-off shorts, and had the long silky blonde hair and golden skin that I used to dream about – my skin being so pale and my hair almost pitch black. She was sitting on the floor with her legs poking across the aisle. Next to her was a thick-set guy in a bright green Hawaiian shirt, with short curly dark hair and fair skin, who was sitting the same way, except that … one of his legs was missing. There was no right leg sticking out from the faded board shorts. I took a second look and saw his left hand was damaged too. The last three fingers were all caught up in a bunch. I blushed with embarrassment when he glanced up and caught me looking. A prosthetic leg complete with matching sneaker was propped up against the bookshelves opposite. I noticed that he had a scar across his forehead and one eye had a kind of milky film over it.

I motioned that I needed to get past them to the kids' section, and the girl looked up and pulled her legs in immediately. I saw then that she was extraordinarily beautiful. A model's face, with perfectly even features, a big wide mouth with full lips. It was hard to turn away from such beauty. Nellie held out her hand and the beautiful girl took it straight away.

'Hey, little one,' she said. 'What's your name?'

'Fenella,' Nellie replied. 'What's yours?'

'Julianne. But I get called Jules.'

'Well, I get called Nellie.' Nellie puffed out her belly importantly, squinting at the girl. 'And I've got a dog.'

The girl flashes me a quick, gorgeous grin. 'Have you now?'

'Yes?' Nellie went all shy and hid behind my legs, but she watched the beautiful girl from behind my right knee. There was something ethereal about her that must have been obvious even to my three-year-old. The huge grey-green eyes with the paintbrush black lashes, the bone structure that made every time she turned her head a cause for wonder.

'What is your dog's name?' the girl asked.

Nellie took a moment to think. 'Streak,' she said, looking up at me for confirmation. I nodded. 'And Mamma sometimes paints my toenails pink,' she added quickly, as though anxious to keep the conversation going. She held out one small grubby foot inside its plastic sandal for the girl to admire, then looked up at me. 'What else?'

'Lots of things,' I say, feeling the familiar rush of tenderness shoot straight through me. Nellie's existence has complicated my own life almost out of existence, and yet even in my darkest hours I can't honestly wish she wasn't around. 'What about the chooks?' I suggest.

She takes a deep breath. 'And I can feed the chooks if Mamma lifts me up to unlock the gate,' she whispers shyly.

'You live on a farm?'

'And we've got two goats.'

'Wow! You have so many interesting things in your life!' The girl had a lovely light laugh that had the odd effect of making me want to cry – the way it just bubbled out of her so sweetly, like music.

The guy was the same, both of them friendly and full of fun. I could see under the damage that he'd been good-looking. He still wasn't bad, with a square chin, a straight nose, wide smile full of straight white teeth. They talked to Nellie about how old she was and what kind of books she liked, and they both tried to include me a few times but I held back. My hair was tied up with an elastic band, my jeans were shabby – straight from Vinnies – and my faded red top had stains down the front. My feet in the rubber thongs were grimy as well. I was conscious of the rough red patch of skin under my eye and around both ears. Since the stint in hospital I'd become very thin as well. Just that morning, Jay had taken a long hard look at me when I came out of the shower.

'Do something with yourself, why don't you?'

'What do you mean?'

'Eat, for a start!'

'I do eat.' But the truth was I barely ate. Food had lost its attraction.

'Too skinny,' he grumbled. 'Fucking you is becoming a chore.'

The insides of my elbows were particularly itchy that day at the library. I needed a fresh tube of the ointment I'd used in hospital, and I was building up to ask Jay if we could stop at the clinic for a prescription on the way home. I stood rubbing the skin, trying not to use my nails, as I listened to the couple chattering to my daughter. As I moved along the shelves picking out books, reading the blurbs and putting them back, I took quick glances at Jay through the glass door of the library, enjoying my momentary freedom as he talked to the bloke on the stairs outside.

But when I heard the girl tell Nellie that they'd be driving down to Melbourne in a few days, a strange tingling sensation began in my toes even before the idea came to me properly. It rose up to my knees and then into my gut and I forgot about the itching. I edged my way closer to where they sat, aware that something was bouncing back and forth in my head, like a giant moth bashing itself against a hot bulb. Back and forth it went, singeing its wings and refusing to give up.

I'd been out of hospital for a few months. Looking back, I see that I'd been waiting for this moment, or one like it. I became quite close to a nurse in there, an older woman who didn't mess about being polite. When I tried lying about the bruises she didn't buy it, and I opened up a bit. Not that I told her everything, but she knew. She told me that I would know when to make a move, an opportunity would present itself, and if it felt right I should grab it with both hands.

When Nellie wandered off to the kids' section I walked back to the young couple. I could still see Jay through the door – he was standing on the steps, deep in conversation.

The amazing thing was that they seemed to understand instinctively when I told them I needed to escape. I don't know if they noticed the red-raw patches of skin on my arms, the fading bruises around my neck or the desperation in my eyes, but they didn't ask many questions. Luck was on my side, because we got nearly ten minutes to work things out. They had come up to Byron to visit the beautiful girl's sick grandmother and would be driving back down south in a few days. They planned to leave very early in the morning – before daybreak – and they would be happy to give me and Nellie a ride. They knew our road, and suggested a meeting spot under the trees just before the dirt track hits the main road.

By the time Jay walked in through the glass doors they'd disappeared behind some shelves, and I was shoving children's books into my library basket.

And so here I am. I tell myself that if they don't turn up then I'll move to Plan B. I'll walk the extra stretch to the main road, we'll hitch into town, and catch the seven a.m. train. I shudder, because realistically I know that waiting on that platform will be like waiting on death row. If push comes to shove, I'll probably decide to go back. If he hasn't woken I might be able to drop the backpack and make up something about Nellie being fractious.

How far now? How far? Surely over this rise I will see the trees that tell me I've reached the cemetery, and from there it's only a little way to where they'll be waiting under the clump of trees.

My heart is racing as I come round the corner. I see a car. Do I automatically assume it is theirs? They told me that they'd be driving his mother's grey BMW, but it's too dark for me to tell the make. This one looks *ominous,* waiting in the dark under the trees, as if it might contain one of Jay's brothers …

I approach tentatively, then stop mid-stride when I see movement. The driver's window comes down.

'Tess?' comes a deep male whisper.

'Yes.'

Elation rips through me, until I see that he is alone. *Where is the girl?*

The door opens and he gets out. He must have his fake leg on, because he moves easily enough in his jeans and windcheater. He smiles and squeezes me briefly around the shoulders, as though this might be some kind of adventure that we can both enjoy. I move away.

'Come on then.'

'But where is … your girlfriend?' I gulp, bending to look into the car in case I've missed her. No one else is there. He's on his own. I try not to panic. I stand still and try to think. What can it mean? Is something dodgy going on?

'Where is she?' I ask again, more sharply than I intended.

'Her gran took a bad turn yesterday,' he tells me. 'She decided to stay an extra few days and then fly down.' He must see that I'm completely unnerved by this turn of events, because he steps back and holds up both hands in a kind of surrender gesture. 'There was no way to let you know,' he says. 'I'm sorry.'

I stare at him, trying to see into his eyes, but it's too dark.

'It's okay,' he adds softly. 'Honestly.'

I hover for another moment before I jump. It's not as though I have a lot of choice. I must trust him or … go back. We stow my bag in the boot and he takes out a blanket. I try to get Nellie out of the stroller, but my hands are trembling so uncontrollably that he has to push me aside to unclip the straps. We fold it up together. Every minute counts. Was that a light? My head jerks to look back up at the track. Nellie wakes up and stares around her, but doesn't cry. Bless her! The guy holds open the back door for us.

'Jules combed the op-shops for a car seat, but nothing doing,' he whispers. 'Sorry.'

'It's okay.'

I climb into the back seat and settle Nellie on my knees and she immediately falls asleep again. The guy shuts the door quietly on us and climbs in behind the steering wheel. The car smells new, seats soft and expensive. He slips the key into the ignition and starts the engine. I take a sniff of the comforting leather and settle back, until I hear the soft click of all the doors locking. Fear rises in my guts again. *Of course they would have contacted Jay after meeting me the other day, just to check out my story! They probably talked it over and had second thoughts. Then decided to betray me. Maybe the girl didn't want to be there when it happened. Jay can be so plausible, handsome and friendly if he feels like it. Instead of going back out onto the road, this guy is going to drive the car back up along the track where I've just walked and deliver me back to Jay. They have it all planned. With Nellie on my lap, what will I be able to do?*

I imagine this so well that it feels as if it's already happening. I tentatively try the doorhandle but it doesn't open.

'I've locked it,' he calls from the front seat. 'Just in case.'

'Okay,' I nod.

Jay will come out to greet us – give the guy one of those quick conspiratorial male smiles. 'Thanks, mate!' He might even chat awhile to make everything seem normal, invite the guy into the house and offer him a drink. 'Tessa's hold on reality is a bit weak,' he'll say apologetically. 'She tends to get confused, you know.' And I'll smile and nod my head because … it might save my life.

But no, the young man is turning the car and driving down the road towards the highway. Relief washes through me when I see the Ballina sign. *So far, so good …* I see his profile in the dark occasionally when he turns his head. His jaw is set and he is concentrating on the road. Once out on the highway he picks up speed and relief floods through me again. I want to ask him if he can see out of his dodgy eye, but I don't.

'Thank you … er … I'm sorry, I've forgotten your name.' Since being in hospital I'm like an old person; people's names sit on the tip of my tongue, refusing to step up. I have to wait for my brain to catch up.

'Harry.' He laughs.

'What time is it, Harry?' I ask.

'Just on five a.m. Jules sends her love, by the way.'

'Oh, thanks,' I reply. What else can I say? *Love?* I try to imagine being loved by someone as beautiful as her. 'I forgot to ask, are you planning to go straight through?'

'See how we go,' he says. 'We'll head south until Grafton, then go west to Glen Innes, maybe head down the New England Highway to Newcastle and the coast road. Then I've got a mate in Gosford.' He smiles and turns around to look at me. 'Might stay a night with him. You okay with that?'

'Yeah.' But I'm not taking any of this in. *Just get me away.*

'Bit longer, but figured it'd be good to see some coastline,' he says easily.

'Coastline,' I repeat stupidly. 'Okay.'

I try to remember a life where I might consider travelling the coastline for the pleasure of it, and I can't. I can't even imagine that kind of life.

'So your name is just Tess, or is it short for—'

'Just Tess,' I cut in.

He catches my sharp tone and shuts up, and I'm grateful for that. The soft purr of the fancy engine is all the noise I need. I peer out the window into the darkness. The traffic is mainly coming the other way. Huge trucks roar towards us and are quickly gone. All good.

An hour goes by and Ballina is behind us. He is following the signs to Grafton as he said. The jackhammering in my chest slows even further.

'How old is she?' The voice in the darkness startles me.

'Three,' I say.

'So how old were you when you had her?'

'Eighteen.'

'Wow.' He whistles, but doesn't say anything else for a moment. 'You must have wanted her bad,' he mutters.

I don't reply, but I smile to myself in the darkness. Eighteen years old. Why would I want a kid? Why would I want someone kicking around inside me, sucking at me all hours of the day and night? Why would I want someone relying on me for food, warmth, comfort and security, only to blame me later when things go wrong?

Beth, Marlon and Salome blamed our mother for *everything*. For what happened to Dad, for our lack of money, for the way the neighbours stared at us in the street. Mostly they blamed her just for being who she was, her wacky clothes and posh voice, her wild temper and the way she sang French songs in the mornings. They missed her, of course – we all did – but unlike them I *got* why she had to leave.

We travel for more than an hour through the darkness with barely another word between us. My arms are numb and aching from holding Nellie, but I don't care. At Grafton Harry takes a right turn towards Glen Innes. These places mean nothing to me, but I'm glad to see the signs, because they show we're heading somewhere. He has the radio on now; its low hum is comforting, going from the news and weather reports to classical music, some guy with a plummy accent making snooty little jokes in between. The darkness is comforting too. Harry drives at a steady speed, except for when we hit sudden patches of fog and have to slow right down as we descend into a hazy gloom. This freaks me out a bit. The huge trucks thundering towards us from the opposite direction are like animals from another age, brainless monsters, rushing out of the darkness and stirring up the panic just under my skin, reminding me all over again that anything can happen … at any time.

At last the day begins to break. I stare out at the faint wash of pink light spreading across the tips of the mountains in the distance, the red sun slowly easing its way over one peak like the mournful eye of a sad god, gradually burning away the fog before us. I'm thinking of Jay waking up and finding me gone. He'll get up, bleary-eyed and start calling out.

Tessa, he'll yell. *Where are you?* He'll be annoyed because there will be no answer, and imagining that makes me want to laugh. No answer, and no smell of coffee in the kitchen, and the fire won't be lit. Nor will I be down checking that the foxes didn't get into the chook pen overnight. And I won't be sweeping down the verandah, either, or making sure the dogs have fresh water. A shot of wild elation mixes with the pool of terror in my gut as I see him moving quickly from room to room, disbelief and fury rising in him like hot steam. *Tess!* My heart pounds as I picture it. Eventually he'll walk into Nellie's room, see the empty bed. *What the hell?* But eventually the penny will drop. And then? How long will it take before he starts thinking straight?

Not long. It won't be long at all. He'll call his mother first off. She lives up the hill from us. *Hey, Mum! Tessa up there?* When she tells him no he'll laugh to hide his humiliation. *Well, what do you know?*

She done a flit, has she? The old bag will be dragging on her first fag for the day. I can see her. The tea in one hand, the fag in the other; her scrawny old neck hooked over the grimy green telephone. *Taken the kid with her, has she?*

Yeah.

Then you'd better go find her, son. Ring Nick and get onto it now. She won't get far.

Of course not.

Calm down. I am sitting in a car that's moving at a hundred and ten kilometres an hour *away … away* from him and his family and the last few years of my life. It's going to work out. It has to work out.

'So, how long were you living out there in the hills?'

'Three years.'

'You came up with him?'

'I met him in Byron.'

'Any family up here?'

'His. Two brothers. Mother.'

'Why?' he asks simply.

'Why what?'

'Why did you go for him?'

'I don't know.'

Trying to think up answers is like wading through swamp water. I want to go back into my own head, to the racing tunnels of thought whirling and dodging each other like cars at an intersection with faulty traffic lights. I have to keep my wits about me. Words are the last thing I need.

'You must have loved him?'

'Yeah.'

He gives a sudden low chuckle as if I've just said something funny.

ABOUT THE AUTHOR

Maureen McCarthy is the ninth of ten children and grew up on a farm near Yea in Victoria. After working for a while as an art teacher, Maureen became a full-time writer. Her novels are firm favourites across generations, and have been shortlisted for numerous awards. The *In Between* series was adapted from scripts Maureen co-wrote with Shane Brennan for SBS TV. Her bestselling and much-loved book *Queen Kat, Carmel and St Jude Get a Life* was made into a successful four-part mini-seres for ABC TV. Maureen has three sons and lives in Melbourne.

Also by Maureen McCarthy

Stay With Me
Somebody's Crying
Rose by any other name
Queen Kat, Carmel and St Jude Get a Life
Careful what you wish for
Flash Jack
Chain of Hearts
When you wake and find me gone
Cross my heart
Ganglands
In Between series